THE SISTERS

D1331587

Also by Sarah Shears

The Fairfields Chronicles

THE VILLAGE
FAMILY FORTUNES
THE YOUNG GENERATION
RETURN TO RUSSETS

and published by Bantam Books

THE SISTERS

Sarah Shears

BANTAM BOOKS
TORONTO · NEW YORK · LONDON · SYDNEY · AUCKLAND

THE SISTERS
A BANTAM BOOK 0 553 40582 9

Originally published in Great Britain by
Judy Piatkus (Publishers) Ltd

PRINTING HISTORY
Judy Piatkus (Publishers) edition published 1988
Bantam Books edition published 1993
Bantam Books edition reprinted 1993

This book is set in 11/12 pt Compugraphic Times
by Colset Private Limited, Singapore

Bantam Books are published by Transworld Publishers Ltd,
61–63 Uxbridge Road, Ealing, London W5 5SA,
in Australia by Transworld Publishers (Australia) Pty Ltd,
15–25 Helles Avenue, Moorebank, NSW 2170,
and in New Zealand by Transworld Publishers (NZ) Ltd,
3 William Pickering Drive, Albany, Auckland.

Printed and bound in Great Britain by
Cox & Wyman Ltd, Reading, Berks.

PART 1

1

'Mother always wears black,' Bertha commented. 'It suits her and she knows it,' she added, acidly.

'Mother is still in mourning for Father,' Ellen reminded her, in her calm, pleasant voice that was never raised in anger.

'For three years? Twelve months is the official period of mourning, so the Queen has decreed, but Mother pleases herself, as we all know!' Jane chuckled.

Grace was silent. She seldom had an opinion, and never asserted herself. A tall, willowy creature, just past her seventeenth birthday, her blue eyes were sad with the memory of that beloved figure, whose manly ghost still seemed to haunt this house of females. His second daughter had been his favourite. Her name suited her. She had little in common with her five sisters, and soon the pattern of her life would be completely changed, though she was still unaware of her mother's plans for her future. It would be the second time in her short life that her familiar little world had been disrupted, and this time it would isolate her from her sisters to an extent that even her own mother had not envisaged.

The four sisters were standing at the drawing-room window watching the independent little figure cross the road. In her thirty-ninth year, Amelia Brent had a proud dignity that none of her daughters could match. The silver hair, piled so becomingly under the smart astrakhan cap, had shocked and surprised her six daughters, three years ago, but the younger girls could now scarcely remember the flaxen hair. The astrakhan coat, the black kid gloves and boots had been worn for three winters already, and would have to last for several more now that their circumstances demanded careful economy. A veil covered her face to protect her fair complexion. In the summer months she carried a parasol.

'Where is she going?' Bertha demanded of her elder sister.

'She didn't say. Possibly to the bank,' Ellen hazarded.

'Does she ever confide in us? I sometimes wonder why she had children, for she's not in the least maternal.'

'Bertha!' Ellen was shocked. She adored her mother, but Bertha only shrugged.

'Well, it's true.'

'I suppose they were hoping for a son to carry on the business, but gave up hoping after Lucy was born?' Jane volunteered.

'What happens to the business when Grandfather and Grandmother Brent have died? Will it be sold?' Bertha was not a favourite with the grandparents, and seldom got invited to the imposing residence facing the park. Grace and Lucy were the favourites.

'It would seem strange to see another name over the entrance, but Brent & Son is no longer appropriate. There *is* no son,' Jane reminded them, quite unnecessarily.

A chapter had closed in the split second that Thomas Brent had drawn his last agonized breath under the flaying hooves of a runaway carriage horse. She would never marry again, Amelia told herself with passionate conviction. Her heart was cold and dead. Thomas had been such a devoted husband, and she had revelled in his adoration. Six pregnancies, and six daughters. They had wanted a son so desperately. Now it was too late. Thomas had been shocked and delighted by his young wife's wanton behaviour in the marriage bed. At an age when modesty was expected, Amelia had slept naked! Her personality was the stronger, and Thomas had been persuaded to remove his nightshirt on their wedding night. Victoria had set a pattern of behaviour for maidens and matrons, but not all had complied to such strict measures. Amelia was self-willed, and too proud to be submissive to a husband. Strict with her daughters, they saw only her authority. The smiles and endearments had been reserved for her husband.

When the children were small, they were handed over to a nursemaid and later to a governess. She supervised both, and expected devoted and loyal service. Only Kate had demanded her attention with her tears and tantrums. Only Kate had climbed on her lap to be cuddled and comforted. Kate was Mother's favourite, and her sisters resented it. But life went on. Her daughters needed her. Mother was indispensable. Her word was law.

Three years ago, she had shed all her tears in the privacy of her bedroom. The nights were long and lonely in the big marriage bed, but the days were occupied in reorganizing a household that had run so smoothly in the past. She had only to keep her hands on the reins. Unfortunately, the proud independence that Thomas had so admired had not endeared Amelia to his parents. On the day of the funeral, she was informed by the family solicitor that her monthly allowance had been drastically reduced. Too proud to complain, she set about the changes in her way of life with a zeal that only her eldest daughter could applaud. The governess, the cook and the housemaid were dismissed with a month's wages to compensate for the shock. Amelia provided all three with satisfactory testimonials. Only Maggie, the scraggy little drudge, who came in daily for the rough work, was retained for her services were invaluable. She was responsible for the family wash on Monday, for scrubbing and cleaning the kitchen and scullery, for washing up, for cleaning the flues and black-leading the kitchen range, and for helping with the spring-cleaning. She was given her dinner in the kitchen, and counted her blessings – so she declared – though Amelia could find nothing blessed in such a life of drudgery, a lazy husband, always finding an excuse to stay at home, and a family of seven children, for whom Maggie worked her fingers to the bone. Among her blessings, however, she counted the generosity of a good mistress, for she was allowed to take home anything in the nature of leftovers from their midday dinner, and that included nourishing soup. She dressed her own children in the cast-off clothing of the Brent sisters, cut down to size and roughly sewn. Even the boys' knickers could be contrived from a dark skirt. So Maggie stayed on, and felt important in her role of the only surviving servant in such a respectable household.

It was customary for the children of the middle class and the upper class to address their parents as Mama and Papa, but Amelia had insisted on Mother and Father since their earliest years. Her quaint idiosyncrasies had been regarded with tolerant amusement by an indulgent husband, and her daughters had been taught to accept their mother's authority as the law of the Medes and Persians. The plump nursemaid to whom they were entrusted in those early years had been an affectionate, warm-hearted girl, and they were not deprived of cuddles and endearments. Cook had been another buxom, good-tempered soul, fond of the children and respectful to her mistress. Jane was her favourite, and it was Jane who remembered the stolen moments in the kitchen, watching Cook roll out the pastry for pies and tarts, preparing vegetables, or basting a sizeable joint of meat. It did not occur to her, nor to Cook, that she was actually storing up useful knowledge in her fertile mind that would prove invaluable at a later date. The smell of the dough, set to rise on the fender, the strong aroma of onions in the stockpot, baked apples stuffed with brown sugar – so many delicious smells to make her mouth water. She was allowed to eat the sugar in the candied peel and a raw carrot as she stood, entranced, at the kitchen table.

'I am going to be a cook when I grow up. The kitchen is the best place in the whole house,' Jane had decided only a few days before the tragedy that would change all their lives.

'Young ladies have other things to do, Miss Jane. There won't be no cause for you to spend your days in a basement kitchen, and your Ma wouldn't allow it,' she added, sensibly.

Jane sighed. 'Mother doesn't understand. She expects all her six daughters to be modelled on the same pattern, but we are all so completely different, each one of us. We are separate individuals, with separate and different minds and hearts and spirits. It bores me dreadfully, the way we are obliged to conform to the ladylike pattern of behaviour.

11

Mother is such a snob. I know she was born in the "upper class", but she married into trade, and that in itself dissociates her from the upper class for ever – unless one of her daughters makes a good marriage, and it certainly won't be Jane! I'm much too ordinary to attract a handsome, wealthy suitor. Grace is the only one of us with a certain distinction and an air of quality that must be inherited from Mother's side of the family. To tell you the truth, Cook, I would sooner have been born into the working class!'

'Now you are talking nonsense, duckie. God knows best, and we all have our proper place in this life.'

'You mean you actually believe in that sentiment the poor little orphans are taught?'

'What's that?'

'The rich man in his castle, The poor man at his gate, God made them high or lowly, And ordered their estate,' Jane quoted.

Cook nodded emphatically.

'Well, I don't, and neither does Mr Dickens.'

'Who's Mr Dickens?'

'He writes the books that Ellen reads aloud in the drawing-room after supper. The everlasting embroidery would be more tedious without the readings. I like it best when Mother plays the pianoforte. She has such a delicate touch. Not one of her daughters has inherited her talent, and that's a pity. We still have to practise for half an hour every weekday, and we are only excused if we are feeling poorly. Taking a walk with our governess, listening to Ellen reading Mr Dickens, the everlasting embroidery, and the sketching that only Grace enjoys – it's all so pointless. I could scream with frustration!'

'But it's natural, duckie, for young ladies to do these things. Now if you was born a young gentleman, it would be a different kettle of fish altogether.'

'I wish we had a brother. How is it possible for Mother to give birth to six girl babies and no boy babies? I don't understand. It's all so hush-hush and mysterious, and nothing is ever explained. Oh, Miss Beresford never misses an opportunity to explain the functions of the birds and the bees, but never a mention of human babies. I want to know how babies are made, and how they are born.'

Cook shook her head. 'Time enough for that, Miss Jane, when you are married. Miss Beresford is quite right.' Then she changed the subject quickly. 'Tell you what, duckie, you ask your Ma's permission to be excused from the drawing-room after supper tonight. It's some time since you made a nice batch of toffee and coconut ice. What jew say?'

Jane's lively little face was lit by a radiant smile. 'I should like that. Thank you very much. It's such a nice change from the boiled sweets Mother likes us to buy. I do wish she would let us spend our allowance any way we please. I even have to put a penny in the collection plate at church on Sunday, and I only receive a paltry fourpence. It's not fair!'

'Your Ma knows best, Miss Jane.'

'But she decides *everything*. Even Ellen is not allowed to have any views of her own, and she is nearly old enough for marriage.'

'It don't seem to worry Miss Ellen. She don't get worked up over things like you do, duckie. She takes life very calm and quiet, do Miss Ellen.'

'Yes, you're right, Cook. I *do* get worked up, but it's because I am so frustrated. If only I could use my hands on something practical. If only I didn't have to

13

practise those interminable scales and five-finger exercises. No wonder Jackie howls.'

'Jack don't have such a bad life. A nice comfortable kennel, two meals a day, bones to chew, and you taking him for a walk every day. Jack is a lucky dog.'

'I worry about him in the Winter, but Mother won't allow him in the house.'

'Only pedigree dogs are allowed indoors, duckie, not mongrels.'

'Is Jackie a mongrel?'

'Yes.'

'How do you know?'

'Just by looking at him. His legs are too short, and his tail's too long.'

'I have never noticed, and I don't mind. I love him just the way he is. Does it take two kinds of dog to make a mongrel?'

'That's right.'

'I'm so dreadfully *ignorant*, Cook.'

'Don't you believe it, Miss Jane. You're the brightest of the bunch in my opinion.'

'You're a darling, and I love you.' Cook was smothered in a warm hug.

'Now you've got jam on your pinny,' she scolded.

Jane laughed and skipped away.

Cook would often recall those stolen moments and warm hugs when she found herself in another household of adults.

The day following the elaborate funeral of the beloved son and heir to the biggest store in town, the cook, the governess and the housemaid were summoned to the morning room at precisely ten o'clock. It was the smallest room in the house, and to Amelia it held the fondest memories of quiet hours of close harmony and companionship in which their

14

children had no place. She would write her letters there, and drink her hot chocolate at mid-morning. Now she had a duty to perform, as distasteful as anything she had encountered in the whole of her married life.

Thomas had always spared her the disturbing elements of his busy day at the store, and when he came home, he left behind the trappings of public life, and clothed himself in the comfort and privacy of The Haven – so rightly named by his predecessor. In this small, private world in which Amelia was mistress, she reigned with the authority of a matriarch, but he was her darling and her best beloved.

When the three women entered the room, she bade them be seated, and they sat down and regarded her with a growing sense of dismay, their hands folded demurely in their laps. In a dress of black alpaca, with only a cameo brooch to relieve the tight-fitting bodice, the blue eyes were kind, not disapproving as they were on other occasions when one or the other had been summoned to this same room. That in itself suggested this was a matter of grave importance. Not only the eyes but the voice was kind.

'You must forgive me, but I am feeling as shocked and distressed at having to tell you this as you will be at receiving it,' she began. 'A month from today, I have to ask you to leave my employ because I can no longer afford to pay you.'

Cook gasped involuntarily. 'It don't matter about wages, Ma'am. I been with you since you was first married, and I couldn't leave now.'

Amelia shook her head sadly. 'I couldn't accept such a sacrifice, Cook, but I am grateful for your loyalty.'

'But – but who will take my place in the kitchen, Ma'am?'

'Nobody can replace you. We shall miss you, but we

15

shall have to compromise and manage without you. I am going to ask a big favour. In the month that remains of your service, will you teach Miss Jane the basic essentials of cookery – nothing elaborate, just plain, wholesome food such as we have always enjoyed? Will you do that for me?'

'Miss Jane? But she's only a child, and she's still in the schoolroom.'

'She is an intelligent child, and there will be no schoolroom.'

'As you wish, Ma'am.' Cook was near to tears.

Miss Beresford controlled her emotions more effectively, but she was grievously dismayed at the prospect of starting all over again with another family. At middle-age, with little to recommend her save the capacity to instruct her pupils with firmness and quiet patience, she could only gloomily foresee a future in a strange household, bereft of the loving and lively companionship of the Brent sisters.

'I understand perfectly, Madam,' was all she said.

Dora the housemaid was snivelling miserably. 'I can't believe it, Ma'am. Only another month. Whatever shall I do? I been 'ere since I left the Orphanage at twelve years of age, and now I be coming up to seventeen.'

'I shall find you another situation, Dora. At your tender age, you have all of life before you, and you mustn't be afraid to take a step forward into the future.'

'But I likes to know where I be going and what I be doing, Ma'am.'

'I know you do, but it's not always possible to please ourselves. We have to compromise,' Amelia pointed out, kindly.

'But somebody 'as to do all the chores, Ma'am,

and the young ladies ain't never done no more than make their beds.' Dora had seen herself as indispensable to this household, and it was a shock to discover she was not.

'The young ladies will share the light work. Maggie will still do the rough. We shall manage. We *have* to manage.'

'Yes, Ma'am.' Dora sniffed miserably, pressing a wet handkerchief to her trembling mouth.

'Do you propose to teach the two younger girls yourself, Madam?' Miss Beresford enquired, quietly.

'No, I do not. Kate and Lucy will finish their education at the Academy for Young Ladies at Hove. Grandfather Brent has kindly offered to pay the fees.'

'I see.' The governess was wondering how the temperamental Kate would react to such an arrangement. Lucy was a gentle, obedient child. There would be no trouble with the youngest of the Brent Sisters.

So they were dismissed – the governess to resume an interrupted lesson, and Cook, pushing the tearful housemaid down the basement stairs.

'Don't take on so, girl. The Mistress don't have no choice, and that's a fact,' she scolded. 'Put on the kettle and make us a cup of tea.'

When the door had closed, Amelia sighed. That was the first hurdle, but she still had to confront her daughters with their drastic change of status. She would wait till this evening, when they were settled comfortably in the drawing-room. It was difficult to anticipate their reactions, but of one thing she was certain: Kate would make a scene.

When all the girls had taken up their needlework or sketching, Ellen opened Mr Dickens's *David*

Copperfield, while Amelia glanced about the room on her daughters' bowed heads, and knew she could no longer postpone the ordeal.

'Just a moment, Ellen, please. There is a very important matter I must discuss with you – all of you,' she added, as their heads were raised and their eyes regarded her enquiringly. 'This morning I had the unpleasant duty of dismissing Cook, Miss Beresford and Dora. They will be leaving us in one month from today.'

The stunned silence was broken by Bertha, as expected. 'Why, Mother? What have they done?'

'Nothing to their discredit. I can no longer afford to pay their wages.'

The stark finality of the situation dropped like a pebble in a pond, and six pairs of eyes searched her face as though she had pronounced the end of the world. In a sense it was the end as they had known it, for nothing could ever be the same again without Cook, Miss Beresford and Dora.

'Are we poor?' Lucy whispered, fearfully, recalling the awful plight of Mr Dickens's Oliver Twist.

'We are not poor, and there is no need to advertise the fact that we shall be living in reduced circumstances. We have our pride, and I expect each one of you to conduct yourself in a ladylike manner.'

'But who will do all the work if you dismiss the servants?' Bertha demanded, suspiciously.

'My daughters,' Amelia answered calmly.

'That doesn't include Lucy and me, of course, does it, Mother? We are too young to help, and we have to continue with our education,' Kate reminded her.

'Quite so, Kate. Arrangements have been made

18

accordingly. You and Lucy will finish your education at the Academy for Young Ladies at Hove. Grandfather Brent has generously offered to pay the fees up to the age of eighteen.'

Kate tossed her dark head and glowered defiantly. 'I won't go! You can't make me!'

'You will do as you are bid.'

Kate threw down her sketching pad and scrambled to her feet.

'SIT DOWN!' Amelia commanded, authoritatively '. . . and listen to what I have to say. Where are your manners, child?'

Kate subsided sulkily, her eyes stormy.

'Must we live there, Mother? I mean, do we come home to sleep?' Lucy ventured.

'You come home for the holidays. It's a boarding school. They do not take day pupils.'

'May I take Teddy?'

'I expect it will be allowed since you are still a minor,' Amelia conceded. Teddy was a much-beloved relic of nursery days, handed down from the eldest to the youngest.

Jane was anxiously awaiting her turn to speak. She had folded up the square of hessian on which she had been working so laboriously, with coloured wools, and now she smiled at her mother with engaging frankness. 'May I do the cooking, *please*? I know how to roll out the pastry and knead the dough for the bread. I have watched Cook and you can learn a lot by watching. Please let me try.'

Amelia returned the smile. She was not unaware of those stolen moments in the kitchen. Very little escaped her vigilant eye where her daughters were concerned. She knew she had an ally in her middle daughter, who seemed to have grasped the situation so sensibly. 'I have already spoken to Cook on your behalf, Jane, and she has agreed to teach you the basic principles of plain cookery during the next four weeks, when you will be excused lessons with Miss Beresford.'

'*Thank you*, Mother,' breathed Jane, shiny-eyed in anticipation.

'Pooh! A fine cook! I'll bet you sixpence she will burn the sausages!' jeered Kate.

'That will do, Kate. Nobody is asking for your opinion,' Amelia admonished – and turned her attention to her three elder daughters. 'I have a very strong feeling, Ellen, that this will not concern you for long. I expect to be hearing of your engagement to Jonathan Cartwright in the very near future?' she prompted.

Ellen blushed and stammered, 'How did you know, Mother dear?'

'How does a mother know when her daughter falls in love? That young man has singled you out for attention since before he went to Sandhurst. The Vicar's youngest son has chosen well. In my opinion, Ellen, you are ideally suited to be the wife of an Army officer, and I am sure his parents will approve of the match.'

'Jonathan had intended to ask Father for my hand in marriage on his next vacation.' Ellen's voice was choked.

Amelia nodded, and controlled her own voice with an effort. 'Your father would undoubtedly have given his blessing, and his wishes will always be respected.'

'Yes, Mother.'

'That leaves Grace and me. We seem to be left with all the chores.' Bertha deeply resented her mother's unquestioned authority, and her voice was sharp with annoyance.

'Quite so, and with Maggie to do the rough, you should be able to manage the rest.'

Bertha shrugged. 'A lot of use Grace will be. I shall be the one to do all the donkey work.'

'It's entirely up to you, Bertha. I have every confidence in your ability to distribute the chores fairly.'

'When Grace gets her head in a book she forgets everything. A pity she was not born into the family of Mr Dickens!'

The object of her derision seemed not to have heard a single word. Crushed by the devastating blow of her father's death, Grace's gentle spirit would need time to recover. Her heart ached, and her sensitive nature would not take kindly to Bertha's strict regime. Amelia had other plans for her charming, ladylike daughter, but it was too soon to disclose them. Grace was much too young and vulnerable to be sent away.

In the month that followed, the normal routine of the household was disrupted by the frequent absences of Miss Beresford in search of other employment. She went forth, armed with a kind testimonial from her mistress, but her acute anxiety must have revealed itself in the several interviews with prospective employers since she had no success till the final week, when she was obliged to accept a post with an Anglo-Indian family, resident in this country for only a few months. Kate and Lucy dissolved into a flood of tears when the tin trunk was carried down from the attic and Miss Beresford started to pack. Too late they realized how fortunate they had been to have a governess who seldom lost her temper or found it necessary to punish her pupils. Their darling

'Berry' had suddenly assumed the nature of a saint, and her plain, bespectacled features a certain beauty of countenance that had gone unrecognized for years. Kate's parting gift of scent – which she never used – and Lucy's gift of Swiss embroidered handkerchiefs – too small and dainty to be of practical use to a person subject to head colds – were graciously accepted.

Among her most treasured possessions, however, and likely to upset her calm demeanour when she unpacked her trunk in a strange bedroom, were the samplers each girl had worked so laboriously during the early weeks in the schoolroom, starting with ELLEN DOROTHY BRENT AGED 6 YEARS to LUCY MARY BRENT AGED 7 YEARS. Lucy had been delicate, and allowed to spend an extra year in the nursery. Jane's sampler was grubby and spotted with dried blood from pricked fingers. Grace had been given full marks for a perfect example of a Victorian sampler, so clean and neat it was difficult to believe that such small fingers had actually compiled it.

With so many interrupted lessons, Ellen was instructed to escort her two younger sisters for walks, and it was Kate who decided where they would walk, and Kate who persuaded Ellen into the daring step of drinking coffee at Kong's.

'Don't be so stuffy, Ellen. It's our last chance to have fun,' Kate had argued, as their dutiful elder sister hesitated on the pavement, breathing the aroma of freshly roasted coffee beans. It would take a stronger character than Ellen to dissuade the self-willed Kate once she had made up her mind.

As for Jane, she was much too busy in the kitchen to spare a thought for her sisters. Every day was a challenge, and her lively mind soon grasped the basic essentials of plain cookery. No elaborate dishes had been served in Thomas Brent's lifetime. Good, nourishing food had been the order of the day, and would continue that way. Their small, select dinner parties had not been renowned for exotic dishes, but for the perfection of Cook's steak and kidney and mushroom pies, and the paper-thin pancakes served with lemon and castor sugar. There would be no more dinner parties, only small, select tea parties when Amelia had resumed her social obligations.

Having made her wishes known to her six daughters, she left them to their own resources, and did not interfere as they arranged their duties accordingly. It was Ellen who was given the distressing duty of escorting Kate and Lucy by train to the Academy at Hove, after Kate's final fruitless attempt to persuade Amelia to change her mind. Now she could settle down to her main duties under the new regime until she married Jonathan. All of three years would pass while he enjoyed his days as a cadet at Sandhurst – the best years of his life, he would discover. The morning room had been converted into the sewing room, and here Ellen was installed with a treadle machine and a pile of bed linen, sadly in need of repair after more than twenty years of constant use. Dora was delighted to hand over the basket of mending that had been yet another chore added to the rest for one pair of hands in a household of young ladies only expected to make their own beds. There would be night-gowns and petticoats to make for her sisters, and alterations to their dresses when a current fashion changed.

Amelia had acquired such an extensive wardrobe from Brent's store, when Thomas died, at the expense of her father-in-law, she had no need to bother Ellen. Indeed, it soon became evident that Amelia had no intention of changing her own routine. She would continue to breakfast in bed, and have cans of hot water carried up to her bedroom to fill the hip bath in which Thomas had found such sensual pleasure. Even in her pregnancies his adoring eyes had seen only beauty in her swelling belly and heavy breasts. As for Bertha, she could fret and frown, and make poor Maggie's life a misery, but the Mistress could always manage to dissociate herself from their bickerings.

Cook's basement bedroom, adjoining the kitchen, would soon be converted to the breakfast-room. Only midday dinner and supper would be served in the dining-room, and afternoon tea, as always, in the drawing-room.

Little overworked Maggie, on her hands and knees, scrubbing the tiled path to the front gate, would push her bucket aside when the Mistress passed by. In her black kid boots, she trod daintily over the wet tiles and lifted her skirts fastidiously with a gloved hand.

'Good morning, Maggie.'

'Good morning, Madam.'

That was all. The proud little figure would disappear through the green gate, and Maggie would wonder what the Mistress found to do now that she had no husband to please. It did not occur to her that ladies of leisure could spend a whole morning strolling on the promenade, greeting their acquaintances, admiring and criticizing the fashionable ensembles while the military band played rousing marches and continental waltzes.

Amelia was a gregarious person, and although she

preferred the company of the opposite sex because they flattered her, she would no longer associate with her late husband's male acquaintances. Her loyalty to her beloved Thomas would be absolute; on that she had already determined.

Smarting under the scolding tongue of the house-proud Bertha, Grace would escape to the world of fantasy. She had long since found a comforting anti-dote to the demands of her more forceful sisters. If she had been allowed, she would have spent her days sketching and reading. Perhaps Mother would no longer insist on a bracing walk, for health's sake, now that she was kept busy all morning with dom-estic chores? she wondered. Draped in a long, white pinafore, her slender hands encased in clumsy house-hold gloves, Grace had already been reminded more than once to use a stiff, not a soft brush for brushing the stair carpet, and how many times must she be reminded to empty the chamberpots?

'Grace is hopeless!' Bertha complained. But Amelia had responded that Grace might be per-suaded rather than bullied into doing her share of the chores. Bertha seemed to have forgotten that it had been Grace who had often rescued her from a strangling, sick headache in her younger days. Pale and shivering, with a throbbing head, the gentle sister knew exactly what to do – persuade the poor sufferer to lie down – draw the curtains – heat a hot brick in the oven – bathe the cold brow with hot towels, and wait for the weak voice to murmur 'Thank you', then creep away.

It was Grace who had helped to nurse Kate and Lucy ill with chickenpox and measles in nursery days, and Grace who put a splint on Jackie's broken leg. And it was Grace who gave Maggie the healing ointment for her chilblains. All this was forgotten by her sisters in the disrupted routine of a household that had always run so smoothly. Only Amelia had remembered, and seen her sympathetic second daughter as ideally suited to be a lady's companion in a quiet household. A semi-invalid of the upper class would appreciate her gentle virtues. Two years, or perhaps three, and Grace would be ready for such a post. It did not occur to Amelia that such an arrangement might not be agreeable to Grace. 'Mother knows best,' as Thomas would say. But Thomas was no longer here to make such a bold statement credible.

They had scarcely settled down to the new regime, however, with Cook installed in her new post at Littlehampton, and the tearful Dora welcomed into the household of Thomas Brent Senior, when Kate arrived, in a state bordering on hysteria. She had run away from the Academy for Young Ladies, but she had reckoned without Amelia's grim determination. Nothing annoyed her more than a disobedient daughter.

'Control yourself, child!' she commanded sternly, with Kate sobbing incoherently at her knees.

'It's so *awful*, Mother! I can't bear it! You cannot conceive how we are treated. I have to share a bedroom with seven other girls – *seven*! The food is terrible, and we are not allowed to speak at meals. It's been bells, bells, all day long, and if you are five minutes late, you get a black mark.' Kate was gulping in a desperate attempt to convey all the hideous tortures of such an establishment, and her innocent blue eyes, flooded with tears, would have moved a less stern parent to compassion.

Amelia hardened her heart. This was no time for

26

leniency. 'Where is Lucy?' she demanded.

'She wouldn't come.'

'Sensible girl.'

'She is everyone's pet.'

'And you are not?'

'I don't wish to be.'

'I am ashamed of you, Kate. You will go back on the morrow, and you will apologize for the disturbance you have caused. I shall conduct you there *personally*.'

'Please don't send me back, Mother darling. Why are you so cruel when I love you so much?'

A wry smile touched Amelia's stern mouth. This child had always been controlled by her emotions. Tears and laughter, and an infinite capacity to dramatize. Was she destined for the stage? An actress in the family? Heaven forbid!

Amelia squared her shoulders. 'Dry your tears, child. Tomorrow is another day. You and I will take coffee at Kong's and listen to the band. What do you say?'

Kate stared at her mother in wide-eyed astonishment, then flung her arms about her neck. 'Am I forgiven?' she asked, tremulously.

'If you promise me to behave sensibly in future.'

'I do. I will. I promise faithfully – and you won't tell Grandfather Brent?'

'No.'

'Were you sent away to boarding school when you were young, Mother?'

'Very young. At the tender age of eight.'

'Why?'

'Because my parents were killed by an avalanche in the Austrian Alps, and I was put in the care of an elderly guardian, who was not particularly fond of little girls.'

'Poor Mother.'

'So you see, Kate, I know all about it.'

'And you didn't run away?'

'There was no place to run. I stayed there till I was seventeen, then I met your father at my first grown-up ball. He was just down from Oxford, very charming, very handsome. We fell in love. You know the rest of the story, child.'

'Why do you never speak of it when it was so wonderfully romantic?'

'There are some things that can never be shared with our children.'

'Cook told me you were disinherited because you married into trade?'

'Cook was an old busybody.'

'Was it true?'

'I suppose so, though I never knew what happened. I had an elder brother, so he would inherit.'

'Uncle Richard?'

'Quite so.'

'He was killed in the Crimea, and his widow married a brother officer.' Kate was quoting the governess. Amelia had not mentioned it. The tragedy had been so far removed from her own safe little world, and the brother and sister were almost strangers.

She shook herself free of such disturbing memories, and stroked the dark head. 'Come, child, put on your hat and gloves. Bertha will be polishing the hall. She takes great pride in her duties. Your sister Bertha is a perfectionist, – and that is more than could be said of Grace, but then we are not all so houseproud. Grace has other worthy virtues.'

'If we went out the back gate we need not step on Bertha's polished floor?'

'Don't be tiresome, Kate. The back entrance is for tradesmen, and for Jane when she exercises the dog.'

'Yes, Mother.'

The scolding was forgotten as Kate followed Amelia through the green gate. It was fun to leave her sisters behind, all busy with their morning chores. She could hear the sewing machine rattling, and Jane shovelling coal on the fire in the basement kitchen. Bertha scowled as they went past. The parquet floor shone like a mirror, and Amelia nodded approvingly at Grace who was dusting the stairs.

'Good morning, Maggie,' said Amelia, as Maggie pushed the bucket aside.

'Good morning, Madam,' came the prompt reply.

'Good morning, Maggie,' echoed Kate – but there was no answer.

'Stuck up little puss!' muttered the old servant, scrubbing furiously at the tiles.

Worthing was a favourite seaside resort, and today, in early Summer, at the start of another holiday season, everything was clean and sparkling in the fresh paint. The striped canvas was new on the deck chairs lining the promenade, from the pier to the bandstand, and the band enclosure was crowded with neat rows of chairs. Not many were vacant as the young widow with the pretty daughter selected two in the centre aisle, and unfurled a dainty black parasol. It was the only black parasol to be seen in the band enclosure on that bright morning, in the lovely month of May, and whispered exchanges reflected on the sadness of such an early bereavement. The silver hair, piled so becomingly under the fashionable hat, enhanced the beauty and quiet dignity of the youthful lines of a face partly hidden by the veil.

But the blue eyes were misty with memories as she sat there, listening to the strains of the *Blue Danube*. Here she had sat with Thomas and their six daughters on Easter Sunday afternoon. If she closed her eyes, she could imagine he was still sitting beside her, in immaculate white flannels, a nautical jacket and boater. He would reach for her gloved hand when the band played a Strauss waltz, and they would exchange a secret smile, remembering they had fallen in love as they circled the ballroom on that memorable night. Her starched petticoats had rustled as she leaned towards him. The dress was an Easter present, and the colour matched her hair that Thomas declared was as golden as ripe corn. What would he think of it now? It was inconceivable that she could wake one morning to find it was silver, yet it had happened.

Everything about her was small and dainty, and not one of her six daughters could boast such tiny feet and hands. The parents were proud of their six daughters, but not absorbed by them. A son would have changed their attitude towards their children, and Amelia would have adored a boy child.

On that Easter Sunday afternoon, only a few short weeks ago, they had spread themselves over a row of deck chairs, shortly before three o'clock, and it seemed there would never be a time when the whole family would not be together, to stroll along the crowded promenade, after one of Cook's satisfying Sunday dinners, enjoying the admiring and covetous glances of less fortunate families. Amelia always chose her daughters' clothes discreetly, from the simple patterns the dressmaker could easily copy. The four elder girls were dressed alike now, in high-necked blouses and ankle-length skirts, for weekdays. For Sunday, they were permitted to adorn their rather prim dresses with a lace collar and cuffs, or hand embroidery. Kate and Lucy had worn the same childish style of dress since their early days in the schoolroom. Now they had been promoted to a more becoming style, as befitted the young ladies of the Academy.

Kate knew she was pretty, and that she and her mother were attracting a deal of attention. If only she hadn't to go back to that hateful place! If only she had breasts like Lydia Maitland, the head girl! It was beastly to be so flat-chested, and to have her hair tied back with a bow of ribbon. She smiled and preened herself when she caught the eye of the youngest bandsman, and her feet tapped to the rhythm of the waltz.

As the last notes faded, polite clapping echoed round the enclosure. Kate was still clapping excitedly when the applause had died away. Amelia opened her eyes and laid a restraining hand on her tempestuous young daughter. But the conductor was smiling and bowing, and they played an encore.

Dancing lessons were included in the curriculum at the Academy, but it was no fun at all dancing with girls. One day she would fall in love, in the arms of a handsome young man as they circled the ballroom, just like Mother. She couldn't wait to grow up. Romantic day-dreams of her future husband had already replaced the adoration of a handsome father. She would not marry into trade, however. A man looked his best in uniform.

She envied her elder sister, Ellen, and couldn't bear to witness the loving glances that passed between Ellen and the young cadet from Sandhurst, who usually managed to seat himself, with a companion, in a convenient position in the band enclosure when they were home on vacation. Mother and Father smiled benignly on the budding romance.

They had known the Vicar's youngest son since he sat in the family pew dressed in a white sailor suit, and fidgeted impatiently till the sidesman presented the collection plate, when he dropped in a penny with a loud clatter. That was Jonathan's big moment in one-and-a-half hours of acute boredom.

There were few opportunities for Jonathan to be alone with Ellen, but he certainly never missed an opportunity to meet her during the three years that followed her father's tragic death. With her sister, Grace, as chaperone, they would meet at a chosen spot on the promenade on Saturday afternoons – the only time the girls were permitted to please themselves – during the Easter and Summer vacations. It was a daring escapade for such a day and age, and the handsome young cadet, with a girl on each arm, would enjoy his self-importance. When Kate reported having seen the trio laughing and chatting together while she sat moodily in the deck chair in the company of Lucy and her bosom friend, Rose Smith, who was spending a holiday at The Haven, Amelia paid no attention. Too often in the past Kate had told tales about her sisters and they resented it.

Amelia was delighted to hear that her eldest daughter was obviously being courted seriously by the Vicar's youngest son. He was a very presentable young man. Ellen was no beauty, but she had her father's distinction, and with her dark hair and eyes, her tall figure and her calm serenity she was so like Thomas.

Jonathan was charming to Grace, but only because he was naturally charming to the opposite sex, as Ellen would discover to her cost soon after their marriage. Jonathan Cartwright could charm a bird from a bough with that irresistible smile. The future, however, was in the lap of the gods, he would remind himself with careless bravado.

'You may invite the young gentleman to take tea with us on the occasion of your next meeting,' Amelia told Ellen. She had been watching from the drawing-room window, and seen them shaking hands at the gate. Then he had saluted smartly, closed the gate, and marched away.

'Thank you, Mother.' Ellen's dark eyes were shining, and her cheeks were flushed.

Grace was looking bored, but then she was not in love with the handsome young soldier or any other gentleman for that matter. She had already decided, since she could never hope to find another to compare with her beloved father, she would remain a spinster. Having made this momentous decision on the day of the funeral, she would abide by it to the end of her days.

But Jonathan soon became a favourite with the other Brent sisters, and even the critical Bertha could find no fault in him. Handing round cups of tea, dainty cucumber sandwiches, and Madeira cake, Jonathan gave the impression that he was enjoying every moment, and that was his secret weapon.

Amelia found herself wishing he were her son. Thomas would have felt the same way.

He flirted with the naughty Kate, made Lucy blush with his teasing, and congratulated Jane on the excellence of the Madeira cake. In every way his manners were beyond reproach, and Amelia was enchanted with her future son-in-law.

Soon after the tea-party, the Sunday School Summer outing provided an even better opportunity for the two young people to be together. Three of the sisters being Sunday School teachers, it was a duty as well as a pleasure to accompany the party of children. They travelled in two wagonettes to the old windmill on the Downs, a favourite spot for Summer picnics. They set forth one hot afternoon in August, with a plentiful supply of bread and butter and two kinds of cake, lemonade for the children, and all the equipment for brewing fresh tea for the adults, carefully packed in the two hampers, stowed away under the driver's seat. The Vicar was in charge of the first wagonette, the Curate in charge of the second.

For many of the children it was the highlight of the Summer holiday, and even more exciting than the Christmas treat in the church hall, when the deserving few were presented with small volumes of good works and moral integrity, such as *Uncle Tom's Cabin*, *The Orphan Sisters*, and *The Crossing Sweeper*.

Jonathan had seated himself next to Ellen in the crowded wagonette, and held her hand all the way. Jane found herself seated beside the Curate in the second wagonette, and nothing could have pleased her more. He was rather an insignificant young man with a nervous stammer, but for Jane Brent he held all the virtues of a good Christian, and she admired him tremendously. Jane was a lively companion, and he was amused by her comments when the tea was spread over the grass, a short distance from the windmill.

'It reminds me of the parable of Jesus feeding the five thousand with two barley loaves and small fishes!' she chuckled – 'only we do have cake!'

'And not m-m-more than fifty children, Miss J-J-Jane,' he reminded her, kindly.

Games were organized by the indefatigable Vicar,

and the children ran races for pennies. The boys rolled down the steep banks, but the girls could only stand by, watching enviously. Even on a picnic a certain decorum must be observed in the presence of the Vicar.

Bertha, and her bosom friend, Norah Styles, were detailed to brew the tea and unpack the hampers, while Ellen and Jane ran about entertaining the children. Jonathan was a great asset, and a favourite with the children.

Hot and breathless, they all assembled in a group for the Vicar's short prayer of thanksgiving, for a fine day, and happy occasion.

Jogging along in the crowded wagonette, Jonathan's arm slipped round Ellen's slim waist. He could feel her heart beating and her body tense at such familiarity. His dear girl would have been profoundly shocked had she known his thoughts! Three years was a long time to wait – too long. His sexual appetite had long since been satisfied by an obliging housemaid.

Three years had passed since Amelia was widowed, and her authority had become more firmly established. There was a hardness about her now that Thomas would have deplored. She had her way about everything, and would not concede the smallest decision to any one of her six daughters. Kate still defied her openly, but the verbal battles were soon over because Amelia held the purse strings, and could threaten Kate with a cut in her meagre allowance. She tolerated the Academy for Young Ladies because she had to, but she was not popular with the girls or the staff, while Lucy had endeared herself to everyone. The orphan girl, Rose Smith, would have spent all her holidays at the Academy but for the intervention of Lucy Brent. And Amelia, remembering her own unhappy childhood, was sympathetic to Lucy's pleas that Rose should spend the holidays at The Haven. Rose was tearfully grateful. She had never loved anyone as she loved Lucy. But Amelia wrote to her youngest daughter, enforcing certain rules and restrictions on their liberty. They must not be allowed to forget to take their share of the chores. They must share a bed, and keep their room tidy, help Jane in the kitchen, and lay the table for meals. They must iron their own clothes, and polish all the shoes. Lucy readily agreed. She would have agreed to anything to have the company of Rose. They were kindred spirits, and had pledged a lifetime of love and loyalty. No thought of suitors or marriage had entered their heads. They were still too young.

Now Amelia was anxious to make provision for her second daughter. Bertha was so aggravated by her sister's dreamy ways and lack of energy, and one couldn't blame her. They were so diverse in every aspect, and it was becoming irksome to listen to the complaints of the dominant sister, and to watch the complacency of the other.

Amelia was determined on her original plan for Grace, and she found what she was looking for in the columns of *The Times* one morning. It read as follows:

Refined young lady sought as companion to semi-invalid. Comfortable house situated in Bayswater, London. Generous salary. Please apply with credentials and photograph to Mr and Mrs Courtney-Halliday, Box 150, The Times.

Amelia was delighted. It was exactly right for Grace. Her six daughters had all been photographed separately, shortly before the death of Thomas, and only the two younger girls had changed in appearance. On her desk was the family group that Thomas had admired so much – a mother surrounded by her six daughters, all looking as solemn as owls, for the professional photographer had not suggested they smile.

Grace might have been spared a lot of heartache if she had been consulted at this stage, but Amelia was so accustomed to deciding what was best for the girls that she took a sheet of the embossed notepaper without giving the matter second thoughts. THE HAVEN, RICHMOND ROAD, WORTHING was a good address, and the Courtney-Hallidays could easily check on their credentials. Thomas Brent & Son was an old-established and superior drapery store. The Vicar would also oblige if called upon.

When she had completed the letter to her entire satisfaction, she enclosed the photograph, and went out to post it. The pillar-box was only a few yards down the road, but she never stepped outside the green gate without a hat and gloves.

It was very satisfying to her self-esteem to have taken the first step to solving the problem of a household so often disrupted by Bertha's angry accusations. One could no longer ignore the atmosphere of positive dislike between the two sisters. They must be separated, the sooner the better.

As she dropped the letter into the box, however, she was suddenly aware of some misgiving. What would Thomas say to such an arrangement? Grace was his favourite. Would Thomas blame her if she had made a sad mistake? The question hung in the air as she walked slowly back to the house and let herself in the front door.

She could hear the girls chatting over their

mid-morning cup of tea in the basement. Removing her hat and gloves, she laid them carefully on the hallstand, glanced at her reflection in the mirror, and went to sit down in the drawing-room to await the cup of hot chocolate that Jane would bring on the small silver tray, with her favourite *petit beurre* biscuits.

Jane was so dependable and so cheerful. There was never any trouble with Jane. The kitchen was her domain, and she spent more time in the basement than any of her sisters. She treated Maggie kindly, and always found something for her basket at the end of the day.

Maggie's children would be waiting outside the back gate of The Haven at four o'clock, their peaked little faces screwed into anxious anticipation. Jack would be straining at the leash and barking furiously. He could hear the children whispering, and scuffling in the loose gravel. Jane insisted that he would not hurt a fly, that his barking was pure excitement and not at all vicious, but even the tradesmen were wary of Jack, and as for Maggie, she scuttled across the yard and through the gate, clutching her battered old hat and a basket of appetizing leftovers.

'What jew got today, Mum?' a piping chorus would greet her as she slammed the gate.

But she stood no nonsense from them, and her calloused hand was hard on exploring fingers. Once outside that gate, Maggie was her own mistress, and the children knew it.

2

Three days later, Amelia received a most courteous reply from Mr Courtney-Halliday. He and his wife would be delighted to welcome Miss Grace into their home, and she would be assured of every kindness. Her duties would not be arduous, and his dear wife was a gentle, uncomplaining lady, who suffered with a weak heart. They would be much obliged if Miss Grace could be available as soon as possible, and would appreciate a telegram announcing date and time of arrival. All expenses would be refunded.

The letter had been delivered on Amelia's breakfast tray, and she could hear Grace emptying chamberpots in the upstairs lavatory. This particular chore was most distasteful to her fastidious daughter, but Bertha had not spared her.

Amelia wrapped a cashmere shawl about her shoulders. It was pale mauve and light as thistledown. She slipped out of bed, opened the door and called, 'Grace, will you come here, please. I wish to speak to you.'

A tall young woman, in a long white pinafore, stood hesitating in the doorway. Mother's bedroom was such a private place, and she blinked nervously at the dainty little figure sitting bolt upright in the exact centre of the huge bed – the bed in which all her children had been conceived and born. The Spartan plainness of her daughters' rooms had nothing in common with this boudoir, with its soft draperies and white carpet.

'Close the door, child, and sit down.'

Grace obeyed. She was not unduly troubled by the summons, for it could only be something that had displeased Bertha, though it was customary to be summoned to the drawing-room later in the day. Amelia's cheeks were pink, her blue eyes shining, and her lustrous silver hair crowned a face that would always be beautiful, even in old age. Glancing apprehensively at the open letter on the breakfast tray, Grace could feel a little shiver of fear travel down her spine, but she waited for an explanation because it was her nature to do so. The hands folded on her lap smelled faintly of the chamberpots. She had forgotten to bring the housemaid's gloves, and dare not evoke Bertha's anger, wasting time in collecting them from the basement.

'It has become increasingly evident that two of my daughters can no longer live amicably under the same roof,' Amelia began. 'Regretfully, therefore, they must be separated. This household is constantly taking sides under the tension of conflicting reports. *It must stop*. I am sending you away, child, for your own good. It has not been an easy decision to take, and a suitable post was not readily available. I do not expect a daughter of mine to take a post as governess, but here is the perfect situation, in my opinion, for a calm, gentle nature such as yours. I will read you the letter that I have just received in reply to my recent application. It is most courteously penned.'

'Please, Mother, don't send me away. I will try harder,' Grace whispered, chokingly. She could not believe it was happening, but she was helpless to prevent it. Underneath that deceptively fragile

40

appearance was a ruthless determination. There was no tenderness in those searching blue eyes or firm lips. Tenderness had no place in Amelia's widowhood. But Grace was too proud to plead a second time, when the letter had been read. If her beloved Father had not died – if Bertha had not been put in charge – if she herself had the strength and energy to accomplish all the household chores she had been allotted – if she hadn't been born with her head in the clouds . . .

She sighed, and asked wistfully, 'When do I leave?'

'I thought Sunday would be the best day to travel. Ellen will accompany you and see you settled. It's only an hour's journey by train, and you must ask for a free Sunday once a month to come home to see us. Don't look so crestfallen, child. A lady's companion has a certain status, you know, and you will not be treated as a servant.'

'No, Mother. I quite understand. Will you excuse me now?'

Amelia nodded, more than a little surprised by the lack of emotion, but then she was not really close to any of her daughters. What had she expected?

Automatically and dutifully, Grace went about her morning chores in the bedrooms. At precisely eleven o'clock, she went downstairs to the basement breakfast room, to join her sisters for their mid-morning tea and biscuits. Her gaze wandered round the table – to Bertha, who was pouring the tea, Ellen, who had left her sewing machine for a short break, and Jane, rosy-cheeked and cheerful, from her warm kitchen. Kate and Lucy would not be home till the end of July for the Summer vacation, so she would not see them to say goodbye. It was the ninth of June, 1870, a date that Grace would remember to the end of her days, and a date that a million others would remember for the passing of Charles Dickens.

'What did Mother want with you, Grace?' Bertha demanded, in her forthright manner. She always went straight to the point, and she always called a spade a spade.

'I am being sent away. She has found a suitable post for me as a lady's companion in Bayswater, London.'

'Why? What have you done?' asked Jane, wide-eyed with curiosity.

Ellen reached for Grace's hand across the table, her brown eyes soft with compassion. Bertha shrugged, and her own grey eyes held a hint of triumph.

'For my own good, she tells me,' said Grace, quietly.

As she spoke, they could hear Amelia's bedroom door close, and shortly after, the drawing-room door creaked open.

'Remind me to oil that door. It gives me the fidgets.' Bertha helped herself to a biscuit, and pushed the plate across the table, but Grace shook her head.

'Are you taking Mother's hot chocolate or shall I take it?' Ellen asked Bertha.

'You take it. She may be a little more forthcoming since you are the eldest.'

Ellen frowned anxiously. 'Do you think she might be persuaded to change her mind?'

'No, I doubt it. Mother never changes her mind.'

'But this concerns us all, Bertha. I know there must be changes in a family, but I thought I should be the first to leave home, not Grace. This is so sudden. We can't spare Grace, she is indispensable.'

Jane agreed.

'Nobody is indispensable,' Bertha argued, her

mind already at work on a plan to recruit Norah Styles –
her only friend and confidante, and probably the only
person to understand that aggressive mentality and not
be offended by it. Norah had been apprenticed to a
dressmaker at the age of fourteen, and usually came
along to help with the fittings. She would be eighteen
now – a big, strong girl, as handsome as a gypsy, who
still had to be reminded not to whistle in the company of
the young ladies.

Grace sipped her tea in agonized silence, while Ellen
climbed the basement stairs with the hot chocolate and
biscuits on the little silver tray.

When she returned, she looked at Grace and shook
her head. 'Her mind is made up, and I am to accompany you to Bayswater on Sunday afternoon.'

Grace nodded. She hadn't expected anything different, but it was kind of Ellen to try. They were close,
these two sisters. They had shared everything since
nursery days, when the nursemaid had pushed them
around in a basinette, and they had been much
admired, the one so dark, the other so fair. The nursemaid always insisted they were good as gold, and gave
no trouble. Then came Bertha, who seemed to be born
with a strong determination to have her own way.
Right from the start she had resented the attention paid
to her two pretty sisters, who walked dutifully on either
side of the basinette, holding the handles. If Grace
tired, the nursemaid would sit her in the basinette, but
Bertha objected so strongly, she had to be removed.

'She's a proper little vixen, that one,' the nursemaid
would complain to Cook, who always helped her with
the pram. Bertha was nobody's favourite, and she
grew into a plain child with spiteful ways, while her
three younger sisters were claiming their share of attention, especially Kate.

'Perhaps it will not be too disagreeable, Grace. It could be fun, living in London, and actually seeing the Queen,' Jane reminded her sister, with her customary optimism.

'It will depend entirely on the disposition of her employer, particularly the wife. Let us hope she will not be too demanding,' Ellen sighed, sympathetically, and added, 'You don't have to stay if you don't like them, Grace. I shall come and fetch you home.' They all knew it was wishful thinking.

'But they must *like* you, Grace, for they engaged you without an interview,' Jane insisted.

'She photographs well. Grace is so *ladylike*!' sneered Bertha.

Grace made no comment. Her head was bowed, and her eyes flooded with tears. Pushing back her chair, she walked away. Jane would have followed her, but Bertha barred the way.

'Let her alone. For the first time in her life she must stand on her own two feet. Don't baby her. She is a grown-up young woman, not a child to be protected and cosseted.'

'But she is so shy and sensitive. What will become of her?' Ellen protested.

'We shall soon see, shan't we?' Bertha had the last word, as usual.

The routine of the household was barely disrupted by the departure of Amelia's second daughter. Grace had accepted the ultimatum with typical composure, and only Ellen was aware of the heartache as they packed the tin trunk in their bedroom. There had been no time to engage the dressmaker, so Ellen had been busy on alterations, and some small adornment to the plainest of the dresses. But Amelia, who had spent more money than she could afford on equipping her two youngest daughters only recently, could not be prevailed upon to spend more.

'The dresses are most suitable, under the circumstances,' she insisted. 'Your mistress will not expect to be eclipsed by her companion.'

But Ellen had contrived to brighten the uniform plainness with bands of coloured braid on the skirts, and lace collars and cuffs. All the girls possessed three sets of Summer and Winter underwear, three cotton night-gowns, and three winceyette. This had not met the requirements of the Academy for Young Ladies, however, and Amelia had been appalled by the list she had received after the girls had been formally enrolled. The dressmaker had worked twelve hours a day for a whole month in the sewing room. A certain status and style had to be observed in dressing young ladies for the Academy. It had pleased Kate enormously, but Lucy had been quite happy in the childish styles of the schoolroom.

No money was spent on Grace's wardrobe, apart from the yards of braid and the collars and cuffs that Ellen had paid for, out of her own small allowance. Grace received parting gifts from Amelia and her three sisters. Handkerchiefs from Ellen, small tins of homemade toffee and coconut ice from Jane, and even Bertha had persuaded herself to part with a cameo brooch. Amelia found she could spare two pairs of new gloves from her glove drawer – not the best quality, but second best.

When the station cab arrived on the Sunday afternoon, and the driver had carried out the tin trunk, Amelia kissed her daughter affectionately on both cheeks, bade her write a regular weekly letter, and watched the departure of the two girls from the drawing-room window. Bertha and Jane were standing at the open gate, and Maggie stood on the pavement with her tribe of children, for Sunday was her free day. Only beds were made and potatoes boiled at The Haven on Sundays.

'Poor Miss Grace. It's a crying shame. She won't last long in London, for she looks that delicate,' Maggie predicted, as Bertha closed the gate.

The two sisters sat with their gloved hands firmly clasped, and watched the flying landscape with misted eyes, both equally determined not to weep. Amelia's stoic example in the past three years had not been wasted on her four elder daughters. Only Kate and Lucy still wept with the uncontrolled abandon of childhood, but would soon learn to control their emotions at the Academy. Not one of her daughters had seen the crumpled little figure buried in the pillow on which her beloved's head had once rested, or heard the stifled sobbing, and they never would. Grief was a very private affair for Amelia.

On this short journey to London by train, Ellen found her thoughts straying, unwittingly, to the long and arduous journey by sea and overland to some remote province of Northern India. She would be separated from her sisters by thousands of miles. It was inconceivable. How had she allowed it to happen? Jonathan had courted her patiently, but persistently, for more than three years, encouraged by the approval of his parents and her own mother. But it was only now, as she travelled to London with Grace, that she fully realized the extent of such a commitment. *Five years, possibly seven*! Jonathan had been rather vague about the exact number of years that his regiment would be stationed in India. Perhaps he had wanted to spare her too much anxiety on such an alarming prospect. He was a dear boy, and they were in love. She would make her solemn vows in the church they had attended since nursery days. It was ordained, from the beginning. She knew every word of the marriage service, and the familiar hymns they would sing. It would be a white wedding, with four of her sisters as bridesmaids. Grace had already decided not to attend her sister's wedding. It was too soon to ask favours of her new employers.

Ellen had turned from the window and was looking at her now with an enormous frown. The train was racing towards London, but her rigid control had not snapped. Outwardly calm and composed, only her eyes reflected the sadness of separation. And Ellen, who thought she knew all there was to know about a sister who had been her constant companion since they shared the basinette, was troubled by such controlled emotion. It was not natural. Were there hidden depths in Grace she had not suspected?

When the porter came to lift down the tin trunk from the rack, it was Grace who stepped out, confidently, and followed his truck down the near-deserted platform. Catching Ellen's hand, she smiled, tremulously. 'Don't worry about me, dearest Nell. I shall cope.'

They took a cab from the station, and held hands all the way, listening to the clop-clop of the horse's hooves. Turning into Hyde Park, they leaned forward, eagerly absorbing a scene so unfamiliar and fascinating. A detachment of cavalry, resplendent in scarlet uniforms, riding two abreast, sat their magnificent mounts with the stiff immobility of toy soldiers. Nursemaids walked their charges sedately in their Sunday best, restraining active small boys with firm hands. There were no hoops today. The Queen

47

strongly disapproved of anything in the nature of frivolity on the Sabbath. Footmen from the mansions in Park Lane were exercising their mistresses' pet dogs, and a procession of open carriages moved at a leisurely pace – the ladies shielding their complexions under pretty parasols, the gentlemen bowing to acquaintances and raising their hats politely. It was like a colourful pageant on this warm afternoon in early Summer. But nobody gave a thought to the discomfort of the liveried coachmen or the sweating cavalry officers in their close-fitting uniforms.

In July and August, the mansions in Park Lane, and the town houses of the upper class would be shuttered. Wives and daughters would be comfortably installed in spacious country houses, enjoying garden parties and tennis parties. Trim parlourmaids would serve tea with dainty cucumber sandwiches and cakes, under the spreading branches of the cedars. The nursemaids would be away to the seaside with their charges – to Frinton-on-Sea and Littlehampton. Husbands and fathers would remain behind, and probably welcome the change from the bustling activities of a big household to the peaceful comfort of their clubs. In late August they would join their wives on their country estates for two weeks before the whole family moved back to London.

But the two young women from middle-class society were beginning to get anxious as the cab turned into Bayswater Road. Grace clutched Ellen's hand more tightly.

'Nearly there,' she whispered, with a little shiver of apprehension.

When the cab swung suddenly into the drive of a house, both were surprised that it was not more pretentious. Indeed, it was no larger than The

Haven, but a different shape, and no wistaria was allowed to climb the walls. Iron railings surrounded the basement area, and a flight of white steps led to a front door with a shining brass knocker and letter box. Striped sunblinds shaded all the lower windows, but the small attic windows under the roof, where the servants slept, were bare. They would be sweltering hot in Summer, and freezing cold in Winter, but servants did not expect to be comfortable.

The door opened as Grace stepped down from the cab, followed by Ellen. They were expected. Somebody had been watching. A pert house-parlourmaid, in long black skirts, a starched white apron, and a cap with streamers, stared at this latest addition to the household with wary eyes. The Master would soon be chasing after this good-looking piece, and she would be kept in her place! These were her first thoughts, and her manner was sulky.

'Good afternoon, Miss.' It was a grudging sort of welcome, and Grace was momentarily hurt by the lack of warmth, till she saw the maid smile at the cabby who carried the trunk, and dumped it in the hall. Obviously it was not their first meeting, and the maid handed over some money that seemed to please him. He winked, and muttered 'Ta-ta for now, duckie,' touched his cap to the young ladies, ran down the steps, and climbed aboard. The whip flicked the horse's flanks and the cab circled the drive, and out through the other gates.

Only then did the maid close the door and give her attention to the new lady's companion. 'This way, please,' she said, and they followed her across the polished hall to a door at the far end, where she tapped and stood back deferentially as it was flung open by the Master of the house, with an outstretched hand, and a curt little bow.

Henry Courtney-Halliday was not a handsome man, and at middle-age, already inclined to portliness, but his lack of height and distinction were more than compensated for by a pair of penetrating dark eyes and black hair, smooth as a raven's wing, on a head too big for his body. He smiled a welcome as he took Grace's hand. Henry Courtney-Halliday was enchanted with the new lady's companion. The photograph had not done justice to the exquisite complexion and misted blue eyes, nor the air of proud dignity as she stood before him. His dear wife did not deserve such a paragon, but he was more than satisfied. His personal choice had been the right one.

'How do you do, Miss Grace.' His cultured voice was deep and pleasing to Grace, at that first encounter with her first employer. He was obviously a gentleman.

'How do you do, Sir,' she answered. 'May I introduce my sister, Ellen?'

'Charmed.' A curt little bow, but no handshake for Ellen.

The initial stages of a new relationship were always tedious, and he was impatient to see the impact of this delightful creature on his ailing wife. It was yet another chapter in a marriage that had turned sour since the birth of a still-born child three years ago. There would never be another.

'Come in,' he invited, cordially. Then he flung a command over his shoulder. 'You may serve tea now, Parsons.'

'Very good, Sir.' Parsons bobbed a curtsey, and hurried away with burning cheeks. It was the end of the intimacy she had enjoyed, and she was so jealous of the newcomer she could have wrung her neck! Such airs and graces. Who did she think she was? A paid servant like the rest of them, and if she expected to be waited on, she would soon discover her mistake. Not that she envied her the job. The Mistress was a poor, weak creature, and she didn't deserve to have such a kind, upstanding gentleman for a husband. Of course he was entitled to a bit of a cuddle. There was no harm in it. Under that frock coat and striped trousers was a strong, lustful body, only waiting to be satisfied. It was as simple as that. No sentiment, no affection. He took her whenever the Mistress had been particularly tiresome – never less than once a week! It was easy to slip into his dressing-room when the rest of the household had retired to bed. The Master and Mistress had not shared a bed since the early stages of her confinement. Now her boudoir was separated by a small bedroom where the companion slept. Perhaps she wouldn't stay. It was a comforting thought. The last one had stayed only a month, and the one before that only three months. They couldn't stand the same old routine, day after day. It was deadly dull. And the Master had not fancied either of them. What a laugh!

Mrs Weldon, the cook-housekeeper, and Harrison, the fat, elderly housemaid, were all agog to hear the latest bulletin from upstairs. Parsons was the go-between, and they suspected her duties had included a bit of 'you-know-what', for she was that saucy.

'What's she like?' Cook demanded, eagerly, pushing the kettle over the glowing coals in the shining range.

'A fancy piece. Looks as if a puff of wind would blow her away. Suppose she thinks she's got a nice cushy little job. My golly!' Parsons scoffed.

'Is she pretty?' Harrison was concerned only with the comfort and pleasure of her poor Miss Beatrice.

51

She was just a clinging vine, and had never been anything else. Even as a little girl she couldn't bear to be scolded. Harrison had started her working life as nursemaid, and taken over the Courtney nursery when the old nurse had retired to a cottage on the estate. The Courtneys were a wealthy county family, and Beatrice their only child. There must have been a handsome dowry, for the Master had been plain Mr Halliday, a mere clerk in a City bank, living in lodgings when they first met. For all her tears and sensitiveness, Miss Beatrice had a will of her own, and it seemed she took one look at the young man who had been sent out to attend her father in his carriage, and lost her heart.

'That is the man I wish to marry, Papa,' she was reported to have said – the coachman often heard more than was good for him – and her Papa had patted her little gloved hand and smiled tolerantly.

'My foolish darling. What will you say next?' he teased.

When he realized she was serious in her intention, he took her away, and they toured Europe for six months. Father and daughter were inseparable. It was a beautiful relationship, but it was not enough. On their return, Beatrice began to toy with her food, deliberately losing weight. In a few months she was so thin and languid, her devoted nurse was frightened that she was going into a decline – a not uncommon state for love-sick maidens in that day and age. So she had her way eventually, but her fond Papa had died of a stroke shortly after the marriage, which was not surprising under the circumstances. Only the Master called her Harrison. Miss Beatrice still called her Nana. As for the weak heart, that was just another device to get her own way, the sly little puss!

So when she asked the question 'Is she pretty?', she was remembering the first of a long line of companions who had nearly wrecked a marriage so precariously balanced on the whims of a very emotional wife. Yet his indiscretions were always forgiven, and it was an open secret that Beatrice Courtney-Halliday still adored her husband.

Parsons was telling them that the new companion was not only pretty, but she was a lady. 'She had only to open her mouth and there was proof,' Parsons insisted, grudgingly, as she took up the heavy silver tray. 'That spells trouble, don't it?' she added.

Cook and Harrison nodded agreement. But it was the Master who had earned Cook's loyalty and devotion.

Into this divided household, the unsuspecting Grace Brent followed her employer with trusting innocence. It was the study, not the drawing-room, into which they had been invited – a man's room, with book-lined walls, leather armchairs, and a bureau that filled the window recess. A rich Turkey carpet covered the floor, and the fragrant aroma of a recently smoked cigar still clung to the velvet curtains.

'Please sit down.' His voice held a gentle note as he addressed the sisters. He could be charming, and he could be boorish, depending on the company he was entertaining. For a man of humble birth, he was surprisingly arrogant, in his relationships with those he had long since considered his inferiors.

It had been a meteoric rise in promotion in that City bank, for the Courtneys had been shareholders for three generations, and a mere clerk could not be permitted to marry into such an influential family. Henry Halliday had been lucky. He was the envy of all the other clerks still sitting on their high stools, bending over their ledgers. But he was no fool, and he knew exactly how to cope with such good fortune. There was a hard streak of ruthlessness in his mentality. 'The Lord helps those who help themselves' could have been his motto.

A member of a gentleman's club in Pall Mall, and dressed by one of the best tailors in Savile Row, there was still a trace of the working-class background in the strong features, and the blunt thumbs on the big, masculine hands.

Both sisters were sitting stiffly upright in the leather chairs, and he smiled reassuringly because he could sense their anxiety.

'I thought we would have a little private chat, you and I, before we join my wife for tea. She gets so agitated over making the acquaintance of a new companion. I must be perfectly honest with you, Miss Grace. There have been several very agreeable ladies in the past, but they have not stayed long. It could be that they found the post tedious and restrictive. Because of my wife's indifferent health, we do not entertain, and we have no visitors. I am obliged to leave her occasionally, on a business trip to the Continent. We have a branch of the bank in Paris, another in Brussels. So you see how important it is to have a congenial and trustworthy companion? You do understand?'

'Yes, Sir, I understand.' Grace was beginning to wonder if she would fit into this household, and whether the wife could be as patient and long-suffering as he had declared in that letter to Mother.

'It's a question of understanding and tolerance,' he continued. 'This heart condition is not serious, but her doctor has advised a quiet routine, and no extra exertion in any way. These frequent changes are disturbing, Miss Grace, for both of us, and I would be most sincerely grateful if you could stay with us for at least a twelve-month. Am I asking too much for you, now that you know the circumstances?'

'No, Sir. I can assure you on that point – that is, if Madam likes me.'

'I have little doubt that she will find you a most agreeable companion.'

'I will do my best to please her, and as for the quiet routine, it will suit me admirably. My sister will confirm I have always been the quiet one in the family. Isn't that so, Ellen?'

'That is so,' Ellen agreed. 'Quiet and kind, and so very sympathetic to illness or misfortune. We are going to miss her sadly, Sir.'

Grace was blushing with embarrassment. 'Really, Ellen, you paint too rosy a picture. Mr Courtney-Halliday will be thinking he has discovered a paragon!'

'I am already inclined to regard you as such, my dear young lady. Thank you, Miss Brent, for confirming my opinion.' He bowed to Ellen and smiled disarmingly at Grace. 'I can hear Parsons. Shall we join my wife for tea in the drawing-room?'

He led the way to the adjoining room and pushed open the door. The maid was arranging the tea tray on a low table, beside the couch. A cake stand stood nearby. A sun-blind shut out the Spring sunshine. The french windows were closed, and the scented, stuffy atmosphere was repellent to the two sisters, who were accustomed to well-aired rooms. Only Mother's bedroom was scented and stuffy, but that was her privilege.

It was an anxious moment for Grace, that first meeting with her new mistress. So much would depend on her reaction.

'My dear, may I introduce Miss Grace Brent?' her husband asked affably.

'How do you do, Madam.' The quiet voice, the gentle manner, and the air of refinement had an instant appeal to the plump little woman with the limpid grey eyes. Her pallid face crinkled with pleasure, and she extended a limp white hand. 'But how *nice*. I feel, indeed, I *know*, we are going to like each other. How clever of you, darling,' she cooed.

And he bent to kiss her cheek, hardly daring to believe his good fortune. The flowered muslin tea-gown was too girlish for a plump, middle-aged, semi-invalid, who indulged in too many chocolates, and her voice was girlish. A pet dog lay in her lap, a King Charles spaniel, who shared his mistress's passion for chocolates. It snarled at Grace as she bent over the couch, and she scolded it playfully.

'Come, sit beside me, and you shall play the hostess and pour the tea,' she invited. 'That will be all, Parsons,' she told the hovering maidservant.

'Very good, Madam,' Parsons replied, and bobbed another curtsey.

It was going to take a little time to feel at ease in a household where the servants were so subservient, Grace was thinking. The servants at The Haven had never curtsied, and there had been affection as well as respect for their employers. But she must not make the mistake of comparing this with her own home. It was a new chapter, and she was determined to be obliging and tactful.

So she seated herself on one of the small gilt chairs her employer had placed beside his wife's couch, and took up the silver teapot.

'How do you like your tea, Madam?' was the first question.

'Weak, with two spoons of sugar,' came the prompt reply.

'And you, Sir?'

'As it comes. I am not fussy. But first pour a cup for your sister.'

The sisters exchanged a meaningful glance, for Ellen normally liked her tea with a slice of lemon. Not today, however.

Mr Courtney-Halliday handed the tea to Ellen with another of his stiff little bows, and pushed aside the porcelain figures and cedarwood boxes of trinkets on the occasional table. In complete contrast to the study, the drawing-room was so feminine and fussy, the Master looked extremely uncomfortable as he lifted his frock-coat over the back of a chair, after he had handed round dainty cucumber sandwiches and tiny iced cakes.

Ellen had been openly ignored by his wife and felt rather foolish, so now he made amends by introducing her as the elder sister of Miss Grace.

'How do you do,' they murmured, with latent politeness.

It was Beatrice who prattled girlishly over the tea-cups, and fed the pet dog with crumbs of cake. Her husband smiled indulgently. It was not often that he saw Beatrice so animated. Would it last? Had she really taken a fancy to this charming creature, and would she monopolize her completely? Beatrice had so many ways of punishing him for his indiscretions. If he had been unfaithful, she had only herself to blame for refusing him a husband's marital rights and privileges. It was humiliating to be banished to the dressing-room. She couldn't possibly know about that delightful widow in Brussels, but she may have been informed on the midnight liaison with Parsons by that last companion he had so disliked. Only a wall had divided them, and their lustful pleasure was not a silent performance! No more of that. He would lock his bedroom door in future, and Parsons could be bribed to keep her mouth shut. She was already jealous of the newcomer, and could not hide her feelings. Even an ignorant servant girl had her pride, he supposed. But he was not a man to lose any sleep over the matter, and when Parsons was dismissed, three months later, for obvious signs of pregnancy, she had no proof to substantiate the claim that the Master was the father of the child. Poor Parsons. Such a pert little madam, and so condescending to the lady-like companion in those early days, before her downfall.

Another house-parlourmaid would be engaged, with no sex appeal, and the episode would be forgotten. Or was it wishful thinking? There were so many subtle ways of punishing an erring husband.

So, on this pleasant Sunday afternoon of early Summer, when the Brent sisters should have been enjoying the sea air, and the military band on the Worthing promenade, they were drinking tea in a scented, stuffy drawing-room, politely pretending to be amused by the girlish prattling of a stupid woman with the mentality of a spoilt child.

Ellen could have wept for the sister she loved so dearly. It was not fair of Mother to send Grace away to strangers, purely on the recommendation of a single courteous letter. She did not trust either of these people, and her intuition could usually be relied upon. Grace was so easily deceived by charming

58

gestures, and could not visualize her role as 'go-between' husband and wife whose marital relationship was so obviously incompatible. Should she warn Grace to be on her guard – or keep her doubts to herself? She decided on the latter, and was consequently troubled with everlasting regret.

Her private thoughts were interrupted a few minutes later by the Master's pronouncement that a cab had been ordered for six o'clock to take Miss Brent to the station. It was exactly 5.25 p.m. by the clock on the mantelpiece.

'Ring the bell, will you, my dear? Parsons can show Miss Grace to her room. She will wish to have a little time with her sister before she leaves.'

Grace smiled her thanks, and when Parsons promptly answered the summons, they followed her upstairs to a small bedroom, adequately furnished, but not in any way comparable to the luxurious boudoir they had just left, or the elaborate ostentation of the drawing-room. The tin trunk had been carried upstairs, to serve as a reminder of their parting. How could they bear it? They had shared a bed since they left the nursery. There was such warmth and comfort in a shared bed.

Now they removed their hats, and sat down on the single bed, draped in a white quilt, that would often be cold and lonely, and Ellen could no longer pretend it was anything but a ghastly mistake.

With their arms lovingly entwined about each other's waists, the dark head and the fair leaned close together. Ellen's voice was choked.

'You could have found a post as a lady's companion in Worthing, my darling. Could you not?'

'I suppose so, dearest Nell, but one never questions Mother's authority. One just obeys.'

Ellen nodded agreement. 'I shall think of you every moment of the day, and I shall pray for you every single night.'

'Thank you. I may be kept too busy to think of you during the daytime, but when the day is over and I close my door, then we can communicate. This will be my private sanctuary. Nobody will disturb me here. I wonder whether I shall be permitted to take a walk on my own some days, or whether I shall be obliged to stroll very sedately with Madam in the park?'

'And that spoilt little dog.'

'We shall not get very far, for he is too fat.'

'So is Madam!'

Now they were giggling like a couple of schoolgirls, but their eyes were wet with tears.

'How soon shall you know the date of your wedding, Nell?' Grace asked, tremulously, for that was yet another milestone in their lives.

'Quite soon. Possibly next week. It has to be a Summer wedding. The regiment sails for India in September.' Ellen shivered, and her arm trembled about her sister's waist. 'I wish I knew what to expect, darling, physically I mean. I do love Jonathan dearly, and we seem to be compatible mentally and spiritually, though I shouldn't brag, for there is so much still to discover after marriage. But the intimate part of marriage is a complete mystery. How *are* babies conceived, Grace, and how *are* they born? We both are so ignorant of the facts of life. Yet we had the example of our parents, who were so obviously devoted. As for Mother, she must have enjoyed the intimacy, for she bore six children, and not once were we allowed to linger near that bedroom door till the midwife permitted us a cautious peep at the new infant. Do you remember your first glimpse of Kate? Wasn't she the most adorable baby? – and the naughtiest?' she added.

Grace agreed.

'Lucy was like a pretty little doll, and so good and cuddlesome,' Ellen mused. 'They will be sorry to have missed saying goodbye to you, but you will be seeing them later, won't you, before the end of the Summer vacation?'

'I – I am not sure. It hasn't been mentioned yet when I shall be free to go home.'

'Then *you* must mention it. One free Sunday in the month is considered a fair arrangement, I understand. Every ser . . . employee is entitled to free time to visit her family.'

'You were going to say servant, weren't you? It's true, dearest. I *am* a servant. I feel like a servant. So would you, under the circumstances. Mother was wrong. The status of a lady's companion is no different from that of a governess, and that means one belongs neither upstairs nor down. Perhaps I should have realized my place in the household, but I did not until I actually heard myself calling the Courtney-Hallidays Sir and Madam. At least I feel no compulsion to curtsey!'

'I can't bear it, my darling, for they are not in the least what we expected.'

'I hadn't really thought about it. I have been in a state of total submission since Mother read me the letter. She must have known I would not question her authority. But, yes, I will mention the free Sundays as soon as we are settled, but not immediately. I have to wait for the right moment.'

'You sound resigned.'

'I am. Here I am, and here I stay.'

The final moments were fraught with the poignant awareness of their immediate separation. There was nothing more to say, so they remained silent, wrapped in each other's arms, till a tap at the door reminded them that their time together was spent.

'The cab's waiting, Miss,' Parsons announced.

'Thank you,' Grace answered.

Ellen arranged her hat on her lustrous dark hair, and pulled on her gloves. They faced each other bravely. It was not ladylike to make a fuss in public, so they embraced for the last time, pledged eternal love, and went downstairs. The drawing-room door stood open, and Mr Courtney-Halliday was posed, in typical masterly attitude, with his hands tucked under his coat tails, and a smile on his sensual lips that did not reach his eyes, for he was not yet sure that the new companion would allow her sister to depart alone. She seemed a charming, docile creature, but one could never be certain. The female sex had a way of suprising one.

The two young ladies looked quite composed, however, as they descended the stairs, so he stood aside for Miss Brent to bid farewell to his wife, then he shook her hand, and thanked her warmly for escorting Miss Grace. The sisters' parting was calm and unemotional, with nothing more than a light kiss on the cheek. So they were going to be spared one of those embarrassing scenes that might be expected under the circumstances.

Parsons was hovering in the background to close the door, but he avoided her suppliant glances. The time had passed for such intimate glances. He had no patience with any female who could not accept the simple fact that the affair was over. Of course he had used her, but she was willing to be used, and he had paid her more than she deserved.

Now he watched every glance and gesture between

these devoted sisters, and was filled with admiration. The cabby opened the door, Miss Brent lifted her skirts and climbed in. The cab moved away, and she waved a gloved hand at the tall, slender figure on the steps. Then she was gone.

Slowly she turned, his wife's latest acquisition, and his heart hammered as he regarded her blanched, stricken face. It was the face he had waited for all his adult life – a sad, beautiful face, with a hint of mystery and aloofness.

'I expect you will wish to unpack, Miss Grace?' he suggested, affably. 'We dine at seven.'

She nodded, too choked to speak, an anguished appeal in her wet eyes, and slowly climbed the stairs.

That first meal with her new employers was an ordeal she could only endure by using her willpower to its utmost. Too proud to weep in their presence, she listened to the inane chatter of the woman she was paid to serve, and toyed with the roast lamb, new potatoes and peas, but shook her head when Parsons offered a dish of strawberries.

'How tiresome. I ordered them especially for you,' her Mistress complained.

'I am sorry, Madam. Tomorrow, perhaps.'

'Tomorrow will be too late. I shall finish them up. I adore strawberries and cream. Isn't that so, Henry?'

'You do indeed, my dear,' he answered, indulgently, as she spooned castor sugar over the fruit, and covered it with cream. She ate with the absorbed greediness of a child, while the little dog sat waiting at her feet to lick the dish clean when she had finished.

Grace shuddered involuntarily. Animals had never been allowed in the dining-room, the kitchen, or the bedrooms at The Haven, and Jackie seemed happy enough in his kennel, with two good meals a day, and bones to chew. It was unhygienic. Mother would be horrified. Grace was surprised that her husband permitted it, but she would soon discover there were certain things he was obliged to overlook or their marital relationship would be quite insufferable.

Coffee was served in the drawing-room. Parsons moved about her duties with the quiet competence of a well-trained servant. Back on the couch, reclining among the cushions, with the pet dog once again installed on her lap, the Mistress asked, 'Will you play for us, my dear?'

Grace was startled into an awareness of her duties. This was obviously one of her duties, to entertain the Master and Mistress with music, after the evening meal. She hadn't her mother's professional touch, but she was easily the most accomplished performer at the pianoforte of the six sisters. Now she was acutely nervous, as she settled on the stool and turned over the scores lying ready.

'Have you a particular preference, Madam?' she asked.

'Nothing heavy. Beethoven and Bach give me a headache.'

'A Chopin Polonaise?'

'That will do nicely.'

The Master was standing beside her, waiting to turn the pages. His wife closed her eyes, or pretended to close her eyes. She didn't trust Henry. He would soon be up to his old tricks again. But he would not be allowed to have his own way with this refined, gentle creature, for whom she had felt an instant liking. He was already showing signs of that devastating maleness that had so attracted her at their first meeting – till she had discovered or thought she had discovered the real Henry, after their marriage. There had been so much to discover about Henry.

For one thing, she was never sure when he was speaking the truth. For another, she had found the intimacy of the marriage bed most indelicate. No gentleman would behave in such a vulgar fashion – but then, Henry was no gentleman. It was a game of pretence between them now, since she had taken to her couch, and even her own doctor was deceived into thinking she had a weak heart. The heart spasms could be controlled, so also could the spells of dizziness. Fainting was an accomplished art that every gentlewoman should practise. Few men could resist the temptation to support a swooning female – and Henry was no exception. He was so ridiculously self-important in his new role at the bank, but she was not deceived into thinking he was loyal to those who had provided the means for such rapid promotion. On more than one occasion she had been suspicious of his plausible excuses for being late home.

She was jealous, of course, and couldn't bear to think he was unfaithful, or to see her companions so charmed by his masculine attraction. She had every right to be jealous. Hadn't she been the means of that rapid promotion and his easy entry into upper-class society? This dignified residence, facing the park, had been bought with her money, and the membership of the gentleman's club in Pall Mall only made possible by the timely intervention of her father.

So she watched Henry through half-closed eyes, and was pleased to see the young woman completely absorbed in the keyboard. She played well, and the Chopin Polonaise was followed by the haunting *Liebestraum*. The short recital ended with a Strauss waltz. Not once had her new companion glanced at her husband till she had finished playing, when she thanked him politely. Henry had behaved with perfect decorum, but it would not last. A leopard cannot change its spots!

'That was charming, my dear,' Beatrice sighed with fatigue. It had been an exhausting day. 'Now I am ready to retire, if you will be good enough to assist me with my toilet. I get so breathless.'

'Certainly, Madam,' Grace replied respectfully, more than a little surprised to be regarded as a ladies maid as well as a companion.

She bade good night to the Master, and followed the Mistress to her boudoir. The sun-blinds had protected the closed windows all day, and the atmosphere was stifling. First the little dog – that answered to the name of Prince – had to be made comfortable under the satin coverlet. Then Grace was initiated into the delicate operation of unfastening hooks to remove the crumpled dress, several petticoats, and the corset. When drawers and stockings had been removed, the plump little body was wrapped in a fussy négligé, and finally the lank, mousy hair was given a hundred strokes of the silver-backed hairbrush, though nothing could ever restore its youthful lustre.

When Parsons delivered a can of hot water, it pleased her to see the ladylike Miss Grace on her knees, removing the Mistress's stockings. It was not the first time a companion had been surprised at the nature of her duties. Parsons could have told her that in this household a companion was regarded as nothing more than a rather superior type of servant.

A few minutes later, she heard the bedroom door close, and shortly after, the study door closed with a

66

slam, always an indication the Master had no wish to be disturbed. He was always the last to retire, and was amply provided with his nightcap of whisky and soda, and dainty sandwiches of Gentleman's Relish. Parsons was free to retire to her own attic bedroom, but she felt the need to share another gossip and a final cup of tea with Cook. They would speculate on whether or not Miss Grace would stay for more than a month. Parsons wondered how soon she would be back in favour. It was not the first time this had happened, and he knew she was waiting and willing. But Parsons had already served her purpose.

As for Grace, she was standing at the wide-flung window, filling her lungs with fresh air. Those long hours of close confinement in stuffy rooms seemed like a penance. Suddenly she was engulfed by a wave of homesickness, and she let the hot tears fall, but covered her trembling mouth lest her choked sobbing should disturb the occupant of the adjoining room. Dear God! How could she bear it? Yet how could she not bear it, when Mother had decreed she must be separated from Bertha?

It had been explained, when Grace had enquired, tactfully, on the nature of her duties, that her first duty of the day would be to exercise the little dog in the park, before breakfast. Her Mistress always breakfasted in bed, then Parsons filled the hip bath with hot, scented water, and laid out warm towels. The morning toilet was a leisurely and prolonged affair, for Madam had to decide which dress to wear, and which of the assortment of necklaces, ear-rings and brooches would best suit the dress she had chosen. She loved her jewellery, and her hands were bedecked with rings, on fingers so plump they could not be removed.

The Master left early for the City, after a hearty breakfast. A tempting choice of lamb cutlets, kidneys and bacon, scalloped eggs, kippers and kedgeree awaited him, in hot dishes on the sideboard. He helped himself, for his temper was short in the early morning, and he was in a hurry. The maidservant hovered in the hall to hand the Master his hat, kid gloves, portfolio, and the current copy of the *Financial Times*. The brougham would be waiting at the front entrance at precisely eight o'clock, and the coachman, who lived with his wife in the rooms over the coach house, would salute smartly, bid his Master a very good day, close the carriage door, and climb back on the box. The suave host of yesterday was replaced by a stern gentleman of the City, who hardly noticed his servants, dutifully kissed his wife's cheek, and greeted the new companion with a brusque 'Good-day to you, Miss Grace'. He was hardly settled in the carriage when he unfolded the *Financial Times*, and his mind from henceforth would be completely absorbed in the day's business. His public life and his private life were segregated in his lively mind, and no thought of his wife or her companion would intrude on his concentration. This was not uncommon in a man of his position. Only the humble clerks would allow their thoughts to wander from their ledgers to sick wives and stillborn children, to poverty and the threat of eviction, and the ever-present phantom of dismissal for a careless mistake. Henry wasted no time on these unfortunates. He, too, had known the anxiety and the grinding poverty of the working class in those early years. He had discarded the memory as easily as he had discarded Parsons.

Henry Courtney-Halliday loved this bustling world of the City – a man's world in which women had no place. Some days he would visit wealthy clients in their own homes, and settle some outstanding matter over a glass of sherry. It was all part of the status he had acquired after his marriage to Beatrice.

The carriage would be at her disposal for an hour every afternoon, for she liked to drive in the park with her companion and the little dog, after her rest. She always complained of fatigue, yet no woman could have been more idle. This restful hour, however, would be the only time during the day when Grace would be free to take a solitary walk in the park, or to write letters, depending on the weather.

Tea was served by Parsons in the drawing-room at precisely four o'clock. Then Grace would read aloud. 'Not Mr Dickens, if you please, my dear. I find his moralizing rather tedious,' Beatrice insisted that first day. She liked French novels, translated into English. They were so provocative. The written word, spoken aloud in the cultured voice of her new companion, was enough to satisfy her limited sensuality. She had no further need to experience such passionate embraces. As for taking a lover, it would be unthinkable to deceive Henry, even if she had the energy.

Grace read well. Indeed, on this first day together, there was nothing displeasing, and her every wish had been anticipated.

Henry arrived home punctually for dinner in a most expansive mood, bearing a large box of her favourite chocolates from a confectioners in the Strand. A musical evening, and so to bed. This would be the pattern of their days, only interrupted by their removal to Bournemouth for the month of August. Henry was bored with holidays, but would join them for a week, then make the excuse that he had urgent business to attend to on the Continent. If Beatrice and Grace had been better acquainted with the business world, they would have known that both Paris and Brussels were deserted by the upper class during the month of August. The saucy Yvette was the distraction. In the chorus of a popular revue, Yvette was engagingly frank and frivolous, with a delightful willingness to take off her clothes.

It was during the last week of August that Ellen was married. Grace had sent money to Jane, in July, to purchase the wedding present of bed-linen. It had taken most of her month's wages, and there had been little money left for the holiday. Since everything was provided and paid for by Madam, Grace was not inconvenienced. A telegram of good wishes was despatched on the morning of the wedding, and Grace found her thoughts wandering to Worthing, from the military band on the promenade to St Matthew's Church.

She could visualize the scene so vividly, for Ellen had written to describe what had been planned. It took all her self-control to sit quietly beside the fussy little woman, in the frilled organdie, nursing her pet dog. She could see Ellen, a radiant bride, in her mother's lovely wedding gown and veil, on the arm of the handsome subaltern, and her four sisters in dainty flowered muslin, with poke bonnets, carrying Victorian posies. Even Bertha might be persuaded to enjoy her sister's wedding, and young Katie would not need to be told she was one of the prettiest bridesmaids ever to follow the bride down the aisle of St Matthew's. There would be a guard of honour, in dress uniform, with crossed swords. It all sounded very impressive.

Grace had been promised a photograph. Mother

70

would be warmly congratulated on this good marriage of her eldest daughter to the Vicar's youngest son. She would play the hostess at the reception, in her own drawing-room, with dignity and charm. There would be no tears when the bride left for the honeymoon at St Ives in Cornwall, and no tears would be shed in public, some two weeks later, when the troopship sailed for India.

Ellen had been grievously disappointed that Grace had not contrived to get home before they sailed. Madam had collapsed in a faint on that particular Sunday, and the Master's pleading that the visit be postponed was not in vain. Her employers had long since discovered that Grace was so vulnerable, so acutely sensitive to anything of a distressing nature, they could call on her sympathy at will. It was so easy to deceive such a gentle creature with a contrived collapse.

When they returned to London in September, the house had been thoroughly cleaned, and the smell of polish and yellow soap still lingered, and fresh air still clung to the curtains, much to the annoyance of Madam, who soon had the boudoir and drawing-room sweetly scented and stuffy.

The coachman had been employed on beating carpets, and his wife scrubbing floorboards and stairs. Parsons was suffering from early-morning sickness, and the state of her mind was bordering on panic as the weeks slipped away, and she could no longer hide her swelling stomach. Only one person in that divided household would feel any sympathy for that unfortunate young woman, but Grace could do nothing to prevent the ultimate discharge and disgrace. The Master washed his hands of her pitiful plight, and, like Pontius Pilate, refused to be involved. As for Madam, she had no pity or patience with a foolish maidservant who allowed herself to be seduced, though she deplored Henry's taste.

'What will become of Parsons?' Grace enquired, anxiously, of Cook, when the friendly cabby was summoned to remove her and her few pathetic belongings one mellow day of early Autumn.

'Don't you fret yourself about that young woman, Miss Grace. She won't starve, not 'er. Likely as not she'll move in with that fellow. She's a saucy minx, and she's got no more than she deserves.'

But Grace could not so easily dismiss the ex-house-parlourmaid from her thoughts. Why should she have to take all the blame? It was her first glimpse of the careless disregard of a maidservant's fate when she 'got into trouble'. Nothing of that nature had ever disturbed the household at The Haven. Thomas Brent had been too devoted to his wife, Amelia, to notice the attractions of any maidservant.

Grace was much concerned by a situation that seemed to lack common decency and charity, and more than a little surprised to discover her employer so susceptible to a pretty face. It did not occur to her, in her innocence, that a lustful man, deprived of the intimacy of the marriage bed, would find solace elsewhere. She had not noticed that he sometimes appeared distracted, and forgot to turn the page of the musical score Madam had chosen for their entertainment. His thoughts would have shocked Grace profoundly. Henry Courtney-Halliday was not only distracted, but desperate. The weeks and months had slipped away, and his wife's companion was so devilishly elusive, he began to doubt his own capacity to capture her. Beatrice monopolized her completely, and the sweet creature seemed quite happy with that arrangement. Not by a single glance or gesture had she indicated her preference for his society. It was humiliating!

The park was shrouded in fog, that fateful morning of late November, when Grace crossed the Bayswater Road with the little dog on a leash. The normal traffic noises were muffled, and the cabs appeared as ghostly shapes, then disappeared. The hooves of the dray horses, pulling heavy loads, had a frightening clarity as they loomed out of the fog.

Grace had tied a veil over her nose and mouth, and was breathing with some difficulty, but it was not the first time she had noticed her breathlessness, even on a clear day. Born and bred on the South Coast, and accustomed to a daily walk, breathing sea air into her lungs, she had not taken kindly to her present stuffy abode, or the restrictions imposed on her liberty. But she had not complained, so why should Madam change the normal routine when it suited her so well? Simmons, the new house-parlourmaid could have exercised the dog without feeling any discomfort, for she was a big, strong woman, with healthy lungs.

So, on this fateful morning, Grace halted at the park gates to get her breath. She could hear the baying of a big dog in the distance, and for some unaccountable reason, she would never understand, Prince tugged the leash out of her hand, and shot off, quicker than she had ever seen him move on these regular morning walks. Now she could hear his excited yapping, then a terrible scream of fright and pain – and an eerie silence. She picked up her skirts and ran, gasping his name, into the blanket of fog.

Not more than fifty yards away she halted, but it

was too late. A huge wolf-hound, straining on a leather strap, stood over the small corpse, and a liveried footman stuttered helplessly.

'It wasn't 'is fault, Miss. That little dog of yours came straight for 'is legs and scared the daylights out of 'im. Bruce is a big dog, but 'e's nervous as a kitten.'

Grace was too shocked and stunned to reply. Bending down, she gathered the warm little body in her arms, the silent tears wetting her cheeks.

'Where jew live, Miss?' the man was asking, and she nodded in the direction of the house across the road.

'You ought not to be out in this fog, t'ain't 'ealthy. You should let a servant exercise the little dog.'

'I *am* a servant,' she whispered, brokenly, as she wrapped the little corpse in her veil.

'I'll see you back across the road,' he said.

Grace thanked him, and he took her arm. The huge dog trotted obediently beside him across the road to the back entrance.

'I 'ope you won't get into trouble, Miss,' he said, kindly. Then he was gone. He really was rather a stupid man, she thought. Trouble? She was trembling in anticipation. This pitiful scrap in her arms had received more affection from his Mistress than her own husband.

The Master had left for the City. The servants were busy in the kitchen. When she pushed open the door, and walked in with the limp bundle in her arms, the three women stood gawping. Then the elderly housemaid, once employed as a nurse on the Courtney estate, threw her apron over her head and wailed, 'My poor Miss Beatrice, my poor baby!'

'Did it get run over, Miss?' asked Simmons, who

had no love for a pet dog that snapped at her fingers when she pushed it aside to place the breakfast tray on Madam's lap.

Grace shook her head.

'Put it in the scullery, Miss. Jackson will bury it when 'e comes back from the City. Madam mustn't see it,' said Cook.

'You ready for breakfast, Miss?' asked Simmons, as though it were a normal day.

'I couldn't eat a morsel.' Grace was still choked with tears.

When she had laid the pitiful little bundle in the scullery sink, Cook insisted, 'Sit you down, Miss, and I'll pour you a nice cup of tea. You look proper shrammed.'

Grace thanked her and sipped the hot sweet tea gratefully. But it was only postponing the moment she was dreading. Would Madam have hysterics or a fatal heart attack? I shall have killed her, Grace was thinking, as she tapped on the door of the boudoir.

A bright fire burned cheerfully in the hearth, and the curtains were drawn against the fog. In the soft glow of the lamp, the Mistress reclined on her pillows, a dainty shawl draped over her shoulders. She was smiling expectantly, waiting to welcome her little darling. Surprised to see her companion so soon back – half-an-hour was the time prescribed for the morning walk – and seeing her arms were empty, she demanded, suspiciously, 'Where is Prince? What have you done with him? Answer me, woman! What has happened?'

'Prince is dead,' Grace whispered.

'DEAD? Then you have killed him, you wicked woman! You always hated my little darling, didn't you? Don't deny it! Don't you dare deny it!'

'No, Madam. That's not true! It happened so suddenly, I could not save him.'

'Don't lie to me! Get out of my sight! GO AWAY! I never wish to see you again!' She was weeping hysterically.

The old woman stood in the doorway, waiting to be reinstated. She had lost face as a housemaid. 'My poor baby,' she soothed, and gathered the sobbing woman into her comforting arms.

Grace slipped away quietly into her own room, and sat down, shivering miserably on the bedside chair. The room was wretchedly cold, for there was no fireplace, but even if there had been, a humble companion was not entitled to a fire in her bedroom. In normal circumstances it did not matter, for she spent her days with Madam in the boudoir and the drawing-room. This was not a normal day, and the close relationship they had established was broken. 'GO AWAY!' Nothing could be more final. But where to go? That was the question to which she had no answer in her present state of mind.

Over and over again she re-lived those few agonizing moments. Why had she let the leash slip out of her hand? Why had the little dog answered that eerie baying in the fog, only to be trampled to death under those huge pads? Why? Why?

The hours slipped away, and she lost all sense of time. She felt so drained of strength. She thought she would never have the energy to get up from the chair and leave the room. It had always been a sanctuary, and the only place in the house to enjoy a little privacy. Here she had written her weekly letters to Mother, to the two girls at the Academy, and to Ellen, *en route* to India. Here she had dreamed her dreams of being reunited with her family, and forgiven for her mistaken belief that Bertha would put up with her languid ways indefinitely. She *was* lazy. She admitted it now, but then she never felt really well, and every chore had been an effort. Bertha was so sturdy, so practical, so very houseproud. Yes, it had been a right decision to send her away. Mother was always right.

In this house she was spared all those dreary chores, but had no liberty, no life of her own. Always at the beck and call of a demanding Mistress, with an unpredictable temper, yet she could be so charming, so generous. No place was perfect. She was a little afraid of the Master. Those dark, discerning eyes could probe the very depths of her being. What did he want of her?

She sat there, shivering and hopeless, till Simmons tapped on the door, and came in with a bowl of hot soup on a tray. It was the very first time a servant in this house had waited on her, and she was so grateful, the tears started afresh.

'Cook says to have this while it's hot, Miss, and why not lie down on the bed, for there's nothing to be done once Madam turns against you, Cook says. She has seen it happen with the other companions. It's just what we've been expecting, Miss. Even if she wasn't blaming you for killing the little dog, it would be something else, Cook says.'

Grace nodded agreement, and thanked the maid. She did not need to be reminded that her prospects were bleak. When she had drained the bowl, she felt a little better, and lay on the bed, still wearing her overcoat. Surprisingly, she slept, and was awakened in the early evening by a fresh outburst of hysterical weeping in the adjoining room. The doctor had been summoned by the old nurse, earlier in the day, and he had administered a sleeping draught. She, too, had slept all afternoon, and now she had awakened to the realization of an empty lap. She wept and moaned that she could not bear to live without her little darling.

Then the front door slammed. The Master was home early. Grace sat up, blinking in the gaslight. The street lamp was so conveniently placed, she had no need of a candle.

'What on earth has happened? Where is everyone?' the Master was demanding of Simmons.

'It's the little dog, Sir. It's been killed,' she answered, as he pushed his overcoat, hat and gloves into her willing arms.

Heavy footsteps bounded up the stairs, the boudoir door burst open, and he shouted irritably, 'Beatrice! For God's sake stop that horrible noise!' Then, relenting a little, he sat on the bed, and was instantly smothered in a suffocating embrace.

'She killed him, Henry – my precious darling!' she wailed.

'Who? What *are* you talking about? Come, control yourself, my dear.'

'That companion you engaged, because she was so gentle and ladylike. I always knew she was deceitful. The quiet ones cannot be trusted. Well, I have seen the last of her. You can pay her wages, and she can get out of the house!'

'Where is Grace?'

'I haven't the faintest idea. She may have left already, without her wages.'

'But you have been so happy with her for the past months. You can't just dismiss her without an explanation. She was so fond of Prince. It must have been an unavoidable accident.'

'She was *not* fond of Prince. She hated my poor little darling. No, Henry, I will not be persuaded to forgive her.'

Henry withdrew himself from her clinging arms, and felt nothing but contempt for the woman he had married, yet he had only himself to blame. Her face was puffy and blotchy, and her eyes still swimming in tears. He found the closeness of her scented body quite nauseating, and he wanted to hear the truth from Grace – unless she had already left. She would be too proud to plead.

He bade the old nurse bathe her Mistress's face, and fetch a tempting supper tray from the kitchen. But when he bent to kiss her wet cheek, she wailed, 'Don't leave me, Henry. I feel so dreadful!'

He patted her shoulder, and signalled to the hovering servant. Then he left them together, and went in search of Grace. There was no answer to his light tap on her bedroom door, so he pushed it open and stepped inside. He stood there, gazing at a wraith-like creature in the gaslight. Her face appeared so drained of colour, he was alarmed. With a finger to his lips, he took her cold hand. She slid off the bed, and he steered her out of the door and down the stairs, still holding her hand. Opening the study door, he pushed her gently inside and closed the door. The glowing fire reflected her ashen face, and he conquered the urge to take her in his arms. This was no time for such thoughts. It was comfort she needed, and reassurance, like a child who has been unjustly punished.

When he had removed her overcoat, he pulled up her chair near the fire, and sat her down, for she seemed incapable of making any independent movement. Then he poured a measure of brandy into a small glass, and put it into her cold, trembling hand. She was still shivering uncontrollably.

'Drink it,' he said. It was an order, and she obeyed because she always obeyed an order. The brandy burned her throat, but after a few minutes, she could feel a pleasant warmth spreading over her whole body, and she stopped shivering.

'Feeling better?' he asked, kindly, and she nodded, tremulously. Now he pulled up a chair on the other side of the hearth, and sat facing her, because he dare not trust himself to sit too close to her.

'First, I will apologize, Grace, for that icy cold room. It had not occurred to me to inspect it. A man leaves that sort of thing to the servants. Is there no fireplace in the room?'

'No, Sir.'

'Then you must be moved. We have a guest room that is never used. Simmons can light a fire and the room will be nicely aired before you retire.'

'What will Madam say?'

'My wife will probably succumb to another bout of hysteria, or a mild heart attack, either of which is unlikely to prove fatal as you yourself have long since discovered. Which brings me to the question of your abrupt dismissal.'

'Will you accept my resignation, Sir?'

'I have no intention of accepting your resignation, Grace, but I should like to hear your version of what actually happened to the little dog.'

Grace told him quietly, and unemotionally. She was drained of tears, and felt only a sense of guilt at her carelessness. The Master listened sympathetically to the pitiful little story.

'It was an accident. It could have happened to Simmons had she been taking the dog for a walk, which she should have been doing in any case. Is there nothing that I can leave to my wife? And why are you so compliant, Grace? Have you always allowed yourself to be dominated by a stronger will?'

'I suppose I have. Mother always decided what is best for all of us, and I have never questioned it.'

'But your sisters? Do they also comply with her wishes with such extraordinary meekness?'

A tremulous smile broke the gravity of her young face. 'Not Bertha, or Kate, and even Jane gets her own way in the kitchen since she was put in charge of the cooking. As for Ellen, she was permitted to marry her young subaltern, but it was not a loveless marriage. That leaves Lucy, the youngest, who is rather like me, though she has become a little more self-assured at the Academy for Young Ladies. Boarding school for girls is, I suppose, a good thing, but I am glad I escaped by being past the age for enrolment when Father died.'

'Is that when your circumstances changed?'

'Yes, the pattern of our lives changed completely, almost overnight. We could not afford to keep the servants, so they were given one month's notice.'

'So if your father had lived, it would not have been necessary for you to take a position of this nature?'

'No.'

'Life is strange,' he mused, his dark eyes approving the delicate flush on her cheeks. She had stopped calling him 'Sir' he noticed. It was only a small step forward, and he was not a patient man. Yet he must not frighten her away. It was so unusual to feel such tenderness towards a young woman. He normally took what he wanted, and paid for it. Even with Beatrice, he could have escaped before he was committed, but ambition had driven him into a situation that was quite intolerable. Yes, he had paid dearly, and was still paying.

'What shall I do if Madam refuses to have me attend her?' Grace was asking.

After a slight hesitation, he answered, 'You can work for me until such time as my wife decides to forgive you.' His gaze travelled round the book-lined room. 'I collect first editions. It's my hobby. I enjoy browsing round the second-hand book shops in Charing Cross Road. But I have no time to catalogue. They are just pushed on to the shelves. Now that is something you could do for me, Grace, and nobody will disturb you here. Keep away from my wife. I shall give orders for your lunch and tea to be served in this room, and you can ring when you feel the need for a cup of tea or coffee. Believe me, this unfortunate incident will be forgotten and forgiven – a week, a month? My wife will tire of all the fussing and petting of the old nurse, then she will ask to see you.'

'Supposing she comes in here and orders me to get out? I can't believe she will just ignore me when she knows I am still living here?'

'Leave it to me. Leave everything to me, in future, Grace.'

'Thank you,' she sighed, gratefully.

'Now, have you eaten anything today?'

'Simmons brought me a bowl of soup, and I have slept all afternoon. I am not hungry.'

'Nonsense! You must eat, or you will be fading away before my eyes. Heaven knows, I have never seen a more insubstantial creature. I do declare you have lost weight since you came to us, and that in itself is embarrassing.'

'Please, do not concern yourself. I have always

been thin, but I am quite strong and perfectly well.'

'Then appearances are deceptive. When I came into your room, you gave me quite a scare. I thought you were ill. But perhaps it was the gaslight.'

'Yes, it would have been the gaslight.'

He smiled indulgently, and his dark eyes were soft as velvet. She could hardly believe he was the same man who could be so callous as to allow a young maidservant to be dismissed without any means of support and no reference when the time came to look for other employment. He was a difficult person to understand, but, she supposed, typical of this day and age, when a man was master in his own home. It was no secret that Beatrice Courtney had fallen in love with the young bank clerk, and threatened suicide if she was not allowed to marry him. The old nurse knew the history, and had retold it on more than one occasion, when the Master had neglected her poor Miss Beatrice, or seen fit to upset her.

She had no respect or liking for the Master, for she remembered a time when Beatrice was a lively, lovable girl, with no thought of hysterics or a weak heart. Of course, she was spoilt, and wasn't that natural, being the only adored child of wealthy parents, and heir to a big estate? It was Cook and Simmons who doted on the Master, and that silly little Parsons. Now the old nurse was reinstated, she would be a little smug towards the other servants. It was, and always would be, a divided household, and Grace was the 'go-between', distressed by the atmosphere of friction and petty misunderstanding between husband and wife.

'Well, that's settled. Now we can eat,' the Master was saying, and he rang the bell for Simmons to serve dinner. He would dine alone tonight, but tomorrow he would be dining at his club, and every night henceforth, till a peaceful relationship was restored between Beatrice and Grace. Women were the most contrary creatures on God's earth, he reflected. If he hadn't intervened so promptly, Grace would have left the house without even an explanation.

'Miss Grace will have a light supper in here, Simmons,' he instructed, when she appeared in answer to the bell. 'Has Madam been attended to?'

'She has, Sir. I will see about the other tray after I have finished serving you in the dining-room.'

'I am in no hurry. Serve Miss Grace first.'

'Very good, Sir. What do you fancy, Miss?' she asked with icy politeness. *Somebody* was stepping out of her place, and no mistake! Simmons knew *her* place, and she also knew which side her bread was buttered.

'Just a boiled egg with bread and butter, and a cup of tea, please, Simmons.'

'Very good, Miss.' She was on the way out when the Master called her back.

'And, Simmons . . .'

'Yes, Sir?'

'We are moving Miss Grace into the guest room. It will be more comfortable. See the fire is lit when you have finished in the dining-room.'

'Very good, Sir.' She bobbed a curtsey and left the room.

'It's coming to something when the companion has to be served a tray in the Master's study – and a fire in her bedroom, if you please,' she exploded.

'I've seen it coming,' Cook replied. 'It don't surprise me, Simmy.'

'For two pins I would hand in me notice, but it doesn't do to be too hasty. After all, no place is perfect. In my last place, I was pestered with four spoilt little brats, always playing tricks when my back was turned. Made my life a misery.' She sighed, in retrospect, took up a tray, covered it with a clean starched cloth, and waited for the egg to boil. No need to brew fresh tea. Cook kept the tea-pot on the hob. It was one of the few privileges the servants enjoyed – cups of tea, at any hour of the day, for they were never surprised by an interfering Mistress.

'Jew know what I think, Simmy?' asked Cook, her arms akimbo on her ample hips.

'No, what?'

'I think that young woman is consumptive.'

'You don't say?'

'Thin as a rake, and pale as a ghost. You mark my words, that young woman won't make old bones!'

3

As the recently married wife of a young subaltern, Ellen's new world was even more strange and bewildering than the one in which her sister Grace found herself. The first glimpse of the troopship at Southampton Docks had been so awesome a sight to a young woman who had travelled no further than London in her short life, she caught her breath on a gasp of fear, but managed to control her agitated nerves, and the question on her tongue – 'What am I doing here?' – went unasked.

On that brief honeymoon, she had soon discovered her husband was not the familiar adoring person with whom she had been associated for more than three years, but an impatient, demanding stranger, who insisted on claiming his conjugal rights. Innocent of the facts of life, and previously concerned only with his charming manners and his dutiful attendance on her wishes as his betrothed, Ellen had only vaguely visualized the intimacy of the marriage bed. Nothing had prepared her for the passionate lover, and if the trauma of their wedding night had to be regarded as an example of the future, then she did not know how she could endure it.

If Jonathan had been an observant husband, he would have seen a sad resignation in the depths of those dark eyes, but Jonathan was not concerned with the deeper elements of life. Being the son of a clergyman had done little or nothing to curb his natural capacity to enjoy life, with a light-hearted approach to anything of a serious nature. Jonathan had a brilliant mind, but lacked the intelligence to understand the limitations of the strict environment in which his young wife had been reared. Like the majority of his brother officers, the courtship had been conducted in the company of sisters, mother or chaperones, and they were seldom left alone before marriage. Ellen's response to his stolen kisses had been nothing more than a fluttering of the heart.

Being a wife was not the romantic dream that her betrothal had promised, but harsh reality. And Mother had been so brave and calm, and her farewell kiss so unemotional, Ellen had reacted in the only way that Mother would expect of her eldest daughter. Well-bred young ladies made no fuss in public, and shed their tears in private. But there was no privacy for Ellen now, and no sister to share the anguish of parting from her home and family.

In the cramped little cabin they had been allocated, she unpacked their clothes, and the few personal belongings they were allowed for the voyage, but it was Jonathan's batman who had shown the practised ease and assurance of a well-trained servant in making the most of such limited space. It was Thompson, whose comforting arm had supported her trembling body when the first vibrations under their feet warned them that the ship was on its way. Jonathan's duties had kept him busy, and it was not his fault he had been missing at the crucial moment of departure. It was one of the earliest lessons Ellen must learn, as the wife of a serving officer in Her Majesty's Royal Fusiliers – a wife was of secondary importance in a soldier's career.

On this long sea voyage, on which she had embarked with dutiful devotion but fearful doubts, Ellen would be shamed by her own inadequate preparations for such an adventure. Hers was not an adventurous nature, and Jonathan had chosen unwisely. She was not passionate, and would never satisfy his demands. And with ever-increasing nausea, from those first throbbing moments, she would know the despair and discomfort of sea-sickness for an interminable six days and nights. If only she hadn't to share this confined space with an impatient husband, who was not only a good sailor, but actually revelled in rough seas and the rocking motion that kept so many of the men groaning in their bunks, and the majority of the women and children wishing they had stayed at home.

It was not Jonathan's nature to sympathize with suffering, since he had never known anything more serious than a mild attack of measles in early childhood. He was proud of his young, healthy body. Not an ounce of superfluous flesh, no sagging muscles, and no need to be ashamed of his nakedness in the swimming pool reserved for the junior officers on 'C' Deck. Born and bred in a coastal town, he had been taught to swim at an early age. Preparatory school, public school, and university, then on to Sandhurst. This had been the pattern of his youth and young manhood. Two other brothers had also followed their particular pattern into adult life, the eldest to be ordained, and the second son to join the ranks of the Civil Service. Jonathan was not even consulted. It was naturally assumed that a third son would follow an army career.

So he left the overworked stewardess to attend to his sick wife, and went on deck to breathe the fresh air. Neither eau-de-cologne nor carbolic could dispel the stench of vomit. And the pallid face on the pillows was totally unrecognizable as the girl he had married.

'It will pass, Ma'am, and you will soon be enjoying the voyage,' the homely stewardess promised.

But Ellen was not convinced till they docked at Marseilles, and her throbbing head and sick stomach began to recover. It would be two more days, however, before she was back on a normal diet, and several hours before she was tempted to try a cup of tea.

It was pleasant to meet the women and children for the first time on deck, and to breathe fresh air into her stifled lungs. Jonathan had gone ashore, after he had settled her comfortably in a deck chair, and he brought her back a present. Wearing her best bonnet, with a shawl round her shoulders and a rug over her knees, she was still looking pretty ghastly, he thought, as he bent to kiss her cheek and dropped a small package into her lap.

'A little present, my love. 'Tis only a trifle, but there was no time to look around.'

She unwrapped the box and found a necklace of coral beads. He insisted that she wore them to enliven one of the plain dresses that Mother had thought suitable for the first part of the voyage. It was kind of Jonathan, and she thanked him prettily, but she did not care for jewellery. Had he never noticed that her only adornment was the cameo brooch? All the sisters had received one from their father on that last Christmas before his tragic death. Now she wore Jonathan's wedding ring, and even that still felt a little strange.

He looked such a picture of radiant health, and so handsome, standing there, she felt at a disadvantage, and determined to prove herself worthy of his love, just as soon as she had fully recovered her strength. She did not need to be told that he had been missing the love-making of their honeymoon, and was feeling deprived. Poor Jonathan. He seemed to be a creature of moods for all his light-heartedness, but of course she had seen only the brightest facet of his personality during their engagement. They both had so much to discover, and it must have been a shock for a newly-wed husband to find a sick wife in her bunk, hardly before they were out of Southampton Water! It should not be too difficult, she thought, for her own temperate nature should balance Jonathan's tendency to fluctuate between ecstasy and despair. His moods were short-lived, and she had already discovered, on their honeymoon, that a quiet manner was the best antidote to a mercurial temperament. Everything he did exacted to the utmost his energy and enthusiasm. There were no half measures with Jonathan.

In some ways it was contradictory and rather puzzling, for the young husband was so very different from the betrothed. Obviously he was not himself aware of the difference, and he expected her, as a dutiful wife, to understand a mentality so alien to her own. Was that why he had chosen her from among her sisters? Had he seen in her steadfast brown eyes a promise of fidelity and devotion? she had asked herself.

The coral beads had been his way of compensating for his neglect and impatience of her sickness. He had been feeling guilty, and was too proud to apologize. Ellen would not exact an apology. She was a reasonable young woman, and extremely unselfish. Being the eldest of six sisters, she was probably maternal, but that would show itself in the birth of their first child – a boy, she hoped, for Jonathan's sake. A man could live again in his son. They had not spoken of children during their engagement. It was not proper. In any case, there had been no opportunity to discuss anything of an intimate nature. As for the brief honeymoon, Jonathan had been much too occupied indulging his young bride's every wish, and his own overwhelming delight in her virgin body. It hadn't surprised him to discover he had married a virgin. Comparing his own wedding night with brother officers on board, he was not the only one to feel proud and superior. Yet he found a certain curiosity and fascination in the relationship between Carstairs and his wife, Sylvia. She had been widowed twice, and was his senior by ten years. He was madly in love with her.

'No pure little virgin for me, thank you! I like to be seduced by a woman who knows all the tricks!' he had boasted. It was vulgar, but it was candid, and Sylvia Carstairs was certainly a handsome woman, with a delightful sense of humour. She did not seem to mind being teased about her reputation.

'How else do you suppose I landed three husbands before I was thirty?' she had retorted, over a glass of sherry in the Officers' Mess.

It was not strictly true, of course, for Sylvia had been thirty for the past five years! But she was not only a good sport, she was a good sailor, and she had enjoyed the congenial company of all the men deprived of their wives during the early part of the voyage. She was bored in the company of women, anyway, and children were just a nuisance.

Jonathan found his glance wandering repeatedly to the elegant Mrs Carstairs in the centre of a noisy group a short distance away. On the arm of her husband, they were comparing the souvenirs they had purchased in the French port they would be unlikely to see again for the next five years. Her rippling laugh had a young inflexion, and her companions were obviously amused.

Looking down at the pale face under the bonnet, Jonathan wished he could join their gay company. Ellen was a dear girl, but so dashed serious and sensible.

He could hear the grooms exercising the horses on the cobbled dock down below. There would be two more ports of call, at Port Said and Aden, but both horses and grooms would be glad to get to their journey's end. The limited deck space allowed only a fraction of the exercise to which these high-spirited creatures were accustomed. Jonathan could hardly wait to saddle Justin for the first canter on Indian soil. What did the future hold? He saw only the excitement of sudden confrontation with warring tribes on the frontier, and none of the boredom of weeks and months of routine training in preparation for such emergencies. The regiment would be his life from henceforth, and the men under his command would recognize and respect his authority. Discipline and devotion to duty were not born in a man. They had to be learned in a hard school, and Sandhurst had prepared him for the arduous responsibility as a junior subaltern.

The rankers' families were accommodated in the well deck. He supposed he should have been more sympathetic to their crowded conditions, but his fastidiousness had been rudely assaulted by the stench, only four days out from Southampton. Some of the women were camp followers and not even married, and they bred like rabbits. There was really no need to feel concern for them, he had persuaded himself. They had never been accustomed to decent living conditions. Born into poverty and squalor, this opportunity to 'follow the drum' to a warm clime would seem like a dream – if they were capable of dreaming.

Jonathan was no prude, and a pretty housemaid at The Vicarage had been seduced in his formative years. Whether or not his elder brothers had seduced Martha, he could not be sure, for they were some years older, but there had been no breath of scandal, and Martha had survived, apparently unscathed, with no illegitimate child hanging on her skirts.

John and David had started on their preparatory school when he was still in petticoats. Such a pretty little boy, and his Mother's darling! He smiled at the memory. Now he was Ellen's darling. His ego demanded such devotion. A mother, a wife, a sister, all were trained to devotion and obedience, but there had been no sisters at The Vicarage. Intelligence was no requisite for marriage, and a 'blue stocking' remained a spinster. Jonathan had simply complied with the wishes of his commanding officer, who expected his junior officers to take a wife on this five-year term of service in India.

'Shall we take a little stroll, my love?' he suggested. And Ellen dutifully put aside the rug and stood up, swaying a little with weakness, after six days and nights of sickness. She hadn't the slightest desire to take a walk, but it did not occur to her to object, and she took her husband's arm. It was not expected or necessary to make polite conversation as they strolled about the deck, only to acknowledge fellow passengers with formal bows, and to look pleasant. Their conversation would always be limited, for their only common interest would be their children and the regiment, and a man did not gossip about his friends, or the trivialities that women were concerned with.

Ellen's early environment had not prepared her for this wider world in which she found herself. Singularly lacking in the need to establish a friendly relationship with any one of the wives enjoying the air on deck, she clung to her husband's arm as they leaned on the rail to look down on the horses.

'A splendid sight, my love,' he pointed out, proudly.

'Yes, indeed, dear,' she agreed. She really believed those horses took priority over wives! Unfortunately, she was petrified of horses, and Jonathan knew it. In her small, secluded world, there had been few facilities for outdoor games for young ladies, and they had enjoyed a quiet game of croquet, or tennis on the grass court in the Vicarage garden. As for accomplishments, Ellen would never make a pianist, no matter how many hours she practised. Dressmaking had been useful for the past three years, but she had not brought the sewing machine.

'Nobody makes their own clothes in India, my love. You simply choose a style you like from a magazine, buy the material in the native market, and have it made up by a native tailor. They are reputed to be absolute wizards, and at very reasonable cost. I shall expect you to choose something a little more modish, my love, for we shall be invited out, and we shall also do our share of entertaining,' he had explained, on their honeymoon. 'With your dark eyes and hair, you would look well in almost any bright colour. Your figure is perfect, whether clothed or unclothed. And no need to blush, my love!'

It was true. His two hands could encompass her small waist, and under the ankle-length skirts and petticoats, her long, shapely legs would do justice to a principal boy in a Christmas pantomime.

Now if Jonathan had cared to discuss religion with his young bride, he would have been surprised at the wealth of knowledge she had memorized from the Bible. She could quote passages from the Old Testament and the New Testament, a number of psalms had been learned by heart, and the exploits of the Israelites, *en route* to the Promised Land, held an extraordinary fascination. Ellen was every bit as familiar with Abraham and Jacob, Rachel and Ruth, David and Jonathan, and the Apostles, as with the characters of Mr Dickens. Only Grace had shared this absorbing interest, and only Grace would have shared in the suffering and misery of the past six days. There had been no letter from her favourite sister, and she was feeling a little worried.

'I do hope Grace is well,' she reflected, as they leaned over the rail to watch the horses.

'Grace? Why shouldn't she be? It's an easy enough post, by all accounts,' he answered, indifferently.

The stewardesses had been right about enjoying the rest of the voyage, and Ellen found herself an interested spectator of the passing scene. Now she could recognize the places that had been nothing more than coloured blobs on the globe in the schoolroom – Sardinia and Corsica, Sicily, the toe of Italy. She was often joined at the rail by a lively small boy, who also found the passing scene quite fascinating.

'But the Mediterranean is not blue, Mrs Cartwright. It's grey,' he observed, and he seemed disappointed.

'Do you think, Clive, it is something to do with the

skies? The skies are grey. I understand the sea reflects the colour of the sky?' she suggested, tentatively.

He looked at her with fresh interest and nodded his shapely head. She could see in his wide blue eyes and flaxen hair the son she hoped for – a small replica of Jonathan, to grow in his stature. Spending so much time with this child, she knew already that she would love being a mother. She might even call her firstborn Clive if Jonathan approved, of course. It was a manly name.

'Were you named after Clive of India?' she had asked, when they first became acquainted.

'Yes, my father chose my name and my mother chose my sister's names – Rose, Violet and Daisy.'

'Flower names.'

'Yes, I think they are silly, but girls are silly, aren't they?'

'I was a girl not so long ago.' She smiled at the scorn in his voice. He would be rather an arrogant elder brother.

'But you wouldn't be silly. You would be very nice,' he decided, gallantly.

She thanked him for the compliment. If only they had had a brother in their family of girls, there would have been no shrinking from the male body and its ugly organ, no need to close her eyes at her husband's nakedness. It had amused him when they were on their honeymoon, but he would not expect her to behave so foolishly now that she was no longer a virgin bride. Soon, very soon now, Jonathan would be reminding her of her wifely duty. The cramped space on the lower bunk would be no deterrent to his passionate love-making. He had been very patient with her indisposition, but there was a limit to a man's endurance, he had also reminded her, when he kissed her good night and climbed into the upper bunk.

A number of wives and children went ashore at Port Said, including Clive, who brought her back a packet of Turkish Delight that he helped to eat. It was a rather gluey substance and not very appetizing, but she had to pretend to like it.

The English nurses who accompanied the families of the senior officers took charge of the younger children that day, and watched them play from the comfort of deck chairs. They were superior young women in their starched uniforms, and stood no nonsense from their young charges. Junior officers could not afford such paragons, and they would employ the gentle Indian ayahs who would spoil their 'Babas', and break their hearts when the time came to hand them over to be disciplined and educated in a cold climate, so far removed from the tropical sun. It was fun to go ashore, but much more fun to be back on board, watching all the funny little men selling their souvenirs and Turkish Delight, Clive decided. Even the starchy nurses were tempted to purchase the stuff, but when they had sampled it, threw it overboard in disgust while their charges wailed in protest.

Wide-eyed with wonder in the Suez Canal, Clive watched the camel caravans plodding patiently along the sandy banks.

'It's just like it used to be when Jesus was a boy,' he reflected. Ismailia, with its palm trees, was another source of wonder, for white children and native children had gathered to wave and call greetings. The strange tongue was all part of the fascination to a child who spoke only the Queen's English.

'My father will teach me to speak Hindustani and my mother will give us our lessons, because she was our governess before she married my father,' Clive explained, carefully.

'Then you and your sisters must be step-children?'

'Yes.'

'Do you remember your own mother, Clive?'

'Yes, I remember she was very pretty, and she smelled nice, but after my youngest sister was born, she lay on a couch, and we hadn't to disturb her. Then one day Father told us she had gone to live in Heaven. Then we were told to call our governess Mother, and I refused. Father gave me a beating,' he added, but there was no malice in the accusation.

'What age were you then?' Ellen was touched by the sad little story.

'I was six and a bit. Now I am seven and a bit. Look! Here comes another ship! It must be coming back from India. Will there be room to pass? Isn't it exciting?' The sad story was forgotten. He was too young to grieve for a mother who was already a pretty ghost with a nice smell.

The canal had widened into the Bitter Lakes, and there was ample room to pass. Some time later Clive told her importantly, 'My father says I am very privileged, for most boys of my age are left at boarding school in England.'

'So I understand.'

'My father has already entered my name at Winchester, because that was his own public school, and you must be thirteen years old before you can start. My father says I can go to Sandhurst when I leave Cambridge. It's all arranged.'

'It sounds splendid.' Ellen smiled at his lively interest in the future, and wondered whether a parent could really predict a child's future with such absolute certainty.

But Jonathan did not allow her to spend so much time with the boy once they had passed Aden, the last port of call before they disembarked at Karachi. He insisted that she spend more time with the group of other young wives to whom she had been introduced at the start of the voyage. Ellen was shy of them and cool in her manner, and her shyness was interpreted as snobbishness. Nothing could be further from the truth. Only one of Amelia's daughters suffered from an exaggerated opinion of herself, and that was Kate. Ellen found the gossip spiteful, and their minds shallow.

On the outskirts of the group – which always seemed to claim the same sheltered corner of the deck and the same deck chairs – the ex-governess, with her three little step-daughters, took no part in the conversation. On more than one occasion, she was reminded of her status by some haughty remark, and Ellen felt sorry for the young woman, and helped to amuse the children. Clive would hang around looking sulky till she joined him at the rail. He seldom addressed the ex-governess as 'Mother' she noticed, and he practically ignored his little sisters. It was a pity, Ellen thought, that the father should have insisted on this form of address so soon after the death of his first wife. It was thoughtless and rather stupid.

The three little girls were alike as three peas in a pod, with only a little over a year between each child. No wonder that poor woman had succumbed to a state of exhaustion after the birth of the third girl. She scarcely had time to recover from the birth of one child before she was carrying another. But that was no fault of the governess – unless the overburdened mother, in a permanent state of pregnancy, had known her husband would turn to the governess for the intimate relationship of which he was deprived, through his own selfishness. It was not a nice thought, and Ellen kept it to herself, but it prevented any friendly attachment with the young woman, under such suspicious circumstances. More than ever she could understand Clive's reluctance to accept the ex-governess as a mother. There was no love lost between them. The boy was polite and respectful because the father would insist on it, but that was all.

'I wish you could be my mother,' had surprised and shocked Ellen one afternoon, when they were watching the ballet of flying fish, leaping and hovering above the calm waters of the Indian Ocean.

'My dear child, you take my breath away! Whatever persuaded you to make such a statement? We are good friends, are we not?'

He nodded, very near to tears, but boys were not allowed to cry.

She caught his hand in a warm clasp, and her voice was gentle as she explained, 'We all have to accept some things we find displeasing, dear. Even grownups can be hurt and disappointed. But this is life. It's not all smooth sailing on calm waters. You remember the rough passage through the Bay of Biscay, and round the Rock of Gibraltar?'

'Yes, but I was not sick.'

'Then you are fortunate to be a good sailor. My meaning has nothing to do with sickness, Clive. I intended it as an example of what to expect as you grow into manhood. Before we could enjoy these calm waters of the Indian Ocean, we had to endure the rough passages. Do you understand what I mean?'

'I think so.'

'I wish I could promise you all plain sailing and

calm waters, but that would be cheating. When I was your age, I thought our safe little world would last for ever. Our parents, my sisters, the servants, and our little dog called Jack. I loved them all, but I could not keep them for ever. I was lucky to keep them all together till I was a young woman. Then, very suddenly, my small world collapsed. Father was killed by a bolting horse. We could not afford to keep the servants, and we all had to take our share of the work. Then my dearest sister, Grace, was sent away to London to be a lady's companion, and I shall not see her again for another five years. I miss my home and my family, Clive. Even grown-ups can feel homesick.' She smiled wistfully at his upturned face.

'I didn't know. I'm sorry,' he said.

She squeezed his hand and pointed to the wide expanse of ocean. 'Let's pretend we are the only people in the whole world. Sailing away to a new land,' she suggested, gaily.

'I'll be Livingstone, and you can be my man Friday,' he shouted, excitedly.

The ex-governess was conscious of a little stab of jealousy. She saw only sulks. Being a stepmother was not an enviable role.

There was a certain sadness in parting from the troopship that had been home for so many weeks. It had seemed there would never be a time when they must step ashore on Indian soil, and start their long trek across country. Rudely disturbed from the pleasant routine of the voyage, the subalterns' wives were faced with no alternative but to travel by camel, slung in a kind of wicker basket, two to each beast. When all were assembled, after gruelling hours of confusion on the sun-baked docks, they set forth in a long convoy, led by the regimental colours, and the

Drum-Major, mounted officers, laden ox waggons, and marching men. Senior officers had brought their carriages to convey their wives and children in comparative comfort, though they complained bitterly of the dust, the flies, and the smells.

The swarms of native servants awaiting them at Karachi trotted along in the rear, barefoot and uncomplaining, the women carrying black-eyed infants no bigger than dolls. It was the first introduction to a country in which the white Sahib had dominance over all but the princely states, and Ellen was not the only woman to be shamed by the arrogance of Her Majesty's regiment, including that of her own husband.

'You are wasting your sympathy, my love. These creatures are less than the dust. They are born to poverty and servitude. This is India. What did you expect?' he retorted at the end of the first day's long march.

'I don't know. I hadn't given it a lot of thought, but Jonathan, they are so *thin*. They look starved.'

'Tough as little mules, and so dashed lazy, they have to be whipped to get anything done.'

'Whipped?' Ellen was horrified. 'You won't whip our servants, will you dear?'

'I shall, if they deserve it. It's the only kind of treatment the native understands. You will be waited on hand and foot, my love. A Memsahib does nothing but give orders.'

'I am not sure that I shall care for that, dear.'

'You will soon get used to it. Now, have you forgotten your promise?'

'What promise?'

He gripped her shoulders and smiled, disarmingly. They were alone at last in their tent on the overnight encampment, *en route* to their destination. Jonathan had just finished his last duty for the day, and given orders they were not to be disturbed. Ellen was weary, and her head was throbbing. It had been a long day in such cramped conditions. Had she promised?

Silently, obediently, she undressed, and lay down on the narrow camp bed the batman had made ready. When the tent flap was fastened, it was stifling hot, and they both were panting and sweating as they made love.

'It's devilish hot, but I do declare, I could eat you – you adorable woman!' Jonathan announced as he smacked her buttocks playfully, and rolled off on to his own narrow bed. In a matter of seconds, he was sleeping soundly, curled like a tired child in the candlelight.

This was her husband, the man she had married for better or worse, till death parted them. It was a solemn thought. If this passionate possessiveness of her body was the only way to keep him happy, then she must submit. It was her duty, but not her pleasure. Did it matter? How many wives could honestly say they found pleasure in the act of intercourse? Perhaps, if Jonathan were not so impatient for her response? On their honeymoon he had time, with caresses and kisses, and whispered endearments. By the end of the week she had forgotten her shyness, and he was enormously pleased with her when she allowed his thrusting tongue to part her lips. Surprised and shocked by her own immediate response, he had no further need of persuasion and patience. His hard mouth, not his caressing hands, had such power over her senses, from henceforth she knew she had no resistance to his mastery. If this was all – this physical desire, without tenderness – then she knew

103

for certain now that she should never have married Jonathan.

Exhausted and deeply troubled by such thoughts, she lay awake, listening to the footsteps of the sentries on guard duty, and the quiet breathing of her young husband. In the early hours of the morning, she was disturbed by a wave of nausea. Staggering to the wash-basin, she was violently sick, but it passed, and she made no mention of it to Jonathan, over a hasty breakfast. It would be the jolting of the camel that had upset her stomach, she decided. In which case, it would have to be endured for a further two-hundred miles or so. What a poor traveller she had turned out to be. The best antidote to an upset stomach was a good dose of Epsom Salts, as Mother would say, so she helped herself from the medicine chest.

Jonathan had awakened fresh and ready for a new day, when the bugle sounded reveille. She had not seen Clive since they came ashore at Karachi. He had acquired a pony, and she supposed he was travelling with the men in the front of the convoy. It would be his first taste of a world in which a youthful Sahib could be regarded as a young prince among the native servants.

When they were settled in one of the bungalows allocated to the junior officers in the garrison town in the North West province of Punjab, Ellen could no longer persuade herself that the early-morning sickness was due to the lolloping gait of the camel. The doctor was summoned – a grey-haired fatherly man, who wasted no time in pronouncing, importantly, 'My dear Mrs Cartwright, I am delighted to inform you that you are suffering nothing more serious than the happy state of pregnancy! And not the first by any means. Indeed, we have quite an epidemic of pregnancies. Your husband will be delighted, I feel sure. A healthy young woman like yourself should have no problems. It's just a question of adjusting to the hot climate. Keep out of the sun. Always take a siesta in the afternoon. Eat what you fancy, and drink plenty of fluids. Remember to insist that all water is boiled. Native servants are careless and lazy. They cannot be trusted. Now I must be on my way.' He patted her shoulder, wished her well, refused a *chota-peg*, but accepted a glass of iced fruit juice. This was not his first assignment in the tropics, and he had seen the health of too many men ruined by over-indulgence in alcohol.

After he had left, Ellen lay for some time on the marriage bed while the fan stirred the humid air. A baby, so soon? Had she conceived on her honeymoon? If only she had Grace, or Jane, or even Bertha with her sharp tongue. She had never felt so alone as during this first hour of the long months of waiting. He was a kind doctor, but how could he be expected to understand a woman's desperate need of a mother, or a sister in this crucial hour, thousands of miles from home? As for adjusting to a hot climate, she knew already she would never like it. Every small effort left her exhausted, and Jonathan had insisted she play her part in the social life of the regiment. Tea parties and picnics, dancing the lively waltzes and polkas in the cool of the evening, and riding. Thank goodness she would be spared that ordeal when Jonathan knew she was pregnant.

She sighed, and gave herself up to a quiet little weep. It was foolish to cry. She should have been feeling so delighted, but that would come later. Just now she was very much afraid of Jonathan's reaction. The doctor could be wrong, and her young husband not yet ready for fatherhood.

When they had settled on the verandah, some hours later, he demanded, 'Well, my love, what did the doctor have to say?'

Ellen's brown eyes were tender, and her rare smile lent beauty to a face that could be plain. 'I am expecting our first child, dear,' she told him.

'That's dashed good news, I must say. All that wretched nausea gave me quite a scare. Thought you were really ill.'

'I should have known it was only what to expect in the early stages, but nobody told me.'

'And you were too shy to ask?'

'Yes. Are you glad about the baby, dear?'

'I'll be glad for your sake, my love.' He leaned over to kiss her cheek. She could smell whisky on his breath. He was always reluctant to tear himself away from the gregarious company in the mess. There were times when he found the quiet company of his wife just a little tedious. 'We must think of a name for our son,' he said.

'Jonathan! It's another seven months – and it could be a daughter.'

'First a son for me, then a daughter for you,' he decided. 'This calls for a toast.'

The bearer was not surprised to be summoned by a shout from the Sahib at this late hour. Sahib liked his whisky and soda, and Memsahib liked her iced fruit juice. Sahib called him 'Boy', but he was already a grandfather. What matter? He had served other Sahibs in other regiments in this garrison town. It was the Will of Allah, for he had been one of the fortunate few to be chosen by the steward, some twenty years ago. So many had been willing, but so few chosen. It was a privilege, and Boy was proud of his position in the household. Always on duty, always respectful, always accepting the blame for the laziness or misconduct of the lesser servants. To see them whipped was customary. It was only what they deserved. This new Sahib was impatient, and his temper was short. Was the Memsahib a little afraid of her lord and master in these sudden rages? Did she try too hard to please him? But that was the custom, even among these overlords of the great Queen Victoria. The woman was a poor creature, and Allah had not intended her to be anything but the bearer of children. His new Sahib had not yet realized that his native servant had such a good understanding of the English language in common use. He was not as humble or as illiterate as Sahib assumed. He knew, for instance, exactly what it meant to be 'less than the dust'. Even the youngest Sahibs would remind their servants of their humble origin, hardly before they were breeched.

So when Sahib raised his glass, smiled at the Memsahib, toasted the Great Queen, then raised his glass again – 'To US, my love,' Boy knew what it meant. Soon an ayah would be engaged, and she, too, would be less than the dust.

Gerry Carstairs and his wife, Sylvia, could be relied upon to enliven the dullest party, so they were always included in the invitations. On the few occasions when Gerry was on duty, there was no lack of escorts for the handsome woman with the wittiest tongue and the wickedest suggestions. 'A brazen hussy!' was the general opinion among the wives, but they dare not raise their voices in condemnation, for their husbands would naturally assume it was jealousy – and they could be right! Yet there was nothing spiteful or vindictive in her mentality. Mrs Carstairs was always the first to call when one of the young wives was reported to be suffering from some indisposition, including pregnancy.

She called on Ellen one morning, and found her seated on the verandah, lovingly engaged on stitching the infant's layette. She smiled a welcome, excused herself from rising, and bade her visitor be seated. For the past three months, Ellen had spent her days quietly, and Jonathan had not insisted on the social round of engagements that was so much a part of the station life. On one of his regular visits, the doctor had prescribed an iron tonic for the blood, and more rest for her swelling legs. Ugly varicose veins were a further excuse to be spared the social activities, and she was enjoying the respite. Her nature shrank from all forms of excessiveness, and it was this moderation that her young husband found so tedious. His gregarious appetite could only be satisfied in the company of men, with the exception of Sylvia Carstairs.

Seated in the comfortable bamboo chair with a cushion at her back, her gloves and sunshade folded neatly in her lap, she was wondering, not for the first time, what had attracted the dashing young subaltern to this quiet, gentle-voiced woman. Had he been looking for a mother for his children, he could not have chosen more wisely, but Jonathan soon became bored with the topic of his pending paternity.

'You are looking very pretty, my dear.' Sylvia believed in flattery whenever she noticed a slight strain in the conversation. Those dark eyes appeared so deceptively undisturbed by the current rumours circulating in their small world, where the slightest indiscretion became a scandal over night. It was true they were lovers, but with Gerry away on another of these mysterious missions to the frontier, Sylvia was bored – and boredom was a deadly state to a woman of her nature.

When there was no response to the flattering remark, she handed over a small package with a charming smile. 'A little gift for the baby, with my love,' she said. It was a silver mug. The other expectant mothers would be receiving one. It seemed a suitable gift for either a boy or a girl. The name could be inscribed later.

Ellen thanked her politely. Boy was hovering behind her chair, and she ordered a *chota-peg* for her visitor, and iced fruit juice for herself, and wondered how long she would stay. It was really quite ridiculous to be behaving with such conventional politeness when all her deepest feelings had been violated by this woman. In her presence she felt very young and vulnerable, and quite incapable of insisting on her rightful place in her husband's affections. Such elegance, such charm, such sparkling vivacity – all had been employed as a topic of conversation since the young subaltern had first introduced her to his fellow officers and their wives on board the troopship at Southampton Docks. Not one of the young wives, for all their pretty ways and girlish chatter, could compete with a woman so obviously attractive to the opposite sex. Ellen was different, and the difference was becoming a little embarrassing. With no mention of husbands, and no children, as yet, to be admired and petted, they had made no contact whatsoever, Sylvia had to admit, somewhat reluctantly, as she prepared to leave.

When she touched the flushed cheek with lips that could part so invitingly for a lover's kiss, she felt the younger woman shrink from her touch, and was momentarily ashamed. Recovering quickly, she smiled disarmingly.

'Goodbye, my dear. Take care.'

'Goodbye, Mrs Carstairs. Thank you for calling.' Ellen returned the smile. Amelia would have been proud of her eldest daughter. 'Discretion is the better part of valour' was one of her favourite maxims. But it was doubtful whether the alluring Sylvia Carstairs would know its meaning.

'Well, my love, how are you feeling?' The question had become a habit, Ellen thought wearily – a habit and a duty. If she had answered him truthfully – that her heart ached, that her swollen stomach was so stretched she thought she must be carrying twins, and that she couldn't bear his deceptive gallantry a moment longer – what would have been his reaction?

'Not too uncomfortable, thank you dear,' she answered, quietly, as he bent to kiss her cheek – the cheek that Sylvia Carstairs had kissed. She shivered involuntarily, and he asked, 'Have you caught a chill?'

'No, no. It's nothing.' If only she had Grace! She was so dreadfully homesick. Five years! It was an eternity. This was not her world. It was alien to everything that had been so dear and familiar. She was a stranger in a foreign country, thousands of miles from home. Then her mother's voice spoke with sharp authority in her subconscious mind. 'Control yourself, Ellen!' A whimsical smile brightened the dark eyes that a moment ago had been near to tears, and Jonathan was shaking his head at her.

'You know, my love, you keep me in constant suspense by your moods these days. The state of pregnancy seems as variable as our English weather!' he teased. 'What have you been doing with yourself all day?'

'The usual – sewing, dozing, drinking pints of iced fruit juice. I had a visitor this morning.'

'Oh, yes?'

'Mrs Carstairs. 'Only the twitching muscle in his cheek revealed his nervousness. 'It was kind of her to call,' Ellen prompted.

'Yes.'

'She brought a silver mug for the baby.'

'How long did she stay?'

'Not more than half-an-hour.'

'Did she mention Gerry?'

'No, it was just gossip, women's gossip. No mention of husbands.'

He sighed, and the little muscle stopped twitching. Then Boy was there, helping the Sahib to remove his jacket, on his hands and knees, pulling off his boots. The drinks were served and he moved away, on silent, sandalled feet, the jacket over his arm for pressing – the perfect valet.

'Not much longer, my love,' Jonathan reminded her as he stretched his long legs in the lounge chair, and reached for the drink.

'Three to four weeks according to my reckoning, but Doctor tells me the first baby is a bit unpredictable.' With her feet on the stool that Boy had provided for her comfort, they were close enough to touch, and he leaned over, lifted her skirt, and stared at the swollen legs and the ugly varicose veins.

'How soon will your legs get back to normal after the baby is born?' he asked.

'I don't know. Shall you mind too much if they don't get back to normal?'

'You had nice legs, my love.'

'Yes.'

He hated ugliness. This woman, with her swollen belly and ugly legs, was not the girl he had married. What did he expect? And wasn't he to blame for her condition?

'Isn't it time you engaged the ayah?'

'Boy has bespoken her. She has been with the children of a Captain Arlington of the Royal West Kents for the past five years, and she is looking for another post. Boy says she has a good recommendation from her ex-mistress.'

'Engage her, then, before she gets snapped up by another pregnant Memsahib!'

'I will speak to Boy in the morning. Where will she sleep?'

'On a mat outside the nursery door.'

'Jonathan!'

'It's customary. Don't look so shocked.'

'I shall never understand it, not if I have to spend the rest of my days here. They are human beings, dear, not animals. Only a dog would sleep on a mat outside a door in England.'

'When in Rome, you do as the Romans. How often must I remind you? Less than the dust, remember, my love?'

She shook her head. 'They are all God's creatures. Have you forgotten so soon the lessons you learned at your mother's knee?'

'I remember only what I want to remember – Daniel in the den of lions, David and Goliath, the mighty Samson, and all those Egyptian soldiers and chariots that were swept away by a tidal wave crossing the Red Sea. Now that was really something to appeal to a small boy, not all that sob stuff about every sparrow that falls to the ground is known to God. If you believe that, you can believe anything!' he laughed. 'Give me the Old Testament if I must read the Bible, I told Father when I was old enough to speak my mind. Barbaric customs and cruel injustice, but not to the people in that day and age.'

'Then you don't find this callous treatment of the natives barbaric?'

'Not in the least, Memsahib!' His blue eyes were mocking.

She sighed. It was no use. They were miles apart, for all their closeness.

'Will you excuse me, dear? I think I shall be more comfortable in bed,' she said. As she struggled to rise, he leapt to his feet to assist her.

'Good night, my love.'

'Good night, dear.' They exchanged a kiss. Another day was over.

Someone was screaming. She did not recognize herself, for she never screamed. But when a small, brown hand, no bigger than a claw, gripped her clutching fingers and a gentle voice repeated, 'Doctor Sahib he come soon, Memsahib,' she knew the screams were coming from her own tight throat, as her contorted body plunged with every agonized spasm.

Nobody had told her the truth about childbirth – that her body would be torn apart. Was it the child fighting and struggling to get out of the womb? Sweat ran into her eyes, and the small hand wiped her brow, repeating, 'Doctor Sahib come soon, Memsahib.'

'Jonathan?' she whimpered. 'Where is Jonathan?'

'You want Sahib? I send for him.'

'No! No!' Her head jerked on the pillow. It was her Mother she wanted now, not a husband or a sister, but a brave, wonderful mother who had borne six children, and *survived*.

When another scream rose in her throat, she clamped a hand over her mouth and it subsided into a moan. She was still moaning when she became aware of another presence in the room. The ayah was pushed roughly aside, and a cup held to her parched lips.

'Drink this,' she was told, and she drank obediently. Had it been poison she would not have refused it. But it was laudanum. This elderly regimental surgeon had seen so much unnecessary suffering he had been powerless to prevent, so whenever possible he administered a draught of this soothing opium drug. 'Old Sawbones' they called him affectionately in the ranks. It was not a pretty name, but it fitted. For a woman in the final stages of a difficult birth, he did not hesitate. There was a limit to a woman's endurance, and this poor woman had obviously reached that limit. He had been detained in the Sick Bay with a fresh case of enteric fever. Those bloody native servants! They should be flogged. Somebody had been careless, and men were dying.

Acting midwife was a role he found singularly distasteful. To amputate a limb was a straightforward operation and he knew how to proceed. Delivering a child was a delicate and hazardous operation, and the final stages saw him sweating profusely. With a complicated delivery, there was always the risk of losing the mother and saving the child, and a husband was not over pleased to be presented with a live infant over the corpse of his wife. The doctor was blamed. No amount of explanation could soften the blow. A surgeon should not be expected to deliver babies. It was an insult to his profession. The fact remained, though, that he had not yet replaced the wife of Sergeant Mallory, a most efficient midwife who had succumbed, surprisingly, to influenza *en route* to their destination. Any woman in the ranks could deliver a child, but they were a slatternly lot, and not to be trusted with the officers' wives.

The ayah poured hot water in the basin, and he rolled up his sleeves, washed his hands and arms thoroughly, and took the clean towel. He hardly glanced at her. Another pair of hands, and brown hands, but he had no choice. She would obey his every command, and it would not be the first child she had helped to deliver.

Now his patient had stopped threshing about on the bed, and lay still, watching him with her anguished dark eyes. Her pulse was weak. He patted her hand and smiled encouragement.

'Be brave. The worst is over,' he lied.

How could it be over till the child was safely delivered? But she trusted him, and that was half the battle.

When at last he held the tiny scrap of humanity in his two big hands, he knew a moment of triumph, as satisfying as the knowledge that he had saved a limb from amputation. The ayah took the child, and when he had cut and tied the cord, he had no further interest in the child, only in the mother.

'A little girl,' he told her, and her tremulous smile was all the payment he needed. It had been a difficult birth, but that was not uncommon for a first child. There would be a second child within the year most likely. The young subaltern would want a son. It was natural. They would drink the health of the mother and the child in the Mess tonight. It was customary.

'Next time, see you deliver a son!' Jonathan would tease. That, too, was customary.

'Why is she yellow, my love?' Jonathan demanded, when he had kissed her cheek, and barely glanced at the tiny scrap cradled in her arms.

'You have a little daughter, Sahib,' Boy had greeted him with the news as he pulled off his boots.

'The Memsahib? Is she . . .?' His heart was racing. He was a selfish brute. He should have been here. Ellen could have died while he lay in the arms of that Delilah!

But Boy was saying, soothingly, 'Memsahib had good sleep, and nice cup of tea. Memsahib very brave lady, Sahib.'

He nodded impatiently. Of course she was brave, and so damned uncomplaining she would not even upbraid him for staying away till it was all over.

'Is she yellow? I hadn't noticed. It must be a touch of jaundice,' Ellen told him, with quiet unconcern, for she could see no flaw in this tiny creature that had nearly killed her mother. She was so happy and relaxed, and she knew for certain, now, that being a mother would satisfy all the inborn maternity in her nature. To be the eldest of six had prepared her for this day. Her dark eyes were tender with love, and soft as velvet. Her smile held a serene, Madonna-like beauty.

'What shall we call her, dear?' she prompted.

He shrugged. 'Isn't it a mother's privilege to choose a name for her daughter?'

'You are disappointed?' She could read his thoughts like an open book. His frank, boyish face was so revealing. In her heart, and in her newfound maternity, he was a child – a grown child, to be spoilt, and allowed to please himself. She would not bind him in fetters of wifely obligations. Or remind him of his duty as a parent, for she knew he was not yet ready for parenthood – might never be ready.

When he sat on the edge of the bed, she touched his cheek and asked, 'Did Boy give you a *chota-peg*?'

'No. I could do with it. It has been a hellish day, for me, also. I was scared stiff you were going to die. You had me in a cold sweat, my love.'

'Poor darling.'

Darling? He was surprised at the endearment. Ellen was not demonstrative. This particular endearment was bandied about so freely among the socialites, it had no meaning.

'Aren't you hungry?' she asked.

'I could do with a bite of something.'

She tugged on the bell-rope, and the summons was answered so promptly she thought Boy must have been standing outside the door, waiting patiently with the *chota-peg* on the little silver tray.

'Kidneys and bacon for Sahib, please, Boy, and I will have tea and toast.'

'Very good, Memsahib.' Boy was devoted to the young Memsahib. She always spoke kindly to the servants, and although Sahib had reminded her on more than one occasion that it was not customary, she always said please and thank you. In this respect she was not obedient to his wishes.

In the servants' quarters, beyond the compound, Sahib never set foot, but his Memsahib, greatly daring, would visit the sick with Boy in attendance, carrying a dish of chicken broth, reputed to have such nourishing qualities. It was a pity it had to be thrown away, for his own people found it so distasteful. Sahib would have raised his voice in anger had he known of these visits, but not his fist. Only the ranker Sahibs beat their wives when they had drunk too much of the cheap, intoxicating liquor they bought in the market. Boy and the other servants despised the ranker Sahibs, with their rough voices and abusive language. The barracks, where they ate and slept and fornicated, was a crowded, verminous place, where discipline was maintained with a ruthlessness that often left the victim unconscious. They had no status, so why did they consider themselves so superior to the natives? That was a question that Boy and the ayahs, who had served the officers of the Great Queen so devotedly, would ask themselves. It was not true to say they were SCUM, or they were BAS-TARDS. Over the years they had acquired not only a useful knowledge of the English language, but had copied their speech and mannerisms. So a feud existed between the rankers and the natives that would never be reconciled because it had its origin in the slums of Liverpool and London, not in the mud huts of a teeming native population. It was a feud of aliens, of hatred, of mistrust – and of the colour of the skin.

Their daughter was baptized Prudence by the regimental chaplain a week after her birth. She was such a puny mite that even the devoted ayah, who adored her new baba, had grave doubts whether she could be reared. Ellen had no such doubts. She paced the verandah every night with the fretful infant, so that Jonathan would not be disturbed, and Ayah could get some sleep on the mat outside the nursery door. To see the child suckling at her mother's breast had a peculiar effect on Jonathan. Was it jealousy?

Ellen seemed to spend so much time nursing and

118

feeding the child, he felt neglected. 'Why keep a dog and bark yourself?' he demanded, irritably one night, when he had awakened to find he was alone in the marriage bed, not for the first time. In his haste to locate his wife, he had stumbled over the sleeping servant, and cursed the poor woman in no uncertain terms. He found Ellen in the rocking chair, humming a lullaby to the baby. Wearing nothing but a diaper, its small damp head lay on her shoulder, and her own head was drooping with weariness. Her startled eyes flew open.

'What did you say, dear?' she asked. Something about a dog, but they had no dog.

'Give her to me.' He spoke with gruff kindliness now, his annoyance forgotten, and Ellen handed over the child with a sigh of relief. She lay in his arms, weightless as a moth. Six weeks had passed since her birth, and she had gained no more than a few ounces. The jaundice had left its mark on her pallid skin, and the little cap of dark hair was damp with sweat.

Prudence – the name suited her, he thought. Such wide-eyed innocence was faintly disturbing to his senses as they stared at each other for a long moment. When the baby's hand reached up to clutch his nose, he chuckled.

'You see, she knows her Papa!' he told Ellen, and they hung over the child together, for the first time, united in parenthood. It would not happen often, not with this girl child. Jonathan was waiting for his son.

'I take her, Sahib?' asked the gentle voice in the doorway. He made no answer, but the willing arms received her baba.

'Come back to bed, my love. I need you,' he coaxed. Ellen must not be allowed to forget that her husband's need was infinitely more demanding than a fretful baby.

Gerry Carstairs was back, and had claimed his wife. Was he really so enamoured of the woman that he could ignore the rumours, malicious and mischievous, that awaited his return? Jonathan wondered. It was a strange relationship, unlike any other among the junior officers. Yet they seemed happy enough, and it could be said they enjoyed a second honeymoon when Gerry returned.

With a small company of picked men, Gerry Carstairs had succeeded where other subalterns, including Jonathan, had failed, and he was due for promotion. His devil-may-care approach to danger had endeared him to his men, and also to the woman who flirted with danger in a different kind of way. Envy and jealousy could be bitter enemies in their small world. Any one of the young husbands who found her mature charms so fascinating, would have been shocked and surprised to be told that Sylvia Carstairs actually despised her easy conquests, and made mock of them in the ardent embrace of her lawful husband. There were no secrets between them, and no inhibitions. Sylvia had found, in her third husband, the perfect complement to her own demanding sexuality, and not one of her lovers could hold a candle to Gerry. So they could afford to be generous in their united front against the spiteful tongues.

But Jonathan's ego had been sadly deflated when, once again, he found himself a rejected suitor. Next time he vowed he would not be such a fool. Sylvia could find her pleasures elsewhere. This she would do, of course, so he would be depriving himself, not her.

'I could wring her neck!' he exploded, when he

found the door locked and the groom leading the sweating horse to the stables. That was two weeks ago, and he was still sulking over her callous indifference to his wounded pride. After all, it had been a much longer period, this time. Gerry had been away for six weeks, and no word had been received of his whereabouts. Had he been killed, or kidnapped? Once he came back disguised as a beggar, in filthy rags, and not even his own wife had recognized him. His scattered platoon had wandered back in pairs, and wild horses would not have dragged any information from their closed lips. Their commanding officer, a shrewd, hard-bitten little man with a strong resemblance to the redoubtable Bonaparte, on horseback, had them all marching and sweating on the parade ground in the heat and dust. It was a boring sort of life, relieved only by the occasional skirmish on the frontier, a few days' hunting, and the annual leave, where the officers joined their wives and children at a hill station. Nobody gave a thought to the families in the garrison, who remained on the plain whatever the season.

The hill station was a pleasant place, with cooling breezes from the snow-capped mountains, and meadows carpeted with wild flowers. Away from the heat and dust of the plain, the baby thrived, and Ellen wished they could stay in that high altitude, for it suited her also. But that was wishful thinking. She felt like a new woman in the bracing air, and enjoyed the company of the other young wives, while the older children rode their ponies, and the little ones romped in the gardens where previous tenants had planted English roses and bright scarlet geraniums.

Playing with her baby, drinking tea on a green lawn, she could almost imagine she was back in

Worthing. Letters from home were often delayed, and the long-awaited mail would bring a batch of letters to read so many times over she would know them by heart before the next batch arrived. The homesickness could be endured – must be endured – now that she had Prue, and another child conceived before Prue was six months old.

But letters from home invariably brought sadness, for there was so much happening among her sisters that she could not share. Grace was unhappy in that troubled household, and could only confide in her elder sister. Jane was engaged to her curate, and only waiting for her eighteenth birthday when Mother would sanction her marriage. The curate would be leaving his comfortable living at St Matthew's. Then it would be a hard life among the poor of London's East End, for Jane's curate was joining the ranks of the Church Army. He knew exactly where God intended he should minister, and had chosen his helpmeet wisely. Jane would promise to love, honour and obey, and keep her vows till death parted them. Bertha's bosom friend, Norah Styles, would take over the kitchen and earn her keep. Mother had no alternative but to agree to this proposal, since there was still no money to pay for servants. Their circumstances had not changed for the better, and Amelia was often financially embarrassed, but too proud to ask for help from her late husband's family.

Kate was being difficult, according to Lucy – had she ever been anything else? She made trouble between the sisters and their special friends. Kate had no bosom friend, and scorned such girlish nonsense. She preferred the company and the flattery of two young 'Varsity undergraduates in their boaters and blazers, but was never allowed to meet them unchaperoned by one of her sisters.

Ellen knew she would *never*, *never* get acclimatized to her adopted country, or to her role as Memsahib. She was English to the core, had no social graces, and had made only one close friend on the station. Madge Bentley, a cherished only child of elderly parents, was even more in need of a staunch woman friend. Both had been persuaded into a way of life for which they were totally unsuited, and both would have been quite content in neat little houses with only one servant, and a husband who travelled no farther than his City office.

When Madge had a miscarriage and lost her first child, Ellen was there to comfort her. Now, in the healthy environment of the hill station, with little Prue chortling in her bamboo crib among the flowers, they both were busy on another layette, and sharing memories of a happy childhood, so different yet so alike in innocence, sheltered from the slings and arrows of a wider world. Neither had been ready for the rigours of Army life. Romantic dreams had promised an idyllic future, and a sort of prolonged honeymoon that no man could provide. As for the alarming intimacy of the marriage bed, it could not be disclosed, even to one's dearest friend.

Clive's stepmother, who was once his governess, was giving lessons to the older children in the mornings, while the ayahs watched over the little ones. But Ellen had not been persuaded to hand over her baby completely to a native servant. Feeding and nursing Prue was her biggest joy, not the duty and the burden the more frivolous young wives seemed to find it.

Prue was still small for her age, but no longer fretful, though not to be compared with the fat, bottle-fed cherubs the ayahs carried around for everyone to admire.

'Memsahib's baba very special baba,' Ayah insisted, in her gentle way.

Loyalty to the families they served so devotedly was expected, but seldom praised or rewarded. On silent feet, their humble status often abused by the heavy children they carried on their hips, was a constant anxiety to Ellen, who could not bear to watch the little tyrants belabouring the wrinkled brown faces with their fists.

When the husbands arrived at the hill station on their annual leave, the quiet hours that Ellen and Madge had enjoyed with the baby and their sewing were suddenly disrupted. The social round of dinner parties, picnics, balls, tennis and polo had a hectic gaiety, and the young subalterns, reunited with their wives and children, behaved with boyish exuberance in the healthy climate. More babies would be conceived, and not only in the marriage bed. Sex-starved men, in holiday mood, would find ample opportunity to make love, in the hills and valleys, under the chilling stare of those snow-capped peaks.

Jonathan saw no reason to be deprived of his pleasure because Ellen was expecting their second child – the son destined to fulfil all his father's ambitions for the future. His baby daughter was rather shy, and when he plucked her out of her crib and tossed her over his head, she cried.

'Take her!' he told the hovering ayah impatiently. 'She has forgotten her Papa.'

'Baba too young to remember Sahib,' she reminded him, deferentially.

He shrugged, and went in search of Ellen. She, too, was shy of this boisterous young husband she had not seen for three months – shy, and more than a little apprehensive that frequent demands on her pregnant body might harm the child in her womb. She was still so ignorant of such matters, so anxious to protect the unborn child. For the past three months she had hardly been troubled by morning-sickness or swelling legs. Surrounded by the young wives and their lively children, she had not been expected to be anything but an expectant mother, or to exert herself beyond a leisurely game of croquet on the lawn, and a quiet stroll after supper. Now, because her husband had arrived and she was so desperately anxious to please him – too anxious, perhaps? – she had lost her serene acceptance of her condition, looked positively haggard, and her legs were swelling.

His wife was not an attractive woman in the early stages of pregnancy, Jonathan was thinking, and once again he was obliged to excuse her from the exhausting round of social engagements provided for their entertainment. When he had made love to her, he kissed her cheek, bade her rest, and hurried away to make up a foursome for tennis, leaving her feeling guilty and depressed. She could, of course, watch the match, if she could summon enough energy and enthusiasm, but she hardly knew the rules of the game, and would probably make some stupid remark.

Gerry and Sylvia Carstairs would be evenly matched against Jonathan and his partner, an athletic young woman with a forceful drive. Being the only girl in a family of four brothers – she had married a cousin at the age of seventeen – Dodie Wentworth had no time or inclination for the normal pursuits of the fair sex, and had somehow managed to avoid the hazards of childbirth. Only she and Sylvia Carstairs could claim such immunity!

It was the start of the tennis tournament, and these four players were high on the list of betting. To back the winners of any and every contest, from marbles to mountaineering, was all part of the holiday mood that infected the hill station now the husbands had arrived. Nothing was too ridiculous, or too difficult, to attempt, and Jonathan, partnered by Dodie, would be hot favourite for more than one contest.

Ellen lay where he left her, stretched naked on the marriage bed, her damp thighs still throbbing from his impatient thrusting. Such impatience had spoiled what might have been a pleasant occasion. Why had she expected it to be different? A husband did not change his habits or his method to suit his wife. Surely she was not going to question his right to the role of her lord and master? That would be a fatal mistake. A woman of her middle-class environment did not question in this day and age, but complied with her husband's wishes. Only the rare exceptions, such as Sylvia and Dodie, could defy the conventions, and, surprisingly, win the applause of the stronger sex. Yet there must be something more to marriage than the bed, Ellen was thinking.

Being a mother had still not completely satisfied that inherent desire for a spiritual or a mental understanding, or a common interest they could share. Perhaps, after the birth of his long-awaited son, Jonathan would allow her to share in his upbringing, at least in his formative years? And she must not harbour disloyal thoughts, for she was not actually unhappy, only questioning Jonathan's lack of interest in anything but her body.

When Ayah brought the baby for her feed some

time later, she found her Memsahib looking serene and pretty in a frilled day-gown after her bath. With the child to her breast, Ellen knew once again the comforting reassurance of motherhood.

'You have another little daughter, Sahib.' Boy spoke with less assurance on this occasion, as he pulled off his Sahib's riding boots, and a *chota-peg* stood ready on the bamboo table.

Jonathan flushed, picked up the glass, drained it and barked, 'Another!'

'Very good, Sahib.' Boy hastened to obey. It was the Will of Allah, the servants were saying, but Allah's Will was often misunderstood by these superior beings who ruled their lives. Sahib's bitter disappointment would have its effect in the entire household. There would be no rejoicing, no extra coin in their meagre wages, and no little Sahib to ride on the shoulders of his proud Papa. Boy had been dreading this moment all day since Doctor Sahib had delivered the child. It had been an easy delivery, and Ayah had reported the birth of a second daughter to the other servants. All had received the news with the calm assumption that Allah knew best about matters of life and death. Memsahib was young, and would bear more children. Next year or the year after, the son and heir would assuredly arrive.

But such faith would not satisfy their impatient Sahib. He had been away from the garrison for more than a month, and had ridden hell-for-leather with his detachment of picked men, to escape the band of hostile tribesmen. Ambushed in a gully, on one of their regular patrols, they had lost three men, but had the satisfaction of shooting down five of their attackers. This was the purpose and the duty of the regiment. Hundreds of miles of frontier had to be patrolled, and casualties were inevitable. For all their intensive training and their endurance, they could not anticipate a surprise attack with any degree of accuracy, and were often defeated by the cunning and daring of these tough little men of the hills who clung like limpets to their shaggy ponies.

Jonathan and part of his detachment had been lucky to escape with their lives. An ambush could mean the slaughter of the British patrol, when the tribesmen fought amongst themselves for the spoils.

For one particular young subaltern, this was to be a homecoming of special significance. The disappointment was so acute, Jonathan slumped in the cane chair on the verandah, and Boy removed the empty glass and brought another *chota-peg*.

Ayah kept the nursery door firmly closed, for little Prue would normally toddle in to welcome Papa, and he would lift her on to his knee to receive a wet kiss on his cheek. But not tonight, no, most certainly not tonight. Sahib would be disappointed a second time, for the newborn child was puny, with the same jaundiced skin as her sister, and the little cap of black hair that would never curl. Why did other men's wives produce such pretty children, with golden curls, blue eyes, and dimples? Jonathan would ask himself, on the morrow.

Slumped in the chair, his lean body damp with sweat, and his handsome face flushed from the third *chota-peg*, he slept till bugle-call with no sense of obligation to the anxious wife, who awaited his coming with the newborn child. Stretching his stiff limbs, he shivered in the cool air of early morning and shouted for Boy, who brought a cup of hot sweet tea, and wished his Sahib a polite good morning.

Few men were at their best in the early morning, and Jonathan, after a cramped night in the cane chair, merely grunted. Fully awake now to the new day, he remembered why he had slept on the verandah, and felt a little guilty.

The servant, who seemed to anticipate his every wish, had instructed a lesser servant to fill a hip bath in Sahib's dressing-room, and to pour the cold water over his head. In a matter of seconds, Sahib was reaching for a towel, and cursing the unfortunate creature who was drenched to the skin. The entire household, as always, had been alerted by these early morning ablutions, but Ellen had been awake most of the night, feeding the baby at regular intervals, and expecting to see Jonathan.

Ayah had picked up her mat at bugle-call, and crept quietly into the nursery. She would not close her eyes again till the sombre notes of 'sun-down' echoed across the plain. This was her life, and she wished for nothing more than a new baba every year, and a kind Memsahib. It was sad to part with her children every five years or so, and to start all over again, but she could not be persuaded to leave the garrison where she had made her home. She belonged here. Those who had sailed across the seas to the country of the Great Queen had died of the cold and the damp, heartsick for the hot, dusty plains.

'Well, my love, is this the son I was promised?' Jonathan teased, looking down on the tiny head cradled in his wife's arms.

'Are you very disappointed, dear?' she asked, reaching out a hand, entreatingly.

He took the hand and kissed it, with a gallantry not often displayed. Ellen sighed with relief, and relaxed.

Sitting on the edge of the bed, with damp tendrils

of hair curling about his ears, and his face glowing from vigorous scrubbing with a rough towel – he couldn't bear a soft one – he looked too young to be the father of two children. He did no more than touch the baby's head, but Ellen was not expecting any demonstration of affection. That would come later.

Little Prue, who adored her Papa, had managed to find a way to claim his attention for a few minutes each day. She was a lovable little girl, and not at all daunted by Jonathan's impatience. He called her by her full name – Prudence – and could see no sense in giving a child a name then shortening it. But Ellen preferred the shorter version, and the servants called the child 'Missy Baba.'

'Have you thought of a name for your second daughter?' Jonathan prompted.

'*Our* second daughter, Jonathan dear,' Ellen reminded him quietly.

'Of course,' he agreed, with a disarming smile.

'Do you care for Matilda?' she asked.

'Not bad. But how many people will call her Matilda? It will soon be shortened to Mattie, and that's not at all pretty for a girl.'

'We could call her Victoria?'

'No, for there are too many Victorias. We must have at least a dozen in the bungalows, and heaven knows how many in the garrison.'

'Arabella?'

'I like it better than Matilda, and everyone will call her Bella, which is prettier than Mattie. Shall we have her baptized in the coming week? If so, I will speak to the chaplain.'

'Thank you, dear. It might be advisable, though I think she weighs a little more than Prue weighed at birth. I wonder why I have such small babies? I am not a small woman.'

'I would not call you a big woman, my love. Tall, yes, but a tiny waist and narrow thighs.'

She blushed. To speak of thighs was embarrassing.

'Never mind, my love. Our son will be a big strapping fellow. You'll see!'

She nodded, tremulously. It would be nice to have a little time to recuperate before the next pregnancy, but it would depend on when she conceived, not on her own preference. While the servants would say it was the Will of Allah, Ellen and the young wives would see themselves as instruments of their husbands.

No mention was made of the recent skirmishes in the hills. Husbands did not discuss such matters with their wives. It was a man's world, completely separated from the small, sheltered world occupied by the women and children.

Only a mature woman like Sylvia Carstairs would share the confidence of her husband and his fellow officers. They found her intelligent grasp of their exploits almost as rewarding as her sex appeal. So Ellen merely enquired after Jonathan's health, and was satisfied that he seemed no worse for the month-long expedition to the frontier.

His commanding officer had been pleased with his report, and had reminded him of his duty to inform the wives of the men they had lost. This was a duty that every officer would have liked to avoid, but he was not allowed to forget his responsibilities. In the overcrowded women's quarters, separated from the men with nothing more than a few yards of canvas strung on a rope, he had been surrounded by a swarm of dirty, barefoot children, and their mothers, in various stages of undress. The stench of urine and unwashed bodies was nauseating to his fastidious senses. Naked babies clung like limpets to their mothers' sagging breasts, and stunted little girls were carrying younger brothers and sisters on their hips. There was nothing to choose between these despised creatures and the natives – but the colour of their skin, Jonathan was thinking.

His manner was brusque as he sorted them out, and left the three widows to console each other. Their loud lamentations followed him on to the parade ground, but he was not unduly concerned about their future. Single men would waste no time in claiming a widow. This was their life. They fornicated and bred, without privacy or embarrassment.

So the months slipped away, and Ellen asked no questions, and turned a deaf ear to the rumours concerning her husband and the fascinating Sylvia Carstairs. Captain Gerry Carstairs seemed to spend more and more time on those mysterious assignments to the native villages bordering the frontier. With his mastery of Pushtu and Urdu, and his cleverness in disguise, Gerry was a legendary character in the regiment, and not yet thirty. The two men were still friends, yet it was no secret that Jonathan was a favoured lover in the absence of the husband.

Jealousy would rear its ugly head, however, when Sylvia decided to tease, and Jonathan found the door locked. Smarting from her rejection, and reminded every day of his bitter disappointment over the birth of a second daughter, he was moody and unpredictable in his behaviour. The servants were wary of his anger, and only little Prue showed no fear of her Papa.

Madge had given birth to a son, and her proud husband was boring all the unmarried men in the Mess with ridiculous comparisons to other offspring of the same age. To hear him talk, you would suppose there had never been another child so perfect in every way. It was not Madge's fault, and she was embarrassed by such effusive baby worship, and rather vexed that a normally attentive husband had failed to notice her exhausted condition in giving birth to such a heavy child. She had suffered a permanent injury, and the doctor had decided there must be no more pregnancies.

If Ellen had envied her friend her adorable cherub, it would have been understandable, but all her mother love was bestowed on her two puny little daughters. Jonathan had waited no more than a few weeks to claim his rightful place in the marriage bed. A second crib was provided for the new baby, and Ayah instructed to pacify her crying and not disturb the Memsahib. It was not Ellen, but Jonathan, who disliked being disturbed, and it was Jonathan who gave orders to the servants.

Ellen had mastered no more than a dozen words in their strange tongue, and her attitude to the servants was much too lenient, in Jonathan's opinion. It was no use. Ellen was in her wrong element, and could not change her nature, even to please her husband.

One night, after drinking heavily in the Mess, he made his way to the Carstairs' bungalow, and found a horse tethered to the rail of the verandah. The servants had retired to their own quarters. No native servants slept on the premises unless there were children, when the ayah slept on the mat at the nursery door.

Trembling with rage and frustration, Jonathan tethered his own horse under the banyan tree in the garden, and waited impatiently in the shadows, listening for the first signs of movement in the bedroom. As he waited, the anger grew hot in his belly, and his head was swimming.

Some time later, a tall figure appeared in the open doorway, ran down the steps, and leapt the rail on to his mount with practised ease. It was Richard Greyson, his hated rival for Sylvia's favours. Raising a hand in salute, he cantered away.

The woman in the doorway laughed a low, chuckling laugh, as familiar as the scent she wore. Naked, but for the flimsy wrap she had thrown over her shoulders, she had no time to close the door. Jonathan was there, forcing her back into the bedroom, a smile on his lips, but no smile in his eyes.

'Johnny! What are you doing here?' Sylvia demanded, fretfully, backing away.

'You bitch! You tantalizing, bloody bitch!' he hissed. He snatched off the transparent wrap, and it fell to the floor, and his eyes raked her perfect body, travelling down from the full breasts to the hips. It was a mature body, but more alluring than any virgin. He stared, hypnotized, his loins aching with desire. Reaching out a hand he touched her thighs, and found them still damp.

'Whore!' he shouted, beside himself with jealousy now.

Pushed roughly backwards on to the tumbled bed, she stared up at his distorted face as he stripped off his clothes. Then he was on top of her, and she was helpless under the fury of his lean young body.

'Johnny, *please*!' she whimpered as he spread her legs. He thrust deeper and deeper, and she cried out with pain, begging for mercy. His breath stank of whisky, his hot hands clutched her breasts, and his hard mouth bruised her lips.

'Johnny, you're hurting me.' She was sobbing now, but his rejected manhood was still not satisfied.

'I'll wring your neck!' he threatened, as his hands closed round her slender throat. A second or two of startled disbelief, and her head fell back, like a flower on a broken stem. The fire went out. Only ashes remained.

'Sylvie! Sylvie! Speak to me!'

It was his turn to plead, but there was no answer.

Horrified, he slid away and stood there for a long moment, choked with tears. Pulling on his trousers, he fumbled for his pistol, and staggered down the steps into the garden.

PART 2

4

The double tragedy shocked the entire regiment. Both were buried quietly in the military cemetery, lying side by side, among the men, women and children who had died of cholera or enteric fever through the years. Captain Gerry Carstairs had not returned and could not be traced or notified. The bungalow was empty and securely locked. The natives averted their eyes as they passed. The Will of Allah could not be questioned.

Boy was sad without his Sahib, and wept over the uniform he sponged and pressed, and the riding boots he still polished. His young Sahib had trained him well. For a bearer to boast of his capabilities as a valet was all to his credit, and he would find no difficulty in transferring to another household when Memsahib and the children had left.

The servants crept about on bare, silent feet, but Ayah, who was taking orders from her Memsahib now, did not hush her babas.

'Thank God they were too young to remember, Ayah,' was all she said. There were no tears. She was too shocked and stunned to weep.

Jonathan's Commanding Officer called in person to offer his condolences, and to explain kindly that she was not to worry. His official report to the War Office would simply state that Lieutenant Jonathan Cartwright had been killed in a skirmish with raiding tribesmen. 'In that way, you will receive a pension,' he added. 'I shall also notify his parents that their son has been killed in action, and you will notify your own parents accordingly.'

'Only my mother, Sir. My father died some years ago.'

'Indeed?' He sighed with relief. She was so calm and controlled. All her sorrow was hidden in the depths of her dark, anguished eyes. For such a young woman, she was remarkably composed – and composure was a rare quality among the wives of his serving officers.

'May I go home now, Sir?' she asked, like a child who had been away too long. But she was all woman – and she carried her third child in her swollen belly.

'Just as soon as it can be arranged,' he promised. 'You will need an escort to Karachi, and once you are aboard a ship, a stewardess will help you with the children, unless you wish to take the ayah?'

'No, I won't take her. After what has happened, she has offered, but this is where she belongs. It would be cruel to take her away.'

'You are probably right. Few natives of India would find our English climate agreeable.'

When Boy tapped on the door and proffered a *chota-peg*, with a polite little bow, the brusque thanks he received surprised and pleased him enormously. Such an important Sahib to notice a servant!

Ellen did not enquire what plans had been made for the servants and the bungalow. It would not concern her. She would be gone.

Only Madge called to see her during those final weeks. She did not bring the child, and their meeting was rather strained. The intimacy they had enjoyed could not be recaptured, and it was a relief when

Ayah brought in the two little girls. Prue was missing her Papa. At the age of two-and-a-half years, she was a lively child with a determined will. She had been told that her Papa was busy on a special duty for the Queen, and since she had only to be lifted up to touch Her Majesty's portrait, she was satisfied with that explanation. Ellen was hoping the child would soon forget in the excitement of the long journey home to England. Bella was toddling, but not yet talking. There was no jealousy between them, and Prue regarded her baby sister as her own special charge.

What would Mother say to such an invasion of The Haven? Ellen wondered. Would they be welcome? Such young children would disturb the peaceful routine of a household, no matter how hard she tried to keep them under her wing. It was not going to be an enviable situation, but she had proved she was not a woman who expected her path made smooth. It would be the house-proud Bertha who would complain if her polished floors and immaculate beds were soiled.

Would the good-tempered Norah intervene? She seemed to have settled in as a permanent member of the household, neither family nor servant. According to Jane, who was a prolific writer of letters, Norah shared a bed with Bertha, and was a most agreeable young woman. They all liked her.

Why did nobody mention Grace, and why had there been no letter from that beloved sister for more than six months?

Jane had married her curate. As the wife of the Warden of a Church Army hostel at Hoxton, she would be sharing the hardships and poverty with which they were surrounded. Dear Jane, so capable and kindly, and so dedicated to good works. Six sisters, all different, all individuals.

Only the servants were there, huddled on the verandah, to watch the little cavalcade start on the first stage of its long journey back to England. It was better so, Ellen thought, for they were an embarrassment now to the regiment. This was the end of a chapter, and there would be no contact at all with this country that had never lost its strangeness, or the regiment that Jonathan had disgraced.

Tucked into the baskets swinging from the camel's bony back, they lurched forward, the camel driver muttered curses, spitting in the dust. A second camel followed with the baggage. The encumbered animals, destined from birth as beasts of burden, stepped cautiously towards the main gate, escorted by two reliable troopers on horseback.

The two little girls laughed and shouted gleefully, but Ellen's throat was choked with tears, and she did not look back or she would have seen the servants crouched on the steps, rocking themselves in submission to the Will of Allah.

Back across the long, weary miles to the port of Karachi, with many halts to allow the little girls to wander, hand-in-hand, to inspect the clumsy beasts, and pat the soldiers' horses. The two men lifted the children down and put them back with kindly patience, and Ellen was also lifted out to stretch her cramped muscles. They drank iced fruit juice and ate tiny sandwiches. The children fell asleep under their canopy, as they plodded on at the same steady pace, till nightfall. A tent was erected, and a meal provided by the troopers, with the expert ease of men long familiar with tents and camp fires. The camel drivers ate a meal of cold rice, curled up beside their beasts, and slept till daybreak, while the troopers bedded down under the stars, each taking a turn to keep watch for thieving robbers.

The lurching motion had brought on the travel sickness that had made the outward journey so unpleasant, and it seemed to Ellen that the child in her womb was protesting at such indignity. The camel was a smelly beast, and they were too close. There was little time to spare for her own condition, however, for there was no ayah to wait on them. One thing she was spared on this homeward journey, and for that she was grateful. No husband was waiting to claim her exhausted body at the end of the day. In her relief, a twinge of guilt would keep her awake as she blamed herself for the tragedy. It need not have happened if she had been a little less devoted to her children, and a little more willing to spend time on her appearance, and the social graces he had thought so important. She had failed as a wife. She would never marry again. Her maternity was too strong.

Even as she mourned her husband, she was still absorbed in her two little girls, and the unborn child. Would it be the boy that Jonathan had wanted? If only he had had a son, everything would have been different. She had disappointed him in every way, yet they had started out with such high hopes.

Lying awake on the narrow camp bed, listening to the quiet breathing of her children, Ellen knew herself to be guilty of betraying her marriage vows – as guilty as that other woman, whose belly was never swollen with child. Three children in three years. Could she not be excused for neglecting Jonathan? The voice of reason was too small. The voice of conscience spoke more loudly. Other women had babies every year and kept their husbands happy. If only she could have these years over again, how differently she would behave – or would she? There is no second chance for anyone. It is an irrevocable fact that we pass through this world but once. Mistakes had to be lived with – big and small mistakes. And to marry into the regiment destined for a five-year term of service in India, was surely the biggest mistake of her young life. Romantic love had not been enough. The honeymoon was quickly over, and a seasick wife in a stuffy, crowded cabin was an ugly sight for a newly wed husband.

Her sister Jane would not have made the same mistake. She knew exactly what to expect from her young curate, who had embarked on a lifetime of service to struggling humanity. They shared a common bond, and were no strangers to the qualities of kindness, thoughtfulness, and faith.

'Jonathan, my poor darling. I am so ashamed,' she whispered. In the glow of the hanging lantern, she could see the two little girls wrapped in each other's arms, and knew an overwhelming sense of loneliness in her solitary state, till the child in her womb stirred, and she was reminded, once again, of her motherhood.

The dock was noisy with winches and shouting white overseers directing the swarm of native porters who staggered up the gangway with heavy loads of baggage, to be dumped on deck for the stewards to handle. It was pandemonium, and the two little girls were frightened of the noise, for now they remembered nothing else but the trek across country, the quiet days and nights, and the lolloping camel. The devoted little woman called Ayah was lost for ever for Prue, and Bella's small world was complete with her Mama and her sister.

When they had been lifted out of the baskets, clutching their rag dolls, the two troopers carried them carefully up the gangway, and stood them down on deck, where they were too frightened to move. Then they went back to help Ellen – a pale, sad-eyed ghost of the young woman who had boarded the troopship at Southampton, less than four years ago. Native porters carried up the baggage, and the camel drivers moved off, leading their patient beasts. They had been paid for their services, and had no further interest in the quiet Memsahib, or the pestering children who had delayed the journey by several days with their fretful demands to be lifted down. White children were spoiled and spoon-fed by their ayahs at an age when native children were already working.

But the troopers were in no hurry to start on the return journey, and when they had handed over the little family to a steward and a stewardess, they saluted smartly and disappeared to the saloon bar. It had been a tedious assignment, and they were glad to be relieved of the responsibility. Their horses would be fed and watered, groomed and exercised on the dock. One of the bullying overseers had recommended two natives who could be trusted to do the job properly, and he had pocketed the biggest share of the payment. How they wished they could stay on board and travel back to England, in such civilized surroundings, but the penalty for desertion was flogging, or death by firing squad. They could be killed by a stray bullet from a sniper's gun, but that was an honourable death. They had taken the Queen's shilling, and there was no escape.

Shy of the bustling stewardess with her pallid face and crackling starched apron, the two little girls clung to their Mama in this frightening new world. But the woman was too accustomed to coping with the spoilt darlings of devoted ayahs on the homeward voyage, and made no attempt to coax them away from their Mama's skirts. She was more concerned with the pregnant mother, and when she had reported her condition to the ship's doctor, she hurried to the galley to make tea and toast, to warm milk for the little girls, and arrange a plate of assorted biscuits that never failed to please children who had not yet seen or tasted an English biscuit. These babies were too young to share the early supper served in the dining saloon. They would take their meal in the cabin, and when they were bathed and tucked in their shared bunk, she would keep an eye on them while the mother joined the other passengers for dinner. But not tonight. These early hours of settling her families in their allotted cabins had to be endured with good grace, for it was enough to try the patience of a saint. It was all part of the job. The wages were small, but the tips were generous, and a widowed stewardess could afford a convent education for her daughter.

A strong stomach was the main credential. A good sailor was born. It was not something you could acquire, like a posh accent. Look at Nelson! It was no secret that the fourth engineer, the youngest quartermaster and Sparkie were throwing up their dinners as the ship rocked and pitched in the ocean, and continued to do so till they docked at Southampton – the poor buggers!

Her bustling cheerfulness could be a little too much for seasick women and children who only wanted to die. Early morning tea and biscuits were discarded in favour of fresh orange juice or lemon barley. The stench of vomit and urine in the stuffy cabins would have turned a queasy stomach, on the final stage of the voyage, for the sickness was as catching as measles. Only rarely did a child escape the epidemic, and then it was not the eldest or the healthiest in the family, but likely as not a puny little boy or girl who actually enjoyed all the rocking and tossing, and would demand sausages and ice-cream!

Ellen was too exhausted, and too sad to appreciate the bustling services of the cheerful stewardess that first evening aboard. When she had washed and fed the children with the milk and biscuits, drunk a cup of tea, and rejected the buttered toast, she undressed Prue and lifted her carefully to the top bunk where she hung over the rail, waiting for Bella.

'Good night, my darlings. God bless you.'

In their strange new world, only Mama had not changed, and their wet kisses were all the reward she needed. In a matter of minutes they had snuggled down like two little birds in a nest, and were sound asleep.

The tea was still warm in the pot, and she was grateful for a second cup. *Petit beurre* biscuits. It seemed an eternity, in another life, when she had taken her turn to carry up the heavy tray with early morning tea and biscuits for Mother – always the first to be served – and her sisters. She sighed, and wondered who would be carrying up the tray. She had brought the silver christening mugs, stamped with their names – Prudence and Arabella.

Stretched on the lower bunk, covered by a freshly laundered sheet, listening to the clanging of winches and the babble of voices on the dock below, Ellen felt only a sense of relief that the first uncomfortable stage of the journey had been accomplished, and she could relax her tired mind and aching body in this tiny private compartment that was no bigger than Jonathan's dressing-room at the bungalow. Jonathan! Would there ever be a time when her last thought at night and her first thought on waking did not reach for his presence? His strong personality had dominated her little world, and her own personality had been dwarfed into a timid resistance to his wishes that only amused him.

'A man must be the master of his destiny, my love, and master of his own household,' he told her, with that supreme arrogance he had developed since their arrival in India. Then why had his weakness for that other woman shattered that destiny, and a single pistol shot ended that promising young life?

She must not allow herself to dwell on that pistol, or the heart-rending picture of his ghastly death. Not a whisper must ever escape her lips, not even in her dreams. Jonathan had been killed, with a number of others, defending the garrison from raiding tribesmen. An honourable death. She had only to repeat what his commanding officer had stated so categorically in the cablegrams. Her mother and sisters would never know the truth, neither would Jonathan's parents. It would be her duty to visit them and share their sorrow. She would write letters and leave them in the purser's office – letters to Mother, her sister Grace, and Jonathan's parents. The mail boat was scheduled to arrive at Southampton a week before their own arrival. Several days would be lost on their recognized stops at Aden, Port Said and Marseilles. Everyone would know she was a widow, carrying her third child. But would everyone welcome her back with such a family?

She could not answer that question. She must 'wait and see', as Mother would say. 'Never meet your troubles halfway, child.' Dear Mother. It would be just like her to see the tragedy of the eldest daughter as nothing more than a cross to be carried with the minimum of fuss and bother. Instead of Jonathan deciding every issue, it would be Mother. She would be back where she belonged, sheltered, protected from the slings and arrows of the past four years, and infinitely grateful. That indomitable little figure – would she still be wearing black? – would be kind, but not indulgent.

They had never been close, the mother and her daughters. The reason for this was simple. Amelia's love for her husband had totally eclipsed the love for her children, six daughters, and no son. It had been a grievous disappointment, almost too bitter to bear. Thomas had not blamed her, but she had known the hope of a son and heir was shattered after the birth of Lucy – and poor little Lucy had been handed over to a nursemaid. Mother was not maternal. They all had discovered it for themselves, and each, in turn, had tried with pathetic eagerness to gain admission to that private sanctum of the heart, reserved for her husband, Thomas.

And there she was, at the end of the long journey, on the station platform, seemingly unchanged – a slight, dignified figure, still attired in black, and looking ridiculously young to have six grown-up daughters and two grandchildren. A porter stood beside her with a trolley, awaiting instructions to collect the baggage from the luggage van.

When she had lifted down the two little girls, she bade them stand quite still while she greeted Ellen with a kiss on both cheeks, that was lacking in warmth.

'Grandma,' Prue explained, bending over her baby sister protectively, as though danger threatened. Bella nodded. Too young to make any comment, she depended on Prue to interpret. Since she left Ayah behind, Prue had taken on the role of elder sister at this tender age.

Ellen was pale and anxious. Her dark eyes held a patient resignation, and the growing anxiety could only be dispelled by a glimpse of her favourite sister. But Grace was not here, and her heart sank. Surely there had been time enough to arrange it? She had not expected Bertha to meet the train, and Jane would be busy at the Mission. As for Kate and Lucy, they were still at the Academy. Grandfather Brent had promised Amelia that suitable employment would be found for the girls when they reached the age of eighteen. He had written it into his Will, so there would be no disagreement after his death. His doctor had warned him that a second heart attack could be fatal. No, she had not expected to see Kate and Lucy till the vacation, but she *had* expected to see her dearest Grace.

Amelia was smiling at her grandchildren and holding out her hands. 'Come along, the cab is waiting,' she coaxed.

'No,' said Prue, shaking her head decidedly. 'Go wiv Mama.' And she took Ellen's hand, and Bella took the other hand, and they clung like limpets.

'That was naughty, my darlings,' Ellen scolded, but it was such a mild rebuke.

Amelia hid her annoyance. She was accustomed to being obeyed. When she had given instructions to the porter, she led the way to the forecourt. The cabby was surly when he saw the pile of baggage on the porter's trolley.

'There ain't enough room for that lot in my cab, Ma'am,' he argued. 'The porter can push it on 'is trolley to Richmond Road. T'aint far.'

'Very well,' Amelia agreed, wishing she had sent Bertha and Norah to meet the train. 'We shall need you both the other end to carry it into the house, for we have no manservant,' she told them haughtily as she lifted her skirts, and climbed into the cab.

The two men exchanged a meaningful glance. It was a common practice to work together and share the tips when it was only a short distance. With a large family to support, the porter would be glad of an extra sixpence. A gentleman would not hesitate to give a shilling, but not this little Madam. He could tell by her manner. Long years of portering had taught him to recognize the type of customer he was dealing with.

Ellen had taken no part in the discussions. She was too exhausted. When she had lifted the children into the cab, they sat demurely, one on either side of her – two quaint little mites in beribboned bonnets, hugging their rag dolls, staring wide-eyed at their grandmother. Their unblinking stares held no fear because they had always been surrounded by love, and Mama was there, a calm, comforting presence with her swollen belly and warm arms.

Bella would remember nothing of that long journey from India or the homecoming. For her, the earliest memory would be at The Haven.

But Prue's memory was longer, and she spoke her thoughts aloud. 'Papa?' she asked anxiously, when the cab stopped at the green gate in the high wall.

'No, darling,' Ellen answered quietly.

Then more strange faces crowded round, and everyone talking at once. Ellen's voice was choked with tears as she greeted Bertha, but her sister's smile was bleak. She disliked children. They were just a nuisance. The entire household would be disrupted by this invasion.

So it was left to Norah, in a white, starched apron, flushed from the heat of the oven, to welcome them with a beaming smile, and to Jane, with breathless hugs and apologies.

'Sorry I couldn't meet you, Ellen, dear. I came on a later train, and took the short cut from the station. Caught up with your porter, staggering under the pile of luggage. I helped to push the trolley, so here we are!' she laughed. In her faded skirts, and the same straw boater she had worn in their bicycling days, her homely face was glowing with pleasure as she squatted on the pavement to embrace her small nieces.

'Hello, I'm your Auntie Jane, and this is Auntie Bertha and Auntie Norah,' she told them. 'You don't have to kiss me if you don't want to,' she added, playfully.

'Jane, dear. They have seen so many fresh faces in the past weeks,' Ellen was saying, glancing at the open gate. Where was Grace? Why did nobody mention her?

Amelia was supervising the cabby and the porter. She led the way down the tiled path to the open door. The neat little garden was unchanged, with its patch of grass surrounded by laurels and a border of London Pride. Wistaria climbed over the walls and framed the windows.

'If you will kindly carry everything upstairs, I will make it worth your while,' she insisted when the cabby removed his cap and scratched his head dubiously.

'It will cost you an extra shilling, Ma'am.'

'Very well,' she agreed.

When they had finished and received their wages, plus the extra shilling, they went away and the door was closed.

'Now,' said Amelia, marshalling her family. 'We are having tea in the dining-room. Norah, will you make the tea. Jane can help. Ellen, you will want to wash the children's hands and faces in the cloak-room, will you not?'

'Yes, Mother.'

When Norah and Jane had hurried down the base-ment stairs, Bertha closed the little gate at the top of the stairs. 'These stairs are dangerous, and the gate will be kept closed. Norah will carry you down for breakfast. Other meals we have in the dining-room,' she instructed in a voice that matched her stern expression.

'Mama carries Prue and Baba,' the child answered, fearlessly.

'You are too big to be carried by your Mama,' Bertha snapped, and averted her eyes from the swol-len belly.

Two high chairs had been brought down from the old nursery, two plates and two mugs decorated with the three bears, and two clean bibs had been provided.

Prue climbed into her chair and pushed the bib away. 'Bib for Baba. Prue have napakin,' she announced in that decisive way that was going to infuriate Bertha.

'She can have mine,' said Ellen, appeasingly.

'Don't be absurd. We are not short of table

153

napkins.' Bertha pulled open a drawer in the side-board, and took out another.

Ellen smiled her thanks, but there was no response in those cold, grey eyes. It didn't surprise the elder sister. She could understand Bertha's resentment. It was natural.

Amelia had settled herself at the head of the table, where Norah had placed the heavy silver tray, silver teapot, and hot water jug. Jane had followed her up with two plates of buttered scones; two plates of dainty bread and butter, a dish of strawberry jam, a Madeira cake, and a fruit cake were spread on the linen cloth that Amelia had embroidered so beautifully.

Prue was reaching for the jam, and Bella licking her empty plate when Amelia bowed her head and intoned, 'For what we are about to receive, may the Lord make us truly thankful.' Ellen put a warning finger to her lips and flushed guiltily. There had been no grace before or after meals with Jonathan. But she was teaching Prue to say 'Gentle Jesus' and 'God bless Papa, Mama, Baba and Ayah,' before the tragedy. She was still saying 'God bless Papa'. How could you explain to such a young child that Papa was no longer here? Now she was worried that she had left it too late. Prue was such a bright, intelligent child. Even the youngest child can be told 'Papa has gone to Heaven to live with Jesus.'

But there was no time for such thoughts. Prue was waving her mug and demanding, 'TEA!'

'Only ladies drink tea. Little girls drink milk,' Amelia reminded them.

'Only a tiny splash of tea, *please*, Mother. It was Ayah who started it.' Ellen could foresee tears and tantrums if they were deprived of their 'tea'. Was it

154

really worth making a scene for such a small favour? She waited anxiously, but all was well. Mother was not going to refuse.

Norah had taken off her apron and was passing scones. She was never at her ease in the company of Mrs Brent. Her position in the household, neither family nor servant, depended on her own sensible behaviour and happy nature. She took no liberties and expected no favours. Norah had no illusions. Bertha's temper was short. She was jealous and possessive. It was a strange, unnatural relationship, and the intimacy they shared in the privacy of the bedroom would have shocked Amelia.

Afternoon tea was a rare treat to Jane these days, and she sipped the strong, sweet tea gratefully. They could only afford the cheapest blend at the hostel, and sugar had to be rationed. Their bread was stale, and spread with margarine or jam. The jam was bought in tins, red and yellow, labelled PLUM and APRICOT. It was nothing more than coloured pulp. Jane's sense of humour had not deserted her, however, and she could often find fun in a situation that would depress her beloved Edward. It was Jane's ability to make a home of a drab hostel, and to see the lighter side of life, that balanced their natures, for Edward was so serious. Both were dedicated to the poor and destitute. Jane had no regrets. They called her 'Missus' and they called Edward 'Guv'. Biting into a buttered scone, she could imagine what Aggie would say about this tempting spread, called 'afternoon tea'. 'Cor, blimey, Missus, I knew you was class, but you ain't never said you was one of the nobs.'

Aggie was a tough little woman, who spent her days in a sacking apron, scrubbing floors and peeling potatoes.

'You are mistaken, Aggie. I am not one of the nobs, and neither is my husband,' she would contradict. 'Any average middle-class family would sit down to a similar afternoon tea.'

But the gap between Aggie's poverty-stricken slum and Jane's respectable middle-class background was too wide to bridge, and Jane was sensible enough to keep them apart. She had made her life with Edward in the teeming streets of London's East End. In a sense, she no longer belonged here, but was just a visitor. She belonged with Edward, where bare-bottomed babies played in the gutter, and barefoot boys played football with pigs' bladders.

Not one of her sisters could survive in such horrific conditions, and she had not invited them to visit her, because they would not understand how anyone in her right mind would actually choose to live there. To be born and bred there was another matter. Babies born in such conditions survived or died, and there was no time for mourning. Dirty, rat-infested hovels had bred a people of surprising energy and stamina. Those who survived clung to life with grim determination, and discovered it was not all misery. Hardship lent a purpose to life shared by the neighbours. Children developed a sturdy independence at an early age. The struggle for survival in the back streets had frightened Jane in those early days, until she realized she was far less likely to be assaulted than in the West End. There was a rough kindliness in the East End that was missing 'dahn West'. The homely young woman, with her cheery smile, gave herself no airs, and the Missus was a familiar figure in her shabby shirts and button boots, on her way to the market stalls to bargain for the cheapest cuts of meat and vegetables for her soups and stews.

Those few years in the kitchen at The Haven had not been wasted. She had only to multiply by a dozen, add a penn'orth of marrow bones and a sprig of herbs to the huge stewpot on the stove to provide a nourishing meal for her hungry family at the hostel. Suet puddings, with black treacle, and jam tarts, helped to fill those empty stomachs. It was plain wholesome food, and nothing was wasted. The 'barrow boys' were not all young and cheeky. The older generation were more respectful and obliging. She knew where to get the best value for her meagre housekeeping allowance, and every penny must be accounted for in the monthly budget for which Edward was responsible. They worked in harmony with the Salvation Army 'lassies' who often had to be rescued from the jeers and jokes of lively youngsters. To save souls was not their only concern, however; sick bodies and hungry mouths had to be satisfied. Their kindly motives and ministrations were often abused, but they went on their way undaunted, and would roll up their sleeves to scrub and scour some filthy hovel with complete disregard for their safety. They worked in pairs, and paved the way for future generations of worthy Salvationists in their poke bonnets. To hold the attention of the Sunday night audience at the street corner they had to compete with the attraction of the public house. There must be singing as well as prayers, and the children would follow the band back to the Citadel – a long procession of prancing barefoot urchins, and skinny little girls staggering under the burden of younger brothers and sisters. This was the way to their hearts, and to Heaven!

Watching her Mother add that tiny splash of tea to the children's milk, she was remembering how the squalling infants in their neighbourhood would be silenced with dirty dummies dipped in sugar, when the breast milk had dried up for lack of nourishment. That fastidious little figure behind the silver teapot had no conception of such disgusting practices, and would not wish to know. Her small world would expand for Ellen's sake to include her grandchildren, but her comfortable way of life would not be disrupted, for she had a way of dismissing anything that threatened her comfort. It would be Bertha and Norah who would be left to cope with this unexpected invasion of The Haven. Two spoilt little girls and another child on the way – and Ellen a widow with her sad dark eyes and air of weary resignation. Three babies in less than four years. It was inexcusable for a man of a cultured background to be so insensitive to his wife's health. In the crowded slums, where whole families slept in one room, and there was no escape from the marriage bed, or the demands of a drunken husband, it was unavoidable.

What sort of husband had he proved to be – that handsome young subaltern, with the charming ways? she wondered. Edward had not liked or trusted the Vicar's youngest son, who knew he could get out of any scrape, being his mother's darling. There had been rumours of a housemaid dismissed in a state of pregnancy after Jonathan had sailed for India.

Edward was kind and considerate. When their first child was stillborn, and the doctor had advised no more children, Edward was careful to prevent conception. Intercourse was not a habit to be indulged in at frequent intervals. When Jane fell asleep over her prayers, after a particularly busy day, she would have to be undressed and put to bed like a tired child. This was the life she had chosen to share with her young curate when he was appointed the Warden of the Hoxton Mission – for better, for worse, in sickness and in health, till death . . .

Ellen was wiping Prue's nose with her own handkerchief. With another child on the way, shouldn't Prue be wiping her own nose? And Ellen was feeding her with a buttered scone, spread with strawberry jam. Could the Indian ayah be blamed for such pampering? If a child had to be coaxed to eat, it was not hungry. Jane could not prevent her thoughts from comparisons. *Their* children, of the slums, were born to hunger and stayed hungry. She had seen mere toddlers fighting for a crust of stale bread. With swollen bellies and rickety legs, they still survived. Such comparisons seemed to separate her more and more from her own family. She was closer now to her adopted family – the flotsam of the streets. They came and went. There was no compulsion. They were welcomed, they were fed. They shared the simple amenities of dormitory bedrooms, and could earn a few shillings helping Edward with white-washing. Those who stayed permanently, and shared the homely comforts of Jane's parlour, would learn to read and write, and jobs would be found for them locally, so they could pay for their board and lodging. Sometimes Jane would be surprised and touched to be pushed away from the kitchen sink, and a pile of dirty dishes would be washed up, while she rested her aching back.

Prue had pushed away the scone and was demanding cake. When it was refused, she threw her plate on the floor, and beat the tray with her small fists.

'Prudence!' Amelia admonished, but Ellen showed no surprise.

'Will you excuse us, Mother?' she asked quietly, as

she scooped the child from the chair, set her astride her hip, and carried her, screaming, out of the room. Bella had found a better place for her plate. It was on her head! Her hair was sticky with jam, so were her face and hands. She chuckled gleefully when Jane leapt to her feet, tucked her under her arm, and carried her away.

'That child is a born clown,' said Amelia, hiding a smile.

From the open door of the cloakroom, Jane could see her sister laboriously climbing the stairs, with the child on her hip. Her screams of rage seemed to echo all over the house, but Ellen, who knew these tantrums were just to attract attention, and there were no tears, stayed calm. If she lost her own temper, then the child would get hysterical. Ayah was not entirely to blame for spoiling her Baba. It was a combination of losing her adored Papa, the long journey home, and all the strange faces. She was still too young to understand what had happened to her happy little world of the garrison, yet old enough to remember the handsome soldier of the Queen who fed her with ice-cream when she was good – and she was always good with her Papa. How could she explain it was because she could not find him that she was so naughty? Mama was kind and patient, but always tired, and Bella was a baby. Nobody seemed to understand about her Papa. Now, in this grand house, surrounded by more strange faces, she would scream until they fetched him.

'My darling, please stop,' Ellen pleaded, breathlessly, as they reached the top landing, and she sank exhausted on to the old sofa in the room that was once the schoolroom. Now it had to serve as bedroom and playroom for the children, and she would sleep next door in the old nursery.

Norah had been busy. Everything was ready. Through the open door she could see the single bed and the cradle, re-trimmed with starched muslin. The child in her womb stirred restlessly, and the child in her arms stopped screaming and stared about her with wide dark eyes.

'Papa?' she asked, with that pitiful persistence that was beginning to disturb even Ellen's self-control.

She shook her head sadly. 'No, my darling. Papa is not here.' And when the child opened her mouth to scream again, she closed it gently with her hand. This was the moment of truth – the truth as told to a child of tender years. Only her own broken heart knew how distorted that truth could be. 'Papa has gone to Heaven, to live with Jesus.' When she took her hand away, she was surprised at the child's question.

'Gentle Jesus, meet-an-mile?'

'Yes, darling.'

Prue sighed, and sucked her thumb. She was satisfied now.

'You're a little scamp!' Jane scolded, affectionately, as she washed away the strawberry jam. If only she could take this funny little scrap of mischief back to the Mission. Edward had not fully realized the cruel disappointment of losing their own child, and then to be told it would be dangerous to have another. What had gone wrong with her healthy body? Had she worked too hard and not fed herself properly while she was carrying? It was too late for regrets, and when her baby niece, still chuckling gleefully, wet her drawers and soaked her best dress, she did not scold, but dropped the small garment in the bucket. She hoped it would not offend Mother when she washed her hands before the next meal, but there seemed no point in carrying it upstairs.

When she hoisted Bella on to her hip, she was surprised to find it was so much easier to carry a child that way. Even so, it was a long way up to the top landing. How tired their young housemaid must have been at the end of a long day to have to climb all these stairs from the basement back to her attic bedroom. Cook had had her bed-sitting room next door to the kitchen – the room that was converted into the breakfast-room when Cook left.

So many changes since Father died, and only Mother seemed unchanged, yet who could tell what she suffered in the privacy of her bedroom? Not one of her daughters could hold a candle to her fortitude and dignity.

The screams had stopped as suddenly as they had started. Ellen was sitting on the old sofa nursing Prue, who had dropped off to sleep, sucking her thumb.

'Here we are at last,' Jane whispered, breathlessly, sitting beside her. 'It's a long way up, Ellen. How will you manage?'

'I *must* manage, dear. The only alternative is The Vicarage, and Mrs Cartwright would not care for it without Jonathan. A daughter-in-law is only tolerated for the sake of the son, not for her own sake. And with these two, and another on the way, it would be an intolerable situation, even worse than this, but I can cope with Mother because I know her ways.'

'Bertha is being difficult.'

'Bertha was always difficult.'

'Mother wishes to speak to you in the drawing-room after you have put the children to bed.'

'Is it about Grace?'

'Yes.'

'Is she ill?'

'Mother will explain.'

162

'I knew something was wrong when she didn't meet us at the station.'

Jane felt uncomfortable under the scrutiny of those dark, searching eyes. 'Shall I undress Bella and put her down to sleep in the cot? Look, she has fallen asleep, poor darling.'

'Please. She seems to have taken quite a fancy to you, Jane. Was she awfully messy?'

'Strawberry jam in her hair, and she's wet her drawers.'

'Oh, no! Where are they?'

'In the bucket in the cloakroom.'

'I must bring the bucket upstairs. It would annoy Bertha.'

'Bugger Bertha!'

'Jane!'

'Sorry. It slipped out. It's everyday language where I come from!' she grinned.

They were still whispering, but the children were so soundly asleep, they could be undressed and put to bed without any further disturbance. Sucking their thumbs and hugging their rag dolls, they looked angelic, but the morning would bring more trouble.

'I'll stay with them till you come back.' Jane slipped a comforting arm about Ellen's shoulders. For a brief moment the elder sister leaned on the younger, then she pulled herself away, smiled tremulously, and left the room.

Amelia was sitting in her favourite chair. She was wearing an afternoon dress of black lace, trimmed with tiny silver buttons, and a black velvet band, fastened with a cameo brooch round her slender neck. With her silver hair piled becomingly on her proud little head, and her blue eyes still as bright as Lucy's, she made a gracious and charming figure in that Victorian drawing-room, so cluttered with occasional tables and *bric-à-brac*. Nothing had changed here since her marriage to Thomas. But her eldest daughter, who would never again have to ask her permission to marry, was looking at her with those dark, searching eyes that reminded her so strongly of Thomas so that she was momentarily flustered, but it quickly passed.

'Have I kept you waiting, Mother?' Ellen was asking, dutifully.

'Not at all. Come and sit down. Are the children in bed?'

'Yes, Jane is staying with them, but they were asleep before we could get them undressed.'

'Tired out, no doubt.'

'Yes. Mother, I must apologize for their appalling behaviour at the tea table.'

'It *was* rather shocking, wasn't it, dear? Should one blame the ayah?'

'I blame myself. I never felt well in India – the climate, the way of life, and homesickness. I missed you all intolerably.'

'And Jonathan?—he loved it, of course.'

'Yes.'

'Was he a good husband, child?'

'Yes, Mother.'

Only a slight hesitation, but it was not lost on Amelia. This woman had suffered. Had it been a mistake, her own mistake, to give them her blessing? She had to admit it had been a mistake to send Grace away, but she couldn't bear to admit her mistakes.

'Mother, what has happened to Grace?'

Ah, she had been expecting that question, and showed no surprise. 'Grace is in Switzerland, at a sanatorium. She is suffering from tuberculosis.'

'Is she – is she going to die?'

'It's a question of whether or not her constitution has been permanently damaged.'

'Have you seen her?'

'No. It happened so suddenly. She collapsed, the doctor was called and diagnosed tuberculosis. You may read the letter I received.' She took it from the pocket of the tea-gown, and handed it to Ellen with no further comment.

Ellen received it with a sense of utter desolation. Her dearest Grace. If only she could weep, but it would embarrass Mother. She must wait. It was a long letter, and it was signed by Henry Courtney-Halliday.

My dear Mrs Brent,

You will wonder why I am writing to you, but what I have to tell you cannot be contained in a telegram, and my dear wife is too distressed to write, and Grace too ill.

She collapsed one evening at the piano, after she had been entertaining us as usual with her delightful playing. It was a great shock, for she had not complained of feeling ill. Looking back, however, on the past year, I do recall that on one occasion I mentioned to Grace that if she lost any more weight, people would think we were ill-treating her. To which she replied, with a shrug, 'Nothing could be further from the truth. You spoil me.' We are very fond of Grace. She has always been treated like a daughter, and she has seemed so happy with us.

Now to explain what has since happened, and, we hope, to put your mind at rest. We shall understand, my dear Mrs Brent, if you feel hurt or annoyed that you were not consulted, but it all happened so suddenly, there was no time to get in touch with you. Our doctor insisted it was a matter of the gravest urgency, since Grace was suffering from advanced tuberculosis, and her only chance at this late stage of the disease would be her removal to a sanatorium at a high altitude. The particular sanatorium he had in mind is situated in most beautiful surroundings overlooking the lake of Thun in Switzerland. The doctor in charge is a Herr Graffner – a German specialist in this disease, and an old colleague of our own doctor, since both were trained at Guy's Hospital. Arrangements were made to receive Grace, and she was conveyed by ambulance, with a trained nurse in attendance. We have since been informed that she stood up to the journey as well as could be expected, and was resting quietly.

My wife joins me in assuring you that Grace will receive the best treatment available, and no expense will be spared. We have been advised, however, not to expect a miracle. Two years, possibly three, before you can expect to have her back with you in Worthing.

May I inform you, with the utmost respect, that a sum of money has been transferred from our London bank to the Zurich branch to cover all expenses, and that such an arrangement in no way reflects on your own capacity or willingness to pay for your daughter's treatment. We will keep in touch with you, and you will be notified immediately of any change in your daughter's condition.

    With kindest regards,

        Very sincerely yours,

           Henry Courtney-Halliday.

Ellen handed the letter back to her mother, too choked to make any comment. The depths of her sadness, revealed in the dark eyes that were so like her beloved husband's, seemed to be accusing her of making a grave mistake in sending Grace away, but she would not dwell on such a fancy. Thomas would *never* blame her.

'You were right, my dearest. You always know what is best for your daughters.'

So she averted her eyes, and looked instead at the travel-stained clothes, and the long slender hands – Thomas's hands – clasped so tightly over the swelling belly. The silence between them was filled with the sense of guilt, though Ellen had not, and *would* not presume to question her mother's decision to send Grace away. The repercussions of such a decision had only just been discovered. Was it too late to save Grace? Remembering the way her new employer had glanced at her lovely sister on that fateful Sunday, Ellen knew it was not the glance of a father but a lover. She had seen such glances in the eyes of her own dear Jonathan, in the early days of their marriage. A man could not hide his feelings like a woman. And her beloved Grace was so innocent, so inexperienced, she would see no danger in such glances. Knowing the relationship to be dangerous, she, the elder sister, had not spoken. So to whom could the blame be attached? Surely Bertha must take her share, since she had started the sad sequence of events with her complaints and her intolerance.

Mother and daughter, in this moment of truth, could have drawn closer together if the right word had been spoken, or the right gesture of reconciliation made, but neither could bridge the gulf that divided them. If it was too late for Grace, it was also too late for Ellen, whose own tragedy was still so fresh in her mind. Yet only Grace could have been trusted with the truth of that particular tragedy. On the long journey home, the thought of sharing the burden with her favourite sister had sustained and comforted her.

In the early days, she had been too shocked to think coherently, but gradually she had realized there was just one person with whom she could share the reality of her disastrous marriage. For it *was* a disaster. She should never have married an army man – a man who must follow the drum and serve his Queen in some foreign land. If Jonathan had known of her reluctance and fear of that act of intercourse, and if she herself had been honest enough to admit she was not the right wife for him, the tragedy could have been averted. But an engagement was so binding, it could only be broken by mutual consent. The scandal and outrage would have seemed disastrous, but nothing to compare with life-long regret.

'Will you excuse me, Mother? It has been a long day,' was all she said.

If Amelia had expected her to explain away her own guilt, she was disappointed. The touch of her daughter's lips on her cheek was cool.

'Good night, Mother.'

'Good night, Ellen.'

Then she was gone. The loneliness of pride and dignity felt like a cloak about her rigid shoulders, and she sighed, involuntarily, as the door closed.

5

The house in Bayswater Road had always been divided, and the servants knew exactly where they belonged. Their loyalty to the Master or the Mistress was a positive and clearly defined fact that kept a permanent breach between Cook and Simmons, and the elderly maid the Mistress still called Nana.

In this divided household, the innocent Grace Brent had no place and no status. She was the 'go-between'. Master and Mistress competed for her company and her favours, and the servants regarded her with suspicion. She was neither servant nor family, and to say she was treated like a daughter was as far from the truth as to claim she was happy. The atmosphere was tense, and although she did her best to please both Beatrice and Henry Courtney-Halliday, she actually pleased neither for more than hour or so each day. They did not want to share her. They wanted to possess her, body and soul. And it was this possessiveness that further weakened a constitution already enfeebled with tuberculosis. Uncomplaining and sweet-tempered, Grace was no match for the spiteful tongue of the spoilt wife, or the duplicity of the husband. Angry scenes disturbed her peace-loving nature. Husband and wife had no control over their emotions, and the servants watched and listened, and made small bets on the outcome of such sparring battles. Hadn't they forecast trouble from the start?

Lady's companions came and went, for the Mistress was hard to please, and it was not the kind of post that suited the average young woman who liked a bit of life. With no visitors staying in the house, and no escape from the demands of the fretful semi-invalid, other young women had either been bored to distraction, irritated by the sameness of the daily routine, or resentful of being classed as a servant, but without the freedom the servants enjoyed in the kitchen, once their duties were finished. Not one of these former lady's maids had found favour with the Master, however, whose roving eye for a pretty face and comely shape had to be paid for in expensive presents of jewellery, flowers and chocolates. Beatrice was no fool, and she knew his weakness, but she had not foreseen the impact of such a lovely creature on her own jealous nature. She blamed Henry for engaging the young person without an interview. She hadn't known about the photograph, but even if she *had* known, Henry would have persuaded her to give it a trial. One could always make some excuse after a month and pay her off, with her wages of course.

But it hadn't gone according to plan, for they both liked Grace Brent. It was impossible to *dislike* Grace. She was charming. She was so ready and willing to please, and she was a *lady*. As for Henry, he could not hide his feelings. Why should he? The photograph had not prepared him for such a vision of loveliness.

'Slender as a wand, and fair as a lily,' he would have described the young woman who walked into his life on that fateful Sunday afternoon. 'Grace by name and Grace by nature,' he told his wife, who had to agree – with certain reservations, being Beatrice!

Yet Grace had seemed completely unaware of her strange fascination, and when a whole year had passed and she was still in residence, neither Henry nor Beatrice could claim to have reached a closer relationship.

After the sad affair of the little dog, on that foggy morning in the park, the servants had expected to hear that the indispensable Miss Brent had been dismissed, and her fate hung in the balance for several weeks. Then she was reinstated. The Master had intervened.

So the weeks and the months slipped away, and Grace had found her Mistress so disturbed by any change in her routine, she had given up suggesting a short holiday, or a free day, to visit her family.

'But you belong *here*, my dear, and I cannot spare you. It gives me palpitations just to think of being handed over to Nana to be looked after. She fusses like an old hen with one precious chick. Her hands shake, and she SNIFFS. Old age, I suppose. She should have been retired years ago, but where could she go? Only to the workhouse. She has no relatives, and there are no cottages on these premises for retired servants. She is such a liability, but I must do my duty. It would be heartless to send her away. The poor creature simply dotes on me, as you have observed. But there is a limit to my patience, Grace, and I will not be left to her fussing for a whole day. I should lose my temper, and when I lose my temper, my heart nearly bursts. It frightens me. My doctor tells me I must not excite myself. It's very bad for my heart. What am I to do with her, Grace? I suppose we could allow her to press my dresses and wash my lingerie, could we not? It would please the poor creature. But nothing more. I will not be intimidated by her tears. And what do you mean about taking a holiday, Grace? Isn't it enough that you and I spent the whole month of August together in that luxury hotel? I could weep with vexation. Were you only pretending to enjoy it for my sake?'

'Indeed not, Madam. I found it most pleasant.'

'*Most pleasant*? Well, nobody could accuse *you* of being demonstrative. Sometimes I wonder whether you even care for me, Grace?'

'I do care, Madam.'

'Really and truly?'

'Yes, Madam.'

'Do you care for my husband?'

'I respect and admire him.'

'You have not answered my question. You must know he is in love with you.'

'No! I am sure you are mistaken.'

'You're blushing, Grace. Of course you know. He gives himself away, doesn't he? The silly man. Those eyes betray him, as I was betrayed once, long ago, into thinking he loved *me*. It was my position in society, my background and my fortune that Henry Halliday coveted.' Tears of self-pity wet her pallid cheeks, and she dabbed at her wet eyes with a perfumed handkerchief. 'My dear, his charm is so deceptive, and you could be so easily deceived. Promise me you will never allow him to take liberties with you, Grace. You must promise me.'

'I do assure you, Madam, nothing is further from my thoughts.'

'Ah, but you don't know how devious he can be when he makes up his mind. There is a hard streak in my husband, and a ruthlessness that springs from his working-class background. He *thinks* he has left it all behind, and the trappings of the upper class can disguise the truth of his humble birth and breeding. Have you noticed his hands? But of course you have, when he turns the pages of your music. Those blunt thumbs, and the chewed nails. He *bites* his nails, Grace. These are not the hands of a gentleman.'

'No, Madam.' Grace had long since discovered it was better to agree with her Mistress. This conversation was conducted in the Mistress's boudoir, and Grace was arranging the frizzed hair becomingly around the plump, pallid cheeks. Their faces shared the mirror, and there was no escape from the scrutiny of those pale eyes. The probing questions were meant to hurt and confuse Grace, for to tell the truth, she *was* attracted to Henry Courtney-Halliday, in a way that was so disturbing to her senses, she had become extremely embarrassed in his company.

It was not often they were left alone, for the Mistress had become suspicious of their relationship. It was a kind of mental torture for Henry, to stand so close to Grace at the piano, and turn the pages of her music, yet Beatrice would not spare him, and almost every evening, after dinner, she insisted on a little music to soothe her nerves before she retired. Reclining on the couch, cursing her new pet, it was not the music she enjoyed so much as the sly satisfaction of watching her husband's acute discomfort. He had never been at ease in her stuffy, scented drawing-room, and had usually managed to excuse himself, but not any more. The occasion was too good to miss, and his obvious delight in the nearness of that sweet creature was also a kind of torture to her own sensibilities. She could see his hand clenched on the lid of the piano, waiting for a nod from Grace to turn the page. His sturdy figure was tense with the effort to control the urge to touch her.

173

Seemingly, Grace gave him no encouragement whatsoever. This was a new experience for Henry, whose sexual appetite had often disgusted Beatrice in the early days of their marriage. She had not wanted a child, and when it was stillborn, and she became hysterical when he approached her, the doctor had advised Henry to abstain from intercourse until her nerves had recovered from the shock of a stillborn child. Since she had no intention of recovering, Henry was banished to the dressing-room, and he found his sexual appetite could be satisfied elsewhere.

Then she was jealous of those other women, for jealousy was inborn, and fostered by an indulgent parent and a doting nanny. It was a tangible, destructive element, and it had already destroyed the last vestige of affection between husband and wife, before Grace arrived. The angry scenes between them were no longer private. Grace was acutely embarrassed, but the servants took sides, and rather enjoyed the verbal battles that could, at any moment, actually come to blows.

During the month of August, Beatrice could claim the whole attention of her companion, and for three weeks they were almost on equal terms, till Henry arrived to spoil the harmony.

'You may call me Beatrice. Relax, my dear. There is no need to be so stand-offish now we are on holiday,' the Mistress had purred, confidentially, as they sat together on the balcony of their suite, overlooking the sea, sipping the hot chocolate the young waiter had just served.

'Hot chocolate in August?' The order had been queried.

'Hot chocolate in August,' the waiter repeated with a shrug.

Why question the fads and fancies of the idle rich? They were paying for it. But what had possessed such a beautiful young woman to attach herself to the idle rich?

Their chairs had been placed in the shade of the striped awning. Madam's orders. She was wearing one of the big, fashionable hats to shield her face from the sun, and she had carried a parasol on their short stroll on the sea front, after a late breakfast served at Madam's bed, and to the companion in the dining-room. The young waiter had watched them from the hotel – the older woman – mutton dressed up as lamb – in frilled organdie, hanging on the arm of the younger, who looked as though a puff of wind would blow her away. In her plain linen skirt and blouse, she caught the eye of every passing male. It hadn't taken long to discover they were not related. The chambermaid had reported that Miss Brent was sleeping in the dressing-room, and was already bathed and dressed when she carried in the early morning tray at 7.30. Madam had ordered China tea and buttered toast.

'I wouldn't 'ave that young woman's job for all the tea in China! That fussy old faggot wants 'er bottom smacked!' Polly reported to the young waiter. Polly was a vulgar little bitch, but he loved her. They were going to be married as soon as they had saved enough. They were saving all their tips. A smile and a bow. 'Yes, Madam.' 'No, Madam.' 'Certainly, Sir. I'll see to it right away, Sir.' It cost nothing, and it could make all the difference between a sixpence and a shilling tip. A waiter and a chambermaid could also have their dreams, and a basement bed-sitting-room would seem like a palace at the end of a twelve-hour working day. Polly actually enjoyed being a chambermaid. And what went on in some of those bedrooms would make your hair curl – according to Polly!

Since the sad affair of the little dog, when Grace had expected to be dismissed, and had actually packed her trunk, she had enjoyed the luxury of a fire in her bedroom and a view of the park.

A Persian kitten, soft as swansdown, had replaced the little dog in the Mistress's affections. It grew into a heavy cat, with too much cream, and seldom left her lap during the day. Yet, for all the pampering and persuasion, it had to be let out at night, or it would disturb the whole house with its yowling protests. Nature had its way. The window must be opened, and the cat escaped. A cat is an independent creature, and cannot be coerced or compelled to stay indoors when night has fallen. Some inborn instinct, stronger than the comfort and luxury of that scented boudoir, would prevail, and Beatrice discovered she had met her match. It was Cook who had to open her window, in the early hours of the morning, for the persistent scratching on the window pane of her attic bedroom disturbed her sleep.

'Drat the creature!' she would mutter, irritably, shivering in a blast of cold air. With a disdainful sweep of its handsome tail, the cat would vanish down the back stairs, and Cook would climb back into bed. The door of the boudoir was left ajar, and it slipped inside with feline grace, sprang lightly on to the bed, and settled down with a satisfied purr.

'Naughty pussy,' Beatrice would yawn, and fondle the cat in her arms. This was the kind of sensuality – the only kind – she enjoyed now. Neither a husband nor a child could have given her so much pleasure.

She found the cat even more affectionate than the little dog, but had to tolerate its strange preference for the roof tops at a certain hour of the night, when Nature called.

During the month of August, the precious cat was left in the care of Nana, but it resisted every attempt to coax it on to her lap, or into her bed. For several days it wandered restlessly about the house, till one of the Mistress's tea-gowns was spread on the couch in the drawing-room. Its nightly routine was unchanged. The house was thoroughly cleaned and Cook and Simmons each took a week's holiday, but Nana was not at all envious. She thanked God on her knees every night that she had been promised a roof over her head for the rest of her days, and was no longer troubled by the threat of the workhouse. The threat had been removed, and her darling child would keep her word. Her life had revolved around Miss Beatrice since that memorable day, at the age of twelve, when she had arrived from the Orphanage, to wait on the elderly Nanny in charge of the nursery. She was so proud of her nursemaid's uniform – so proud to be allowed to wash, starch, and iron all the dainty petticoats and frocks, under strict supervision, of course – so proud to walk sedately beside the bassinet she cleaned every evening, in readiness for the twice daily walks round the estate.

It had been a revelation to discover the extent of the parklands and gardens that surrounded the Big House, and the number of servants employed. Her own small domain of the nursery suite was more than enough to fill her days with joy and contentment. Discipline was expected, for she had been reared in a hard school, and she expected to have her ears boxed if she forgot her manners, and to forfeit her supper if she was careless. This was the punishment she tried to avoid, for she was always hungry, and it seemed such an age to wait till breakfast. She was growing fast, and the undernourished waif from the Orphanage developed a few curves and budding breasts in that first wonderful year in service. She answered to the name of Fanny in those early years, and fell in love with the stable boy who would have tumbled her in the hay if he had had half a chance! But he in turn was cuffed and bullied by the head groom, likely as not to push his head in a bucket of water in one of his black moods. The head groom was responsible to the Master, and the Master was a most impatient gentleman, with a biting tongue, if he was kept waiting. So protocol was established, and a servant was a servant. In the servants' hierarchy, a stable boy and a nurserymaid had no status, and no time to play. Work was their destiny. They were born to a kind of slavery, and had no opportunity to escape – not that Fanny would ever have contemplated such a drastic step. She had no wish to escape.

When the stable boy was killed by a kick from a vicious hoof at the age of fifteen, Fanny swore to be faithful to his memory. The pattern of her life was changed, however, with surprising suddenness when the old Nanny had a stroke, and Fanny found herself, at the age of eighteen, in complete charge of a five-year-old, very spoilt little girl, and a nurserymaid, aged twelve. From henceforth, there could be no other life for 'Nana'. And fifty years later, grey-haired and crippled with rheumatism, she wondered how much longer her poor Miss Beatrice could ignore the fact that she, too, was no longer young.

During the second year at that house in Bayswater,

Grace began to dread the hour in the drawing-room after dinner, when she sat at the piano and played the kind of music her Mistress liked. Her tastes were light rather than classical, as was her choice of books. Anything that required serious thought or study was termed 'heavy'. Even certain pieces by Chopin were disqualified. But it was a strain, and the hour seemed interminable.

Mentally and physically she suffered, but Amelia's strict training in childhood would not allow for any obvious signs of that suffering in public. If only she could have confided in just one person. If only Ellen had not sailed away to India for five long years. If only Mother had allowed her to stay in Worthing, to breathe that invigorating air into her lungs.

It was becoming more and more difficult to disguise her breathlessness, and the cough was beginning to annoy her Mistress. Various remedies had been tried, to no avail. If the doctor had been consulted in these early stages and the disease diagnosed, her gradual decline could have been avoided. But Grace was not expected to be ill, and when Beatrice suffered a heart spasm, or some minor ailment, she claimed the doctor's full attention. Grace was there only to chaperone, not to make any comment. Her role in the sick room was to fetch and carry.

When the Master concerned himself with the health of his wife's companion, his concern was misinterpreted, and Beatrice was suspicious. Perhaps if she had been in a household less frequently disturbed by angry scenes and petty jealousies, Grace might have had a better chance of recovery, or the disease could have lain dormant. Poor Grace! She was accused of being sly when she hid her feelings, and 'stand-offish' when she continued to address Beatrice as 'Madam'. But her unpredictable Mistress changed her mind as often as she changed her clothes.

For Henry, the strain was intolerable, and he was tempted beyond endurance – tempted to tap on the closed door when the stifled coughing in the adjoining room kept him awake – tempted to discover whether Grace felt anything more than gratitude for his intervention on more than one occasion – tempted to touch the silken tendril of hair on her slender neck as he stood beside her at the piano. What was he waiting for? he asked himself, as he tossed restlessly in his lonely bed in a fever of frustrated desire. Even when he was making love to his mistress, it was Grace he held in his arms, and her slender form he caressed. He did not need to strip her naked to prove that his vivid imagination had not played him false. That virginal body would be so lovely, he would pledge himself for the rest of his days. Hopelessly in love for the first time in his life, his dreams were haunted by visions of Grace in various stages of undress. And while he lusted after her with increasing torment, Grace avoided him. It was not his nature to wait or to plead, but he would have gone on his knees to Grace if she had shown the slightest indication that she cared. Waiting for her response was driving him mad.

So, at the end of that second year, he began to find excuses to stay away from time to time. A business trip to the Continent could always be arranged, and Beatrice did not question anything in connection with the bank. She knew they had branches in Paris, Brussels and Zurich, and that Henry was entrusted with investments for important clients. In this respect he was indeed completely trustworthy, never allowing his private affairs to interfere with his public image. It was probably because he found Grace so elusive that he wanted her so desperately. Other women had fallen too easily for his masculine charm, and a certain recklessness had swept him into the arms of the wealthy Beatrice Courtney and consequently to a position of authority at the bank. Ambition had been the spur in those early years, but when ambition has been realized, and marriage turns sour, it has to be replaced by something equally desirable – and that, for Henry Courtney-Halliday, was Grace Brent.

So, into the third year, Grace's only indulgence was a quiet hour in her room after lunch, reading, or writing letters. She received letters regularly from Amelia, Jane and Lucy, and after long weeks of anxious waiting, several letters would arrive from her dearest Ellen.

Reading between the lines, she could sense a homesickness in the elder sister, so far away, but for Ellen, her husband and children, especially the children, would compensate for the loss of Mother and sisters. For Grace it was quite impossible now to visit The Haven, even for a few hours, for Mother would detect that she was unwell, and keep her at home. Then the trouble with Bertha would start all over again, and to be a semi-invalid, spared all but the lightest chores, would be even more aggravating to that particular sister. Mother no longer expected her to visit, and the distance between them had widened, so that it now seemed she was as far removed as Ellen.

It was an extraordinary state of affairs, but time had slipped away. Grace had been too complacent, and Beatrice too demanding. Now it was too late. Bloodstains on her handkerchief had to be hidden from the prying eyes of Simmons, who cleaned her room. To wash and dry the handkerchiefs in her bedroom had to be accomplished after she had retired for the night. Nothing much escaped that observant house-parlourmaid.

'That cough don't get no better, an' she don't eat enough to keep a sparrer alive,' she told Cook.

'It's like I said, that young woman won't make old bones,' Cook reminded her.

They did not speak of it to the old nurse, however, for she would soon be off to the Mistress, tittle-tattling. There was trouble enough, heaven knows, Cook declared, what with the Master giving orders one minute, and the Mistress countermanding them the next.

'It never used to be like this, not afore that young woman arrived. You would think, to look at 'er, she wouldn't say boo to a goose. She never answers back, an' she seems 'armless enough, don't she? But it's the quiet ones that 'as to be reckoned with,' Cook insisted.

'Since that affair with the little dog, when that young woman should 'ave been dismissed an' sent packing, instead of given a fire in 'er bedroom, an' 'er lunch on a tray in the Master's study, things 'ave gone from bad to worse.'

'Taking liberties,' Simmons muttered. 'I don't like it.'

'No more do I. There's the Master like a bear with a sore 'ead, an' all 'e wants is what a gentleman is entitled to. Then why don't she give it to 'im and 'ave done with it?' Cook's outspoken views on sex would embarrass Simmons, but she agreed, on principle, because they both felt sorry for the Master.

'Do she keep 'er bedroom door locked?' was a question that could not be answered. It was a matter for speculation over the tea-cups, when the old nurse had retired to bed – whether or not that shy young woman who kept the Master dangling, like a fish on a hook, locked her bedroom door.

When she slid to the floor, it made no more sound than a leaf falling to the ground. And when Henry lifted her in his arms, he was shocked and horrified by the weightless burden he carried from the room.

Beatrice made no move from the couch, but called after him, 'Take my smelling salts. No need to fuss. It's just a fainting turn.'

He was not listening. He was shouting for Simmons, and she ran from the kitchen to stand beside him at the bottom of the stairs.

'Miss Brent has been taken ill. Have someone fetch the doctor immediately – and get Mary. She will know what to do.'

Simmons was so agitated, she forgot to bob a curtsey. Mary was the coachman's wife, a sensible little woman they always called on in an emergency. She helped in the house, doing jobs like polishing silver and cleaning windows, washing lace curtains, and helping Cook with her preserves.

Laying her gently on the bed, Henry stood there, looking down at her, choked by compassion and a feeling so alien to his nature, he did not recognize it as tenderness. Dropping to his knees, he took her limp hand and whispered, brokenly, 'Don't leave me, Grace. I need you. I love you.' But there was no response from that waxen face on the pillow, and her eyes were closed. It could have been a corpse lying there, but a faint pulse was beating in her thin wrist. He was still kneeling beside the bed when Mary spoke from the doorway, hesitating for a moment, not wanting to intrude.

'Has she fainted, Sir?' she asked, quietly.

Without turning his head, he answered her in a low voice. 'It's not a faint. I think she is dying.'

'Shall we cover her up with the eiderdown, Sir? And shall I ask Cook to send up a hot brick from the oven?' She always put them in after dinner, ready to heat the beds.

He nodded, and she tucked Grace under the eider-down, and bustled away.

Left alone again, till Mary came back, his whis-pered plea – 'Don't leave me, Grace. I need you. I love you,' was like a prayer, but he wouldn't know how to pray. He didn't believe in God. A man was master of his own destiny, and when he died, that was the end.

'Stay with her till the doctor comes,' he instructed Mary, and walked slowly out of the room. She drew up a chair and sat down beside the bed. Now she could hear raised voices in the drawing-room, and it saddened her. Marriage without love, or sympathy, was a mockery, and she was sorry for both. In their humble abode, over the coach house, she had made a happy, contented place for the two of them. Their only regret was having no child, but if it was God's will, He knew what was best for each one of His children. At the moment, however, she could not see His purpose in striking down this lovely, innocent young woman, but it would be revealed, of that she was certain. In the meantime, she would say a little prayer.

Henry was pacing up and down the room in great

184

agitation, his hands clenched behind his coat-tails.

'Sit down! You are making me nervous. Must you disturb the whole house just because Grace has fainted?' Beatrice demanded.

'She hasn't fainted. She has collapsed. She could be dying, and you lie there, quite unconcerned.'

'Don't be ridiculous! Of course I am concerned. And don't shout. I have a headache.'

'It's you that's shouting – and it's your fault. Blast you! Couldn't you have seen she was ill?'

'How dare you speak to me in that tone of voice, Henry. I will not tolerate such rudeness.'

'I shall speak to you in any way I choose. You have not bought me with your blasted money!'

'Where would you be without my money, Henry Halliday? In the gutter!'

'Never!' he growled, his eyes blazing.

'If Grace is ill, you must send her home. She hasn't been much use to me lately. Always tired, and nothing to say for herself. I find her company rather tedious, if you must know.'

Henry had to walk away he was so enraged by her callousness. Pacing up and down the hall, he waited for the doctor. Simmons hurried past with a hot brick, wrapped in flannel, then slipped back to the kitchen to report to Cook.

'I never seed the Master so upset. If she dies, I reckon we shan't see much of 'im in the 'ouse, for she's the only attraction, as we both know.'

'If she dies, the Mistress will be blamed, and our lives won't be worth living, for she's been the go-between and the peace-maker, that young woman, though we 'aven't always appreciated the fact.'

Simmons stood there, wringing her hands, waiting to answer the doorbell. But when the bell rang, it was the Master who flung open the door and greeted the doctor impatiently.

Surprised by the unexpected discourtesy, and even more surprised to be shown into the bedroom of the companion and not the Mistress's boudoir, the doctor quickly focused his whole attention on his patient.

Mary stood up, dropped a curtsey, and stayed in the room, as chaperone, while Henry stood at the foot of the bed. If the doctor thought it unseemly for the Master of the house to remain in the room, he was much too discreet to say so.

The pulse was weak. He lifted the eyelids and dropped them again, stripped off the eiderdown, and unfastened the brooch at the neck of the blouse. Why did women have to throttle themselves? he wondered, as he held out the brooch, and Henry took it. It was a cameo brooch, and Grace wore it every day, but no other adornment. Some sentimental reason, he supposed.

When the buttons of the blouse, the camisole, and the chemise had been unfastened, and the flat chest exposed, the doctor took out his stethoscope and sat on the edge of the bed, his face creased into frowning concentration. Henry stood transfixed, staring at the breasts he had wanted to cup in his hands, and the white flesh he had lusted after for so long. But now he only wanted to protect her, even from the professional gaze of the doctor, for she would be so distressed to have her nakedness exposed. Modesty was a word that Grace had known since nursery days. 'Cover yourself, child!' was a command as familiar as 'Sit up straight, Miss Grace. Don't loll.'

When the doctor's hands explored the lower part of that pitifully wasted body, Henry shivered in an

186

agony of self-reproach. How often, in the past, he had seen her stripped of her clothes in his imagination, and his own hands exploring. If this was his punishment, he accepted it now, and was shamed by the revelation.

When the doctor had finished his thorough examination, Mary poured water into the basin and handed him a clean towel. He nodded curtly, then turned to the silent man at the foot of the bed. The dark eyes held an anguished appeal. So *that* was the explanation. They were lovers. Well, it was none of his business, and he couldn't blame the man, with a wife who was always ailing. Once a woman took to her couch and turned herself into a semi-invalid, she stayed that way. Beatrice Courtney-Halliday was one of several patients he would like to shake, but had to administer advice and soothing medicine, while their long-suffering husbands paid heavily for his services.

Leaving Mary at the bedside, he followed Henry out of the room, down the stairs, and into the study, where they stood facing each other, Henry still clutching the cameo brooch, waiting for the verdict. One word was sufficient for Henry to draw in his breath with a gasp of dismay.

'Tuberculosis.'

'How – how serious?'

'Very serious indeed. This should have been diagnosed and treated a couple of years ago. It may be too late. She must have been passing blood at this stage of the disease. You've seen nothing?'

'No.'

'And your wife?'

'She would have mentioned it.'

'Blood stained handkerchiefs have to be washed by someone.'

'She would wash them herself, in her bedroom.'

'A resourceful and courageous young woman?'

'Yes.'

'Don't look so despairing, my dear fellow. While there is life there is hope. We must get her away.'

'Where?'

'To a sanatorium. I know of such a place. It is situated near Grindelwald in Switzerland, and run by a former colleague of mine, a German who trained with me at Guy's, who specializes in this disease. Mind you, it will cost a pretty penny, but he is one of the best, if not *the* best authority on tuberculosis in Europe.'

'Would you entrust your own daughter to this man if she had the disease?'

'Without a second's hesitation.'

'Then please arrange it, as soon as possible, and spare no expense.'

'You can leave it to me.'

Henry sighed with relief, and asked, 'Can I offer you a drink, doctor?'

'Thank you.'

'Port? Sherry? Whisky?'

'Ah, a drop of Scotch would be nice.' He sat down, wondering what his patient would say when she regained consciousness, and discovered what had been arranged. Much too ill to protest, and probably glad to get away from an unhappy situation – unhappy and unhealthy. Morals were not his concern, but sometimes he was forced into thinking that men were selfish brutes. In her distress, this Grace Brent would have suffered agonies of mind, if she loved this man. Tuberculosis could develop in a weak constitution, under the strain of such emotional circumstances, but there was no need to burden this

188

poor fellow with his own private meditations.

When they had finished their drinks and the doctor had reaffirmed that he would get in touch with Dr Graffner immediately, they shook hands, and he was shown out by Simmons. Mrs Courtney-Halliday had not appeared, and had not been consulted. He wondered what her reaction would be.

Henry was also wondering, but he hadn't long to wait.

'Well, I hope you are satisfied now that you have disturbed the entire household. I suppose she is now recovering nicely, and taking a little refreshment.' Beatrice sneered.

'Grace is very seriously ill. The doctor has diagnosed tuberculosis.'

'What did you say?'

'You heard what I said. Why ask me to repeat it?'

'Tuberculosis? But how dreadful. You must get her away, Henry. Get her out of the house. It could be contagious. I could have caught the germ, being in such close contact.' She looked at him in wide-eyed horror, ready to indulge in a fit of the vapours.

'Control yourself, Beatrice. Your fears are groundless. The doctor has confirmed the disease is not contagious, but it could be hereditary.'

'Even so, I shall not feel safe until she is out of the house.'

'You are unlikely to meet her. She will stay in her room, with Mary in attendance, until she leaves.'

'Are you sending her home?'

'No, to a sanatorium in Switzerland. She must have specialized treatment in a high altitude.'

'And are you prepared to pay for this extraordinary gesture?'

'Yes. I shall pay.'

'Then there is no more to be said.' She yawned. 'Send Nana to me. I feel quite fatigued with all this fuss and bother.'

Henry made no reply. His anger had evaporated. Stunned and shocked by the events of the past couple of hours, he went back to his study, locked the door, sank into a chair, covered his face with his hands, and wept – the first tears he had shed since his longed-for child was still-born. Without Grace his life would have no meaning. Shuddering sobs shook his heavy body, and he gave himself up in despair.

A week later, Grace was on her way, and they had exchanged no more than a few words. A trained nurse had taken over from Mary, and was travelling with Grace to the sanatorium. The letter he composed so carefully to her mother was a travesty of the truth, but what else could he say?

He was living at his club in Pall Mall now, but he was not neglecting his duties at the bank, for habit was strong in him. He had avoided Beatrice for the whole of that interminable week, and Simmons had reported that Madam was indisposed.

Not a word, nor a glimpse of him in eighteen long months, and suddenly he was there, kissing her hand, his dark eyes searching her face with that remembered scrutiny that had once embarrassed her. Now, surprisingly, she was no longer embarrassed, and only a little disturbed by his presence. A lovely warmth was spreading over her whole body, and she smiled a welcome.

'Half-an-hour, not a minute longer. I have my orders!' His voice was jocular. He was bursting with life and vitality.

190

'Such a short time, and you have come all this way,' she whispered.

He nodded. 'Don't worry, my darling. I shall come again, as often as that fierce Herr Doktor will allow. There will be urgent business that will bring me to Zurich, and it's no distance from there.'

My darling? He had called her his darling. A faint blush stole over her pale cheeks. He was still holding her hand, and it trembled in the clasp of his warm fingers.

'How are you feeling, Grace? You are looking better than I expected,' he lied gallantly. She looked so frail and lovely he had to conquer the urge to take her in his arms. 'Nothing of a disturbing nature,' the good doctor had reminded him. Patience was a virtue he had been practising for a very long time, and now there was no hurry. They had all the time in the world to get to know each other – the real Grace, the real Henry – hidden beneath a veneer of polite formality in the house at Bayswater. They were together at last, in this incomparable landscape, where time stood still, and where the silence was broken only by the tinkle of cowbells.

'Did you know the rules were so strict? – that all letters were censored, and no visitors allowed for the first year, and only by consent for the second year?' Henry asked.

'I was not told anything. Is that why you didn't write?'

'Of course. What could I say that would pass the censor, the censor being Herr Doktor, I presume?'

She shook her head at him. 'It doesn't matter now you are here.'

'It's been an eternity. I couldn't go through it again. I thought you were going to die.'

'I couldn't die till I had seen you again – and now . . .'

'And now?' he prompted.

'I am going to get well and strong. You will see. The next time you come we will take a little walk. Now, tell me all the news. What is happening at the Bayswater house?'

'I have no idea. I have been living at my club since you went away.'

'You have left your wife?'

'We are living apart, by mutual agreement. Beatrice has refused to divorce me, but she may change her mind. Would you marry me, Grace, if I was free?'

'Yes, Henry' – the merest whisper. They were not allowed to kiss. They could only hold hands, but eyes could speak, and hands could cling, and there was hope in their hearts.

'Shall I tell you what I have been planning?'

'Tell me.'

'I have sent in my resignation. I am no longer a director of the bank. The Zurich branch have offered me a post in a minor capacity. Shall you mind being the wife of a humble clerk, my love?'

'I wouldn't mind if you swept the streets.'

'Ah, there speaks the voice of my true love. I am not a poor man, Grace, and my investments in railway shares, brewery shares and Government Stock are as safe as the Bank of England. I have rented a little house in Zurich, and engaged a kindly little woman as housekeeper. I shall be living there in the New Year, so you see, my love, I have not been wasting my time.'

Grace felt a glow of pride in his willingness to forfeit so much for her sake. Choked with emotion, she could only say, 'I think you are wonderful.'

'Of course I am wonderful, and you don't know the half of what I am capable of doing, now that I have your promise, my adorable Grace. Here is nurse with your hot chocolate. Do I smell coffee, nurse?'

'You do, Sir. Herr Doktor sends his compliments, and wishes to remind you that you have only ten minutes more.'

'Too bad, but I shall be back.'

'I hope so, Sir. Miss Brent has been so brave and patient, she deserves a little happiness.'

Henry thanked her, and she slipped away. Ten more minutes, and she hadn't opened the present he had brought. It was a quilted dressing-gown in a pretty shade of blue, trimmed with swansdown, and matching slippers.

'It's beautiful, Henry. Thank you, my dear. I have been clinging to my old dressing-gown because I couldn't afford a new one, but I've had it since I was in the schoolroom, and it's beginning to look a little worn.'

He smiled indulgently at her pleasure. 'I've something else for you, and I nearly forgot to give it to you.'

'My cameo brooch! Where did you find it?'

'It was never lost. I have kept it all these months. You mustn't cry, my darling, or the good doctor will forbid me to see you.'

'I'm not crying.' She was smiling through her tears.

'I love you so much,' he said.

'And I love you,' she whispered.

'Only three more months, then no more parting. Drink your chocolate, dearest. It's getting cold.'

He was so gentle with her, this man who could be so rough and rude. She watched him walk away with a jaunty step. Dwarfed in the lofty magnificence of those three mountain peaks, she saw him as a giant among men – her dear Henry!

6

'Couldn't you have kept an eye on Grace?' Ellen asked, in a low voice, when she had rejoined her younger sister in the bedroom.

'I *did* write, Ellen, soon after you went away, to ask when I could visit her, but she wrote back to say it would not be convenient to visit her, but would I write, as she would like to receive letters. I felt rather hurt, but supposed there must be a very good reason. This letter from her employer explains it. She was already feeling ill, and didn't want me to know.'

'I don't trust that couple, Jane. I didn't like either of them, and was very reluctant to leave her there. Poor darling, if she dies, I shall blame myself.'

'It was not your fault. If anyone is to blame it's Bertha, for it was her complaining that gave Mother the idea to send Grace away. I suppose they are doing their best now, if they are paying all the expenses, for Mother certainly couldn't afford to pay for a private sanatorium in Switzerland.'

'Neither can I afford to visit her. Oh, Jane, what is happening to us? We used to be such a united family. Now we are separated, and coming home is not what I expected. We are not welcome here, but where else could I go?' Ellen asked, forlornly.

'It must happen to all families, Ellen dear, the good times and the bad. We are not unique. Nothing is perfect, and we are not saints. We all make mistakes, and your biggest mistake was to marry Jonathan.'

'You *knew*?'

'Yes. Edward was afraid you would regret it. He told me Jonathan could not be faithful to any one woman, and he was actually boasting of his conquests when he was engaged to be married.'

'You could have warned me?'

'Would you have listened? You were in love.'

'And being in love, I was blind to his faults. Yet he was not entirely to blame. I was the wrong wife for him. Some women would have enjoyed being the wife of an Army officer, drafted out to India with the regiment, but I was not one of those women, Jane. There is no glamour in a garrison town, thousands of miles from home. I was lonely and homesick, and never well.'

'The babies came too quickly.'

'No, for me they saved a situation that was always disastrous. I love my babies, and I am glad there is another on the way. I didn't take long to discover I was a better mother than a wife. Even my feelings for Jonathan became maternal when Prue was on the way.'

'That doesn't surprise me, Ellen. Being the eldest of the family, you mothered us all, bless you, for we didn't get a lot of affection from Mother, did we?'

'Mother is not maternal, Jane, but she must have been a wonderful wife. Father adored her.'

'Grace was his favourite, wasn't she?'

'Yes, I think she was,' Ellen sighed. It had been an exhausting day, and reading that letter from Henry Courtney-Halliday had saddened her.

'Why don't you get into bed? I will ask Mother to

excuse you. I shall be leaving soon, for I don't stay to supper. Edward gets anxious about me if I am out after dark.'

'You are not nervous?'

'No, I don't seem to suffer from nerves, do I?'

'I wish I had your courage and your faith. To choose to live in the slums, and to be so obviously happy, seems to prove that you made no mistake in your marriage.'

'No, we suit each other very well. We are doing useful work, and serving God as well as some of his more unfortunate children. I wouldn't change places with anyone. Of course, it's hard work and there is always an element of danger, but then I was not looking for an easy way of life. I like a challenge.'

Ellen smiled wanly at her younger sister, who had met the challenge and conquered it. To have failed in her own marriage was Ellen's most bitter reproach. She kissed Jane affectionately, and knew she had found an ally. 'Take care. God bless you.'

Then she was gone, running down the stairs, eager to be on her way back to London's East End, to misery and poverty, gaiety and cheerfulness – back to Edward.

Jane missed her usual train, and had to wait an hour for another, so it was dark when she arrived, and the street lamps shed only a faint glow on the wet pavements. The drabness of her surroundings always struck her most forcibly after spending a day at The Haven, enjoying the comfort and luxury of a middle-class home. But tomorrow was a new day, and she was not afraid of the lurking shadows because Edward would be waiting to welcome her, and Aggie would be serving supper to the lodgers.

She could usually switch her thoughts from one

place to another as soon as she set foot in the East End, but tonight she was worried about Ellen and Grace, and still thinking of them when she pushed open the door of the Mission. The house reeked of kippers, and Aggie was slumped on a kitchen chair, surrounded by dirty dishes.

'Cor, blimey, Missus, am I glad to see you,' she wailed. 'I ain't 'arf been worried.'

'Why, what's happened?' Jane's voice was brusque, for it didn't take much to upset Aggie, and the cluttered kitchen was depressing.

'It's the Guv what got 'isself mixed up in a fight at the Adam and Eve, an' got 'is face slashed with a razor.'

'A *razor*?' Jane's face blanched, and she leaned on the table for support. 'When did it happen? Where is he now?'

' 'Bout an hour ago. They took 'im orf to the 'orspital. Blood all over the plice,' she added, with gloomy relish. 'The coppers collared the bloke what 'ad the razor, but 'e was yelling that 'e never meant it for the Guv. It were a mistake.'

'Why does *he* have to get mixed up in these brawls? It's so *stupid*.' Jane sighed in exasperation. It was not the first time he had been attacked, *by mistake*. Last time it was two black eyes.

'Bloody swine! I'll come wiv you to the 'orspital, Missus.' It was Bill, one of the permanent lodgers in the doorway, cramming his mouth with jam tart.

'Thank you, Bill,' said Jane gratefully.

' 'Arf a mo, I'll just tell two of them lazy buggers to give Aggie a 'and with the washing up.' He disappeared into the living-room, and came back dragging two of the younger boys by the scruff of the neck. When he had rolled up their sleeves and shoved them at the kitchen sink, he took Jane's arm and they went out together.

As they passed the Adam and Eve, the door swung open to admit another customer. Someone was playing a mouth organ, and the crowd of men at the bar were laughing and shouting.

'They don't care, do they, Bill?' Jane's voice was choked with tears.

'Bloody bastards!' Bill muttered, savagely.

There were twenty beds in the crowded ward, and the strong smell of antiseptic and disinfectant did not entirely disguise the smell of urine. It was a cheerful place, however, with red blankets and green distempered walls. Edward had just been wheeled in from casualty, and tucked into the bed behind the door – one of several 'emergency' beds that were seldom empty in this big general hospital in the heart of the East End. His head was swathed in bandages. One eye was blinking rapidly, and his mouth trembled on a smile when he saw Jane.

'My poor darling.' She knelt beside the bed, took his limp hand and pressed it to her cheek. Gulping back the tears, she asked, 'Does it hurt dreadfully?'

'Yes, it d-does.' He always stuttered when he was nervous, her poor darling, and this was a nerve-shattering experience. Then he greeted Bill, and thanked him for escorting his wife to the hospital.

'You give us all a bloody awful shock, Guv. My Gawd, talk about a bloody mess.'

'You w-were there?'

'I just come in for me reglar 'alf pint, when it 'appened. You was right in the thick of it, Guv. That poor bugger is going to get 'isself 'urt again, I told meself. But it 'appened too quick for me to do anythink abaht it. So 'elp me.' Bill had not lowered his

199

voice, and every word was audible in the quiet ward. Night Sister frowned disapprovingly, but Bill was not aware of giving offence, for swearing was as natural as breathing.

As for Edward and Jane, they had long since given up correcting such language. To be always sitting in judgement on the men and women they were here to save was not their intention, and if they seemed more concerned with bodies than souls, God would understand. They were practising Christians, as were the Salvation Army lassies with whom they worked so agreeably. Jane did not scrub floors, or rescue battered wives from drunken husbands. She was too busy making a home for the men and boys who would otherwise have been sleeping in doorways, and begging a crust of bread from someone as poor as themselves. Not that the crust would have been refused. The poor help the poor.

Edward's eye was closing. The soothing draught of laudanum was making him sleepy.

'Come along. My patient must rest. You may see him again tomorrow evening at seven o'clock,' said Night Sister, authoritatively.

Jane's gentle kiss did not disturb him, and they followed Sister out of the ward.

'Now don't look so worried. Your husband is suffering from shock. He will be feeling better tomorrow,' she told Jane, soothingly, as they stood together in the corridor.

'Is it a bad wound, Sister – and is the eye damaged?'

'It was a nasty gash. He had thirteen stitches in his cheek, and he may lose the sight of that eye.'

'Thirteen stitches?' Jane echoed. 'That means he will be scarred for life?'

'I'm afraid so, though the scar will fade in time and not be so conspicuous. The surgeons will operate on the eye later in the week. We can only be thankful he was not blinded by the attack. I have known it to happen. A razor is a dangerous weapon.'

'Yes, Sister,' Jane agreed. She was feeling sick, and wanted to get away. 'Thank you, Sister,' she added as an afterthought, and took Bill's arm. Outside the main gates she was sick in the gutter.

'You'll feel better nah, Missus. Better up than dahn,' said Bill, with gruff kindliness.

As for feeling better, in all her short life Jane had never felt more wretched. In the drizzling rain, with a splitting headache, exhausted by the day's events, she staggered towards home, clutching Bill's arm.

'A nice cup o' char, an' you'll be okey-doke, Missus,' said Bill. 'But it's a bloody shame about the Guv. I reckon 'e'll 'ave ter wear one of them black eye shades, an' wiv a bloody great scar, 'e's going to look like a bloody pirate!'

Jane choked on a laugh. Talk about a Job's comforter!

But the kitchen was clean, and the kettle on the boil. Aggie had recovered, and they sat down to a pot of tea while Bill recounted all the grim details, for Aggie's benefit, and they both enjoyed the doubtful privilege of informing the rest of the household after the Missus had retired to bed.

Shivering in the flickering light of a single candle, Jane undressed, and knelt to say her prayers, but her mind was a blank and no words came, so she climbed into the big lonely bed. They had not been separated for a single night since their marriage, and the sagging flock mattress sank lower into the broken springs. Everything in the house had been in use for more than thirty years, and there was no money for replacements. With Edward beside her, it didn't seem to matter, but tonight it mattered terribly, and she wept for the comforts of that home she had discarded with such strong convictions. Why did God allow it to happen? Why? Why? Why?

When Norah had served the simple supper of poached eggs, cheese and biscuits and cocoa, Amelia retired to the drawing-room, while Bertha helped Norah to wash the dishes and lay the breakfast. When they had finished these chores, they retired to bed, for Norah was not invited to the drawing-room and Bertha refused anything that did not include Norah. Nothing had actually been said, but Norah seemed to think it would be 'taking a liberty'. Amelia could be haughty and dignified, so Norah was taking no chances. She had Bertha, she had a good home, and was not overworked. She was happy and contented. The unnatural relationship they shared was the only happiness Bertha had known. Her sulky temper and jealous nature, even in childhood, had not endeared her to her sisters. Only Norah, from a working-class family, rather rough in her ways and with little education, had found her way into Bertha's heart.

Her views on marriage were shared with Norah. They found in their virgin bodies a purity and joy they could never have found in marriage. Yet they *were* married, in a sense that was totally satisfying to both. They shared an intimacy they considered superior in every way to the marital relationship between a man and a woman. The bedroom they shared was a private sanctum where they found what was lacking in their other relationships. At the end of jxthe day, Norah could claim an equality that was pleasing and satisfying to her generous nature. It had been an eventful and disturbing day, with the screaming children and the letter from London. Bertha was upset. Her conscience was troubling her.

'I shall be blamed if Grace dies, for it was me who persuaded Mother to send her away.'

'Of course you won't be blamed, my dearest Bert. Your Mother always has the last word on everything, as we both know. Don't distress yourself. Come and lie down. With all this worry and that nagging conscience, I can see you in bed tomorrow with another sick headache, and poor old Norah doing all the donkey work!'

Bertha's rare smile was sweet, and her plain face had a kind of beauty that her mother and sisters would not have recognized. Gradually her taut nerves relaxed, and they lay together, listening to the strains of Chopin.

Amelia always played Chopin when she was disturbed – and the letter had disturbed her conscience. Could she really blame Bertha?

At the top of the house, the children slept their deep, innocent sleep, and their young mother lay awake in the adjoining room with the door open, and a nightlight burning, for Prue was afraid of the dark. Little Bella seemed fearless, thank goodness, but then she was too young to be disturbed by the sudden disappearance of a beloved parent, and the long journey home to another strange world, peopled entirely with white faces, and no Ayah. So Ellen lay awake at the top of the house, grieving for Grace, and the child in her womb stirred restlessly. One day the memories of that traumatic experience would fade, and she would find happiness again in her growing children.

She hadn't really expected to be welcomed with open arms, and Jane had been kind. Dear, practical Jane, in her shabby clothes and her shining face. How different they were – the six sisters – with only the bond of family to hold them together.

It was Norah who climbed the stairs with a can of hot water and a cup of tea for Ellen at seven o'clock the next morning, and Norah's homely face that greeted the two little girls as they stared, unsmiling, at the tall figure in the long, white apron, only dimly remembered from the previous day. Ellen appeared at the open door and accepted the tea gratefully. It had been a long night, and she was ready now to face the new day.

'Prue want tea,' said the child, reaching for the cup.

'You shall have a sip of mine, darling,' said Ellen, appeasingly, and poured half the tea into the saucer. 'Wait a minute, it's too hot.' She blew on the tea to cool it.

Then Bella found her voice and shouted, 'TEA! TEA!'

Ellen smiled indulgently at her younger daughter. 'Clever girl. Now say Mama.'

'TEA!' She was nearly tumbling out of her cot in her excitement. So Ellen almost emptied the cup to fill another saucer for Bella.

'You spoil them,' Norah scolded, affectionately. 'Auntie Norah will bring you tea tomorrow in your own mugs,' she promised the children.

'You can't, not with the can of hot water. I shall come down for it, Norah. You mustn't wait on me,' Ellen protested.

'I have two good hands, haven't I? A small tray with three mugs of tea in one hand, and the water jug

204

in the other. Nothing could be simpler.'

Prue stared at her with hostile eyes. She had no intention of being friendly with someone who seemed to have taken Ayah's place. Was she a servant? Only servants wore long white aprons and served early morning tea.

But Bella had enjoyed the tea in a saucer. She was feeling surprisingly independent this morning because she was not sharing Prue's bed. So she held up her arms and demanded, 'OUT!'

Norah lifted her out. She was very wet, and smelled of ammonia, but Norah didn't seem to mind.

'It's my fault. I forgot to lift her last night. But I shall do the children's washing. We are still missing Ayah,' Ellen sighed. 'Naughty Baba,' Prue scolded, feeling very superior.

Cuddled in her mother's arms, her small world was complete.

'Breakfast at 8,' Norah reminded them, as she dropped Bella back in her cot and hurried away.

Amelia was served breakfast at 8.30. It never varied – seven days a week – a boiled egg, toast and marmalade, and a small pot of tea. The dainty china, pretty traycloth and matching napkin pleased her fastidiousness. The teapot was covered with a cosy, and a matching cosy covered the egg. Bertha had been pleased to hand over this duty to Norah, for she had resented her mother's privileged status to take breakfast in bed when they had no resident servants. But Amelia was conservative in her habits, and saw no reason why she should be deprived of this small luxury after the house-parlourmaid had been dismissed.

With her breakfast tray she also received *The Morning Post* and any letters that had been delivered.

At precisely 9.30, Norah delivered a can of hot water. The quiet routine of the small household had only been disrupted when Kate and Lucy were home for the holidays. Now it would be permanently disrupted, for Ellen and her children were here to stay, and another child on the way. The shocking behaviour at the tea-table had been a foretaste of what to expect.

'They are spoilt, troublesome little nuisances,' Bertha told Norah. 'Why haven't they gone to the Vicarage? Surely Jonathan's parents should be responsible for his widow and children?'

But Norah would be the 'go-between'. She felt sorry for Ellen. That wet little bundle she had lifted out of the cot had already endeared herself on this first morning, with her warm hugs and slobbering kisses. You could not blame the children for being spoilt with such an indulgent mother and adoring native servants.

When Bertha saw Ellen carrying Prue downstairs on her hip, leading Bella by the hand, she demanded, 'What's wrong with that child's legs?'

'Nothing. She is frightened of stairs. We lived in a bungalow in India.'

'Then the sooner she gets used to them the better. You shouldn't be carrying such a heavy child in your condition,' snapped her sister, irritably, and went to stand guard at the little gate at the top of the basement stairs. 'Norah will carry you down to the breakfast-room,' she told Prue, who clung like a limpet to her mother.

So Norah carried Bella. It was going to be difficult to keep the peace, Ellen was thinking, with Bertha so bossy and disagreeable. But there they were, and here they would stay. It was their home, and they had

206

every right to be here. For the sake of the children she must not be intimidated by this strong-willed younger sister.

Maggie had been at work since six o'clock. It was 'washing day', and the 'whites' were bubbling in the copper. Soon she would be sitting down to a breakfast of bacon and fried bread that Norah had cooked. It was keeping hot in the oven. She came through to the breakfast-room to greet Ellen and the children – a quaint little figure in a sacking apron tied over her white apron, and her hair screwed into a tight bun.

'It's nice to 'ave you back 'ome, Miss Ellen, an' the dear little children, bless their little 'earts.'

They stared at her with wide dark eyes, while their mother smiled her sad, sweet smile. Bertha was anxious to get on with the breakfast, and shooed Maggie away. The high chairs would remain in the dining-room, but Norah had discoverd a couple of old cushions, and Ellen lifted up the two little girls, then sat down between them to prepare the boiled eggs and fingers of bread and butter. First Prue, then Bella, but Bella was accustomed to waiting. Then Prue decided she would also be fed with the egg, like her baby sister, and sat there, pouting her small stubborn mouth.

'Can't that child feed herself?' Bertha demanded.

Ellen made no answer. Prue was being difficult. She was remembering that Ayah had fed her. She liked being fed, and she liked being carried.

Bertha was pouring tea, and had to be reminded to pour a dash of tea in the children's milk. Ellen was determined to avoid another scene, so she went on spooning the egg into Prue's mouth. Then she spread two slices of toast with butter and marmalade, and cut them into fingers.

'Your own egg will be stone cold,' Bertha grumbled.

If this was a foretaste of mealtimes, her patience would be sorely tried. And what would Mother have to say, as she presided over lunch and tea in the dining-room, when her eldest grandchild had to be fed like a baby?

Ellen changed the subject quickly, and asked, appeasingly, 'When will it be convenient to do the children's washing?'

'You must wait till Maggie has finished in the scullery,' Bertha snapped.

'I will help to hang out, then she should be finished by ten o'clock,' said Norah, helpfully. 'The children can stay in the kitchen and watch me do my baking.'

'Prue stay wiv Mama,' said the child, decidedly.

'Not in the scullery you won't, my child. It's too dangerous.'

Bertha and Prue exchanged hostile glances, and Bella's attention wandered from the last spoonful of egg, and it dribbled on the clean napkin tied around her neck.

'Dirty Baba,' Prue scolded, and Bella chuckled.

'Hurry up, my darlings. We can't sit here all day,' Ellen reminded them, as she hastily scooped out her own egg. It was very lightly boiled, and she was feeling rather sick this morning.

'Can I help?' she asked, when they had finished.

'No, thank you. We can manage. We are used to managing,' said Bertha, meaningly.

'What you really need, Ellen, is a young girl to take the children to the park while you are busy with your morning chores.' Norah was suggesting something that seemed impossible on Ellen's limited income, until Amelia solved the problem by allowing Lucy to leave the Seminary for Young Ladies, when her sister Kate left, and since her bosom friend, Rose, now a

Ward of Court, had no close relatives, it was arranged that she should act as nursemaid in return for her board and lodging, and a shilling a week for pocket money.

Trouble was expected with Prue, of course, but Rose had a gentle nature and a way with little children so that even the stubborn Prue found herself demanding to be included in the games of 'ring-o-roses' and 'hide and seek'. Rose was still a child at heart, and glad to be finished with the boring lessons in deportment, music and dancing considered necessary to a well-bred young lady. In her true element now, and with her bosom friend Lucy willing to share her bedroom, Rose asked nothing more of life.

A doll's bassinet had been discovered in a cupboard and claimed by Prue, because Bella was still too young to push it. But Bella was a happy, friendly child, and so accustomed to giving up her toys to Prue, she made no fuss, but proudly accepted the dog's lead, for they always took Jackie to the park. He was getting old, and his pace was slow, so they suited each other very well. 'Dog' was another word to be added to Bella's limited vocabulary.

Prue had to be coaxed to leave her mother, to feed herself, to dress herself, and to walk downstairs, and it was not all achieved in a few days, or even weeks. Rose's patience seemed inexhaustible, however, and Ellen blessed the day when she joined the household. Soon there would be another child, and Rose would be indispensable. She was shy of Amelia, and wary of Bertha, but since she only encountered them at meal times, it was not too worrying.

Now it was Kate who disturbed the peace – a Kate who had grown into a very attractive young woman, fully aware of her attraction to the opposite sex.

Kate was not altogether pleased with the long-standing plan that Amelia had made with Grandpapa Brent, and would have preferred to take her time over choosing her own employment, but Amelia still held the reins, and had no intention of allowing her two youngest daughters to please themselves. They were allowed to choose which department they would prefer, however, at the big drapery store in the High Street. Kate had chosen Millinery, and Lucy had chosen Children's Wear. Both would be apprentices, waiting on the Manageress, dusting and tidying away the unsold articles. They would not be allowed to serve a customer for the first year of their apprenticeships.

Kate was indignant. As a grand-daughter of Thomas Brent, she had expected preferential treatment, but Grandpapa Brent had other views. His own son had started as an apprentice in Gentlemen's Wear, taking orders from the Manager of the department for five years before he was promoted.

'Five years' apprenticeship!' It seemed a lifetime to Kate. 'I shall be married when I'm twenty-one, then I shall please myself,' she informed her mother, on their way to the store where Grandpapa had arranged to meet them and introduce them to the General Manager – his only concession to their status.

'When you are married, my child, you will obey your husband and abide by his wishes,' Amelia reminded her wilful daughter.

'Were you always compliant to Father's wishes?' Kate asked innocently.

'Your father was an exception to the general rule, and he always allowed me to decide what was best for you girls.'

'Then I shall marry an exception!'

'My dear child, you have just finished your formal education. Now you are starting on your career in business. This is no time to talk of marriage.'

'We senior girls at the Academy talked of little else. It was the main topic of conversation.'

'Really, Kate! And you, Lucy?' Amelia asked, turning to her youngest daughter, who was even more reluctant than Kate to make her début in the world of business, but for a very different reason. Acute shyness would make every hour of every day an embarrassing ordeal.

'I am unlikely to attract a future husband. I am much too ordinary,' she murmured.

'That is a foolish remark, child.'

'Well, look at me, then look at Kate. There is your answer, Mother.'

'Your future husband will make his choice of a suitable wife, not by comparing you with Kate, but by assessing your own particular qualities, my dear. Gentleness, docility, and a sweet countenance are very appealing. You do not have to be beautiful to attract your future husband. Be yourself. Be natural. But really, you are much too young to be troubling yourself about a husband. Concentrate on your work. Learn all you can. It will please Grandpapa.'

'Yes, Mother,' Lucy agreed, obediently.

The cab that was taking them to meet their destiny was nearing the centre of the town, and Lucy wanted to cry.

They were both there in the vestibule – Grandpapa and the General Manager – standing side by side, with their hands tucked under their coat-tails, and very similar in appearance, white-haired, portly and dignified. The General Manager had started as an apprentice, and Grandpapa would point him out as a living example of conscientious application, and a dedicated affection for Thomas Brent & Son. They both inclined their heads in a stiff little bow as the trio approached, led by Amelia, who touched her father-in-law's cheek with her cool lips, then introduced her daughters, for it was several years since they had met. There was no close relationship, and the link between them had been broken when his only son had died so tragically.

Thomas Brent Senior had been bitterly disappointed in his grandchildren. Not a single male among that litter of females!

Kate and Lucy curtsied prettily, and he had to admit, somewhat grudgingly, that they did their mother credit, and it was not such a bad thing to have them join the firm.

They all shook hands with the General Manager, who led the way to his office. Curious glances followed them from behind the counters, and young apprentices busied themselves in tidying articles already tidy.

Grandpapa and Amelia took the two chairs, and the two girls were left standing, with the General Manager attentive to every word that fell from his employer's lips. Thomas Brent was his God, and the store his life-blood. A confirmed bachelor, he had no other interest but his church on Sunday, where he officiated as churchwarden, with the same solemn dignity.

'I have allowed the girls to choose the department they would prefer. Miss Kate has decided on Millinery and Miss Lucy on Children's Wear. Apart from that concession, they will be treated exactly the same as your other young apprentices. No favours, Hudson. Is that understood?' The voice of authority was harsh.

'Perfectly, Sir,' came the prompt reply.

'Hand them over to their respective seniors for the recognized period of five years. No need for you to bother yourself. You could, perhaps, ask young Gregson to keep an eye on them. He is shaping well as your assistant, is he not?'

'Very well indeed, Sir.'

'Splendid. Then that's settled.' He beamed benignly on his grand-daughters, patted their gloved hands, bade them wait for Mr Hudson's return, and marched out of the office.

'Oh, *Mother*! I know I am going to faint. I feel so frightened,' Lucy whispered.

'Nonsense, child. Pull yourself together,' Amelia insisted. Nothing must go wrong at the last moment. Her girls were lucky. There must be scores of more suitable applicants, but her father-in-law had kept his promise.

'Don't be such a baby, Luce. They can't eat you.' Kate didn't care two hoots. Nobody was going to tell *her* what to do!

When they had been escorted to their respective departments and introduced to their superiors, they were left to their fate. Amelia was escorted to the front entrance, a cab was called, and she departed with a sense of having done her duty as her beloved Thomas would have wished. She, too, had felt faint in that office where her husband had sat not so long ago, after he had become Assistant Manager.

Dismissing the cab in the next street she decided to take her chocolate at Kong's and then stroll on the promenade. She was not needed at home. They could manage without her. A letter from Jane this morning had been a little disconcerting, but her practical young daughter was quite capable of coping with any emergency. A slight accident, and Mother was not to worry. Edward was being treated in hospital, but would soon be home. Jane was a good girl. She wrote regularly every week, and visited her mother once a month. There had never been any trouble with Jane, thank goodness. Heaven knows, there had been trouble enough with Ellen and Grace, and trouble of a different kind with Bertha, so full of resentment, so disagreeable. Six girls was a big responsibility, but she had done her best.

Sipping the hot chocolate in the comfortable surroundings of the old-established coffee house, Amelia was remembering the stricken face of her youngest daughter as she left her with that stern-looking individual in charge of Children's Wear. But she had never pampered the girls, and for the most part, they had all been obedient to her wishes. Lucy must learn that life is not a bed of roses. She was so like Grace in appearance and temperament. As for Kate. A smile touched her tight lips. She had no fears for this particular daughter in that strange world in which she found herself. Her wilfulness would soon provoke that haughty madam in the trailing skirts. Imagine it – a *train*! And such an air of graciousness in front of Grandpapa and the General Manager. It was quite ridiculous. But her naughty Kate would not be intimidated. Kate knew she had a distinct advantage in being the grand-daughter of Thomas Brent, whatever he may have said to the contrary, and being Kate, she would make good use of it! If she found a career in business not to her liking, she would find a husband to rescue her, for Kate could charm a bird off a bough when she set her mind to it. She had charmed her father with her pretty ways as a little girl, but he had not seen her tears and tantrums. She was jealous of Grace, her father's favourite.

Jealousy had been at the root of all the tears and tantrums as a child, and in adult life it would destroy any relationship that threatened her own happiness.

That first day seemed interminable to both girls, and it didn't take long to discover they were resented by the other apprentices who were wary of them because of their relationship to their august employer. A cloak-room was attached to each department, and here they were instructed to change into grey dresses, covered by grey pinafores.

'For all the world like charity orphans!' Kate would relate at supper that evening.

Completely ignored by the haughty Manageress, their duties were explained by a senior apprentice, and both girls had only a glimpse of the customers being served at the counters, for they spent most of the day in the stockrooms and fitting rooms. Joining the other apprentices for a frugal lunch of bread and cheese and cocoa, they would see the bent heads and hear the whispered conversation. Lucy was embarrassed and near to tears, but Kate tossed her head and stuck out her tongue at the sly glances – a shocking gesture for such a well-bred young lady!

They were not allowed to leave the premises in the lunch hour, and the time would have dragged but for the intervention of the Assistant Manager, who came to talk to them. They had been introduced to him that morning. His shy manner and good looks – blond hair and dark blue eyes – had endeared him to the apprentices, but the senior staff and male employees were very unfriendly. There was a reason for this, as Kate would soon discover, when he escorted them home after the store closed at eight o'clock. His mother had been widowed when Basil was in his first year at Oxford, and being an only child, he left Oxford and returned home to Worthing, where he learned they had been left almost destitute by a feckless husband and father, and that he, Basil, was expected to start work immediately at Thomas Brent's Drapery Store. It did not occur to him to ask how or why it had been arranged. His mother had not divulged that she had once been engaged to marry Thomas Brent Senior, but had been prevented because he was a tradesman, and her family were upper class. On the strength of this early relationship, Mrs Gregson had been interviewed privately, and promised an early appointment for her son. The General Manager was not consulted, and consequently indignant, for he naturally assumed that his assistant would be chosen from those who had served their apprenticeships. In his opinion, this shy young man with the cultured voice and hesitant manner, was a most unsuitable candidate, and he was not prepared to like him, or to train him.

In a sense he was as unhappy as Lucy, for he had made no friends, and had only the company of his mother on Wednesday afternoons – early closing day – and Sundays. He welcomed the arrival of the two Misses Brent, and to escort them home was a pleasure, not a duty.

'Who was the young man talking to you at the gate this evening?' Amelia asked, at the supper table at the end of the first interminable week.

'Young *gentleman*!' Kate corrected. 'That was Mr Basil Gregson. He is Assistant Manager to Mr Hudson, and we were formally introduced the first morning after you had left.'

'I see.'

'We felt so sorry for him,' Kate continued. 'He

was so enjoying Oxford, but felt it was his duty to come home to Worthing when his father died very suddenly of a heart attack. Mr Gregson is an only child.'

'Very commendable.'

'Yes, but he doesn't care for business. It was not the kind of future he had anticipated.'

'And what was that?'

'Mr Gregson is a poet. Several of his poems have been published.'

'Poems? Was he expecting to make a living out of it?'

'Well, not exactly, but with his allowance, he could have managed quite nicely. Only there was no allowance, not a penny piece, for either of them. It was a ghastly shock,' Kate explained, dramatically.

'What are they living on then?'

'Mr Gregson's salary, and an allowance from his maternal grandparents.'

'It surprises me that a young gentleman of such good standing confides his private affairs to comparative strangers.'

'I think he had to tell *someone*, Mother, and he knew we could be trusted.'

Lucy had taken up the story on his behalf. 'He feels so uncomfortable, so embarrassed. Doesn't he, Kate?'

'Why?'

'Because, like us, he was just installed, and Mr Hudson was not consulted. Everyone is suspicious, and we are most unpopular.'

'Your Grandpapa explained that you were to be treated like all the rest of the apprentices, and no favouritism.'

Kate shook her head. 'It makes no difference. We

are completely ignored, and so is Mr Gregson. Naturally we became friends. He has asked us to meet him at the bandstand tomorrow afternoon, and we have agreed.'

'Without my consent?'

'Mother, we are not children. We are in business all the week; and we are entitled to a little pleasure on Sunday.'

'Don't be impertinent, Kate! You are still minors, and as such you will be obedient to my wishes. It is out of the question, unchaperoned.'

'Then will you accompany us to the band, and we will introduce Mr Gregson? *Please*, Mother?'

'*Please*,' Lucy echoed.

Amelia looked from one to the other, and sighed for the days when her daughters had obeyed her without question.

'Very well,' she agreed, reluctantly.

Then Kate's arms were around her neck in a throttling hug. 'Thank you, Mother darling. I love you,' she declared, passionately.

'You love me when it suits you, child,' Amelia retorted with a twisted smile, and waited for some response from her youngest daughter. How different they were. Two completely different personalities.

'Thank you, Mother,' said Lucy, quietly.

The first impression of Basil Gregson on that Summer afternoon was favourable. He was strikingly like Jonathan Cartwright in appearance, but the shy manner and diffident smile were not Jonathan's. He had left his mother sitting in the garden with a book, feeling rather sorry for herself at Basil's neglect. In consequence, he was feeling a little guilty. Like the two girls, however, he considered he had earned the right to a little pleasure after that interminable week at the store.

Surprised to see Mrs Brent with her daughters – having no sister, and no previous experience with the opposite sex, he was not aware of the importance of a chaperone. The formalities having been observed, Amelia led the way to their accustomed places, sat down in a deck chair, and left the young ones to arrange themselves accordingly. Soon they were happily settled, with Mr Gregson sitting between the girls, and Kate chattering. The arrival of the bandmaster would stop all the chattering.

Amelia lost herself, as always, in memories of those earlier years with Thomas beside her, and their six girls spread out along the row of deck chairs. Such happy days. Now her two youngest daughters had grown up, and Kate had surprised her with this pre-arranged rendezvous with young Gregson. But it was not the first time that Kate had persuaded Lucy, and her friend Rose, to a rendezvous on the promenade when all three were on holiday from the Academy. During the Summer vacation, the undergraduates from Oxford and Cambridge flocked to the seaside to enjoy the delights of bathing and flirting with all the pretty girls. When the girls had tired of the young men in boaters and blazers, there had been Jonathan and his friends in their smart uniforms from Sandhurst.

When Ellen became engaged to Jonathan, there was no need for secrecy, and Grace acted as chaperone. Grace always had a good influence on these lively subalterns, who could suggest outrageous plans. Grace was so ladylike.

Seeing the mischief in Kate's sparkling eyes, Amelia could forecast an early defeat for Mr

Gregson, if he should have decided to remain a bachelor. Kate could be quite irresistible, and she was looking particularly attractive today, in a fashionable hat she had purchased at a discount only yesterday. She had spent most of her first week's wages on the hat, and hadn't enough left to pay the few shillings agreed upon for her board and lodging.

Lucy had not been tempted to spend more than a shilling on ribbons for her two little nieces. In her schoolgirl boater and 'Sunday-best' dress she had worn at the Academy, Lucy looked very young and childish, while her sister, Kate, only two years her senior, had quite an air of sophistication. Ellen had been bullied into re-styling the Sunday best of Academy days. With flounces of a contrasting colour, adorned with tiny bows of ribbon at hem and sleeves, and a necklace of jade beads borrowed from Ellen, Kate was in her true element – and Mr Gregson was enchanted.

'Would you care to take tea with us, Mr Gregson?' Amelia asked graciously, when the National Anthem had been played and they were ready to leave.

'Thank you, Ma'am. I should be delighted,' he answered, without a second's hesitation. It was only when Amelia took his proferred arm, leaving the girls to walk together, that Basil remembered his mother. She knew he was meeting the two Misses Brent, for he had made no secret of the *rendezvous*, but to be left to eat her Sunday tea alone would be bitterly resented. The little maidservant she was training was allowed to go home on Sunday afternoons. A child of thirteen, she missed her family. And her mistress missed the services of her elderly Cook and houseparlourmaid. She could no longer afford their wages. The meal would be laid ready in the drawing-room.

220

She had only to brew the tea. But she felt vexed at her son's neglect.

When he came home, he would find her prostrate on the couch with one of her severe headaches. It was her only weapon, as a wife and mother. Men were so selfish, and had to be reminded of their duty. Basil should be grateful for the appointment that had cost her dearly in loss of dignity, for Thomas Brent had treated her with cool condescension. Now Basil was complaining of an unfriendly atmosphere. It was all very upsetting. For the next two hours or so Basil would be enjoying the company of a family of girls, including two very small girls.

Prue had squealed 'Papa!' as soon as he stepped inside the gate, and flung her arms about his legs. He lifted her up and told her, gently, 'I am not your Papa.'

She stroked his face, while her eyes brimmed with tears. 'Papa gone to Heaven. Live wiv Jesus,' she said, forlornly.

He still held her, and carried her into the house. Ellen was also startled by the likeness to Jonathan, but soon realized it was only superficial.

When they sat down to tea, Prue insisted that he take the chair between the two high chairs, normally reserved for Rose. Kate and Lucy, on the opposite side of the table, would have liked to receive a little more of his attention, but he was too busy, spreading strawberry jam on buttered scones, and wiping sticky fingers on his own clean handkerchief. Kate was pretending to be amused by the precocious Prue, but her thoughts were ugly. Children were a nuisance. It was never too early to remind them that 'children should be seen and not heard' at meal times. Why didn't Ellen correct them? If this was a foretaste of future

Sunday tea-parties, Kate decided she would have to take the initiative in planning to meet Mr Gregson on Wednesday afternoons as well as on Sundays. Perhaps they could hire a bathing machine. That would be daring and tremendous fun. And fun she must have if she had to endure that horrid Miss Bennet and her bossiness. To be subjected to so many rules and regulations when she thought she was finished with discipline, after leaving the Academy, was quite intolerable.

When tea was finished, they left Norah and Bertha to clear the table, take everything back to the basement kitchen, and wash up.

'Should we offer to help, Kate?' Lucy whispered.

'Don't suggest it, or they will expect it every time,' Kate whispered back, under cover of the confusion in getting the children out of their high chairs.

Sunday evening, after tea, was the only time they were allowed into the drawing-room, and Amelia played simple hymns for their benefit. They sat on Mr Gregson's knees, and were very good until it was time for bed, when they had to be dragged away, and he promised to say good night when they were in bed.

'Such a fuss and pother!' Kate whispered, when they were led away with Ellen and Rose in attendance.

'They don't often have a man to make a fuss of them,' said Lucy, who was so fond of her very young nieces, and inclined to spoil them.

'Neither do we!' hissed Kate, impatiently.

Now Amelia had claimed his attention, to turn the scores of her favourite Chopin preludes. Kate sighed. It was so boring, and not a bit what she had anticipated. Under the circumstances, it could hardly have been any different, but Kate was feeling neglected.

She knew she was looking her best today, and he had admired her new hat, but it was not enough. She couldn't bear to share anything as a child, and hadn't changed much. Now she would have to share him with Lucy, and she wanted him for herself. 'Two's company, three's a crowd' was an absolute fact. She couldn't bear it if he liked Lucy best. It would be so humiliating, for Lucy was such a MOUSE. She had no conversation, and had barely said a word all afternoon. Shy girls like Lucy had been compelled at school to choose a subject and talk on it for five minutes, but it hadn't made any difference. '*Somebody* has to listen when others want to talk,' Lucy had argued. She could be right, of course.

Kate sighed, and fiddled with the little bows on her dress. She wondered if Mr Gregson had noticed her figure. She was proud of her tiny waist and thrusting breasts. Without her clothes she was really beautiful. Now that she hadn't to share a room, she could admire her reflection in the mirror without some stupid girl bursting in and pretending to swoon with shock! Of course she was vain, and she didn't care two hoots what they said about her. She loved scent and jewellery, but neither could be worn by the slaves of Thomas Brent & Son.

Because her thoughts were so often reflecting on the opposite sex, she would dream that she was being caressed by a passionate lover, or that she was married, and discovering the secrets of the marriage bed of which she was so ignorant. Once she dreamed she was Cleopatra, and her lover was Mark Anthony! Any handsome man, dark or fair, could be made to fit the role. Mr Gregson, for instance?

On the following Wednesday afternoon, equipped with bathing costumes, rubber caps and towels, the two girls made their way to their beach. Mr Gregson had already booked a bathing machine, and paid the charge. He was sitting on the steps, looking very pleased with himself, dressed in white flannels, a college blazer and boater.

If only there had been two Mr Gregsons, Kate was thinking, as he sprang to his feet, doffed his hat, and smiled disarmingly. He was rather a darling, and it was going to be fun for Kate, but not for Lucy. She hadn't been at all keen on the plan.

'The tide is just right for a swim,' he told them.

'But I don't swim,' Lucy shivered, and cast a fearful glance at the vast expanse of water.

'Neither do I, but I should love to learn,' said Kate.

'Then I will teach you,' he said.

And Kate was delighted.

'I will sit here and keep guard on the door,' he told them, as they went inside.

It smelled of damp bodies and damp towels, and Lucy was reluctant to take off her clothes. They were not familiar with the beach and the sea, since Amelia had not cared to sit in a deck chair and watch their frolics when they were small, and had not trusted them to the nursemaid. Amelia liked her comfort, and a deck chair on the promenade, listening to the band, was more to her taste.

The bathing costumes and caps had been purchased at the store on a credit card, to be paid for at the end of the month. The system had been introduced by Thomas Brent Junior, and Mr Gregson had informed the girls. Kate would find herself in trouble later for it was so deceptively easy, in theory, but not to be recommended for spend-thrifts – like Kate. Lucy had hoped to escape the bathing by having no costume to wear, but even Kate could not defy all the conventions by bathing alone with Mr Gregson, so she had purchased two costumes and two caps, rather ugly mob caps that covered all their hair. The black costumes covered their slender bodies, and were fastened with frilled elastic below the knees. They were hardly recognizable as the two pretty girls who had entered the machine, and were very conscious of their odd appearance as they stood, giggling, in the doorway.

'I'll be with you in five minutes,' said Mr Gregson, hiding his amusement as he disappeared into the bathing machine. When he reappeared, he, too, was also revealed as a different being, in a black costume draping his long, lean body. Feeling conspicuous, he ran down the steps and dived head first into the incoming tide. He was a strong swimmer, and he left the girls gasping with admiration at the water's edge. He was quickly back, however, with plastered hair and glowing face.

Reaching out a hand to Kate, he grinned boyishly. The wet costume clung to his body, and two pairs of startled eyes gazed in horrified fascination at the ugly shape of the male organ.

Flushed with embarrassment he dropped his hand and turned away, but Kate called after him, 'Wait! Please wait. You promised to teach me to swim.'

'So I did,' he said, and seemed to recover his composure. Taking her hand, he waded with her out into deep water, and Lucy watched from the water's edge. Kate was so fearless. If only she had a small measure of her confidence, life would be so much simpler. Every single day she suffered agonies of shyness in the Children's Wear Department, where she had not yet experienced the trauma of actually serving a customer. Now that her bosom friend was engaged with the children, they met only for breakfast and supper, and both were so tired at the end of the day, they dropped off to sleep as soon as their heads touched the pillows.

A short distance away, Kate was lying on her stomach, her legs and arms flaying the water, and her chin supported by Mr Gregson.

Still shivering as the water lapped over her buttocks, Lucy's thoughts were chaotic. Nakedness was something to be avoided, and even to undress in front of Kate had been embarrassing. Sharing a bedroom with Rose presented no problems to their girlish modesty, for they pulled on their drawers under the folds of voluminous nightgowns, and pulled them off the same way. Acting as chaperone to Kate on the Summer vacations had not prepared them for serious attachments. It had all been very light-hearted and frivolous. Now Rose had found security and happiness with Ellen and the children, and would not need a husband. For Lucy, however, the sudden plunge into the adult world of Thomas Brent & Son had been quite frightening. And now her emotions had been disturbed by something that seemed so crude and ugly that her first tender thoughts of love had been disturbed. In his company, her heart fluttered like a trapped bird.

But it was Kate who walked close beside him on the pavement every evening as he escorted them home, and Kate who laughed and chatted with such engaging frankness. Now it was Kate lying on the water, and their two bodies in the clinging costumes would not hide, but reveal, the shapes of a man and a woman. A small twinge of envy was quickly dispelled. Kate had always taken what she wanted, even as a small child, and she would continue to do so. If she had wanted Rose for a friend, she would have lured her away, but Rose was not her kind, so she was left alone.

Scrambling to her feet, she ran back up the steps, went inside, and closed the door. When Kate joined her some ten minutes later, Lucy was fully dressed and ready with an ultimatum.

'I don't like it, Kate, and I am not coming here again.'

Kate snatched off the ugly mob cap and shook out her hair.

'Don't be so mean, Lucy. You know I couldn't come here alone. Hand me that towel, and turn your back if you do not care to see your own sister stark naked.' She stepped out of the wet costume, and stood there, admiring her breasts and pink nipples. 'Pretty, aren't they, Lucy? Mr Gregson thinks so!' she giggled. 'You're blushing, Luce. I suppose I should be the one to blush, but then I see nothing to be ashamed of. And it may surprise you to know that Bertha and Norah are not ashamed of their nakedness. I had a headache last night, and went into their room to borrow the stick of frozen eau-de-cologne to rub on my forehead, and there they were – starkers! – in a loving embrace. "Get out! How dare you come in here without knocking," Bertha hissed. I thought she would have a fit, but Norah calmed her. I didn't get the eau-de-cologne, and as soon as I was outside the door, I heard the key turn in the lock. I had forgotten what I was doing there, I was so flabbergasted. I mean to say, would you believe it of Bertha, the sourpuss? Wonder if Mother knows they behave that way when they are alone together? I bet you sixpence Bertha will be as sweet as pie to me now in case I should tell on her. It would serve her right if

227

I did, but I shall keep her on tenterhooks. Can you understand it, Luce? For I can't. What pleasure could you get from showing your naked body to another woman?'

'It's – it's indecent.' Now Lucy was blushing for Bertha and Norah, but Kate was more concerned with her own affairs.

'You didn't mean what you said about not coming here, did you, darling?' she pleaded, humbly.

'*If* I come, I shall not get undressed or go in the water. I shall sit on the steps and watch.'

'So you shall, my pet. And you won't tell, promise?'

'I promise not to tell.'

Kate sighed ecstatically. 'It was absolutely divine, Luce, especially when he floated me on my back, and smiled down at me. He has the most devastating smile, hasn't he? And what do you think he said? "You are very beautiful, Miss Brent." Wasn't that sweet of him when I knew I was looking positively hideous in that ugly cap? But then I realized he was not looking at my face but this.' She smiled at the memory, and patted her breasts with the towel.

'Do get dressed, Kate. Mr Gregson will be waiting to come in,' Lucy urged.

'Shall I invite him in? What a lark! Don't look so alarmed, my darling little prude – I am only teasing' – and she flung on her clothes, opened the door, and ran to meet him with his big bath towel.

Lucy followed her down the steps, and averted her eyes as he hurried inside. The two girls were seated on the breakwater when he came out, his damp hair fitting his head like a little golden cap. Leaning on the breakwater, he addressed Lucy.

'I fear this has been a very dull afternoon for you,

228

Miss Lucy. Will you permit me to make amends by offering you tea at Kong's? They make delicious chocolate éclairs. I often took Mother there in the vac.'

'That would be absolutely divine, wouldn't it, darling?' Kate enthused.

Lucy raised her eyes and met his tender glance. He had called her 'Miss Lucy', not 'Miss Brent'. Had Kate noticed?

'Thank you, Mr Gregson,' she answered shyly. When he helped them down from the breakwater and squeezed her hand, she told herself, 'He *does* like me a little.'

He carried all the towels and wet costumes in a roll under his arm, and swaggered with self-importance, escorting two pretty girls into Kong's. When he had pulled out their chairs and they had seated themselves, he pushed the damp bundle under his own chair and greeted the hovering waitress politely.

'What would you like, Sir? Crumpets? Scones? Buttered toast?' she asked, surprised to see him with two of the Brent girls. In all the years she had served him since he was a little lad at preparatory school, he had always been accompanied by his mother.

The girls decided on crumpets and the chocolate éclairs. Looking about the crowded room, Kate recognized the Manageress of Millinery with an elderly gentleman who seemed very attentive. She was old, of course. She must be thirty-five or possibly forty? Under the buzz of conversation and the rattle of teacups, she whispered. 'Don't look now. The corner table behind the palms.'

After a moment, Mr Gregson glanced in their direction. 'Could be her Papa?' he suggested, blandly. He was not interested, and so completely absorbed in his young companions. He couldn't make up his mind. In Kate's company, on that first swimming lesson, he had been ready to fall in love. Then Lucy was there, with her quiet charm and shy smile. But he didn't have to decide, not yet. He would enjoy the company of both. It would boost his morale to be seen escorting the grand-daughters of his employer. They were well known in the town. So many people remembered the happy young couple, with their six daughters, strolling on the promenade and listening to the military band on Summer Sunday afternoons. In the Winter, they would walk briskly, the girls muffled in warm capes, knitted caps and mittens, and their mother in furs. Now here they were, grown up young ladies taking tea at Kong's.

Kate was pouring tea and chatting brightly. Lucy listened, and could think of nothing to say that would interest Mr Gregson. But it was enough to meet his glance and touch his hand, over the dish of crumpets and the plate of éclairs. The merest touch of his long fingers made her tremble. Was he aware of causing such a tumult of emotion in her fluttering heart?

'We must do this again, Miss Lucy, mustn't we?' he was asking.

She nodded, starry-eyed.

He escorted them home, and they went in the back entrance. The costumes and towels would dry on the line in the yard. Jackie barked furiously at the intruder, but Lucy soothed him. Mr Gregson was pushed outside by a giggling Kate, and the door closed on his laughing face.

Rose had taken the two little girls to the Vicarage, only a few days before Ellen's son was born. Grandmama Cartwright had been suffering from a nervous

230

breakdown since her adored Jonathan had been killed in India, and she kept to her rooms. The Vicar was kind, but rather absent-minded. So Rose found herself, for the first time, in complete charge of the children in the old nursery suite at the top of the house. Cook sent up their meals, and they used the back stairs.

Prue's tears and tantrums were not unexpected, since she had never been separated from her mother, but Rose was gentle, and she soon forgot to ask 'When are we going home?'

As for Bella, she could live anywhere if 'Woz' was there. Instead of going to the park with the doll's bassinet and Prue's hoop, they went to the beach with buckets and spades, and Rose took off their shoes and socks, and tucked their frocks in their drawers. She helped them to make sand pies, and they paddled in the little waves that were lapping the water's edge.

When it was time to go home, Prue cried.

'But you want to see your baby brother, don't you? He is two weeks old already, and he hasn't seen his sisters,' said Rose.

'Has he got a name?' Prue was only mildly curious. She liked living at the Vicarage with Rose and Bella.

'His name is Thomas,' said Rose.

'Why?'

'Because his grandpapa and his great-grandpapa were called Thomas.'

'Why?'

'Questions! Questions!' Rose chuckled. Soon it would be Bella asking 'Why?' Then it would be Thomas. This was her life, with the family at The Haven.

So they went home, and climbed all the stairs to the top floor where their radiant mother lay back on her pillows, nursing her baby son.

'Well, my darlings, here he is at last. Come and kiss your little brother,' she invited, her dark eyes tender with love.

Prue backed away and clung to Rose. 'Take him away!' she sobbed. 'No want boy baba.'

Ellen's eyes clouded with pain and disappointment. Prue was jealous.

Bella was lifted up to plant a wet kiss on the baby's cheek. He opened his eyes, and she found the words. 'Boy baba.'

'Put him back in his crib, please Rose,' said Ellen, sadly, and Rose took him in her arms and laid him down. She thought she had never seen a more perfect child.

'Come to Mama, my darling,' Ellen coaxed.

Prue climbed on the bed, sobbing hysterically, but choked on a sob when she found the swelling breast still damp from the baby's mouth. Ellen held her breath. Prue was suckling, her teeth sharp on the soft flesh. It was quickly over, and her breasts were covered in the loose wrap.

A pair of dark eyes looked up at her, flooded with tears, and a small voice pleaded, 'Love Prue best, Mama. Love Prue best.'

PART 3

7

'Edward needs a holiday,' said Jane.

'You *both* need a holiday,' Nell insisted. Under her
Salvation Army bonnet, her grey eyes shone with
kindliness on this murky day of early Autumn. They
were good friends, and Nell was one of the few
people that Edward would see since he had been dis-
charged from hospital. With a black shade over one
eye – he had lost the sight of that eye – and a livid
scar on his cheek, he was acutely sensitive to his
disfigurement.

Edward had always suffered from bouts of depression when only Jane was capable of persuading him
he was not a failure, that he was loved and respected.
As a young curate he had suffered agonies of self-
doubt under the spiritual guidance of a learned but
unsympathetic pastor. An unhappy childhood had
been dominated by a dictatorial parent who had sent
him away to boarding school 'to make a man of him'
at the age of six. Jane knew his sad history, and her
heart had ached for the shy young curate she had first
met when teaching the Sunday School children. His
stammer had been such a handicap in his own class
of small boys; children are cruel, and Edward was a
butt to be tormented. From that Summer day of the
Sunday School outing to the old mill, when Jane had
sat beside the young curate in the crowded wagonette, and held his hand and watched the twitching

muscles on his lean, sensitive face, she was his willing, devoted slave. Without Jane, it was doubtful whether he would have found the confidence to take over the Mission in the East End. Yet he was not lacking courage, for he did not hesitate to rescue an illtreated wife from a brutal husband, or to interfere in a drunken brawl. It was a desperate kind of courage that Jane deplored. Would he have rushed into the fray at the public house if she had been there that evening? Because she had missed her train and had had to wait an hour for the next, she had been too late to prevent this ghastly accident. Now he was like a child, depending on her for everything, and she was so tired.

So she looked at Nell across the kitchen table, poured more tea, and echoed, 'We both need a holiday.' Then she shook her head. 'It's quite impossible, Nell.'

'Nobody is indispensable, Jane. If I could get permission to stay here for a couple of weeks while you are away, Aggie and Bill would support me, wouldn't they? And I wouldn't be too proud to ask for a little help with the washing up. What do you say, Edward? Would you trust me to keep the banner flying in your absence?'

His crooked smile was the first she had seen since he left hospital. 'Your b-banner and ours are as one, my dear Nell, b-because we serve the s-same God,' he answered quietly, and Jane leaned over to kiss his scarred cheek.

'Where shall we go, darling?' she asked, eagerly.

'Not to The Haven. I sh-should frighten the ch-children,' he said.

'There is plenty of room at the Vicarage. Perhaps they would allow us to use the nursery suite that Ellen borrowed last month for Rose and the children? We could offer to pay.'

'I wou-wouldn't like to ask.'

'I don't mind asking.'

'Wou-wouldn't it seem an impertinence? I w-was only the humble cu-curate, dear.'

'And a very conscientious curate you were, too! The Reverend imposed on you.' Jane was fierce in condemnation of treatment she considered had taken unfair advantage long before they were married.

Nell was amused, as always, by the undefeated spirit of this small, brave woman, not more than five feet tall, and afraid of nothing, unless it were rats and spiders. Even the determined step of a Salvation Army lassie had been known to falter in the presence of a rat or spider! 'I must go,' she said. 'Let me know what has been decided. In the meantime, I will ask the Major's permission to deputize in your absence.' She kissed them both and went her way, lifting her long black skirts off the dirty pavement, to reveal a pair of shining button boots. The familiar bonnet would soon meet up with another, for they worked in pairs like nuns. It was safer.

So the holiday was arranged, and they were on their way the following week, with Edward still a little apprehensive at the liberty they had taken in asking such a favour of the Reverend. But that learned gentleman was surprisingly receptive, and they were welcomed with a hearty handshake. No mention was made of Edward's changed appearance. There was no sign of Mrs Cartwright, but they hadn't really expected to meet her.

'Step inside, my dear fellow,' he invited, 'and I will summon Cook to explain about the provisions she has provided for your use.'

237

When she appeared, in prompt response to the Master's summons, he bade them enjoy their vacation, and disappeared into his study. Cook bobbed a curtsey and they followed her upstairs. The big, rambling house that had once echoed to the shrill voices and scampering feet of three noisy boys, was silent and gloomy. Only the nursery suite still held the ghosts of children, and bright fires burned in the kitchen and the old nursery.

While Edward sank thankfully into the rocking chair, Jane went to inspect the larder, and gasped at the food that had been provided.

'The Reverend said as 'ow you would like to cook your own victuals, Madam. Martha will carry up the coals and fresh milk every day. You won't 'ave no trouble. There's plenty more where this lot came from. We keep a good table. The Reverend won't 'ave no skimping.'

'Skimping!' What would Aggie say to such extravagance? There were joints of meat, poultry, an assortment of cheeses, farm butter, baskets of vegetables and fruit, pickles, chutney, jam and marmalade, crusty home-baked bread, a fruit cake and an apple pie.

'We couldn't possibly eat all this, Cook. It's much too generous, and we couldn't waste it.' Jane wished she could bring her hungry lodgers from the Mission to share such a feast.

'If you'll excuse me saying so, Madam, but you both could do with a bit of feeding up, for you're that thin.'

Jane laughed. Compared to the buxom little figure beside her, she *was* a bit of a scarecrow, and Edward was like a beanpole.

'There won't be no waste. We feed the poor with

238

the left-overs. The Reverend won't 'ave anybody turned away empty-'anded. The children know where to come when they're 'ungry.'

'Hungry children in Worthing?'

'You'd be surprised, Madam. Some of them back streets is swarming. Cheap labour for them big 'otels on the promenade. They get stood off in the Winter. That's when we open up the soup kitchen. There now, shall I put the kettle on? You'll be wanting a nice cup of tea.'

'Thank you, Cook. You are very kind.'

'It's a pleasure, Madam.'

When she had bustled away, Jane pushed open the kitchen window and leaned out. She could smell the sea. Evening shadows were falling across the neglected garden, and a small Summerhouse was almost submerged in trailing vines. A blackbird sang ecstatically on the top branch of the tall elm tree. It was so peaceful.

'Shall we take a walk to the beach before breakfast, darling?' Jane suggested, handing Edward an early cup of tea the following morning.

'Su-such energy!' Edward stifled a yawn and reached for the eye shade.

'I just thought . . .' She hesitated. He was so acutely sensitive, she had to tread carefully.

'That we are unlikely to meet many people at this hour? You are ri-right, of co-course, my dear, bu-but then you always know wh-what is b-best for me, don't you?'

'I'm sorry, Edward. You must please yourself. Stay where you are till I come back. I shan't be long.' She was dressed and splashing her face in the cold water from the jug in a matter of seconds. She moved so quickly, was so assured, it made his own movements seem more slow and clumsy. He knew he had hurt her, but he let her go, and she left the room without another word, without a kiss. She always kissed him when she went out. He could hear her running down the uncarpeted back stairs. Then she was gone, and he wanted to call her back. 'I don't deserve her,' he thought, and a wave of depression swept over him.

Hurrying down one of the side streets that led to the sea, Jane was choked with tears. She tried so hard to please him – too hard, perhaps. Was she stifling him with such a protective love? It was very difficult to know what he wanted, for he was so moody and unpredictable. 'Time would heal,' they had told her in the hospital, but the sight was gone from that eye, and the age of miracles was past. No Jesus of Nazareth walked the streets of London's East End. Being a Christian had not prepared her for this acute loneliness of spirit. Was her faith as strong now that it had been so cruelly tested as before the accident? she asked herself. She had always taken the initiative with Edward because she was the stronger character. That was a reality she had accepted when they were married. He leaned on her, he drained her dry, but what else could she do? Her heart ached for him. Edward was her child now – more child than husband.

It was good to walk on the wet sands, carrying her shoes and stockings. The beach was deserted but for an old woman feeding the gulls. The wind tore at her skirts. It would be too bracing for Edward, but she would do this every morning and leave him in bed. Tomorrow she would not feel hurt. It was foolish to be so sensitive to his remarks. Her poor darling! He was probably weeping with self-pity at this very moment. She would take him in her arms and comfort him. He was her life. She turned and hurried back to The Vicarage.

'Shall you mind, Edward, if I leave you for a couple of hours or so, this afternoon? I would like to see my new nephew. Mother seems to think he is the most wonderful child who ever lived. But it's natural, isn't it, in a family of girls? I wish you could come with me, but I'm a little afraid of Prue's reaction. She is such a nervous child.'

'She w-would probably have one of her scr-screaming f-fits. No, you go. I w-will amuse myself w-with Mr Dickens's *David Copperfield*.'

'But you like me to read to you?'

'My d-dear girl, the t-time has come to read to myself. You've b-been spoiling me.'

'It won't strain your good eye?'

'Don't f-fuss, Jane.'

'Sorry.' She smiled at his peevishness and changed the subject.

The morning had slipped away most peacefully. She had cooked the chicken, with roast potatoes, baked onions and mushrooms. The apple pie was delicious, and Cook had sent up fresh cream with the milk. They had played cribbage and dominoes, two of the games that Jane had discovered in a drawer. In a sprawling, childish hand on the box of dominoes, Jonathan had written, 'This is the property of Jonathan Cartwright.'

'That was t-typical of Jonathan. He was a very p-possessive little b-boy,' Edward remembered. 'Couldn't b-bear to share anything. Didn't s-seem to change much as an adult.'

'You never liked him, did you, darling?'

'No.'

241

'His poor mother was completely shattered by his death. It's so sad. She seems to have forgotten her other sons.'

When Jane had washed the dishes, she left Edward with *David Copperfield*, and hurried along to The Haven. The back gate was unlocked, and Jackie's tail was soon wagging when he recognized her voice. He hadn't forgotten that she took him for walks, once-upon-a-time. A dog has a long memory.

When she had petted him, she greeted Maggie, vigorously scrubbing the back steps.

'Still scrubbing, Maggie?' she asked.

'It's me job, ain't it, Miss Jane?' she answered, cheerfully. 'I'm lucky to 'ave me 'ealth and strength. Your poor Mr Edward. It don't bear thinking about, do it? They must be savages up the East End.'

'Not savages, Maggie. It's the only kind of life they know. They were born to it.'

'You ought never to 'ave gorn there in the first place, Miss Jane.'

'A woman goes where her husband goes, Maggie.'

'Like poor Miss Ellen. Now they really was savages, for they killed that nice young hofficer what was only doing 'is duty. It's sad that 'e never lived to see little Thomas, for 'e's a proper little duck.'

Bertha put a stop to the chatter on the back steps when she opened the kitchen window and called, meaningly, 'There's a cup of tea waiting, Maggie, when you have finished the steps.'

'I don't take no notice, Miss Jane. Miss Bertha's bark is worse than 'er bite,' she confided.

They were making blackberry-and-apple jam in the kitchen. It was a homely smell that brought back memories of Jane's own busy years in this same kitchen, when she had stepped straight from the schoolroom into Cook's long white apron. Norah and Bertha had gathered the blackberries in Goring woods. With a glut of apples this year, windfalls could be picked up in any orchard.

'You will find Mother in the drawing-room. She wants to see you before you go upstairs,' said Bertha, carefully scooping hot jam into the big jars that Jane remembered from early childhood.

Mother was playing *The Moonlight Sonata*, and the strains seemed to float in the air as she climbed the basement stairs. It was one of her favourites, and only Grace had inherited that delicate touch on the keys. They all had to learn. It was one of the compulsory subjects for well-bred young ladies, but Jane could only remember the slogging obligation of that half-hour daily practice on the schoolroom piano. Nobody would dream of interrupting Mother when she was playing. It was one of the laws of the Medes and Persians, and there were quite a number to be remembered by a family of six girls graduating from nursery to schoolroom before they were considered fit candidates for the drawing-room.

Hesitating now in the dark recess at the top of the basement stairs, Jane heard the front door opening, and Rose came in with the two little girls.

'Grandmama play,' said Prue, in a loud whisper, but she was quickly hushed, and they climbed the stairs in single file, with Bella in the middle. It was a long, slow process, but Rose did not hurry them.

When the final notes had died away, Jane tapped on the drawing-room door. She was a visitor now in this house, and waited to be invited in by a mother to whom all the courtesies were strictly paid, and of whom no liberties were taken.

Seated at the piano, her slight figure and proud

little head had not changed with the years. While her elder daughters had been caught up in tragedy and an illness that could still prove fatal, and Jane was still coping with a husband whose nerves were shattered by his disfigurement, Amelia seemed strangely detached from their lives. When Jane had kissed her cheek, she asked, 'You haven't brought Edward?'

And Jane answered dutifully, 'No, Mother. He would not take the risk of frightening the children.'

'Prudence might find a black eye shade frightening. Bella would probably want to see what was behind it. She is full of curiosity.'

'They have just come in. Rose seems to manage them very well. They went straight upstairs.'

'Their table manners have vastly improved.'

'And the baby?'

Amelia's expression softened. 'Adorable. Already showing signs of strong will. If he is kept waiting when he is hungry, we hear his roaring all over the house! And why not? He knows his importance in this house. So does Prudence. Now Ellen has to cope with jealousy.'

'Jealous? Of Thomas?'

'Jealous of Thomas,' Amelia echoed, disapprovingly. 'That child reminds me so much of Kate at that age. She needs a firm hand. If Ellen continues to indulge her, then Prudence will grow up to be a most objectionable young woman. The spoiling was started in India, of course. Native servants have a reputation for spoiling English children. Arabella was too young to be influenced, she adores Thomas. Are they feeding you properly at The Vicarage?' Amelia could always switch her mind so quickly from one subject to another.

'We are fed like fighting cocks,' Jane answered, truthfully.

'The Vicar called one afternoon to see his grandson. He asked about the christening. It has been arranged for Sunday week. Poor man. I thought he would break down when he took Thomas in his arms. "It could be Jonathan. The likeness is quite remarkable," he said. I suggested that Mrs Cartwright should see him, but apparently she has not been told of his birth, as he thought it was inadvisable. It seems so sad. In my opinion, it is just what she needs. Who could resist an innocent little child?' she sighed, and asked, 'Are you staying to tea?'

'No, thank you, Mother. I must get back to Edward. I left him reading Mr Dickens's *David Copperfield*.'

'Give him my love.'

'I will.'

Before the door had closed on her daughter, Amelia had already turned back to the keyboard, and Jane climbed the stairs to the strains of Brahms' *Lullaby*.

Amelia's thoughts were back with the infant Thomas – that 'boy baba' whose earlier arrival could have changed the lives of his parents and sisters. The native servants would say it was the Will of Allah, but Ellen still questioned a God who allowed her to conceive Bella before Thomas. If Jonathan had not been disappointed for the second time, he would be alive today.

They heard her coming, and were grouped on the top landing – the little family who would never be complete or united because of jealousy. Jonathan had left a bitter legacy to his eldest daughter, that threatened to disrupt another generation.

But Jane had been warned, and it was Prue she cuddled first, not Thomas. When the child's arms clasped her neck in a throttling hug, and a small voice whispered in her ear, 'Love Prue best, Auntie Chane,' she could understand Ellen's indulgence. Then it was Bella's turn. Finally, when the two little girls had finished their hugging and kissing, Ellen laid the baby in her arms, and she looked down on a cherubic boy-child, who gazed back at her with Jonathan's blue eyes, and waved a chubby fist. The sweet baby smell was not for her, and this was not her world. She kissed the damp cap of golden hair, and handed him back to Ellen, too choked to speak. Then she waved goodbye, and hurried back to Edward – her man-child. Her feet clattered on the bare stairs, and she called out, cheerfully, 'Edward! I'm back!'

There was no answer, and she stood in the open doorway, panting for breath, staring into the empty room. The fireguard had been carefully placed in front of the fire, Mr Dickens's *David Copperfield* had been dropped on the floor beside the armchair. Panic seized her. Where had he gone? He had hardly dared to take a step without her since he came out of hospital. Would he be in the Summerhouse?

She turned and ran back down the stairs, across the garden, into the tangled shrubbery. The Summerhouse was empty, damp and chilly. She shivered. Where does one start searching for a missing husband? she asked herself, as she climbed the stairs for the second time.

Picking up the book, she turned the pages, and found the bookmark had not been removed. So he hadn't intended to read. What had happened to change his mind? Now she imagined all kinds of horrors – he had been knocked down in the street and was lying unconscious in a hospital bed – he had gone for a swim – but he couldn't swim!

She stood there, staring at the fireguard. It was so unlike him. She was the one to remember such mundane necessities as fireguards. She was the practical one. Then why was her mind a blank, and why was she crying?

It seemed an eternity that she stood there, but it could have been only a few minutes. Footsteps clattered on the stairs, but when he stood in the doorway, she did not move towards him. He was carrying several packages, and he looked very pleased with himself.

'W-what's the m-matter? W-why are you crying?' he demanded, authoritatively.

'I thought – I thought – Where have you *been*?' she wailed.

'Shopping,' he said.

'*Shopping*?' But he never went shopping. She always did the shopping in the market. It was a woman's job. She shook her head. Nothing made sense, and she did not recognize this new independent husband.

'Sit d-down, my dear. You l-look as if you have seen a ghost.' He pushed her into a chair.

'I have seen a ghost!' She was laughing and crying, a weak, silly woman, not at all practical.

He dropped his packages on the floor, sat on the arm of the chair, and hugged her shoulders. 'W-what you n-need is a nice c-cup of tea,' he decided, gallantly – and went to the kitchen to put on the kettle. The tea was weak and very sweet. She liked it strong, unsweetened. But it tasted like nectar because it was only the second cup of tea Edward had made. The first had been equally surprising. She had had a tooth pulled, and was feeling faint. It was a long time ago. They had been married for only a week!

It was bliss to lean against his shoulder. She had not realized how near she was to breaking point until she found him gone. Holding Ellen's baby in her arms had been an emotional moment – a climax to weeks of emotional strain and anxiety. She knew that something had happened in her short absence, but she would not question him. He would tell her in his own way, in his own time.

After a few moments, he dropped his arm from her shoulders, picked up one of the packages, and laid it in her lap. 'A present for me? But it's not my birthday?' Edward always had to be reminded about birthdays. Men were not expected to remember.

'A p-peace offering,' he said.

'Have we been fighting?'

'I w-was unkind.'

'Darling, you didn't mean it.' She was touched by his confession. It was not easy to apologize. But this was so altogether unexpected, and so *unlike* Edward.

Her hands trembled as she unwrapped the paper – Thomas Brent & Son. 'You went *there*?'

He nodded.

'A *blouse*! Darling, it's beautiful. What a lovely surprise. And my favourite colour.' She kissed his scarred cheek.

'Kate ch-chose it. I asked to s-see her and L-Lucy.'

'That was brave of you.'

'Not really. A p-polite young man went to f-fetch them. I was s-seated at the counter. Kate came b-bounding in, all airs and gr-graces. That awful uniform! Isn't she p-pretty? She g-gave me a kiss and told m-me I looked very handsome w-with the eye-shade. Then she introduced the young m-man as her

248

beau! P-poor fellow, he was quite embarrassed. But he soon r-recovered and t-told me he had the honour to sh-share the affection of the two Misses Brent! Then L-Lucy appeared, rather sh-shy, and we sh-shook hands. I th-think I like Lucy best. The blouses were spread all over the c-counter. Everyone was st-staring at us, and the g-girls had to report back to their d-departments.'

It was a long and agonizingly slow story, but Jane listened patiently. It was not often that Edward was so expansive. The nervous stammer was such a handicap.

When he told her he had invited the girls to tea, with the nice Mr Gregson, she was delighted. 'I will ask Cook to make something special,' she told him.

Then he showed her the presents he had bought – for Nell, an embroidered tablecloth from the Linen Department, a beer mug for Bill, and a cup and saucer for Aggie, from a gift shop in the Arcade, both inscribed 'A PRESENT FROM WORTHING'.

Nell had promised to keep in touch. There would probably be a letter tomorrow. The Mission and the East End seemed to be in another world, and they sat there together, in quiet contentment, staring into the fire.

It was Edward who had removed the fireguard and shovelled on more coal, and Edward who made toast for their tea, kneeling on the rag-rug that the boys' old Nannie had made, all those years ago. Jane had intended to take presents back for Nell, Aggie and Bill, but Edward had forestalled her, and chosen so sensibly, she did not mention her own intentions. He wanted her to try on the blouse after tea, so that he could admire it, and she kept it on till bedtime, while they played their games of cribbage and dominoes.

From time to time he would ask if she was really pleased with it, and she would reassure him that she had never possessed such a beautiful blouse.

This need for reassurance was more like Edward, and when he sat waiting for his cocoa and biscuits at ten o'clock, and watched her bank up the fire, place the fireguard in position, turn out the lamp and light the candle, then she knew that her brief spell of spoiling was over!

The shopping expedition, however, had given him the confidence he needed to show himself in public again, and while she prepared a special tea for their visitors on Wednesday afternoon, he went off to the beach to sit on the steps of the bathing machine, watching Kate and Mr Gregson. The season was over, and the patient old mare would soon be drawing the machines to the top of the beach for the Winter months. Kate was showing off her figure in the clinging costume in a rather shocking manner, as she waded ashore, and Mr Gregson plunged into deeper water and was soon lost to view.

'Shall we leave them to walk back together?' Lucy suggested, and took Edward's arm. More than ever now, since the swimming lessons had started, she was aware of the attraction between the two. But Lucy was not a fighter, and she accepted defeat without a struggle; that was exactly what Kate had expected.

Walking back to The Vicarage with Edward, she appeared to be the same demure little sister-in-law he had known since he first became acquainted with the six sisters at The Haven. He could not know that she was suffering the heartache of first love, and that her small, safe world had become so alarming since she had left the Academy and been plunged into the jungle of Thomas Brent & Son. It had all happened so quickly. She had lost Rose to Ellen and the children, and she had met Mr Gregson. In her misery and loneliness, she would have found Edward a sympathetic companion. But she saw him as someone in need of sympathy, not providing it. Poor Edward.

Jane thought her youngest sister was looking pale and tired, and so much like Grace she feared for her health if she had to remain at the store. Lucy had always been frail. It seemed only yesterday she was being fitted for her new dresses at the Academy, and now she was a grown-up young lady.

'The fire looks cheerful, Jane,' she said. 'It was chilly on the beach today, though the sun was shining. They call it an Indian Summer, and Kate says the water is still warm, but she was shivering when she came out.'

'Can she swim?'

'Yes, but she pretends she is frightened, and she gives a little scream when Mr Gregson leaves hold of her.'

'And we both know Kate is frightened of nothing, don't we, Luce?'

'She told me she was only pretending, and made me promise not to tell Mr Gregson. As if I would!'

They went through to the bedroom, and she took off her hat, laid it carefully on the bed, and gazed at her reflection in the mirror. 'I wish I was pretty, like Kate,' she sighed, wistfully.

'You *are* pretty, dear. It's a different kind of prettiness, more genteel, like Grace.'

'But Grace is tall and dignified.'

'You are small and dainty, and your hair is the colour of ripe corn. What more do you want?'

'I want to be dark and glamorous and naughty, like Kate.'

'Silly pet. We don't want two Kates in this family. Look at me. Plain Jane and no nonsense.'

'I like your face, it's a happy face, and you have nice eyes.'

'Thank you.'

'Bertha is really plain, because she is so disagreeable.'

'Yes, I suppose so. The good looks are not fairly distributed in this family. Ellen is very attractive, with her tall figure and expressive dark eyes. Grace is most distinctive and ladylike. Then comes Bertha and me, the two plain ones, then Kate, who is really quite a beauty, and you, Lucy, like a fairy child.'

They giggled and hugged each other. It was like old times. Jane was wearing her new blouse with the cameo brooch, and Lucy was still wearing her cameo brooch. They were sentimental over these brooches. Kate had discarded hers some time ago.

They sat on the bed and talked – about Thomas and Amelia's absorbing interest in her first grandson, and about the relationship between Grace and Mr Courtney-Halliday. Wasn't it rather unusual for an employer to pay all the expenses of a private sanatorium in Switzerland? Was he in love with Grace?

'But he is married, Jane.' Lucy's innocent blue eyes questioned the right of a husband to love any other woman but his wife.

'It *does* happen,' her more worldly sister was not so shocked. And all the time Lucy was listening for Kate and Mr Gregson. They were taking their time.

When their footsteps clattered on the stairs, Lucy caught her breath. They were laughing as they burst into the room. Kate's laughing face was glowing with health and vitality, and her eyes sparkled with excitement, like a mischievous child. She snatched off her hat and tossed it to Edward, who caught it neatly and tossed it to Jane, who took it straight through to the bedroom and laid it on the bed beside Lucy's. The boaters were identical in shape and size, yet they looked different, even on the bed, and seemed to be stamped with the personalities of the two sisters.

Kate was lifting her skirts, dancing round the tea-table. Mr Gregson, who was carrying the roll of damp towels and costumes, stopped laughing when he saw Lucy hovering in the background. The meaningful glance they exchanged was intercepted by Jane, busily playing the hostess.

'Poor little Luce. She is no match for Kate,' Jane thought. Even her staid young husband had been captured, and they were capering round the table together. Kate was flirting deliberately to tease Lucy and Mr Gregson.

'Give me those damp towels and costumes, Mr Gregson. They will dry in the kitchen,' said Jane, and added, with a touch of bravado, 'Must we be quite so formal? This is not Thomas Brent & Son!'

'You may call me Basil, Madam!' he retorted, with a gallant little bow.

'And you may call me Jane,' she answered, bobbing a mock curtsey.

'And you may call me Kate!' her younger sister mimicked, still dancing Edward round the tea-table.

'And you, Miss Lucy?' Basil asked, with a gentleness he did not need for Kate.

Lucy nodded. Her cheeks flushed with the schoolgirl blush over which she had no control.

But Kate was not going to have it all her own way, Jane decided. She took Basil to the kitchen to collect the dish of muffins, keeping hot in the oven, and gave Lucy the job of brewing a pot of tea. Without the presence of Kate, Lucy forgot her shyness, and enquired politely after the health of Basil's mother.

'She is suffering from one of her bad headaches, and I was loath to leave her,' he answered. It was not strictly true. He was glad to get away from her nagging tongue. She was jealous of his friendship with the two Misses Brent, and fearful of the day when he would announce his betrothal to one or the other. The tears and headaches that had once proved such an effective deterrent to her son's pleasure had been used too often. Now she was left alone on Wednesday afternoons as well as Sundays. Every week he was growing more like his father – a selfish, ungrateful monster! she told herself on that Wednesday afternoon. And when her son had left the house, she rose from her couch and paced up and down in a state of great agitation. What had she done to deserve such unhappiness?

There was an atmosphere of bygone days in the old nursery, and the ghost of Nannie seemed to preside over the tea-table, that afternoon in early Autumn. The firelight flickered on the rocking horse, and Lucy could imagine the little boy who would grow up to manhood, unsuspecting of his cruel fate, riding that rocking horse with the same recklessness that he would ride the black stallion across the Punjab plain. The memory saddened her, but Kate had no time for ghosts. She lived every passing moment, and her daydreams revolved about her own person. She could not wait for things to happen naturally, but had to prod and poke to help them along.

'What shall we do on Wednesday afternoons, Basil, now the season is over?' she was asking, as Jane poured the tea and Edward handed round the dish of muffins. She had no hesitation in adopting his Christian name, and Basil answered her question with hardly a pause for consideration.

'There is always the theatre, Kate.'

'The theatre?'

'Yes, there is an excellent theatre in Brighton. Were you never taken there from the Academy?'

Kate giggled. 'Young ladies from the Academy, my dear sir, were taken to the Pavilion on an educational exercise. That is all we saw of Brighton.'

'Then I shall continue with your education and introduce you to the theatre. You will enjoy it, Kate – and you too, Lucy.'

'Should I? Would Mother allow it? She is inclined to be a little old-fashioned.'

'I will approach her with the proposition on Sunday afternoon, if I am still being invited to take tea with the family?'

'Of course. Mother quite approves of you!' said Kate, saucily.

'And you mustn't disappoint Prue,' Lucy reminded him.

'Tell us about the theatre,' Kate demanded. 'I can hardly wait to sample it. Mother has never encouraged us in any kind of public entertainment. We always had to entertain ourselves on Winter evenings. Until we attended the Academy, we had not even seen a school play, or charades, because we had a governess.'

'But she did make her puppets, and she helped us with the scenery,' said Lucy, quietly.

'Puppets!' Kate's tone was scornful.

'I liked the puppets. I still have Little Nell,' said Lucy.

'Little Nell of Mr Dickens's *Old Curiosity Shop*?' Basil leaned towards her.

She nodded.

'We were brought up on Shakespeare and Mr Dickens,' Jane chuckled. 'Ellen would read aloud to us, after tea, while we were busy with our needle-work.'

'Did I ever finish that horrid sampler?' Kate interrupted. She couldn't bear to be left out of anything.

'I finished it,' Lucy confessed – and Basil smiled at her approvingly.

As an only child without the companionship of brother or sister, he found the family at The Haven a fascinating study. Never a dull moment in that lively household on Sunday afternoon, and now the added attraction of the adorable baby boy, who was carried downstairs to be admired and petted. Only little Prue turned her head away. A quaint child, full of character, but as temperamental as a prima donna.

'Tell us about the theatre,' Kate insisted, her eyes bright with anticipation of the forthcoming treats. 'It won't be all Shakespeare, will it? I find him exceedingly dull.'

'Dull? Anything but dull – the greatest dramatist in the English language. I am surprised at you, Kate. His characters are true to life, and he has the most amazing talent for suspense.'

'Hear! Hear!' Jane clapped her hands. 'I wish I could join you on those Wednesday afternoon excursions.'

'Couldn't you?'

'Alas, no. It would be quite impossible. Think of the expense. If you ever come to London, Basil, you must let me know. It would be a rare treat to see a West End play.'

'It would give me great pleasure,' he bowed.

'We were lucky to be allowed this holiday. Where we come from a holiday is something as remote as Peking,' she reflected. 'Isn't that so, Edward?'

He nodded agreement, but did not attempt to enter the conversation. Jane understood. They exchanged a smile and a shared intimacy that none of the young people had yet achieved. What did the future hold for them? Jane wondered.

'Go on, Basil,' Kate prompted, impatiently.

'We shall see a varied selection of plays and players at the Brighton Theatre. There are excellent repertory companies that tour all over the country. They have quite extensive repertoires, and are usually stage managed by a husband and wife who play the leading roles, and the rest of the cast are trained to play the minor roles. Actually, it has not changed very much since Elizabeth's day. Actors and actresses are usually born to the life. We met quite a number in Oxford, and they wouldn't have changed places with any one of us. It's a hard life, with few comforts in dingy lodging houses, and they earn hardly enough to keep body and soul together in these travelling companies, but they were a cheerful crowd.'

'Shall we see *Romeo and Juliet*?' asked Lucy, shyly.

'You will. It's a perennial favourite,' Basil assured her.

'I expect I shall cry. It's so very sad.'

'Silly goose! It's not true,' scoffed Kate.

Lucy appealed to Basil.

'It would be based on fact, though I wouldn't like to swear to its authenticity. There could have been two families of noble birth that were sworn enemies, and two young lovers, pledged to die. Shakespeare's

Juliet is a tragic creature, whether or not she actually existed. His Juliet was only 15, but I have seen some convincing portrayals by actresses who were no longer young. Clever make-up, of course. I love the theatre. It's a magic world, and there is little enough magic in our lives today,' he sighed.

'Go on,' Kate prompted, pressing his hand affectionately.

'There is always a pantomime for the Christmas season. Last year it was *Robinson Crusoe*. I saw it three times.'

'Oh, *Basil*!' Kate giggled. 'Imagine a grown man seeing a silly pantomime three times!'

'If a certain young lady is too sophisticated for such childish entertainments, we will leave her at home!' he announced, airily.

Kate liked being thought sophisticated, but nothing would keep her at home. In Basil's lively company, she would never be bored. He was such a darling!

When they had finished tea, the three younger people had to leave, for the evenings were drawing in, and the lamp-lighter would be going on his rounds with his long pole to light the gas. Basil was escorting the girls back to The Haven. By the time he had walked home, he would find his mother had retired to bed.

It had been a pleasant interlude, and he was in a mood to play the dutiful son. Talking of the theatre had revived old memories of his boyhood, and the companionship they had enjoyed. It was natural that he now enjoyed the company of the younger generation, but Mother was spoiling that enjoyment by her selfish attitude. Were all mothers so possessive of their only sons? he wondered. Neither Mother nor

258

son would see themselves as the guilty party. Both were at fault, and the breach could be permanent.

Jane lit a candle and led the way down the back stairs. She kissed her sisters and they promised to keep in touch, but it would be left to Lucy to write an occasional letter. Only Mother and Ellen were writing to Grace, and Amelia received a formal report from Mr Courtney-Halliday once a month.

With a girl on each arm, Basil was feeling important. Escorting the two pretty Brent sisters was an enjoyable occupation, and a number of young men at the store would have welcomed the opportunity. Still talking of the theatre, they reached the green gate of The Haven, faintly illuminated by the street lamp. They had already planned their first excursion to Brighton for the following Wednesday afternoon. As soon as the store had closed, they would meet at the staff exit, and hurry to the station. With a picnic lunch to eat on the train – provided by Norah, it was assumed – Basil would be spared the cost of a meal. All this had been decided by Kate, but Basil still had to obtain Amelia's permission. It was just like Kate to take it for granted that Mother would be agreeable, Lucy confided to Rose that same night, as they undressed for bed.

'It's a daring plan, Luce, and you must not be too disappointed if your mother disapproves,' Rose cautioned. She had never seen Lucy half so excited, or so pretty, with her flushed cheeks and sparkling eyes. Mr Gregson was obviously fond of both girls, and seemed to treat them both with the same courteous attention. But Rose was not happy about the arrangement. Somebody would get hurt, and it would not be Kate.

* * *

Nobody warned Basil that to introduce such a secular topic as the theatre on a Sunday evening would be most unpopular, and that he stood the risk of losing the hospitality he was enjoying so much.

When they had finished tea, they all trooped into the drawing-room, and Amelia seated herself at the piano. Ellen was nursing Thomas in his long robes in the chair nearest the piano. Like a little prince, he stared wide-eyed at the assembled company, and turned his eyes towards his Grandmother when she started to play. While her slender hands found the keys of the familiar children's hymn – 'Jesus loves me this I know, For the Bible tells me so, Little ones to Him belong, They are weak, but He is strong' – she gazed tenderly at her adored grandson.

Rose was nursing Prue, and Norah nursing Bella.

'Want Miss Muffet,' Prue announced, decidedly.

'Hush, pet,' Rose whispered. Prue had never been hushed in India, and still saw no reason for it now, even after several months at The Haven.

Amelia ignored her and went on playing. Ellen looked anxiously across the room at her elder daughter, shook her head, and smiled. Sunday was a difficult day! Prue joined the family for the church parade now she was four. It was never too early to start teaching a child the significance of the Sabbath – according to Amelia. But Prue, completely fascinated by the solemn procession of choirboys, exclaimed excitedly, 'Look, Mama! Boy babas in nightshirts!' It was embarrassing, for the Brent pew in the centre aisle was once again the focus of attention.

There had been a time when Thomas and Amelia Brent, accompanied by their six young daughters, all carrying prayer books, in their Sunday best, had

260

occupied that pew. Then it had been Kate who caused a disturbance on her first attendance by refusing to part with her penny when the collecting plate was handed round. How was she to know that Papa, who had given her the penny, was a churchwarden? Threatened with expulsion, Kate was reasonably well behaved in future. To be left behind with her little sister, Lucy, and the nursemaid, was a disgrace she could not have borne. Now it was Prue, and her voice had a penetrating clarity that native servants had hurried to obey.

Ellen was not really listening to the hymn. They were all expected to sing. She was wondering if it would ever be any different. The atmosphere of dissension between her Mother and her eldest daughter was so tangible, there was no pleasure in these Sunday evening invitations to the drawing-room. Yet she could not entirely blame Prue, for Mother's preference for her grandson was all too obvious. It was a relief when they were excused and climbed the stairs, with Rose, to their own quarters at the top of the house, where they could behave naturally.

After they had left, Amelia played a harvest hymn: 'We plough the fields and scatter, the good seed on the land, But it is fed and watered by God's Almighty Hand,' they sang.

'When are you going to ask?' Kate whispered in Basil's ear.

He was wishing now he had got it over when he first arrived, but the two little girls had been hanging round his legs, demanding all his attention.

Kate sang like a choirboy, Norah's deep contralto drowned Lucy's piping treble, and Bertha was singing out of tune. Basil hummed. He had long since forgotten the harvest hymns, and he had no voice for singing. To tell the truth, he was a little bored with the hymn singing.

'Now we will conclude with the evening hymn,' Amelia decided. And once again the sisters were singing.

Now the day is over, Night is drawing nigh,
Shadows of the evening, Steal across the sky.

When Norah and Bertha had been excused for washing up, Kate prompted, in a hoarse whisper, '*Now*, Basil, *please*!'

Basil coughed politely. 'May I ask a favour, Mrs Brent?' he began, as she surveyed her depleted family from the piano stool.

'You may, Mr Gregson,' she answered, graciously, giving him her whole attention.

'Will you allow me to escort Miss Kate and Miss Lucy to the Brighton Theatre on Wednesday afternoon?'

She frowned, her blue eyes hostile. 'The theatre? We do not discuss such topics on the Sabbath, Mr Gregson. It is a matter of principle. My dear husband strongly objected to anything of a secular nature being introduced, and we have brought up our daughters to respect our wishes. If you have nothing more to add to our Sunday observance, then I will bid you good evening.'

Now he could understand why the girls were so obedient to her wishes. Her severity was not something to be ignored. Those blue eyes that had gazed so tenderly on her infant grandson could be cold as steel.

'I beg your pardon,' he faltered. 'I did not mean to offend you.' He stood up, bowed stiffly, and walked towards the door.

'No! Mother please, *please*!' Kate implored, and

darted across the room to fling herself at Amelia's knees. Tears of rage and disappointment poured down her cheeks. Lucy was crying quietly.

'Wait, Mr Gregson. Sit down. Perhaps I have been too hasty.'

When he had resumed his seat, she invited, 'Now, tell me why is this matter so important to you and my daughters?'

'Because we desperately need some diversion on Wednesday afternoons, now the Season is over and there is no more bathing till next Easter. I suggested the theatre as an alternative for the Winter months.'

'I see. So the favour you are asking is not for this week only?'

'No, Mrs Brent.'

Kate and Lucy were holding their breath, but Basil was being very brave.

'I have always loved the theatre, Mrs Brent,' he continued. 'It transports ordinary mortals like ourselves into a realm of make-believe, and we need that make-believe in the world we are living in today, which demands all our time and energy. If we are to give of our best to our work, not only our bodies but our minds need refreshment. Thomas Brent & Son, like Shylock, exacts its pound of flesh!' He grinned, boyishly, and went on, 'Yes, we can see Shakespeare. It's not all frivolous. These travelling repertory companies have an excellent repertoire. The plays are first class. There is no trash. The Brighton Theatre has a long-established reputation. I would not allow your daughters to see anything of which you would disapprove. Certain London theatres cater for a different class of people who prefer their entertainment to be a little more sensational, even a little vulgar, but not the one we shall patronize. I give you my solemn oath, dear lady, that neither their dignity nor their morals will be offended by any performance to which I shall escort them.'

Amelia's stern expression had softened. She smiled at his eloquence. 'Very well. You have convinced me, Mr Gregson. But mind you do not keep them out late. They have never been accustomed to evening entertainment outside the home. This is, well, quite revolutionary!'

'It will always be the matinée. You have my promise.'

'Oh, Mother Darling!' Kate interrupted, unable to control her excitement a moment longer. 'I love you so much.'

'I dare say, now that you get your way with me.' And Amelia removed the clinging arms from her neck, and accepted a kiss from Lucy.

She had surprised herself, and the young ones, by her acquiescence, but having given way, she did not wish to be reminded of the fact. If only Kate could be a little less emotional and a little more rational. Without a firm hand to guide and discipline, she still could embarrass them by some foolishness, for in some ways she was no older than Prudence, and even that emotional child had stopped screaming since Rose was installed as nursemaid.

So she shook hands with Mr Gregson and allowed Lucy to show him out, but kept Kate in the drawing-room. If she could have seen her shy little daughter enfolded in the arms of that young gentleman, Amelia would have changed her mind!

'Oh, Basil!' breathed Lucy, ecstatically, taking his hand and leading him across the hall, into the lobby with its faint glimmer of light from the stained glass panes in the window. She wore her hair down on

264

Sunday, tied with a blue bow, and up all the week. She looked no more than twelve, and he saw her as an excited little girl who had just been promised her first visit to the theatre. So when she spun round and flung her arms round his neck, he was not too surprised. She was so small and light, and when he swung her off her feet, his hands about her tiny waist, his senses were disturbed, but only by her innocence and purity. She had Amelia's blue eyes, but Lucy's eyes would never be hostile or cold as steel, or stern with disapproval. All the sensitivity in her gentle nature was reflected in those blue eyes. He kissed her trembling mouth and smiled down at her that disarming smile that could melt the bones of the young apprentices as well as a certain spinster in charge of Haberdashery.

'Dear little Lucy,' he murmured.

And she gazed up at him with adoring eyes – this God-like creature who had actually achieved the impossible by overturning one of the unchanged laws of the Medes and Persians! For the first time in her young life, the image of Kate was behind her. But Basil was mistaken, she was not a child – she was a woman.

Not even to Rose could she speak of those precious few moments alone with Basil. It was too sacred. Nothing seemed to have changed. She was a quiet, obedient daughter, and a quiet, obedient apprentice, but she was living in a dream world now, her secret locked in her heart. No further evidence was required. Basil had kissed her and called her his dear little Lucy.

Walking back to The Haven after the store had closed on Monday and Tuesday, Kate still walked beside Basil, who was on the outside of the pavement. They would share a joke, and laugh together and they teased each other, but Lucy had no sense of being neglected. She was sorry for Kate who saw herself as Basil's intended betrothed.

When he left them at the gate and raised his hat in farewell, had she imagined that his glance was a little more intimate, and the pressure of his hand just a little more sustained for her than for Kate?

She saw in every glance in her direction, as he strolled nonchalantly through the department, a message intended for her alone – his dear little Lucy.

They left the store on Wednesday afternoon and hurried to the station, the girls hanging on his arms, and all three exclaimed in delight when they discovered the first play of the Autumn season was to be *Romeo and Juliet*. The long queue at the box office was an indication of its popularity, especially with the fair sex. Schoolgirls, middle-aged matrons, and plain spinsters, all saw themselves as Juliet.

Seated between the two girls, Basil could feel their excitement as they waited for the curtain to rise. Kate was flushed and starry-eyed, Lucy was pale and tense. When the orchestra had assembled and the overture silenced the chattering audience, Lucy sighed and relaxed. For Kate the play was a fascinating drama and she enjoyed every moment. For Lucy, it was reality, and the age-old tragedy of the young lovers a heart-breaking experience. She suffered every emotion Juliet suffered, and knew she would die the same death if she were threatened with separation from her betrothed. In her innocence, she could not distinguish fact from fantasy.

She was hardly aware of Basil taking her cold hand in a warm clasp, and oblivious of the fact that Kate was clutching his arm, and had dropped her head on his shoulder. Torn between the childish appeal of

Lucy and the impudence of Kate, Basil was enjoying himself tremendously. It was going to cost more than he could afford from his meagre salary, but it would be worth every penny. On one side he could feel Lucy shivering in a state of great agitation, on the other, the heat and vitality of the irrepressible Kate.

8

For Amelia, her small world was complete now that she had Thomas. There had been something lacking in a family of six girls, a disappointment and sadness that had lingered through the years. Now her life was fulfilled, and all his needs ever her pleasure to provide. She was always thinking of ways and means to curtail the housekeeping expenses so that she could afford to buy Thomas a new toy or a pretty frock to adorn his adorable little person. Now she was often seen in Infants Wear, a department of Children's Wear at Thomas Brent & Son, where the Manageress would attend her in person. Amelia was not an easy customer, and a lavish display would be spread on the counter for her inspection. Sometimes it was her own young daughter who was bidden to fetch and carry, and Amelia would incline her head in acknowledgement. Nothing more. Her sense of propriety was always rigidly observed.

When Basil had seen her seated comfortably, he hovered at a discreet distance, to escort her to the front entrance and call a cab. He would carry her packages. Amelia had never carried the smallest package in all her married life. When she required to purchase goods in other departments, they were delivered to the house. She would always be 'young Mrs Thomas' at the store.

Anything she purchased for Thomas, however,

had to be delivered personally, and Ellen would carry him down to the drawing-room to receive the gift. At that tender age, he was interested only in the wrapping paper, and she loved to see him tearing it off and throwing the contents on the floor – his blue eyes dancing with mischief. Amelia would pick it up and pretend to scold, but Thomas knew already that he was her darling. So they played the game together till he tired.

His first tooth was a miracle, his first steps watched and applauded. His first word 'WANT' was a topic of conversation in the drawing-room. And Amelia, who had seldom praised or rewarded the efforts of her own young daughters – that had been left to the nursemaid and the governess – was fast becoming a doting grandmama. Ellen was of no consequence. Amelia's personality had always been strong, and only Kate had had the audacity to challenge it. As for Rose, she had accepted her humble status with 'Master Thomas'.

The washing and ironing had been trebled since his arrival, and a new bassinet had been ordered to convey his small person to the park. He was a heavy child to carry up and down the stairs, and when he struggled in her arms, she was terrified that she might drop him. He would be breast-fed up to the age of eighteen months, lowering Ellen's strength, and depriving the two little girls of her company. There were no regular feeding hours. Thomas was fed when he was hungry, and the entire household heard his yells. When he had been fed and rocked to sleep, usually by Bella, she would gaze fondly at her cherubic baby brother and whisper, 'boy baba'. She loved him dearly, and never tired of playing with him.

'Thomas is naughty, isn't he, Mama?' Prue would

pronounce – but not in the presence of Grandmama! It was a few days before Easter, and the Millinery Department of Thomas Brent & Son was buzzing with customers. A new hat for Easter was a necessity, not a luxury, for ladies of the upper class, but the majority of women would 'make do' with a bow of fresh ribbon, or a spray of artificial flowers, all of which could be obtained in Millinery.

The Manageress was in one of her bad moods, and her assistant was lying down with a sick headache. The two apprentices, Kate and her friend Dora, were busy in the workroom with re-trimming and all the tedious little jobs that kept their hands employed, but left their thoughts free to wander.

Kate was bored and restless. Beyond the muslin curtains that draped the window, the sun was shining. The sea would be sparkling. It was Spring, the season when young hearts beat faster, and Nature bestowed her blessing on trees and flowers. Kate had enjoyed the theatre during the Winter months, but now her thoughts were racing ahead to the start of the 'Season', the military bands, the Sunday parade on the promenade, and a new dress and hat for Easter Sunday. She could hear a deep, masculine voice among the chatter of feminine voices in the salon – a spacious, carpeted showroom, sprinkled with little gilt chairs. A tempting display of new models was dispersed on glass-topped counters. They were frequently re-arranged. Every customer was entitled to the same courteous service, whether or not they purchased. Certain ladies of leisure would amuse themselves for an hour or more, trying on hats, then calmly walk away without so much as a bow of ribbon or a spray of flowers.

A masculine voice in Millinery? Kate was intrigued,

for rarely did a husband accompany his wife on a shopping expedition. Their customers were invariably mothers and daughters, with the mothers making the final choice, like Amelia.

Taking a peek round the open door, Kate could see a tall, distinguished gentleman in the conventional frock coat and striped trousers, carrying a cane, gloves and grey top-hat, strolling nonchalantly about the salon, while a fashionably dressed lady sat waiting for attention, drumming impatient fingers on the counter. Quite obviously she was not accustomed to be kept waiting. The Manageress, already engaged with a difficult customer, was looking harassed. With only a second's hesitation, Kate marched out from her enforced confinement into the limelight – an impulse she was never allowed to forget for the rest of her days!

With a respectful curtsey and a charming smile, she addressed the impatient customer in a manner that would have pleased Grandpapa Brent enormously.

'Good afternoon, Madam. Can I help you?' Her clear, young voice brought instant reaction. The gentleman swung round, stared at the attractive young woman dressed like an orphan in drab grey, and strolled back to join his sister. The Manageress swung round with a rustle of alpaca skirts, her face a study in shock and indignation. Miss Brent was taking a liberty that would be reported to the General Manager.

'*That* – I wish to try *that* one,' a haughty voice interrupted – and a wave of the hand indicated a youthful model, adorned with poppies and cornflowers.

Kate hurried to do her bidding, placed a mirror

conveniently, and stood by, her eyes bright with interest while the lady removed her own hat and placed the other on her arrogant head. As she lifted her hands to arrange the hat Kate was quick to notice the rings on her fingers – but no wedding ring. So they were not husband and wife! Could they possibly be brother and sister? In Kate's very limited encounters with the brothers of the young ladies at the Academy, she had seen nothing but their boredom, disdain and ridicule.

'Don't just stand there, girl! Fetch more hats!'

Kate jumped to attention. 'Yes, Madam,' and she scurried away to collect three of the most exclusive models. The gentleman had drawn up a chair, draped his coat-tails over the back, and was leaning forward attentively on the silver-topped cane.

'How do you like it, Charles?' asked the lady.

'Just a little, shall we say, frivolous, my dear? Hardly your style,' he answered, dutifully. Since the word 'frivolous' could never have been applied to Eleanor Lefeaux, even in her extreme youth, she snatched it off, took a second hat from Kate, and a third, all of which were rejected, politely but firmly by the gentleman, with amused grey eyes. Charles Lefeaux was enjoying the little tableau. Really, she was a strikingly pretty girl, and not in the least intimidated by his sister's haughty manners. In fact, she seemed to be enjoying it as much as himself, darting about the Salon to return the rejected hats to their original stands, bringing more hats, and presenting them with such charming courtesy. Could he detect a hint of mockery in those dark, eloquent eyes? – or just youthful pleasure in a situation an older person might find tedious? He liked the way she glanced in his direction. No modest maiden this with downcast eyes. He found himself comparing her with the young ladies of his acquaintance whose fond mamas would persistently parade them for his benefit. They were no match for Eleanor, bless her! They were happy enough in their unmarried state, and had no desire for change.

Eleanor had mothered him since their parents died of typhoid in East Africa. That was twenty years ago – a hell of a long time. But he was not smothered by her maternity. He had his club, his constituency, and the House of Commons, all of which provided a good excuse to be late home for dinner! At the age of forty, with splendid health and a light-hearted attitude to life, indulged by Eleanor since Varsity days, he was wondering whether a mild flirtation with a little shop girl might prove amusing. So he prolonged the situation till a dozen or more hats had been tried, then finally gave his approval to an elaborate creation that would catch the eyes of his sister's faithful *beaux*. Oh, yes, she *had* a *beau*, but the poor fellow was much too mild. No man should make a doormat of himself, Charles contended.

'You don't think it a little too fussy?' Eleanor was asking, anxiously.

'Not at all, my dear. It is most becoming,' he assured her, gallantly.

'I will take over here, Miss Brent.'

Kate had forgotten her superior, but the authoritative voice could not be ignored. As always when she was enjoying herself, she looked no farther than the present moment, saw no danger or recrimination.

'Madam has decided,' she answered, with much satisfaction, curtsied prettily to the lady and gentleman, and walked away with a jaunty air. Even in that drab, grey uniform she was dashed attractive,

Charles Lefeaux was thinking. That glossy hair, black as a raven's wing, fitted her proud little head like a cap. The straight fringe had almost touched her eyebrows, and her lashes were long and thick. Her movements had been quick and decisive. There had been no hesitation in her manner, and not once had she consulted the older woman with the sweeping train, so obviously in charge of the department and so obviously annoyed!

So much he had noticed, yet still attentive to his sister. What age would she be? – eighteen? nineteen? Rather young to have adopted that short hair style. Had she copied it from that well-known actress, currently playing in the West End? His thoughts had wandered, and Eleanor was waiting. No mention had been made of payment. Two guineas? Three guineas? No matter. The account would be rendered in due course.

'Come, my dear.' He smiled and proffered his arm.

Back in the work-room, the other apprentice greeted her with wide-eyed admiration. 'Oh, *Kate*, how did you dare? I nearly swooned when I saw you actually serving that lady. You know what will happen now? SHE will report you to Mr Hudson, and you could be dismissed,' she whispered.

'Who cares? It was fun.' Kate's cheeks were flushed, and her dark eyes danced with mischief. She was so saucy, so daring, Dora couldn't bear the thought that she might lose her. Perhaps it made a difference being the grand-daughter of Mr Thomas Brent.

Their whisperings and giggles stopped abruptly when the Manageress swept in, carrying the hat and an embossed card. 'Pack this hat, Miss Brent, and have it delivered immediately to this address. I will deal with you later,' she added, acidly, and swept out. A moment later, her voice was silky and ingratiating. 'Good afternoon, Madam. Can I help you?' This was her life. She had served her apprenticeship and risen to her present exalted position, with a short train to add to her dignity, in fifteen years.

Kate was staring at the card. 'CHARLES PERCIVAL LEFEAUX, MP, 17 ONSLOW SQUARE, LONDON, SW.' On the reverse side was scribbled 'Miss Eleanor Lefeaux, c/o Marine Hotel, Worthing.' When she had packed the hat in tissue paper in one of their prettiest hat boxes, stacked on the shelves, she rang the bell for a delivery boy, and wished she might be allowed to deliver it, if only to see that amused glance and hear that deep, masculine voice once again. 'He likes me,' she told herself, convincingly, as she stitched a large bow of satin ribbon to a drooping brim, and draped the crown with matching tulle.

'If SHE could see you now, Kate!' Dora spluttered in a fresh fit of giggles, for Kate was preening herself in front of the mirror. She loved trying on the hats. It was the only entertainment in the long, tedious hours they spent in the small stuffy room behind the muslin curtains.

'One of these days I shall have hats for every occasion,' she announced dramatically, adjusting the brim at a more becoming angle over the fringe of hair. 'I shall have my gowns made by the Court dressmaker in Mayfair, and buy my lingerie at Lafayette. I have not yet set foot in the streets of London, but I shall – the West End, Piccadilly, Mayfair, Bond Street – the very names are music to my ears. I have heard all about it from the girls at the Academy. Imagine actually *living* in London! Such exquisite delight. How I envied them, Dora. But I never got invited to their homes because my bosom friend one week could be my bitterest enemy the following week,' she sighed, regretfully, and continued, 'They said I blew hot and cold, like the wind – as if it were my fault. We cannot change the personalities we are born with. Not that I want to change. I like myself too well, especially since I cut my hair. What else could I do when Mr Gregson dared me? I can never resist a dare! Now Mother is not one to swoon, but I do declare she very nearly did last evening, when I walked into the drawing-room to bid her good night, curtsied prettily, and confronted her with my new image. Usually so calm and controlled, her expression was a study in shock, horror and indignation. "How *dare* you, Kate! How *dare* you, without my consent?" she demanded, after she had recovered her breath. "I want to be different, Mother," I told her. "Why must you be different?" she asked. "You are one of my daughters. Nothing can change the fact that you are one of the Misses Brent at The Haven." "One of the *six* Misses Brent originally. I wanted to be the only adored daughter of my parents. I wanted that from the time I had to share the bassinet with Lucy. I wanted you to love me best," I told her, Dora, for it was true. "I want, I want. You cannot go through life just taking, not giving, Kate. It's greedy, it's selfish," she insisted. She had recovered her poise, Dora. She was once again the mistress of a situation that had momentarily unnerved her. "You have my permission to withdraw, Kate," she said, coldly, and turned her back on me. I went upstairs, choked with tears, Dora. I wanted to be admired and

loved, but once again I had blotted my copy book.'
Kate sighed. 'There must be a little demon inside me,
for I cannot help myself. Is it so very wrong to want
to be loved and admired? To me it is natural.'

Dora shook her head. 'I don't know, Kate. I don't
feel that way, but then I am so ordinary, aren't I?'

'Yes, you are,' Kate agreed, with devastating
frankness – and they were giggling again.

Basil had witnessed the little drama. Standing
quietly and unobserved, he was both surprised and
jealous, for he recognized the gentleman from photographs in the London press. Only recently he had
been photographed with a pretty debutante riding in
the Row. A man-about-town, one of the privileged
class, seen in all the right places with all the right
people – Ascot, Goodwood, Cowes, and the theatre.
His name had been linked with a certain well-known
actress, currently playing in the West End. There was
a resemblance since Kate had cut her hair, but the
actress was years older than Kate. To be jealous of
Charles Lefeaux was ridiculous, but the feeling was
there. The glances they had exchanged while his companion was preening herself with all those ridiculous
hats, had not gone unnoticed. A spark had been
kindled between them. Knowing Kate, it could be
fanned into a flame. Her beauty was not her only
attraction. It was her personality, her sense of fun
and sheer devilment.

For almost a year he had regarded himself as indispensable to the two Misses Brent. Every Wednesday
and Sunday they had spent many delightful hours
together. He was a welcome guest at The Haven, and
approved by that stern matriarch who ruled their
lives. He was fond of both girls, and the relationship was most cordial. His feelings for Lucy were

protective. She was just a child. For Kate, his feelings were those of any normal man for a very attractive young woman. He recalled how she had teased him in that clinging bathing costume. The Summer season was starting, but it was too early for the bathing machines. They must wait till Whitsun to continue with the swimming lessons.

Now he could hardly wait for the store to close, when they would walk back to The Haven together, and it would be his turn to tease. If she blushed, then he would know he had not been mistaken in his interpretation of those glances. Yes, he was jealous – jealous of Charles Lefeaux's rank and position in society – jealous of his seniority and experience – jealous of the poise and arrogance he himself was lacking. As he escorted the arrogant couple to the front entrance, he was seeing Charles Lefeaux as a potential rival, and his heart was hammering. But he was too well-trained and too dependent on the job to allow his private thoughts to intrude. With a disarming smile and a courteous little bow, he intoned, respectfully, 'Good afternoon, Madam. Good afternoon, Sir.'

Now his hands were clammy with sweat as he stood on the forecourt, watching them walk away towards the promenade. The lady had opened her parasol. The gentleman donned his silk hat with a sweeping gesture. He walked with a swagger, swinging his cane – his hated rival for Kate's affections!

'An agreeable young woman, my dear,' said Charles, conversationally, as they strolled along the promenade.

'Who?'

'The gal who served you with the hats.'

'Yes, obliging enough.'

278

'I wonder why they dress their apprentices in those drab uniforms? If I had my way, they would all be wearing something pretty, with frills and furbelows and mob caps.'

'Not suitable for business, Charles. Too much like milkmaids.'

'Yes, I suppose so. Did you notice her hair?'

'Whose hair?'

'The gal who served you with the hats.'

'No, should I have noticed?'

'It was cut short with a fringe. Very fetching.'

Eleanor turned her head to look at her brother with the indulgent eyes of an adoring elder sister. She had been getting him out of awkward and embarrassing situations since he came down from Oxford, and invariably it was a female who had to be mollified. On one occasion, a young woman had to be bribed – it cost £100 – a lot of money, but worth every penny. The scandal of a bastard child would have ruined his chances for a seat in Parliament.

'My dear Charles, you are *quite* incorrigible!' she scolded – and changed the subject. 'Are we playing cards with the Pendletons after dinner?'

'If you wish.'

The Pendletons were deadly dull, and it would be a boring evening, but it was Eleanor's only vice, so he shouldn't complain. They had been meeting the Pendletons at the Marine Hotel every Easter for the past decade. They managed to avoid them during the day, but it was impossible to ignore their presence in a public drawing-room. Besides, an MP had a certain obligation, a certain image, and the Pendletons were dyed-in-the-wool Liberals. It was pleasant to be thought a good fellow and a generous host – and he could afford to be generous on inherited wealth. It was not even necessary to visit Africa. The gold was there, had always been there, and would go on being there, presumably.

The military band, the first of the season, attracted a large audience. The deck-chairs had been re-covered in striped canvas. The sun was shining, the sea sparkling. It was a pleasant place to be, and Eleanor was an endearing companion. Then why should his thoughts wander to a certain young woman in a drab grey uniform, with saucy eyes and a most enchanting smile?

They sat for a while, listening to the band. It was too early for tea, and Eleanor liked watching the parade on the promenade. Worthing was a popular resort, and Easter brought early visitors from London and the Midlands. The bathing-machines had been freshly painted. They were lined up at the top of the beach. Bathing was not a pastime that he cared for. It always seemed singularly embarrassing to expose oneself in those hideous costumes in order to take a dip in the sea. He wondered if the pretty apprentice liked bathing.

Lucy was in bed with a sick headache on that Easter Monday, and they had promised to meet Basil for coffee at Kong's.

'He will realize that something has happened to prevent your meeting, wait half-an-hour, then walk along here to find out,' said Amelia, sensibly, for Kate was so vexed. 'You may invite him to lunch,' she added, surprisingly. 'Then you could both take a walk with Ellen and the children in the park. Mr Gregson is very fond of the children and they are fond of him.'

Kate sighed. It was not going according to plan,

and there would not be another Bank Holiday till August. If only Mother was not so conventional, so strict about a chaperone. It was not 'seemly', she insisted, for a young lady to be seen alone with a young gentleman unless or until they were engaged to be married. It was so *stupid*, so unfair. Sometimes she wished she had been born in the slums, where such formalities were not observed, according to Jane.

Her sister Jane was quite an authority on matters that were strictly 'taboo' at The Haven. She had a sort of earthy valuation of human behaviour, and the facts of life were no mystery to her. Even so, she had not actually explained the relationship between a man and a woman that produced a child. The marriage bed remained a mysterious and utterly fascinating subject, not to be disclosed by either of her married sisters.

Ellen, with three children, was still rather a prude, and Kate could not begin to understand how Jonathan had persuaded her to take off her drawers. 'Cover your private parts child,' had been so much a part of their early training, even little Lucy had been shocked when she discovered Kate removing her nightgown before she had pulled on her drawers.

'I haven't any private parts,' Kate had protested in the nursery – and was still protesting! 'I shall tell your Mama' was a threat that Kate had found rather exciting. The punishment was an occasion for tears and tantrums, and Mother could usually be persuaded to change her mind!

Going to the theatre with Basil and Lucy had taught her to use her emotions subtly. A clever woman could get her own way with a man by devious means. Tears and tantrums were childish. It was not even necessary to be strictly truthful. White lies were permitted. Yes, the theatre had been an education as well as entertainment. She knew for certain now that she had the talent for acting she had always suspected. Mother would never allow one of her daughters to act in public, but she *did* allow charades at Christmas now they were grown-up, and now it was Prue and Bella who amused themselves with the puppets.

'Did you get into trouble for serving that customer?' Basil had asked, as they walked home together that evening.

'Who told you?' Kate fenced.

'I saw you.'

'You did? What did you think of me?'

'I thought you had the making of a very efficient Manageress one of these days.'

'It was fun.'

'Yes, I could see you were enjoying it.'

'You actually *served* a customer, Kate?' asked Lucy, incredulous at such daring.

'I did, *and* sold one of the most expensive hats in this season's collection.'

'What happened? Were you reported?'

'Of course. That's why you had to wait for me. I was receiving a lecture from Mr Hudson.'

'Did he reprimand you very severely?'

'No, he was quite charming. "Sit down, Miss Kate. I have been asked to speak to you on the matter of serving a customer in the first year of your apprenticeship. Perhaps you do not fully appreciate the importance of such a ruling? It has been in force since your great-grandfather's day, and has never been changed. It so happens that you were able to satisfy a rather difficult customer, and that you actually sold

her one of the new models. That is really most credi-
table, Miss Kate. But I must have your promise not to
repeat the performance. If you recall, your grandfather insisted that you and Miss Lucy must be
treated like all the other apprentices – Ahem''.'

Kate was a born mimic, and they laughed at her
clever portrayal of the General Manager.

'He wouldn't dare dismiss you, Kate – a grand-
daughter of Thomas Brent! You and I, and Lucy,
hold a trump card,' said Basil. 'Not that it helps. In
fact, it's more of a hindrance. We will never be popular, so we may as well accept the fact. Old Hudson
will never forgive me for stepping into the shoes of a
certain worthy young man who had served his apprenticeship. What can't be cured, must be endured,
as Mother would say. Incidentally, I thought Mr
Lefeaux was rather amused by your performance,
Kate.'

'You know him?'

'Everyone knows Charles Lefeaux. Be careful,
Kate. He has a somewhat dubious reputation with
the fair sex – and you were flirting.'

'Me – flirting? Mr Gregson, you are mistaken.'
Kate's wide-eyed innocence was most convincing,
but Basil was not deceived. His naughty Kate!

'Who was the lady?' he asked, as they sauntered
homewards.

'His sister – Miss Eleanor Lefeaux. It was on the
card.'

'A haughty madam.'

'Very haughty.'

'But you were not intimidated?'

'No, should I be intimidated? Humility is not one
of my virtues, Basil, as you may have noticed?'

He nodded.

'I shall die of fright when I have to serve my first customer,' Lucy interrupted.

'Then you must find a husband, darling, and you won't need to work,' said Kate, airily.

Lucy blushed. Kate didn't know about the poems. Rose had delivered them to the bedroom on the Sunday evening, after Basil had climbed the stairs to say good night to the two little girls. It was a pocket-size volume with a note attached:

My Dear Lucy,

I thought you would like to read my poems since I have heard you quote Coleridge and Wordsworth. Not that I can claim to compare with those illustrious gentlemen. I should value your opinion, Lucy. There is no hurry to return them, but please keep them to yourself, for even a very inferior poet is sensitive about his scribblings!

Yours very truly, Basil.

It was an honour, of course, and Lucy was thrilled, but just a tiny bit disappointed. She had read the poems through several times, but still couldn't make up her mind whether they were too intellectual for her limited intelligence, or deliberately obtuse. If these were Basil's private thoughts, then she had to admit he was an enigma, and not the person she had begun to love at their first meeting. Yet it made no difference. She did love him dearly. In some respects, she loved him more for harbouring thoughts that were 'not quite nice'. It made him more human, less God-like.

The truth of that saying 'Every man is an island' was suddenly revealed. In her new adult world, she had been surprised and hurt by the unfriendly attitude of the other apprentices, but Kate had reminded her that she would have reacted the same way had she not had the advantage of being a Miss Brent. Kate was so realistic. It made life so much simpler. Hugging her secret, Lucy would listen to their foolish talk and not feel jealous. She had the poems. Basil had known she would be pleased and proud to read them, and that Kate would probably make fun of them. She was such a tease.

The sick headache would be hereditary, Amelia had decided, for she herself had suffered from the same distressing malady in her younger days, and four of the girls had occasionally to spend a day in bed.

Lucy's attacks were more frequent since she had started out in business. The poor child was not happy at the store, and a sick headache was a kind of escape. Lemon barley was provided to settle the stomach, and the curtains were drawn against the light. Rose, on her way down to breakfast, had reported that Lucy was indisposed, and Amelia had looked in on the invalid – for so her youngest daughter saw herself – and found her in tears.

It was Bank Holiday, and she couldn't bear it, she sobbed. The room was stuffy, and the faint smell of warm blood told its own tale. Menstruation was not a topic to be discussed, however, and Amelia had been singularly embarrassed to be confronted by Kate, in hysterics, at the age of thirteen.

'I don't want to be a woman! I won't put up with it! It's horrid and messy, and my stomach hurts!'

What a fuss and pother! In a family of girls, one must expect to have a daughter who rebelled against nature. Kate had put herself to bed for a day every month from henceforth, and could not be persuaded or bullied to get up. One of the sisters would take up a tray, four times daily, for Kate did not lose her appetite.

Lucy had revealed that Kate had behaved in exactly the same way at the Academy. Menstruation was *not* an illness, it was pointed out. But Kate was adamant.

The warm Spring sunshine on that Easter Bank holiday tempted Ellen to lift Thomas from his nest of shawls in the bassinet, and lie him on a rug spread on the grass, where he kicked and chortled happily. It was a pleasant change from the confined space of the rooms at the top of the house. Little girls were bowling their hoops on the paths, and old men, smoking clay pipes, sat on the benches.

Bella was playing with Thomas, Prue and Rose playing hide-and-seek with Mr Gregson and Kate. The children called him 'Greggy', and he didn't seem to mind. He was such a charming young man, and so good with the children.

'Now it is our turn, Prue. I will hide with Auntie Kate, you will count ten, then start to search for us,' he was explaining. Prue was dancing with excitement. How she loved to be the centre of attention. It was not really so surprising, this jealousy, for Thomas did get more than his share of it, and already seemed aware of his importance in the household. How Jonathan would have loved his son, and how the family's future would have changed had he still been alive today.

Sad thoughts were not so frequent now. Time *does* heal. Ellen's children demanded so much of her time and energy, and Thomas was such a greedy child, bless him!

Kate was being very obliging today. A creature of moods, she was not always patient with the children.

Poor Lucy, such a shame to be confined to bed on this very pleasant Bank Holiday. Her little sister was in love with Mr Gregson, but he was in love with Kate. Ellen recognized all the symptoms, but said nothing. It was only recently that his preference for Kate had been so obvious, and when Lucy became aware of it, she would be terribly hurt. Yet who could resist Kate? Never a dull moment in her company!

She had taken Mr Gregson's hand and they had disappeared into the shrubbery. Behind a bush of flowering forsythia, Kate whispered urgently, 'Kiss me, Basil.'

He blushed easily, and she giggled at his embarrassment. 'Miss Brent, you are a very forward young woman!' he chided, and her arms crept round his neck.

'Kiss me!' There was no time to waste. That bothersome child would count to ten much too quickly. She was wearing scent today, and the perfume had an intangible quality that matched her glowing personality.

Their lips met in their first kiss, but he had always known it would be exciting, since the swimming lessons. Nothing had prepared him for the passion in her wet, clinging mouth, however, or her thrusting breasts. His senses were reeling as his arms enfolded her tiny waist.

'Kate, my adorable Kate!' he murmured.

Prue's shrill voice pierced that exquisite moment. 'TEN! I'm coming!'

'Little baggage,' muttered Kate, crossly, as they leapt apart.

There was no break in the fine weather, and Whitsun saw the bathing machines dragged across the shingle to the water's edge, in readiness for the first customers.

It was Wednesday afternoon, and the girls had arranged to meet Basil. He was sitting on the steps of the bathing machine he had hired, gazing out to sea, anticipating the moment when his adorable Kate would be lying on the water, completely at his mercy. He was feeling in a teasing mood, and she would beg for mercy as he let her sink, then catch her up in his arms at the last second. That passionate kiss in the shrubbery at Easter Bank Holiday had aroused his latent senses. Never had he known such ardent emotion. He was ashamed of his thoughts, for they were no longer pure, and a tormenting anguish in his loins had to be quelled before he could sleep. Masturbation had been practised at public school, but now it was not enough, and his young, virgin body craved intercourse with that other young, virgin body.

Kate's voice, Kate's excitement, Kate's eagerness for the first swim, all combined to set his pulses racing. And dear little Lucy, who had read his poems and praised them. He sprang to his feet, swept off the boater, and bowed mockingly. He looked very young today in the college blazer and the boater, the girls were thinking. They both adored him.

'You were dreaming,' said Kate, with a meaningful glance. She knew that kiss had had a disturbing effect on his lighthearted approach to their relationship, and she had intended that it should. If she had to take the first step towards a closer intimacy, then so be it. So far and no farther. She knew she had already aroused the desire to possess, but she had no intention of allowing it to happen. Her ignorance of the facts of life was not at all obvious, and she could always pretend to be well informed on such matters. It was fun!

'Basil was dreaming of me because I liked his poems,' Lucy was thinking, as he turned his gaze on her childish prettiness. They would sit together on the steps while Kate was undressing. He would hold her hand, and she would read in the blue eyes that matched her own a promise of future happiness.

But he was thinking of Kate, and remembering how the clinging costume shaped her breasts and thighs in a tantalizing near-nakedness.

'We will have tea at Kong's, Lucy,' was all he promised.

Eleanor Lefeaux had been called to the bedside of their old nannie, suffering from some incurable malady, and would probably remain with her for a week or more. She lived in a tiny cottage in Somerset, so there would be no room for Charles, even if he felt inclined to accompany his sister on this mission of mercy.

'What shall you do for the Whitsun break?' Eleanor had asked, anxiously.

'I shall pop down to Worthing for a breath of sea air, since the weather is so agreeable,' he answered.

'You may meet the Pendletons at the Marine Hotel. They often spend a few days there. This lovely weather is sure to tempt a lot of people to the coast.'

'Indeed they will,' Charles agreed. He had no intention of meeting the Pendletons. He would avoid them. For six weeks he had not been able to dismiss the charming picture of that delightful child from his mind, and he had been wondering how to approach her. It must be done diplomatically, for her name was Brent, and she must be a relation of the owner of the store, and not just an ordinary shop girl. This was a golden opportunity. He hadn't yet decided how, when or where they could meet, but he had never allowed himself to be deterred by circumstances. A pretty face was like a magnet, and if the owner of the pretty face was obliging with her favours, the affair could be quite rewarding. Sometimes it had proved a mistake, and the female in question had embarrassed him with her tears and supplications, long after the affair had died a natural death. It was then that Eleanor usually managed to disentangle him.

So, on this Wednesday afternoon, with a twinge of excited anticipation, he sauntered nonchalantly along the promenade – every inch a gentleman and a man about town – in his formal dress and grey topper. It was too early in the season to adopt Summer attire. 'Ne'er cast a clout till May is out, Master Charles,' as Nannie would say. His wandering thoughts were suddenly rivetted at that precise moment by the pleasant sight of two pretty girls in print dresses and straw boaters, hurrying across the shingle towards the bathing machines. They were carrying towels, so they were going to bathe. He shivered involuntarily. It was much too early in the year for bathing. The water would be dashed cold. My golly, they had some pluck.

Leaning on his cane, he stood watching the girls, for they made a pretty picture, lifting their skirts, skipping over the pebbles. Their happy laughter floated back to him, and he was momentarily aware of his lonely state. Then his heart missed a beat, and his throat went dry. One of the girls had snatched off her boater as they reached one of the bathing machines, and the sunlight caught the shining cap of black hair. It was Miss Brent! A young man, suitably attired in flannels, blazer and boater, came into focus, swept off the boater, and bowed. It was the bow that distinguished him from other young men. It was the good-looking young man who had escorted them to the front entrance of Thomas Brent & Son six weeks ago. Now all three were laughing, such young, unaffected laughter. He supposed the store must be closed, and they were feeling happy and carefree.

It had never occurred to him to enquire into the number of hours that shop assistants were confined to their particular premises, or to wonder about the housemaid who lit the fires and carried up hot water for their baths. It was not the concern of the upper class – the ruling class.

Their young laughter was irritating. Could it be a twinge of envy in his manly breast? Ridiculous! It was many years since he felt the urge to compete with another for the favours of a certain popular young actress. So it *was* envy!

Still leaning on his cane, he stayed to watch, reluctant to miss any stage of the little drama, yet more and more aware of his solitary state. He could not see what was happening now, and it was all of ten minutes before a solitary figure, in an ugly costume, wearing a mob cap, stepped down and stood, hesitating, on the edge of the water. In such a disguise, he could not see whether it was Miss Brent or her companion, but one or the other had funked it at the last moment. Then a second figure, the young Adonis, joined her, also attired in an ugly costume, took the girl's hand, and they waded into deep water. He could hear the girl's shrieks as she was suddenly plunged into the sea, and he felt the shock of such a sudden baptism, and knew for certain it *was* Miss

Brent. How he wished he had brought the binoculars he always carried when he attended race meetings. It was tantalizing to see nothing more than the heads bobbing about. Squeals of protest floated up to him. Now she seemed to be lying on her back, and the young man bending over her. Was he touching her intimately? Was he kissing that laughing mouth? He was up to no good, the young scoundrel! Could they possibly be engaged? It was a disconcerting thought that he might be too late.

And now he could not bear to contemplate defeat, even before he had introduced himself. It was a challenge. What had that young scoundrel to offer such a charming girl? He had *youth*. The answer to the question was there, before his eyes. It was torture to watch, yet he could not drag himself away.

He wondered what the other girl was thinking. She would be sitting on the steps of the bathing machine, supposedly acting as chaperone. What a farce! If Miss Brent's parents could see their daughter now, they would be absolutely horrified. If I had such a lovely daughter, I would lock her in her bedroom, he decided. A daughter? That was a cruel reminder he was old enough to be her father. But he didn't look his age. He was a tall, handsome, distinguished figure with charming manners, and a seat in the House of Commons. To compete for her favours, he was willing to forfeit almost anything. It had suddenly become of vital importance. Before he returned to town he must talk to her, persuade her, convince her – of what? He sighed.

They were coming out of the deep water now, hand-in-hand. If only he had those binoculars! Yet he knew exactly how that clinging wet costume would shape her breasts and thighs. Either she was a brazen

292

little hussy, or they were engaged to be married.

When he had seen her safely to the steps of the bathing machine, the young man turned back, and dived head first into the deep water. He was a strong swimmer, thrashing the water with a powerful back stroke. Showing off to the girls, the conceited young puppy! Still unable to tear himself away, he waited again for a full twenty minutes, when they appeared, fully dressed, the young man carrying the towels. Charles turned his back, and was lost in the crowd on the promenade. Now he knew exactly the right approach to make. It was such a novel experience, he was quite elated.

Following the trio at a discreet distance, he saw them enter the coffee shop where they also served teas. He followed them in, and saw them immediately seated at a table in the far corner, and settled himself at a small, individual table just inside the door, and ordered tea and toast. They were obviously hungry. The waitress served them with a hot dish, probably muffins, and a plate of cakes. Miss Brent was pouring tea, facing him across the crowded room. Her cheeks were glowing, and the fringe of hair very becoming under the straw boater.

Taking a small notebook and a fountain pen from his pocket, he wrote a brief note, folded it precisely, beckoned the waitress, and gave her the note, together with half-a-sovereign, and instructions to deliver it immediately to the young lady pouring the tea. He always believed in tipping generously.

'Yes, Sir. Thank you, Sir.' She bobbed a curtsey and hurried away.

He imagined the look of surprise on that glowing young face. When she had read the note, she looked up. Their eyes met and held. He smiled and bowed.

She handed the note to the young man. His damp hair fitted his handsome head like a golden cap. He, in turn, handed the note to the other girl, and they put their heads together and whispered. He had invited them all to have dinner with him at the hotel, this evening. Would they accept? Miss Brent inclined her head, graciously. All was well. Again he smiled and bowed, then retrieved his hat and cane from the hat stand, and walked out, with a jaunty air.

'What an infernal cheek. We haven't even been introduced!' Basil was most indignant, and more than a little apprehensive. The fellow had such an air of well-being, such self-assurance.

'Don't be so stuffy, Basil. I think it was rather a cute idea to write a note.'

Everyone seemed to be watching.

'Showing off! Conceited ass!'

'I do believe you are jealous, Mr Gregson!'

'Of course I'm jealous. I thought you liked me.'

'I *do* like you. What makes you think the invitation was meant especially for me? We are all invited.'

'The note was addressed to you. How does he know your name? Does he think he has only to beckon and you are ready to fall into his arms?'

'Really, Basil! Now you are being stupid. We are simply invited to dinner with Charles Lefeaux, and you imagine some ulterior motive.'

'It does seem rather a strange way of getting to know you, Kate,' Lucy interrupted.

'There you are. Lucy agrees with me, don't you?'

'Yes.'

'And you don't want to dine with Charles Lefeaux at the Marine Hotel?'

'I shall be absolutely petrified. It's so grand, and I have never ever drunk a cup of tea or coffee in a small hotel, and neither have you, Kate.'

'That is so, and that is why I do not intend to refuse this invitation.'

'Shall we let her go alone?' Basil teased.

'You wouldn't be so mean, would you? Of course I could not go on my own. *Please*, Luce. Be a darling,' Kate entreated.

'Mother may not allow it.'

'Of course she will. Charles Lefeaux, a Member of Parliament! She will be most impressed. You know what a snob she is.'

'So we go?' Basil sighed. 'Why does she always get her way with us, Lucy?'

'Because you love me, you know you do.' She smiled at them, and when she smiled, she was irresistible.

'It means our best togs and a cab both ways. Can we afford it?' Basil was looking worried.

'Perhaps Mr Lefeaux will pay?' Kate suggested, airily.

And that is exactly what he did, for he was standing on the steps of the hotel, with that bland smile on his handsome face. He flung open the door of the cab, assisted the two girls to alight, paid the cabby, and bade him return at precisely ten o'clock to convey his passengers to their respective homes. It was all done with such easy familiarity and such a minimum of fuss, one recognized immediately the superior air of a gentleman accustomed to receiving guests and ordering cabbies.

'Come along,' he said, 'and we will introduce ourselves.' He took the girls' arms, leaving Basil to follow. A page boy had swung open the doors, another was waiting to take the girls' wraps and Basil's hat. They all were wearing their Sunday best, but only

Kate was ready to enjoy herself. Lucy was too shy and nervous to appreciate such ornate surroundings, and Basil was looking sulky.

When the formal introductions had been made, the attentive page led the way to the restaurant, where they were greeted by the head waiter. They followed him to the reserved table, situated near a window overlooking the promenade. A small orchestra played Strauss waltzes in an alcove behind the potted palms. Curious glances had followed their progress across the restaurant, and it was assumed that Mr Lefeaux had tipped the head waiter handsomely, for there was a strict ruling that guests must dress for dinner. Immaculate in tails, wearing a white gardenia in his buttonhole, Mr Lefeaux obviously intended to put the young people at their ease. Such pretty girls, and such a good-looking young man. Could they be related? Their table was the focus of attention and much speculation, as Kate quickly realized, but Lucy was too shy to lift her head and Basil still sulky.

The head waiter was French and the menu was French; Basil and the girls had suddenly forgotten all they had learned of the language, but their embarrassment was only momentary.

'Will you order for us, please, Mr Lefeaux?' said Kate, with charming *sang-froid*. And only Kate would fully appreciate the variety of dishes, and the excellence of the fare that was served by the two young waiters under the supervision of their superior. The portly wine waiter, dressed for the part, poured a little wine in a glass for Mr Lefeaux to taste and approve. Then their glasses were filled. White wine with the fish course, red wine with the meat course. Kate was fascinated. It was her first taste of sophisticated living, and she was enjoying every second.

Neither Lucy's shyness nor Basil's sulks could spoil her pleasure. Two glasses of wine and she was chattering and giggling, a third glass and she was inviting Mr Lefeaux to supper at The Haven the following evening! Such audacity! Basil was disgusted. He had refused a second glass of wine, and was feeling very righteous. But Mr Lefeaux was a gentleman, and knew the invitation must come from a parent.

'Thank you, Miss Kate, but I have to return to Town in the morning. Duty calls,' he explained, smiling into her sparkling eyes. She was a captivating creature, and he was falling in love.

The two hours had seemed an eternity to Lucy, but all too short for Kate, who would have lingered over the farewells but for the reminder that Mrs Brent would be waiting to retire. Mr Lefeaux kissed the girls' hands most gallantly, and expressed a wish to renew their acquaintance on his next visit to Worthing.

Lifting his hand in salute from the front steps as the cab rolled away, he sighed with relief, and retired to his room to enjoy a nightcap of whisky and soda. It had been a deuce of an effort with that boorish Gregson, a red hot Radical, airing his views on social reform, slum clearance and such unlikely subjects for a friendly little dinner party. The pretty little mouse of a sister to Miss Kate had hardly opened her mouth to venture an opinion on any subject. Then he relaxed with tender thoughts of that charming child for whom he felt a real affection, and the strongest desire to know more intimately. If Eleanor had not returned by the end of the month, he would certainly spend another weekend in Worthing. The bandstand, on Sunday afternoon, would provide as good a place as any for a *rendezvous* with the trio, when he would contrive to take a chair next to Kate and slip a little note into her hand, begging for the pleasure of her company for dinner that evening.

While he reclined comfortably in an armchair, planning his next move, Basil was complaining to Kate about her shocking behaviour. 'You're drunk, Kate. I do declare your behaviour was most embarrassing,' said he, with the righteous indignation of one who had refrained from over-indulgence.

'Three glasses of wine is insufficient to reduce me to a state of drunkenness, Mr Gregson,' Kate retorted, with some heat. 'You have absolutely no right to criticize, so there!' Her cheeks were flushed, her dark eyes black as onyx. He had never seen her so animated, so desirable. His hated rival had actually encouraged her to take that third glass of wine because he was enjoying her lively company.

'You were flirting with Lefeaux quite deliberately, Kate.' He was so vexed, he could hardly contain himself.

'Who cares? I *like* him, and he likes me.' Kate tossed her head.

'Of course he likes you, because you are young and very attractive, and he sees you as a new plaything to amuse and entertain him in his bored middle-age. You don't suppose he would want to marry you, my flighty Kate!' Basil sneered.

Now Kate's eyes were blazing. 'How dare you! For that insulting remark, Mr Gregson, I shall not speak to you again until you have apologized!' And she closed her lips, and refused his hand when they alighted from the cab. Pushing open the green gate, she ran up the path and rang the bell.

'Don't look so worried, Lucy dear. I shall apologize on the morrow.' Basil's lips brushed her cheek. The cabby waited patiently. The gent at the hotel had instructed him to see all three of the young people to their respective homes, and made it worth his while with an extra large tip.

Lucy swayed, and laid her head on Basil's comforting shoulder. Her head was throbbing, and her stomach queasy from too much rich food.

'My poor little Lucy,' he murmured, tenderly.

If Kate really liked Mr Lefeaux, perhaps she could have Basil, she was thinking as he climbed back into the cab and blew a kiss.

Amelia sent Lucy straight to bed. Too much excitement and the unaccustomed food and wine all combined to upset her delicate constitution. The following day she was prostrate once again with a sick headache. This gave Basil the opportunity to apologize to Kate as they walked home together that evening.

'Will you forgive me, Kate, for my boorish behaviour. You had every reason to be angry,' said he, humbly.

But Kate was not so easily persuaded. 'Was it necessary to be quite so objectionable?' she demanded, haughtily.

'I couldn't bear to see you flirting with Lefeaux.'

'I flirt with whom I like! You behave as though you have a right to dictate to me just because of that one kiss in the shrubbery.'

'The fact is, I am jealous of Lefeaux.'

'That's being stupid.'

'I love you, Kate, but what can I offer you compared with Lefeaux? I feel so inadequate.'

'You are so sweet. I do like you an awful lot, Basil.'

'Enough to be betrothed?'

'That would be fun.' I should have two *beaux*! she was thinking. 'Perhaps we could keep it a secret? We mustn't hurt Lucy.'

'No, of course not. How long would you want to keep it secret? Until I could afford to marry you? Mr Hudson is due for retirement in two years. Then I step into his shoes, and my salary will be substantially increased.'

'Two years! I couldn't keep a secret for two years, and any way, it's not very complimentary to your betrothed. I mean, a girl likes a ring on her finger to prove she is pledged.'

'Does she? Then you must have a ring, my dearest Kate. And you will marry me when I am promoted to General Manager?'

'I should love to marry you, darling, for I don't intend to spend the best years of my life as an apprentice in Grandpapa's silly old drapery store. Where should we live?'

'With Mother. I should still have to support her, and I couldn't afford to run two homes. You do understand?'

'Would she like me?'

'She would love you like a daughter. She has always wanted a daughter.'

'Isn't it exciting? When do we buy the ring?'

'I shall need a little time to save the money.'

'You haven't a banking account?'

'No.'

'Neither have I. But it won't matter, darling, being poor, I mean. I do love you, terribly.'

'And I love you. I didn't realize quite how much I loved you till I saw Lefeaux appraising you that day you served his sister with the hat. Since then, I have regarded Lefeaux as my rival – a hated rival, for your affections. We don't have to meet him again, do we, dearest?'

'Not by appointment, but if we should meet by chance when he is visiting Worthing, we could hardly ignore him. It would not be polite.'

'Very well, we will acknowledge him with a little bow. No need to get into conversation with the fellow.'

Kate was beginning to wonder what marriage to Basil would be like if he was already being dictatorial, and not yet betrothed. I shall get my own way. I always have, she decided.

Inside the green gate they embraced and stole a furtive kiss, then Basil slipped away.

Behind the drawing-room curtains, Lucy was watching. Her headache was better, and Amelia had suggested she came down to supper. What did it mean? Had Kate stolen Basil for herself?

The following weekend, Charles Lefeaux was once again at the Marine Hotel. Eleanor was still visiting the old nannie, who was hanging on to life with the stubbornness of the very old, because her nursling was there to talk of the old days, and hold her hand.

So Charles 'just happened' to be strolling in the vicinity of the bandstand on the Sunday afternoon, a little before three o'clock, and his tall, distinguished figure in formal dress could not be overlooked.

Basil was glowering as they stopped to acknowledge his bow and the doffed hat, and the deep cultured voice exclaiming, 'My dear young friends, we meet again. This is altogether delightful.'

'Good afternoon, Mr Lefeaux,' murmured Kate and Lucy.

Basil still glowered. With a pretty girl on each arm,

however, he felt infinitely superior to Lefeaux, who was ignorant of the fact that one of the pretty girls would soon be wearing his ring.

The older man was not so easily discouraged. It was not the first time he had met with opposition of this nature. His courtship of Kate would be conducted with the utmost discretion and diplomacy. He actually enjoyed a little opposition. It added spice to an affair of the heart. Gregson was too young to hide his feelings, poor fellow.

'May I be permitted to join your company?' he asked, with smooth courtesy.

'Yes, you may,' Kate answered, with engaging frankness. Lucy smiled agreement. Basil scowled.

The bandsmen were assembling in the bandstand, and they took their seats. The two girls left a vacant chair between them for Basil, and Charles Lefeaux seated himself next to Kate.

'Mother used to accompany us on Sunday afternoons in the Season, but now she prefers to walk in the park with our sister Ellen and the children,' Kate explained, breathlessly, as soon as they were settled. The close proximity of her two *beaux* accounted for the breathlessness. Such darlings, both of them! There was no hurry to make up her mind which she preferred. Until she was pledged to Basil, with a ring on her finger, he must not be allowed to dictate. Her feet tapped to the rhythm of the *Blue Danube*, the popular Strauss waltz requested at almost every performance. She wondered what it would be like to dance with Mr Lefeaux. She had danced with Basil on several occasions at the Assembly Rooms, when the play at the Brighton Theatre was a repeat performance, sharing him with Lucy, who, surprisingly, was a much better dancer, and it had proved a little disconcerting. Being a wallflower for alternate dances was not Kate's idea of pleasure. The Assembly Rooms seemed to attract parties, or groups of people, who danced with each other. She turned her head to smile at Mr Lefeaux, and found he was staring at her with an expression that could only be described as flattering.

When Basil was talking to Lucy in the interval, Kate took the opportunity to tease Mr Lefeaux about his frequent visits to Worthing. 'Do you find the sea air beneficial to your health, Mr Lefeaux?' said she, with a saucy look.

'Beneficial to my health and my heart, Miss Kate,' he murmured, his eyes twinkling with amusement.

It was his good humour that appealed to her, for there was no denying Basil could be sulky. Then she felt a light tap on the chair, and looked down to see a note dangling in his fingers. She dropped her own hand, took the note, and tucked it into her glove. They exchanged a secret smile. There was no need for words. Eyes could speak.

She had drawn off her glove, and the touch of her fingers had sent a shiver of excitement down his spine that was quite unexpected at such short acquaintance. She had an astonishing appeal to his senses. Intellectually, he assumed she would be a bit of a scatterbrain. But who wanted intellect in a very attractive young woman? She was wearing the same hat and dress that she had worn to dinner at the hotel. So was her sister, Lucy. Gregson was in his Summer attire, as were the majority of the men – flannels, blazer and boater – it was almost like a uniform at this popular seaside resort. He liked to be different. For one thing, the day for blazers and boaters was gone. A man of forty would feel ridiculous in such youthful garb.

His thoughts were decidedly sensual, and her

nearness so disturbing, he could not restrain the impulse to touch her fingers again. Between the two chairs, their fingers entwined in an intimacy that brought a flush to Kate's cheeks and an awareness to her virgin body that was totally unlike anything she had known with Basil. If this was courtship, it was most disturbing to her light-hearted intention to enjoy the company of both Mr Lefeaux and Basil. His long, sensitive fingers clung possessively. She had not known that entwined fingers could also speak, as well as eyes. They both were staring fixedly at the conductor, but seeing nothing of his immaculate military uniform. Neither could have told you what was being played. The small, ringless fingers could be the fingers of a child, Charles was thinking, but there was nothing childish in their communication.

He could feel her responding to his touch in a way that was refreshingly different from the others who had captured his heart for brief periods of recent years. She was so natural, so unaffected, so altogether delightful, he would not relinquish her fingers till they stood up for the National Anthem. With a sense of loss and loneliness, he followed her out of the enclosure. Smiling and bowing, he watched them walk away.

Basil's step was jaunty. With a girl on each arm and an open invitation to take tea at The Haven, he was feeling a little sorry for Lefeaux.

The note was burning a hole in her glove – or so it seemed to Kate. Hurrying upstairs to her bedroom, she opened it and read:

My dear Miss Kate,
   May I presume to suggest another meeting without your sister and Mr Gregson? It would give

me much pleasure. Dinner, I suppose, would be out of the question? I shall be taking a little drive in the late evening. (There is a brougham permanently housed at the hotel for the use of residents.) I will be in the near vicinity of The Haven, in Richmond Road, at the hour of ten o'clock, and will wait half-an-hour. Dare I venture to hope that you will join me?

Your sincere admirer, Charles Lefeaux.

Kate's heart was racing, and her cheeks so flushed with excitement, she called in the cloakroom before joining the family in the dining-room, to sponge her face with cold water.

'Come along, Kate. You're keeping everyone waiting.' Amelia's voice was sharp with annoyance. Punctuality at meals was one of her strictest rules.

The two little girls had claimed Basil, and he was seated between them. Thomas was ensconced in the armchair, supported by a heap of cushions, and given a silver spoon to bite on. He was never happier than when he was surrounded by the entire family. Only Prue ignored him, but it was hardly noticed for he was so adored by the rest of the family. Even Bertha had finally succumbed to her cherubic nephew, and had actually taken her turn to nurse him, in the drawing-room, on Sunday evening.

'When he is two, I shall take him for a little drive in the morning, in the station cab,' Amelia had informed Ellen. 'He always notices the horses when we are out, and waves his arms excitedly. That would be hereditary, would it not? Jonathan was so fond of his horses.'

'I expect so, Mother,' Ellen had replied, for she seldom, if ever, disagreed with Amelia.

With so much attention focused on the children, Kate could concentrate on the charming epistle, now transferred to the warmth of her bosom. By ten o'clock, the whole family had retired, but could she get out of the house without disturbing anyone? It would be a very daring escapade. Her eyes wandered to the french windows. Yes, this would be the only way out, just by lifting the latch. The front door would be bolted, and the back door would alert Jackie, who was still capable of arousing the household with his fierce barking.

Such a darling man to suggest such a daring escapade! Basil would never have dreamed of such an unconventional *rendezvous*. Sitting between Prue and Bella, he was completely absorbed in spreading strawberry jam, and wiping sticky fingers. Dear Basil. He was rather sweet, but just a tiny bit stuffy. It all seemed very tedious that Sunday evening – singing hymns with Mother at the piano – Thomas being passed round, to be cuddled on each lap in turn – Basil, with a child on each knee, reading the same Bible stories that Ellen had read to her younger sisters in nursery days. They lingered over the farewells to Basil at the front door. His chaste kisses were deceptively brotherly, since both Kate and Lucy had been fondly kissed on at least one occasion.

When he had gone, Norah carried up the hot cocoa and poached eggs for supper, and another Sunday was slipping away, and, for Lucy, a dreaded reminder of another working week and the traumatic experience of serving customers under the supervision of the Manageress, or a senior apprentice. Her shyness was painful to herself and the customer. The general opinion was that she would never make a sales girl, but Lucy Brent was a grand-daughter of

Thomas Brent, and could not be dismissed for incompetence. Neither could Kate Brent be dismissed for being too forward, or for lack of respect to the head of department. Yet she could sell a customer an unfashionable hat or a hat that was totally unsuited to the wearer, with her charming and confident manner. Indeed, she enjoyed selling hats. It was fun.

As the grandfather clock struck the hour of ten in the hall, bedroom doors were closing, and Kate was standing at her window in a fever of excited anticipation. She would wait twenty minutes to make quite certain everyone was in bed, and also to tease Mr Lefeaux, who would assume she was not coming! The gas light in the hall was always left on, turned low, at Amelia's instructions. She gave no reason for this, and nobody questioned what would seem to be an unnecessary extravagance.

Tying a chiffon scarf over her head and draping a dark wrap about her shoulders – a reminder of the Academy – Kate opened her door and listened. Not a sound. Now she could proceed, cautiously, down the stairs, across the hall, into the dining-room. The window latch lifted easily, and she crept out, across the small square of lawn to the green gate. It swung open with a loud creak, and she glanced up anxiously at Amelia's window. There was no movement of the curtains, so she stepped out and closed the gate carefully.

A few yards down the road, she could see a tall figure, standing beside a carriage, with a coachman on the box holding the reins and a whip. Reflected in the street lamp, they had a curious immobility. She picked up her skirts, and ran, like an eager child, into his warm embrace. His arms closed about her. She could smell whisky on his breath as he bent to kiss her mouth.

'My adorable Kate,' he murmured, and lifted her into the carriage. It was so terribly romantic, with the shimmering path of moonlight across the water, the clip-clop of the mare's hooves, and the waves breaking on the shingle. The hotels were still brilliantly lit along the promenade.

'The night is young, my darling girl,' said Charles, as he removed the chiffon scarf and rumpled her short hair. Then his hand slid inside her wrap and cupped her breast, while his other hand slipped round her tiny waist. She trembled, in the innocence of unexplained emotions, and wound her arms about his neck.

'Kiss me again. I like your kisses, Charles,' said she.

'Do you, by jove!' said he, with a chuckling laugh.

Their lips met and clung, and Kate shivered in the strange sensuality of his probing tongue. It was very disturbing, even a little frightening, to feel the dampness in her private parts. It was not menstruation; that was last week.

When his hand slid slyly under her petticoats and almost reached her calico drawers, she pushed him away, and gasped, breathlessly, 'Please take me home.'

'You're a naughty girl, Kate. I thought you wanted me to make love to you?'

'Not like that.'

'My precious innocent, there is no other way. I was not going to hurt you.'

'Are you courting me, Charles?'

'Of course I am courting you. Isn't that why we are here? Why, Kate, my darling, you are crying. What have I done? Have I frightened you? Please don't cry.'

'I'm sorry,' she whispered.

He dried her eyes and ordered the coachman, 'Home, James!' in a jocular manner, for her benefit.

He certainly hadn't expected tears from this particular young lady. It was disconcerting, for now he could not suggest another meeting. So be it, he thought, dispassionately.

The coachman touched the mare with his whip, and grunted, 'Git up there, Bess.'

They trotted along at a brisk pace. They sat holding hands. There was nothing more to say. A short distance from the green gate, they pulled up. Charles lifted her down, kissed her tenderly, and bade her farewell. Was it really farewell?

Too choked to speak, Kate picked up her skirts and ran. She did not look back, and she crept in the way she had crept out.

In that short hour she had been initiated into a disturbing awareness of her own virgin body. That probing tongue, and those exploring hands. She wanted to respond. She wanted him to touch her intimately. Every pulse in her body had wanted to respond. Every question could have been answered. But it was too soon, too sudden, and Charles too impatient. Surely such intimacy should be reserved for the marriage bed? If he had touched her private parts, could she have a baby? What a ghastly thought!

She climbed the stairs slowly, her cheeks wet with fresh tears – tears of misunderstanding and regret. Would she ever see him again?

In the silent house, the family slept, and not one must ever be told of the night that Kate crept out to meet her lover. Her lover? Could this be love? – this compulsive desire to melt into the body of a man, who was almost a stranger?

She lay on her bed, and wept.

9

Three months had passed since that fateful night. It was the height of the Summer Season, and Worthing was swarming with visitors, many of whom could afford only one day at the seaside, and that was August Bank Holiday. Cheap excursions brought Londoners from the East End, who crowded on the pebbly beaches between the pier and the bandstand, because they felt safe in a crowd. Born and bred in tenements and hovels of Stepney, Hoxton, Bermondsey, children were much too awed by the size of the ocean to do more than paddle their dirty feet on the very edge of the incoming tide. Their happy squeals echoed to the farther beaches where middle-class families, who could afford to spend a week in lodgings felt so superior to the noisy hoydens from the slums.

The children spent the day splashing in the water, collecting shells and seaweed to take home, and stuffing themselves with meat pies, cockles and mussels dowsed in vinegar, washed down with bubbly ginger-pop. To be sick on the train on the homeward journey was no disgrace, but proof of a capacity to fill an empty belly on one day in the year.

The military band was nothing more than an accompaniment to their noisy enjoyment. They had their own Salvation Army bands to see them off and welcome them back to London Bridge and Cannon

Street. Shrill Cockney voices proclaimed derisively, 'Gahn! They ain't a patch on the Army!'

In the select area of beach some distance from the bandstand, customers were taking their turns to hire a bathing machine. The woman in charge was beating on doors and demanding that the occupants should hurry for they had overstepped the prescribed hour. Basil was there, with Kate and Lucy. They had brought a picnic lunch, and would listen to the band in the afternoon. Charles Lefeaux had not been seen since Whitsun, and every Sunday afternoon, Kate looked in vain for that tall, distinguished figure, smiling and bowing at their approach. There had been no more invitations. He had disappeared, and left a puzzled young woman, still in doubt about her reaction to his extraordinary behaviour.

Basil was obviously delighted to have the girls to himself again, and Kate was soon persuaded to forget her more sophisticated *beau* in a frolicsome game with Basil in the water.

'Kate, stop throwing water over me, and call a truce,' said he, gripping her shoulders.

She laughed and struggled free.

'Kate – *I have the ring*.'

Her glowing face was suddenly drained, and she stared at him in wide-eyed dismay.

'The ring I promised, the betrothal ring. Aren't you pleased?' He was puzzled by her manner, and more than a little piqued since it had taken all his carefully hoarded shillings.

Then she smiled, and kissed his sulky mouth. 'Pleased? I'm absolutely thrilled, Basil darling,' she lied. 'It's not a secret any more, is it, darling?' she asked, when Basil had slipped the ring on her finger that same evening, inside the green gate.

Lucy had hurried indoors, with small gifts for the children – beads for Prue and Bella, and a carved horse for Thomas. The gift shop in the Arcade did a roaring trade on Bank Holidays.

Basil had taken the precaution to measure Kate's finger with a length of thread, so the ring fitted perfectly. A circle of garnets surrounded a single pearl, and the gems sparkled in the gas light.

'It's beautiful, darling. I can hardly wait to show it off to all the girls in Millinery tomorrow. I was the only one not wearing a ring. Even funny little Dora is betrothed to one of the apprentices, but he bought the ring in the gift shop, and the stones are artificial. How soon can we be married, darling?'

'It's like I said, Kate, dearest. We have to wait two years for Mr Hudson to retire, then I step into his shoes as General Manager.'

Kate sighed. 'It seems an eternity, and I do love you an awful lot.'

'And I love you. The time will pass. We must both start saving now.'

'Saving? Why must we save if we are going to live with your mother?' Kate was dismayed at such a prospect. She spent more than she could afford on clothes, and was always in debt to Amelia for her board and lodging. 'Have you told your mother?' she asked.

'Not yet, but I shall tell her tonight. I thought I would ask her if she would let us have the spare bedroom for our personal use as a sitting-room. We could remove all the old furniture into the box room, and purchase some new pieces from Waring & Gibson. Household linen we will purchase from the store, and get the staff discount.'

'Your mother may not want to turn out her own

furniture into the box room. Some women are very sentimental over their possessions,' Kate suggested. It was not very romantic, this talk of saving, and a sitting-room to themselves in his mother's house. 'You seem to have given it a great deal of thought, darling,' said she.

'Naturally, it's a very serious step we are taking, is it not? A betrothal is binding, and now you are pledged to me, my dearest, there must be no more flirting with men like Lefeaux.'

'That is most unlikely, since he seems to have disappeared.'

'That is all to the good. He probably realized we were pledged.'

'But we were not pledged three months ago. In fact, I wouldn't have been at all suprised if you had proposed to Lucy.'

'She is a very sweet child, but much too young to be pledged. Now I must leave you, my love. One more kiss. Parting is such sweet sorrow, as Will Shakespeare would say.'

Jane had taken the opportunity to visit the family on Bank Holiday. In a crowded compartment, surrounded by slum children, she was nursing a baby and joining in the bawdy music hall songs on the excursion train to Worthing. Amelia would have been horrified to see one of her daughters in such low company, for she hadn't actually visualized Jane at the Hoxton Mission. Jane had not invited any of her family to visit her, and Amelia had not suggested it. Her natural self-indulgence rejected anything of a disturbing nature, and she excused her negligence over Jane's environment in much the same way as she had excused herself from visiting Grace.

Lucy had already greeted her sister and given the children their gifts when Kate came in. It was near the children's bedtime. Bella and Thomas were romping on the white carpet in the drawing-room, and Ellen was reading a story to Prue. Amelia's objections to the children in the drawing-room were noticeably more lenient since Thomas had shown a preference for that soft white carpet!

'Where is Mr Gregson? Is he not coming in to see the children?' she asked Kate.

'Not tonight. He has promised to take his mother to a concert at the Assembly Rooms.'

'Very noble. It is gratifying to hear of a young man so concerned for the comfort and happiness of his widowed mother.'

'*And* for his future wife. Mother, we are betrothed. Look! I am wearing his ring!'

'Betrothed? Isn't that rather presumptuous of Mr Gregson? With no father to approach, it would seem to me to be polite to ask my consent. I am surprised at Mr Gregson, and surprised at you, Kate – though perhaps not so surprised, since you have a way of disregarding my wishes.'

'Don't be cross, Mother darling. I thought you would be pleased to have Mr Gregson for a son-in-law?'

'That's beside the point. Really, Kate, you are quite incorrigible.'

Kate was too excited to be deflated by such criticism. The ring sparkled on her finger. Even Thomas wanted to inspect it.

'Sit down, Kate. I want to hear what has been arranged.' Amelia was offended. She liked to be consulted and this was altogether unseemly.

Kate sat down on the piano stool. She loved an

audience, and they all had stopped what they were doing to listen!

'We have to wait two years, for Mr Hudson to retire, then Mr Gregson will be promoted to General Manager,' she explained, airily.

'And where will you live?' Amelia demanded.

'With his mother.'

'Has *she* been consulted?'

'Not yet.'

'So all this has been arranged without her knowledge? Really, Kate. You take my breath away with such blatant audacity.'

'Sorry, Mother,' said Kate, with a mischievous smile.

'May I see the ring, please Kate?' Lucy interrupted. Pale with shock, she gazed at the symbol of love on her sister's finger. 'It's very pretty,' was all she said, but her blue eyes were stricken, and she was choked with tears. 'Will you excuse me, Mother?' she asked, quietly – and left the room.

The Summer Season was drawing to a close. Kate was still enjoying the Wednesday afternoon bathe with Basil, but now they were betrothed, it was not thought necessary for Lucy to chaperone, so she spent the afternoon in a deck chair, listening to the band, and day-dreaming of what might have been without a sister who had her way with everything, including Basil. She met them for tea at Kong's.

In Kate's company, she had seldom had much to say, so her silence was not so obvious, but she was so tired and listless, Amelia was concerned for her youngest daughter, who was getting to look more and more like her sister Grace.

'She is absolutely useless as far as selling is

315

concerned, but what can one do with a grand-daughter of Thomas Brent?' the Manageress of Children's Wear confided to her deputy. Whenever possible, Lucy avoided meeting Basil face to face. She hurried away from the store at closing time, and walked home alone, and on Sunday afternoons she accompanied Ellen and Rose and the children to the park.

Basil was missing her quiet company, and her agreeable manner. Kate was so unpredictable, and for all her charm, she had not endeared herself to his mother.

'She is much too gushing for my liking, and I do not wish to be called darling by a young woman who is almost a stranger,' his mother complained.

His love for his mother seemed to have undergone a change of recent months, and they were once again as devoted as before he joined the firm of Thomas Brent & Son. So he found himself torn between the two, and inclined to defend his mother's point of view.

As for Kate, she was finding the betrothal extremely tedious. He was so deadly serious, and she still wanted fun. To spend every evening in his company was boring, for they just took a walk on the promenade, and nothing happened – nothing at all!

When the Season was over and there was no more bathing, they would take a walk till tea-time. The theatre would be an extravagance they could not afford, Basil had decided. And with no band on Sunday afternoon, they would take another walk. If he mentioned walks again, Kate said she would scream!

On alternate Sundays, they were taking tea with Basil's mother. The prospect was bleak, and terribly, terribly boring, Kate was thinking, as she stood, waiting for a customer, one Wednesday morning, staring out of the window at the few late visitors in the High Street.

A deep, masculine voice arrested her attention. 'Madam, have I your permission to speak to Miss Brent?'

'Mr Lefeaux!' she gasped.

'Certainly, Sir,' the Manageress answered, affably.

And there he was, smiling and bowing, with teasing eyes. 'How do you do, Miss Brent,' said he. 'I trust I find you well?'

She was blushing like a silly schoolgirl, and her heart was racing. Her dark eyes searched his face. 'I – I thought . . .,' she stammered.

'You thought you had seen the last of me?'

She nodded, her hand on her mouth.

He stared at the ring on her finger, and frowned. 'Gregson?' he asked, his voice low.

'Yes,' she whispered.

'I must speak to you privately, Kate. The store closes at one o'clock on Wednesday, I recall. I shall be waiting for you at the front entrance.' A curt little bow, and he was striding away across the salon, and Kate was near to swooning for the first time in her life.

'Sit down, Miss Brent.' Someone pushed her on to a chair. The salon was swaying, and her heart was beating like a little hammer under the drab, grey pinafore. The deep, masculine voice seemed still to be talking. 'I must speak to you privately, Kate.' This was mastery of a different kind. His personality was stronger than her own, and she recognized his superiority. He would beckon, and she would follow. 'I shall be waiting for you at the front entrance.' It was a command, not a request.

He was striding up and down the pavement, and he

asked, curtly, 'What is that you are carrying?'

'My towel and bathing costume, and a packet of sandwiches. Basil is expecting me. We always bathe on Wednesday afternoon, and eat our sandwiches on the beach.'

'You can leave it with the porter.' He did not offer to carry it, and she did not expect it.

'Where are we going?' she asked, breathlessly, for she had almost to run to keep up with his long, loping strides.

'Back to the hotel to lunch,' said he.

'But I am not dressed for the hotel.'

'You look all right to me.' His casual glance did nothing to restore her self-possession. She had never felt so intimidated.

He marched into the foyer as though he owned the place, swept aside the small page, and indicated the porter. When she had deposited the bundle with the porter, he took her arm and they went through to the restaurant, and were shown to the same table as they had occupied that evening with Lucy and Basil. The few guests were scattered around the dining hall today, and all were in holiday attire, so Kate's print frock and boater were not so conspicuous.

When the head waiter presented the menu, she announced, with a touch of defiance, 'I will just have a mushroom omelette and a chocolate ice-cream, if you please.'

Charles Lefeaux raised his eyebrows. 'Madam has ordered. Make it two mushroom omelettes, Gaston,' said he.

'Very good, Sir.'

The wine waiter was hovering. 'Yes, the usual, Pierre.'

Then he whispered, confidentially, 'Have a bottle

318

of champagne sent up to my room.'

When he turned to Kate, his mood had changed, and his eyes were teasing. 'What prompted you to choose a mushroom omelette and a chocolate ice-cream?' he asked, amiably.

'Because it's a special treat for my birthday, when Mother takes me to Slater's for lunch.'

'Indeed?'

She nodded. She had already recovered her self-possession, and she did not intend to lose it again!

'Poor Gregson. Poor fellow! Such a shame to keep him waiting,' Charles was saying. And he lifted her hand to inspect the ring. 'A tawdry toy, my dear. It has no value.'

She flushed angrily, and retorted, 'You are mistaken, Sir! This ring is a symbol of our betrothal. We are pledged to be married.'

'Your eyes are black as onyx when you are angry, Kate.' He smiled indulgently. 'Ah, here come the omelettes. I must say they look most appetizing, garnished with grilled tomatoes and French beans. Yes, Pierre, you can pour the wine.'

They did not linger over the meal, and Charles pulled a face at the dish of ice-cream Kate was eating with such relish. The young waiter was instructed to bring a platter of assorted cheeses and fresh rolls.

When they had finished, he took her hand, and she found herself in the lift.

'Where are we going?' she asked for the second time that afternoon.

'Wait and see, my sweet,' he teased.

The wine had put a sparkle in her dark eyes and a flush to her cheeks.

Still holding her hand, they walked down a long, carpeted corridor to a door numbered 123. He

319

opened it, pushed her gently inside, closed it, and turned the key in the lock.

There was no escape, but did she want to escape?

Removing the straw boater, he rumpled her hair playfully, and she laughed up at him, unafraid, and beguiling. Momentarily shamed by her extreme youth, he quickly dismissed his doubts, kissed her warm mouth, and let her go. He watched her covertly, as she wandered about the room, admiring the comfort and elegance that money could provide. Like a child inspecting every novelty, she turned on the tap over the wash-basin, and gasped with surprise as the hot water gushed out. Washing her hands with the lavender soap, she selected a towel and dried them carefully.

Waiting impatiently, he stood there, a handsome figure in his silk shirt and white cravat. Frowning at her reflection in the mirror, she picked up one of the silver-backed hair brushes and brushed her hair. To tantalize him further, she went to the window and looked out on a sparkling sea. Now she remembered Basil. He would be swimming, and it was the last opportunity this season. Would he be very angry, or sulky?

'Kate, come here.' That was Charles being masterful again. She shrugged. Let him wait!

'Do I have to fetch you?' His voice was threatening, but she still did not move.

When he dragged her to a chair, sat down, and pulled her across his knees, she struggled frantically.

'You behave like a child, you will be treated like a child,' he said, and lifted her petticoats. She kicked and struggled as he pulled down her drawers and inflicted three smart slaps on her bare buttocks. He could feel her shoulders quivering, and he thought she was in tears, but when he turned her over, she was laughing.

'You little demon!' He kissed her laughing mouth and silenced her. Her arms crept round his neck, and when he unbuttoned her dress, she made no protest. She knew she was being seduced, like one of the heroines in the cheap novelettes the girls smuggled into their beds at the Academy. She would not be ashamed of her nakedness because she knew her body was perfect.

When he laid her on the bed, she closed her eyes while he undressed because she did not want him to see her reaction to her first glimpse of a naked man. It was all so sudden and unexpected, she had no time to fortify herself against the shock!

Then he was there beside her, kissing her breasts, caressing her young, virginal body, whispering endearments. And when he entered her, the pain and the pleasure had an immeasurable ecstasy, and she knew for certain now, she could never again be deprived of it for the rest of her days.

They slept, exhausted, and woke to drink the champagne. Aware of Kate's initial shyness over his nakedness, Charles pulled on his dressing-gown, and brought the champagne to the bed.

Kate looked like a child with her tousled hair and flushed cheeks, but she was all woman, as their ardent love-making had proved, and he was completely and utterly entranced.

'Now that I have seduced you, my sweet, you will have to marry me,' he said, as calmly as though he were speaking of the weather.

'*Marry you*!' she gasped. 'But I am pledged to Basil.'

321

'Do you really want to marry that conceited young pup?'

'I am not sure. We have to wait two years. It's a long time to wait.'

'Two *years*? My darling girl, you and I could be married in two *days* by special licence.'

The bubbly champagne was tickling her nose and making her feel quite light-hearted.

'I want you, Kate, and I have got to have you,' he said, with the air of a man who has always got what he wanted. Kate had met her match. Marriage to Charles would be a battle of wills, but it would never be dull. 'I want you Kate,' he insisted. It was not love, but this compelling desire of the senses was the strongest emotion she would ever know.

'What will your sister have to say?' she asked, coyly, dropping the sheet to expose her young pointed breasts with their pink nipples.

He put down his glass, and bent to kiss them with his wet mouth. She shivered, and his mocking eyes teased her. 'My sister will say I have taken leave of my senses, and she could be right.'

'Will she remember me, Charles?'

'I doubt it, my sister is never familiar with the people who serve her, unlike her brother! Oh, Kate, my adorable Kate, it's going to be fun. You and I together will shock all these stiff-necked colleagues of mine, and all those fond mamas, so desperate to find husbands for their stupid daughters. I shall be called a cradle snatcher, and a doting old fool. What do I care? You will keep me young. What do you say, my sweet?'

'I would sooner be an old man's darling than a young man's slave.'

He threw back his head and roared with laughter –

a deep, masculine laugh, her father's laugh, when she sat on his knee and flirted with him because he was the only man in her small world, and she liked men best! Yes, it was going to be fun. She sipped the champagne.

'You don't care much for that, do you my sweet?' said Charles.

'Not much,' she confessed.

'It's an acquired taste. You will get used to it. Now, you had better get dressed and I will telephone for our dinner to be sent up. In the meantime, you can write your letters to Basil and your mother. Use the hotel notepaper in the bureau.'

'What shall I say? My mind is an absolute blank.'

'That's the champagne, but I am not concerned with the state of your mind, my darling girl,' he chuckled. 'Just say you are eloping with Mr Lefeaux, and we are being married on Friday. Hurry up, then the fellow who delivers our dinner can take your letters and have them delivered this evening. It will be worth a handsome tip, will it not? We shall have to buy you some clothes before we present ourselves to my dear sister,' he added, as an afterthought – and picked up the telephone.

It had been a disappointing afternoon for Basil. He had waited some time for Kate, then decided he could not miss this last opportunity of a swim this season, and he had paid for the bathing machine. So he went in alone, and kept a sharp look-out on the beach. Kate was so unpredictable, anything could have happened, or she could simply have changed her mind. He would meet Lucy for tea at Kong's, and perhaps she would know what had happened to Kate.

The water was chilly, though the sun was shining.

Only two of the bathing machines were in use today, and the beach was almost deserted and rather depressing.

When he had taken a brisk walk along the promenade, he made his way to Kong's, and sat down to wait for Lucy. Again he waited for some time, feeling rather foolish, before ordering a pot of tea for two and buttered toast for one. Customers were streaming in now, so the band session must be over. Still no Lucy.

When he had drained the last drop of tea from the pot, there was no excuse to reserve the other seat any longer, and the waitress was hovering. So he paid the small bill, left a penny tip for the waitress, and walked out, feeling neglected and looking sulky.

Since he first became acquainted with the Brent sisters, he had enjoyed their company on Wednesdays and Sundays, and the warm hospitality of The Haven. Should he go there now and enquire what had happened to the girls, or go home to his mother?

Still feeling disgruntled, he wandered down the beach, sat down on the steps of the bathing machine, and threw stones in the water in a desultory manner. Long afterwards, he would wonder what had prompted him to return to that particular place at that particular time.

Was it Fate or Providence that he should be sitting there, on a deserted beach, when a slight, girlish figure, in a print dress and straw boater, rushed past, hesitated on the brink of the incoming tide, then plunged in.

'Lucy!' he gasped. 'Lucy!' he yelled, and dashed after her. She sank before he could reach her, but he hauled her out. Fully clothed, they both were sucked into the water. Lucy was a dead weight in his arms, but he dragged her ashore, struggling and panting, and lay exhausted on the shingle, still clutching the limp, bedraggled form. Had she fainted? She couldn't possibly be dead – or could she?

Gazing down at her white face and streaming hair, he was choked with an overwhelming compassion. His dear little Lucy. What had prompted her to such madness? Groping under her petticoats, the camisole, and the chemise, he found her fluttering heart under his cold, wet hand.

'Lucy,' he breathed. 'You mustn't die. Forgive me, dear. I was a blind fool. It's you I love.'

Then he carried her up the beach, laid her gently in a deck chair and ran to find a cab.

'Hurry, man, hurry! It's a matter of life or death!' he urged.

'My Gawd!' muttered the cabby, and climbed down from the box, and followed Basil across the promenade. 'She looks a gonner to me, guv,' he said.

'No, she's alive. Her heart is still beating,' Basil insisted. 'Help me carry her to the cab. If we fold the chair flat, it will make a stretcher.'

Several people stopped to stare curiously at the little procession, then moved on. When the cab drove off, Basil gave his own address. It would be a shock to Mrs Brent, but he hoped his mother would not be annoyed at the intrusion. After a few minutes, Lucy opened her eyes, stared blankly at Basil, and closed them again. After that, she seemed to drift into a coma, and lay passive in his arms.

When the cab pulled up at the house, his mother peered from behind a curtain, then hurried to the door as the cabby was assisting them to alight.

'Will you pay him, please, Mother. He has been very helpful.'

She did as he asked, then closed the door, and followed him into the drawing-room. The girl lay on the couch, limp and bedraggled.

'Who is she? Who is this girl?' his mother demanded.

'It's Lucy, Kate's younger sister. She – she tried to drown herself. It was a miracle that I saw her, but I was only just in time.'

'Poor child. Why should she want to take her own life?'

Basil shook his head.

'We must get her undressed and into a warm bed, and then you must get out of your wet clothes.' His mother seemed to have taken charge of the situation, and Basil was relieved, for he was feeling the after-effects of his own part in the rescue operation. 'Carry her upstairs, dear, and put her on the bed in the spare room, and leave her to me,' she instructed.

He did as she asked, but still lingered by the bedside.

'Take a bath towel from the airing cupboard and give yourself a brisk rub down. When I have settled Lucy, I will make you a hot drink. Go along now. We don't want a second casualty.'

'Thank you, Mother.' He kissed her gratefully. She returned the kiss, and wondered if this girl was in love with her son. Then she remembered the letter that had been delivered and decided it could wait.

The girl had not stirred. She looked very young and frail lying there, and not in the least like her sister for whom she had felt a positive dislike. Stripping off the wet clothes, she rubbed her dry, wrapped her in a warm blanket from the airing cupboard, and put her to bed. She stood there, looking down on the dead-white face and the long, flaxen hair, spread over the pillow. 'Poor child,' she murmured, and went down-stairs, leaving the door open.

When Basil came down, wearing his business suit, she had brewed a pot of tea and made toast. They sat down at the kitchen table. (The little maidservant had been sent home with a heavy cold.)

'Will she be all right, Mother?' he asked, anxiously.

'I think so, but we must get the doctor.'

'Yes. I will call at the surgery on the way to The Haven. Mrs Brent will be wondering what has happened to the girls. Mother, I shall tell her Lucy fainted. I don't want them to know what actually happened. We may have to keep her here for a few days, then Mrs Brent will be calling. Will you confirm what I shall tell her about the faint? If we could keep the truth between the three of us?'

'Yes, we will do that,' she readily agreed. 'A letter came for you from the Marine Hotel,' she said, and went to fetch it.

'Who would be writing to me from the Marine Hotel?' he wondered, as he tore open the envelope and read the brief contents.

'Well, would you believe it? Kate has eloped with Lefeaux!' He laughed mirthlessly, and passed the note to his mother. She read it aloud.

Darling Basil,
    I am going away with Mr Lefeaux. We shall be married by special licence on Friday.
    Please forgive your loving Kate.

The ring was enclosed.

'Loving!' scoffed his mother. 'She doesn't know the meaning of the word! That girl is utterly selfish, my dear boy. If you had married her, she would have made your life a misery. In my opinion, you have had a lucky escape.'

But no man likes to be rejected. He *had* loved Kate. Few men could resist her. Lefeaux was a man of the world. It surprised him that such a man had offered marriage when he could afford to keep a mistress. But Kate was cunning as a little fox, and she would have told him she was 'pledged to Basil Gregson'. Besides, she had the ring. He turned it over in his hand and remembered the weeks he had stinted himself of all but the barest necessities. Now Kate would have diamonds.

'She's a bitch!' he exploded. 'Lefeaux doesn't know her like I do, and she will lead him a fine dance if she doesn't get her own way.' He put the ring in his pocket and stood up, wearily. 'I must be getting along to The Haven now. I wonder if Mrs Brent has received a similar note?'

'That poor woman, with six daughters. I don't envy her.'

'She holds the reins, and in her quiet way is quite formidable. But this is one occasion when she has to admit defeat. Keep an eye on Lucy, will you, Mother?'

'You can leave her to me. I am glad you brought her here, my son. I was getting a little morbid, spending so many hours alone. It takes time, dear, for a mother to adjust to her new status when her only son becomes so immersed with his betrothed.' She smiled, whimscally.

'I'm sorry, Mother. I've been a blind fool.' He hugged her affectionately and she was happy again.

'Doctor has been called out on an urgent maternity case. I will send him along when he gets back,' the doctor's wife informed Basil.

Norah answered the door at The Haven. 'Is anything wrong, Mr Gregson? Where are the girls?' she asked.

'May I see Mrs Brent, please, Norah. She will explain everything later.'

She tapped on the drawing-room door, announced the visitor, then disappeared down the basement stairs. 'That was Mr Gregson. He looked ghastly. Wanted to see Mrs Brent,' she told Bertha, who was knitting Winter vests for the children. The breakfast-room, with a bright fire, and two old wicker chairs, was a homely room, and they felt comfortable there.

'May I come in, Mrs Brent?' Basil was asking.

Amelia was seated in her favourite chair, an unopened book on her lap. She looked very calm and composed, sitting there, in the firelight, but he knew that she seldom betrayed her real feelings. 'Come in, Mr Gregson. Sit down. I was expecting you. Mr Gregson, I must apologize for my daughter, Kate. It must have been a grievous shock to receive such news. As for me, I am no longer shocked or surprised by Kate. To tell the truth, I am prepared to like this Mr Lefeaux for taking her off my hands. Tell me, what is he like? You have met, have you not?'

'Very charming and agreeable. A gentleman, a Member of Parliament, and old enough to be Kate's father.'

'A bachelor?'

'As far as I know. There is a sister, but no mention of a wife, that evening he invited us to dine with him at the Marine Hotel.'

A smile trembled on the stern mouth. 'The little minx. She threatened to find a husband that very first day. She hated being an apprentice, and Lucy hated it. I must think of something more congenial. Did you bring Lucy back with you?'

'No, she fainted this afternoon while we were having tea at Kong's. I called a cab and took her home to Mother. It was so much nearer than bringing her here, and it might have startled you.'

'That was very thoughtful of you, but I trust Mrs Gregson was not inconvenienced?'

'Not at all. Lucy was sleeping when I left, but I took the liberty of calling a doctor. The faint lasted for some time, and she looked quite ill.'

Amelia sighed. 'Lucy has worried me for some time. She is rather frail, and so acutely sensitive that anything of a disturbing nature in her department upsets her for several days. The sick headaches have become more frequent of late, but I am inclined to think it is a kind of escapism. My poor little Lucy has always suffered from Kate's domination, so Kate's marriage could be a blessing in disguise. The doctor may advise rest for a few days. Will that inconvenience your Mother?'

'Mother is already prepared for that, and perfectly agreeable.'

'That is most kind. Please convey my grateful thanks. You will keep in touch, will you not?'

'I shall call again tomorrow evening, rather late I'm afraid, since I cannot get away from the store till eight o'clock, and have then to go home to see how Lucy is progressing.'

'I quite understand, Mr Gregson. You are looking pale and tired. It has been a disturbing day for you. Can you let yourself out?'

'Certainly. Good night, Mrs Brent.'

'Good night, Mr Gregson.'

He bowed, and walked away.

Such a nice, well-mannered young man, she thought, but perhaps not *quite* the right type for Kate.

It was late evening when the doctor called and apologized for the delay. It had been a difficult birth, and the midwife could not cope alone, he explained. 'But all is well. The farmer has the son he was hoping for,' he told Mrs Gregson, as he followed her up the stairs.

Lucy was feverish and complaining of pains in her chest. When the doctor had finished his examination with the stethoscope he patted her head, told her to keep warm, and he would call again on the morrow. Lucy smiled feebly. She felt so ill, she thought she might be going to die. She didn't want to live. There was nothing to live for. Kate was going to marry Basil, and she was hopelessly incompetent in Children's Wear. Nobody loved her.

It had taken her all afternoon to find the courage to drown herself. But she was still alive, so somebody had rescued her. Weak tears wet her pallid cheeks. What was she doing here, in this strange bed, and who was the strange woman?

'You have a very sick young woman on your hands, Mrs Gregson,' the doctor was saying. 'You say she fainted?'

She hesitated. One did not lie to one's doctor.

'It was not a faint, doctor. She tried to drown herself.'

'Ah, I could tell it was something more serious. She seems to be in poor shape constitutionally, and this near drowning could have aggravated the condition. Was it your son who rescued her?'

'Yes, doctor.'

'Very praiseworthy.'

'Is it a bad chill, doctor?'

'It's pleurisy.'

'*Pleurisy*?'

He nodded. 'She ought not to be moved, and she will need careful nursing. I may have to drain the fluid, but we will see what rest can do. I am always reluctant to use the needle. Rest is a great healer. Keep her quiet, and keep her on fluids – chicken broth, beef tea and such like. She ought not to be left at night. How will you manage?'

'I shall sleep on the couch in her room.'

'I could find you a night nurse?'

'No, thank you, doctor. We shall manage.'

'As you wish. I shall be calling every day for the time being.'

'Thank you, doctor. Can I offer you a cup of tea? I'm sorry I have nothing stronger.'

'Thank you, but my wife will be waiting. She will have a meal ready. She never knows when to expect me.'

'Who would be a doctor's wife?'

'Who indeed?' he chuckled, amiably.

Basil was hovering in the kitchen, waiting to hear the diagnosis.

'It's pleurisy. I had to tell the doctor the truth,' his mother explained.

He sighed. 'I suppose so. Is pleurisy very serious? I mean, she is not going to die, is she?'

'It is serious, and she will need careful nursing, but we won't let her die, my son.'

'I blame myself. This would never have happened if I had not pledged myself to Kate. I must have been mad. Now it's too late.'

'Too late for what?'

'To tell Lucy I love her and to ask her forgiveness.'

'It's too soon. You must give her time to recover from such a traumatic experience. You must be patient.'

332

'I'll try. I feel so ashamed. If she dies, I shall never forgive myself.'

'She is not going to die.'

'You sound so convinced.'

'I am. That young woman is going to live to discover the best years of her life have still to be lived, and I am going to enjoy nursing her, if only Mrs Brent will not interfere. Isn't she rather a dominating person?'

'She is inclined to play the stern matriarch, but it doesn't always go according to plan. She nearly lost Grace, and it was a big mistake to have Kate and Lucy apprenticed. They are totally unsuited to such a life. Kate had the audacity to find a husband, but Lucy's way of escape could have proved fatal.'

'Well, she is not going to dictate to me in my own house!'

Basil smiled. It was good to see his mother in such an optimistic mood.

'Is doctor sending a nurse?' he asked.

'No, I told him we could manage. I shall sleep on the couch in Lucy's room, and you can take a turn to sit with her on Wednesdays and Sundays. She won't need watching constantly. She will sleep a lot in between the bouts of pain, and doctor will give her sleeping drafts. Don't worry. We shall manage.'

'Oh, *Mother*! What should I do without you?'

'Or me without you. We need each other, my dear. No matter whether you marry a Kate or a Lucy, please make room for me. I promise not to be a nuisance.' She was near to tears, and he hugged her affectionately. Surely there would be room in this house for two women?

He followed her upstairs. A night-light was burning on the bedside table, and in its faint glow he could see Lucy's hair spread on the pillow, and her waxen face. Her eyes were closed, and his mother put a finger to her lips. But Lucy was not sleeping, and her eyes flew open with a sudden, stabbing pain.

'It hurts,' she whispered.

'It will soon be better, dear.' His mother's voice was gentle. 'Would you like a little broth?'

Lucy shook her head and moistened her lips. 'Water.'

'I'll get it,' said Basil, eagerly, and raced back down the stairs. He watched his mother lift the girl's head and put the glass to her lips. His heart ached with love and pity, but she did not look at him, so he crept away and left them together.

Amelia took a cab to visit her sick daughter. Basil was at work, and when his mother opened the door to her visitor, the two women eyed one another suspiciously. The cabby had been told to wait. It was a good sign that the visit would be a short one.

'Good morning, Mrs Gregson. I am Lucy's mother,' said Amelia, importantly.

'How do you do, Mrs Brent. Please come in,' Basil's mother invited.

'It is most kind of you to have my youngest daughter here after that unfortunate affair with Kate.'

'That was nothing to do with Lucy. She is here because she fainted in the tea-shop, and my son brought her home. We did not know, of course, that she was suffering from the early stages of pleurisy, but it would have made no difference. Here she is, and here she stays until she has fully recovered. My doctor insists she must not be moved.'

'I see. I had thought to take her home with me, well wrapped in blankets.'

'It is out of the question, Mrs Brent. Lucy is a very

334

sick girl. Come and see for yourself.' And Mrs Gregson led the way upstairs.

Lucy greeted her mother with a blank stare. Basil's mother placed a chair at the bedside, and Amelia sat down.

'How are you feeling, child?' she asked, pushing back the damp hair from her hot forehead. There was no response.

'She has only just woken up. She is always like this. Her medicine contains laudanum,' Mrs Gregson explained.

Amelia frowned. 'I trust your doctor knows what he is doing?'

'He certainly does. I would not presume to question his diagnosis or his treatment.'

'I have always treated the girls' ailments with the good old-fashioned remedies and have seldom found it necessary to call in a doctor. Lucy suffers from an inferiority complex, and her illnesses are often of the mind. That is to say, they are imaginary.'

'Are you suggesting this illness is imaginary?' Mrs Gregson exclaimed, indignantly.

'I am just explaining what has happened, on more than one occasion. A mother is the best judge of her children's behaviour is she not?'

'I have sometimes wondered. My own son has a way of surprising me. I thought I knew him, but he lost his head completely over your daughter Kate.'

'Kate? Where is Kate?' Lucy murmured.

Amelia glanced at Mrs Gregson. Had Lucy not been informed of Kate's elopement? How very odd. 'Kate is taking a little holiday with a friend from the Academy who lives in London,' she improvised. 'You will see her when she gets back.'

Lucy closed her eyes, and her mother's voice

faded. She did not want to see Kate. She had stolen Basil. Weak tears wet her cheeks.

'Don't cry, child,' Amelia admonished and kissed the wet cheek. 'I must apologize for my youngest daughter, Mrs Gregson. She has never learned to control her tears.'

'Why should she? I always thought tears were a woman's prerogative?'

'Not in my house,' said Amelia, decidedly, as she walked away.

Three weeks had passed, and there was little change in Lucy's condition. The doctor had called twice daily during the first ten days, but it had not been necessary to use the needle.

Basil had taken over his duties in the sick room on Wednesday and Sunday afternoons, and also on two nights during the week, when he dozed on the couch while his mother slept in his bed, and he called her if anything of a delicate nature was required.

Lucy was a good patient, in fact, she was too good, for she seemed to be drifting in a state of weary resignation, like a very old woman who had reached the end of her days.

When Basil showed the doctor out on the third Wednesday afternoon, he laid a fatherly hand on the young man's shoulder, and asked in his blunt fashion, 'Are you in love with that young woman?'

'Yes, Sir,' he answered, without a second's hesitation.

'Take my advice. Declare yourself, or she will slip away.'

'It's not as simple as that, Doctor. You see, I was betrothed to her sister, Kate, but she eloped with an older man.'

'Does Lucy know of this?'

'No, Sir.'

'Why not? What are you waiting for?'

'We thought, Mother and I, to give her time to recover.'

'That girl will never recover unless she has a reason for living. She has lost the will to live.'

'I am not at all sure that Lucy loves me.'

'Then ask her, man! Ask her! This is no time for doubt and regret. Lucy is a sweet child, but she needs the love of a good man as urgently as a plant needs the sun. Why do you suppose she tried to take her own life? Because you were pledged to her sister, Kate. What other reason could there be? It takes a lot of courage to take your own life, no matter what the cynics say. Off you go, my boy. Waste no more time!' He climbed into the gig, lifted a hand in salute, and drove away.

Basil climbed the stairs slowly. The doctor had been very convincing. Lucy had not moved. Propped against the pillows, she looked very young and vulnerable. Dropping on his knees beside the bed, he took her limp hand and held it to his cheek. 'I love you, Lucy.' His voice was choked. 'You mustn't love me. You are pledged to Kate,' she whispered.

'Not any more. Kate has married Lefeaux.'

'I don't believe it.'

'It's true,' he insisted.

Once again her eyes flooded with tears.

'There, my love, cry on my shoulder.' His arms cradled her thin shoulders. She had a sweet, clean smell about her, like a baby freshly bathed. Her nightgown was changed every day, so were the sheets.

'Can you forgive me, my dearest? It's you I love. It was madness, but it has passed. Will you trust me, sweetheart? Could you love me?'

337

'I have always loved you,' she told him, as he wiped the tears from her pallid cheeks.

He wanted to protect her from all the slings and arrows that frightened her, and her weakness with his strength. There was nothing he would not do for her.

'I – I don't want a ring,' she murmured.

'Only a wedding ring, dearest. We will be married as soon as you are well.'

She sighed ecstatically, and he kissed her with a tenderness that Kate would never know.

'A quiet wedding, child? Most certainly not! For Mr Gregson's sake, if not your own, it must be a social occasion. The store will be closed on Boxing Day, and all the staff will want to attend, now that he has been promoted to General Manager. Poor Mr Hudson, the heart attack was so sudden, but he had no time to suffer. Grandpapa Brent has promised to pay all expenses, including the reception at the Marine Hotel. We must let him have his way, child. Besides, you would not wish to disappoint Prudence and Arabella, who would expect to be bridesmaids. Thomas is a little young for a page, but perhaps he could scatter rose petals if someone held his hand?' Amelia paused for breath, her blue eyes flashing imperiously. She was determined to get her way about *this* wedding. Hadn't she been deprived of two special occasions, with Grace getting married in Switzerland to that divorced Mr Halliday, and Kate eloping with Mr Lefeaux?

Three months had passed since Lucy took her first weak steps in the bedroom. She still looked frail, and quickly tired, but there was no doubt about her happiness.

Lucy listened to her mother with polite interest,

but she was no longer intimidated by her strong personality. She knew that her future mother-in-law was getting her own way about sharing the house, and that Basil was pleased at the prospect of sharing the house with his wife and mother.

Since her illness, Lucy had clung to Basil's mother, and had not returned to The Haven. The relationship between the three was most cordial, and Mrs Gregson had found the daughter she had always longed for. Kate would not be attending the wedding, so there would be no embarrassment. The couple would be enjoying a delayed honeymoon in Paris over Christmas and New Year. So, Lucy reminded herself, this would be the last time that Mother would get her own way. Her youngest daughter would be a married woman, obedient to her husband, not her mother. No longer an apprentice but the wife of the General Manager, her status was an enviable one, though some would say that Lucy Brent was a mouse compared to her dashing sister Kate. Be that as it may, Basil would never again lose his head over an attractive girl, and there would be plenty for a handsome man to choose from at Thomas Brent & Son.

The secret of Lucy's attempted suicide would not be divulged. It was safe with the doctor. As for the cabby who helped carry her to his cab that evening, he would never have recognized that poor, bedraggled creature in the radiant bride, in white satin and orange blossom, posing for her wedding photograph on the steps of the Marine Hotel.

It was Charles who had prompted his young wife to write to her mother some weeks after their wedding. Like an excited child with new toys, Kate was lost in wonder and delight at the novelty of her life.

Amelia read the scrawled epistle with obvious displeasure. All that money that Grandpapa had spent on her education, and the child could not even write a legible hand!

My darling Mother

I trust you have forgiven me for distressing you. Charles is a wonderful husband, and I am terribly happy. To go back to the beginning. We were married at Caxton Hall with two of Charles's politician colleagues as witnesses. Since the House was still sitting, our honeymoon had to be postponed till the Christmas Vacation, but we spent a long weekend in Scotland where a cousin of Charles's lent us his hunting lodge. We travelled up on the night express from King's Cross and had our own Pullman sleeping car. The lodge was completely isolated and rather primitive. We seemed to be the only two people left in the whole world. The hills and glens were breathtakingly beautiful. Everything was provided for our use, including peat for the fire, and a row boat for the loch where Charles caught fish. One quickly tires of such primitive conditions and a diet of oatmeal porridge and fried trout! Charles enjoyed every second, but I was glad to get home – home being this big, comfortable house in Onslow Square. I have to be most diplomatic to avoid trouble with the servants, who are accustomed to taking orders from Miss Lefeaux. She is a very haughty lady, and was not at all pleased to discover her brother had married the apprentice who sold her the hat at Thomas Brent & Son! Charles advised me not to make changes at present because his sister will probably marry a faithful swain. And then I shall be mistress. We have a cook, two maidservants and a gardener-handyman, also the daily cleaning woman who reminds me of Maggie. We shall do more entertaining when the sister has left. At the moment, Charles and I often dine out after a show. I love the theatre. It is all so terribly thrilling and exciting. As for Bond Street, I cannot tear myself away from the shops, but I am not allowed to go shopping on my own. I have to wait for Charles to escort me. He likes to choose my clothes, even my lingerie, and is not at all embarrassed! One afternoon I sat in the Visitors' Gallery in the House of Commons, listening to a speech by Mr Gladstone (The Grand Old Man). It was terribly impressive, and I felt so proud and important when Charles raised his hand in salute from the back benches. My darling husband will never make history. He is too lazy! But I adore him, and he adores me. Isn't that terribly nice! Please give my love to everyone and kiss the children for me.

Your ever loving daughter, Kate.

The letter was passed round the drawing-room and caused only a mild flutter.

'In my opinion, Mr Lefeaux is a brave man,' Bertha commented, acidly.

Thomas stole the show at Lucy's wedding; not yet breeched, he wore a frock of white pique with a wide belt and a sailor hat with a wide brim that Rose carried, as well as the basket of artificial rose petals. With his golden curls, pink cheeks and innocent blue eyes, he looked angelic, but Thomas could be a fiend if he was crossed in any way, and the whole family were on tenterhooks that he might suddenly decide to fling the rose petals at the congregation!

The two little girls looked charming in their poke bonnets, muslin frocks with blue sashes, white mittens, and white kid slippers. For Ellen, it was a reminder of her own wedding, with St Matthew's sweetly scented with massed carnations, the choir-boys in their clean starched surplices, and the strains of the *Wedding March* as her pretty little sister walked down the aisle on the arm of her proud young husband – who so nearly married the wrong girl.

The Vicar – her father-in-law – was an old man now, and his wife still confined to her room. But the sadness reflected in Ellen's dark eyes was soon dispelled, for there was Thomas, the centre of attraction, as always, and not for the first time it seemed to her bemused senses that Jonathan's spirit lived again in his son. His every gesture was familiar, and the disarming smile nobody could resist, that is, nobody but his sister, Prue. It was a thorn in the flesh, this jealousy that had reared its ugly head the day that Prue found her mother cradling her new baby brother in her arms. It was stronger than Ellen's loving assurance and Rose's devotion. Between the two, Bella stood firmly, and quite independently on her two small feet, and her sunny nature often quelled the stormy scenes in the nursery, for Bella loved everyone. Prue's passionate nature would allow for no compromise. She wanted *all* her mother's love and attention, *all* Rose's devotion, *all* of Bella's sweet affection. But Thomas was the spoilt darling of the entire household, and Grandmama was foolishly indulgent to her grandson.

Prue had long since given up trying to please her. It was no use. To see her baby brother taking his morning drive to the promenade in the station cab with

Grandmama was too provoking to be borne in silence!

'It's not fair! We should take turns. That horrid child is Grandmama's pet!'

Ellen was secretly in sympathy with her first-born, but helpless to alter a situation that could only worsen. Not one of her daughters had been loved as Amelia now loved her grandson. She saw the Hand of God in the birth of this boy child, as compensation for her own repeated disappointments.

Great preparations were being made for Thomas's third birthday. It would be another of those special occasions that all the family would celebrate. Amelia had summoned all her daughters, and would accept no excuses. Grace and her husband would travel from Switzerland, Kate and Charles from London's West End, Jane and Edward from London's East End. Those two sisters had not met since their nephew's second birthday, and much water had flowed under the bridge since then – as Bertha would say.

Norah had been instructed to bake a cake, cover it with pink icing, and to decorate it with silver balls to read THOMAS. AGED THREE YEARS. In the centre of the cake would be three little candles for Thomas to blow out. He was a manly little fellow for all the spoiling, and he would be breeched on his third birthday. He walked proudly and independently, and talked as fluently as his sisters. Brighteyed and eager, with splendid health, he seemed to be blessed by the gods. Nothing was denied him, and he was never punished. His naughtiness was excused.

'Boys will be boys,' Amelia reminded Ellen and Rose, who thought a very moderate spanking would not come amiss. But Thomas had known at a very early age that Grandmama was his ally.

Poor Maggie would be seen scuttling out of his way with her bucket and scrubbing brush on the tiled path that led to the green gate, for Master Thomas, in a mischievous mood, had been known to swamp the path and the sacking apron with a playful kick from his little kid boot. It was fun. Everything was fun.

His doting grandmother hid a smile behind her gloved hand. Ellen and Rose, however, who were left to deal with him for most of the day, were often at their wits' end. Prue's naughtiness at the same age could be blamed on tragic circumstances, and the child's fruitless search for her adored Papa. In every other aspect, Prue was now a reasonable, well-behaved little girl, already taking first lessons with Ellen. But the jealousy was like a curse on the relationship of sister and brother, and the little boy delighted in provoking his sister. He knew his importance in the household long before his third birthday.

In his high chair, seated beside Grandmama at the head of the table, he was encouraged to take an active part in the sugar biscuits. 'Children should be seen and not heard' did not apply to Thomas.

Kate's empty room was being prepared. It was time he had a room of his own, Amelia had decided. It would also be convenient to pop into Grandmama's bed, to share her early morning tea and biscuits.

The rocking-horse was the biggest and most expensive present. Amelia could not have borne it if any member of her family – and most likely Kate – had managed to produce something even more costly. So she took the precaution to mention it in her letters of invitation to her daughters. It was delivered from the best toy shop in town soon after breakfast. Norah and Bertha would have carried it upstairs, but Thomas insisted on taking his first ride in the hall, and there it stayed all that day.

'It will ruin my polished floor!' Bertha complained, but nobody took any notice. It was the child's birthday, and Grandmama had said he could do exactly as he pleased. Everyone gathered round to admire the young horseman in his first pair of breeches.

'Give your sisters a turn, darling,' Ellen requested, when it seemed he would never stop.

'No, it's mine!' came the prompt reply. So they drifted away with Rose, to play with the other toys.

All the smaller presents had been unpacked in the drawing-room before breakfast, including parcels from Auntie Grace, Auntie Kate and Auntie Jane, delivered by post, but all had been pushed aside when the rocking-horse arrived. Thomas was passionately fond of horses, yet another indication of his extraordinary likeness to the father he had never known.

Bella found the clockwork train quite fascinating. Prue was engrossed in a colourful picture book of wild animals.

'You can have it,' said Thomas, magnanimously. 'I only want the horse.' Thomas was not interested in books, only when they belonged to his sisters. His small hands seemed to delight in destroying things. Nothing was safe from his grasping fingers. But today it was the horse that responded to his grip on the reins. It was a real horse!

'Watch me! Watch me!' he cried, his curls flying.

'I am watching you, my darling,' said Grandmama.

When his head began to swim, he climbed down and went back to the fort and soldiers he had

345

discarded when the rocking-horse arrived. They lay on the floor, side by side, and Bella was entranced with the little engine on its endless journey round and round the track.

'It's my train,' Thomas reminded her.

'I know. It's only borrowed,' Bella agreed, amiably.

The morning drive was halted at Kong's that morning, for hot chocolate and sugar biscuits. After lunch, Thomas decided to help Auntie Bertha and Norah to prepare the family tea. Up and down the basement stairs they went, with Thomas climbing on Norah's strong back for the downward journeys. She was a jolly soul, and laughed heartily as the boisterous small boy bounced on her back.

'It's my birthday, Auntie Norah,' said he, with throttling arms about her neck.

'Norah is not an auntie,' said Grandmama decidedly.

'Norah is not a servant,' said Auntie Bertha, even more decidedly.

'What is she then?' Thomas asked Rose.

'Norah is a friend,' said Rose.

The first to arrive in mid-afternoon were Jane and Edward, and Thomas squealed with delight at the funny uncle with the black eye-shade he was seeing for the first time, thinking he was dressed like a pirate especially for his birthday. It was fun! Everything was fun today!

As for the tea, spread on a starched white cloth, that was special, with three kinds of jam, dainty sandwiches spread with Gentleman's Relish, scones, bread and butter, sponge cake, three kinds of biscuits, jelly, and the handsome cake in the centre of the table.

'You kiss the ladies and shake hands with the gentlemen,' Grandmama had explained.

Thomas was wearing a paper crown on his golden curls to welcome the guests. Each in turn had to watch him gallop his horse across the hall.

'Such a noisy little boy,' whispered Edward, who had a headache. He often had a headache, poor man, since the accident.

The front door stood open for a whole hour so the children could race out as soon as they heard another cab. Grace was the next to arrive with her husband, and Ellen was the first to welcome the sister she had not seen since the day they parted in London. It seemed a lifetime ago. Both sisters wept emotionally, and hugged each other. Then Henry had to be introduced to the entire family, all on the pavement.

'It's my birthday,' Thomas announced, importantly, shaking hands with another new uncle, who immediately started to kiss his sisters-in-law.

'What a lovely family you have, my dearest,' he said to his wife, who was rather shy.

Amelia kissed her daughter affectionately. She had hardly dared hope to see her again, and was surprised to see her looking so well. 'Why, child, you are quite brown,' she exclaimed.

'Like a gypsy,' said Grace.

They were still on the pavement when a second cab drew up, and out stepped Lucy and Basil. More hugs and kisses, and more joyful tears.

'Imagine my little sister Lucy a married woman.' Grace was once again overcome with emotion, and Henry had to find a clean handkerchief.

'Why are they crying?' Thomas demanded.

'Because they are so happy,' Uncle Henry explained.

347

'I laugh when I'm happy,' said Thomas.

'Very sensible. As man to man, I heartily approve of such sentiments.' Uncle Henry was rather portly, and a little pompous.

It was nearly four o'clock and still no Kate.

'Isn't it just like Kate to be last to arrive, to claim all the attention,' Bertha grumbled

Everyone seemed to be talking at once, and paying no attention to Thomas. 'It's my birthday,' he reminded them, yet again. 'Come and watch me gallop my horse.' And he dragged two of his uncles indoors. His excitement was infectious, and both were laughing. Mr Gregson was Uncle Basil now, because he had married Auntie Lucy.

'If they are not here by four o'clock, we will start tea,' said Grandmama, who was wearing a new afternoon gown the colour of violets in honour of her grandson's third birthday. Her daughters were surprised and delighted, for Mother had worn nothing but black since Father died.

When all were seated round the long table in the dining room, and Thomas in his high chair at the head of the table with Grandmama, another cab drew up at the green gate. The front door stood open, and Kate stepped inside, followed by her tall, handsome husband. They tip-toed across the hall and Kate laid a restraining hand on Charles's arm. Her eyes danced with mischief. They stood there, framed in the doorway, smiling at the assembled family. Charles swept off his grey topper, and bowed. Kate curtsied prettily.

'Bravo!' Henry leapt to his feet, eager to kiss the new arrival. All the uncles were on their feet, and Thomas climbed up in his high chair to get a better view. Was this beautiful lady, dressed like a princess, his Auntie Kate?

'It's my birthday!' he shouted, above the clamour. 'Many happy returns of the day, my darling.'

Smothered in a fond embrace, and the feather boa about her shoulders, he wrinkled his nose. 'You smell nice,' he said – and wondered why everyone laughed.

THE END

THE FAIRFIELD CHRONICLES

BY SARAH SHEARS

Set in the heart of the Kent countryside and spanning the period from the turn of the century to the end of the Second World War, Sarah Shears introduces us to the inhabitants of Fairfields Village. As we follow the changing fortunes of the villagers we see how their lives and loves become irrevocably entwined over the years and watch the changing patterns of English country life through the eyes of one of our best-loved novelists.

THE VILLAGE
FAMILY FORTUNES
THE YOUNG GENERATION
RETURN TO RUSSETS

Published by Bantam Books

THE GREEN OF THE SPRING

BY JANE GURNEY

A heartwarming saga of love and separation during wartime.

The carefree days of lazy picnics and house parties end abruptly with the outbreak of war in 1914.

Separation and the testing of young promises form the trials of war as much as trench casualties and Zeppelin raids. Whether from the 'Upstairs' world of the Brownlowes or the 'Downstairs' domain of Mrs Driver's kitchen, each of the inhabitants of Maple Grange is affected by the conflict in Belgium and France, and in ways that they could never have foreseen . . .

A Bantam Paperback
0 553 40407 5

A SELECTION OF FINE NOVELS
AVAILABLE FROM BANTAM BOOKS

THE PRICES SHOWN BELOW WERE CORRECT AT THE TIME OF GOING TO PRESS. HOWEVER TRANSWORLD PUBLISHERS RESERVE THE RIGHT TO SHOW NEW RETAIL PRICES ON COVERS WHICH MAY DIFFER FROM THOSE PREVIOUSLY ADVERTISED IN THE TEXT OR ELSEWHERE.

☐	17632 3	DARK ANGEL	*Sally Beauman*	£4.99
☐	17352 9	DESTINY	*Sally Beauman*	£4.99
☐	40429 6	AT HOME	*Charlotte Bingham*	£3.99
☐	40427 X	BELGRAVIA	*Charlotte Bingham*	£3.99
☐	40163 7	THE BUSINESS	*Charlotte Bingham*	£4.99
☐	40428 8	COUNTRY LIFE	*Charlotte Bingham*	£3.99
☐	40296 X	IN SUNSHINE OR IN SHADOW	*Charlotte Bingham*	£4.99
☐	17635 8	TO HEAR A NIGHTINGALE	*Charlotte Bingham*	£4.99
☐	40072 X	MAGGIE JORDAN	*Emma Blair*	£4.99
☐	40298 6	SCARLET RIBBONS	*Emma Blair*	£4.99
☐	40321 4	AN INCONVENIENT WOMAN	*Dominick Dunne*	£4.99
☐	17676 5	PEOPLE LIKE US	*Dominick Dunne*	£3.99
☐	17189 5	THE TWO MRS GRENVILLES	*Dominick Dunne*	£3.50
☐	40364 8	A SPARROW DOESN'T FALL	*June Francis*	£3.99
☐	40407 5	THE GREEN OF SPRING	*Jane Gurney*	£4.99
☐	17207 7	FACES	*Johanna Kingsley*	£4.99
☐	17539 4	TREASURES	*Johanna Kingsley*	£4.99
☐	17504 1	DAZZLE	*Judith Krantz*	£4.99
☐	17242 5	I'LL TAKE MANHATTAN	*Judith Krantz*	£4.99
☐	17174 7	MISTRAL'S DAUGHTER	*Judith Krantz*	£2.95
☐	17389 8	PRINCESS DAISY	*Judith Krantz*	£4.99
☐	17503 3	TILL WE MEET AGAIN	*Judith Krantz*	£4.99
☐	40206 4	FAST FRIENDS	*Jill Mansell*	£4.99
☐	40361 3	KISS	*Jill Mansell*	£4.99
☐	40360 5	SOLO	*Jill Mansell*	£3.99
☐	40363 X	RICH MAN'S FLOWERS	*Madeleine Polland*	£4.99
☐	17209 3	THE CLASS	*Erich Segal*	£2.95
☐	17630 7	DOCTORS	*Erich Segal*	£4.99
☐	40262 5	FAMILY FORTUNES	*Sarah Shears*	£3.99
☐	40261 7	THE VILLAGE	*Sarah Shears*	£3.99
☐	40263 3	THE YOUNG GENERATION	*Sarah Shears*	£3.99
☐	40264 1	RETURN TO RUSSETS	*Sarah Shears*	£3.99

All Corgi/Bantam Books are available at your bookshop or newsagent, or can be ordered from the following address:
Corgi/Bantam Books,
Cash Sales Department,
P.O. Box 11, Falmouth, Cornwall TR10 9EN

UK and B.F.P.O. customers please send a cheque or postal order (no currency) and allow £1.00 for postage and packing for the first book plus 50p for the second book and 30p for each additional book to a maximum charge of £3.00 (7 books plus).

Overseas customers, including Eire, please allow £2.00 for postage and packing for the first book plus £1.00 for the second book and 50p for each subsequent title ordered.

NAME (Block Letters) ....

ADDRESS ....

....